Praise for Whi

Majestic

"Combining meticulous research, vivid characters, an engrossing mystery and convincing documentation, Strieber has come up with an intriguing, intelligent, exciting novel."
—*Washington Post*

"Engaging as science fiction, unnerving as possible fact . . ."
—*New York Times Book Review*

"A thrilling, frightening, and worthwhile work."
—*Chicago Tribune*

Communion

"If Whitley Strieber isn't fibbing in his new book *Communion* . . . then it must be accounted the most important book of the year, of the decade, of the century . . ."
—*The Nation*

"Strieber comes through as both sensible and sincere . . . His book deserves to be taken seriously."
—*Boston Herald*

Also by Whitley Strieber
available from Tor Books

Catmagic

WHITLEY STRIEBER
THE WILD

TOR ®

A TOM DOHERTY ASSOCIATES BOOK
NEW YORK

This is a work of fiction. All the characters and events portrayed in this book are fictitious, and any resemblance to real people or events is purely coincidental.

THE WILD

Copyright © 1991 by Wilson & Neff, Inc.

All rights reserved, including the right to reproduce this book, or portions thereof, in any form.

A Tor Book
Published by Tom Doherty Associates, Inc.
49 West 24th Street
New York, N.Y. 10010

Cover art by TK

ISBN: 0-812-51277-4

First edition: April 1991

Printed in the United States of America

0 9 8 7 6 5 4 3 2 1

PART ONE
CITY LIFE

Life along the vertebrae of the earth,
brown and slow, concentrates in the cracks,
boiling down to harder forms,
skin to stone, finger to claw.

    —Robert Duke,
       "Silent Transformation" (1987)

CHAPTER ONE

CINDY AND ROBERT DUKE WERE IN THE FIFTEENTH year of a good marriage when something unusual happened.

They had a twelve-year-old boy named Kevin Thomas for his paternal grandfather; they had an apartment in New York City; Bob had sold stock, brokered insurance, sold bonds, was now a computer consultant. He had never been much good at making money, but until now he had managed.

Argument was past, anger was past, the sweated skin of Cindy's girlhood was past, and they were really learning one another, growing close in ways so deep that they spent a lot of time infected with secret laughter.

Cindy was heavier than she had been when they used to traverse Manhattan on roller skates, two cheerful Village types, a young poet and his wife. The need for money had ended those days; Bob was a poet now at night only.

Recently Cindy had made a private decision
that she would allow herself to widen out a little,
to find in the long curves of a bigger body a
comfort she had suspected but never dared try.

Bob liked scallops and steak, he liked game and
on occasion hunted grouse in the Catskills, where
they were members of a hunt club. Cindy cooked
the game intricately, her recipes running to Italy
and garlic, and much invented, all good, the birds
properly brown, the skin crisp and salty, the flesh
tender and sweet, and her quail were delicious in
steaming piles. They both liked to dig into home-
made ice cream with the ice-cream paddle in the
middle of the night. Young Kevin had read all of
Jack London and Mark Twain. Recently he had
turned—or been driven—to Kafka.

Kevin smelled often of oil paint and his art
teacher fluttered when speaking about him. Cindy
disliked the man, but the school administration
loved him. She was tortured with thoughts of
kidnapping or more subtle predation, the caress,
the boy gladdened by the attention and then the
hands against his naked skin, and the parted
cracks, the cries, the awful memories for her little
son.

She was a heavy sleeper, and did not know how
difficult it was for her husband at night. He would
read, he would lie looking at her, he would make a
deer's soft whistle when the shadows from the
street trembled on the bedroom ceiling. Drawing
down the sheets, he would see her golden body,
and touch the down on her thigh, and listen to her
weighty breathing. He loved her, he understood
that, to distraction and to the exclusion of all
others. Once he knew her, other women had come

to seem ciphers.

Now he sat beside her on a bench at the Central Park Zoo while Kevin sketched a tapir. Bob detested zoos; Cindy and Kevin loved them. When he was much younger, Bob had spent time in the wilderness. He had camped and hiked and canoed. The wilderness haunted him. Wolves haunted him. Freedom haunted him.

It was an October Saturday, the third of the month. Cindy held a copy of the *Times* in her hands, twisting it until the ink was smeared. Bob ate the last of Kevin's Cracker Jacks.

"Look at that," she said.

"What?"

"That wolf is watching us."

She was right: it was staring past the children, the men and women, the candy-apple stand, the popcorn vendor, the whole free crowd. From its prison, it was staring not at them, but at him. The wolf was staring straight into the eyes of Bob Duke.

All of his life Bob had been fascinated by wolves. He enjoyed being near them so much that he had tried to track them. Often, he dreamed about them. In his childhood he had fantasized that he was a magic wolf, and could run through the night sky.

He was unsettled by the feeling this poor, imprisoned wolf communicated to him. As he stared back he tore into the Cracker Jacks box. "Why doesn't it look at somebody else?"

"You're the only poet."

He shot an angry glance at her. He could not help his infirmity. All of his life he had been a poet, unpublished, ignored, but nevertheless on the perfectly valid path of a poet. He hated his own love of poetry. Give him instead a good spreadsheet and some numbers to crunch. He was a bitter man.

There was only one way to describe the look in the eyes of the wolf: horrible.

In this regard it was brother to all the creatures here. Bob could feel the unfocused moaning of the place, the yearning toward a thousand different instinctual freedoms: to run, to hunt, to hide or fly. Love of trees, of animals, of the whole intricate, savage reality of the wild had always sustained Bob.

As a boy in Texas he had watched the night sky, the racing moon, and dreamed his dreams of the wild.

There was one dream he would never forget. Even though it had happened when he was eleven, it was still vivid in his memory.

In this dream he had been a wolf. He had been awakened in the thick night by an amazing, intoxicating odor. His eyes had snapped open and his whole body had been quivering. The moon had shone down like the eye of some wild god. Waves of fierce pleasure had surged through him, deranging his senses, overwhelming his childish fear of the dark.

He had leaped out of bed, unlatched the screen window with fumbling, desperate fingers, and rushed off into the night. He remembered scuttling across the porch roof beneath his window, then leaping into the moon-silver air. He'd landed as gracefully as an animal on all fours.

Then there were dew-damp leaves slapping his face, and the pulsing, rushing of a beautifully muscled body, his heart breaking with obscure passions of overwhelming power, odors of the night filling his brain, intoxicating him—and then, for the first and only time, he was alive.

It was like leaping and crawling at the same time. The world was transformed by a great magic, the moon spreading its glow everywhere, and he was happy, all the cares of a dull childhood gone, and he was suddenly free in the night and he threw back his head and shook his body and he howled out the piercing joy that filled him blood and bone and soul.

Then he was awake. True, his pajamas were covered with grass stains and there was a dried leaf in his hair. True also, it was seven o'clock in the morning and he had a math quiz to look forward to.

He had gone off to school, smell of paste, math exercise book, the classroom shades drawn against the glory of the morning sun. But forever after, he had wondered if perhaps, for a little while in the dead of the night, he had been a wolf.

It was truly an intoxicating thought, a delicious thought. Man into wolf. Running. Howling. Leaping on the quaking innocent.

But he had never really escaped that classroom he entered on the morning after his magic, and now the caged wolf's eyes mocked him for it. And he thought, You, are you a man who became a wolf, locked in there now?

It was hideous to think that he might be looking at someone who had a name and a past, who had tasted the freedom of the wild only to be locked up like this, a sort of double prisoner.

"Let's get Kevin and go. It's lunchtime."

"We've only been here ten minutes."

The wolf's eyes bored into him. He imagined long, thin claws extending out from the center of those eyes and into the center of his brain, and forming there a molten spot. "The animal's angry," he said.

"I don't blame him. He's in a zoo."

"I hate this place."

"It's only a perfectly ordinary zoo. Anyway, Kevin's in the middle of something exciting. Look at him."

Bob envied and loved his son's ability to draw and paint. But for a child of twelve, why such furies? He made Francis Bacon look cheerful. His son would climb into his lap and they would read together, and Bob would wonder what tormented the boy, who read Kafka's "Hunger Artist" in a solemn, priestly voice, perhaps even in the voice Kafka had heard while he was writing it. Another jumbo jet would roar over the house, and to the west the sky would mutter, another restless night.

Bob was trapped between the staring wolf and his son's obvious excitement. When he moved, he was captured by his wife's cool hand, which squeezed his own. "Relax. It's a sunny day."

"The cages get to me."

"It's *only* a zoo!"

"Oh, come on, Cindy, can't you feel the anger? What about that wolf? You can feel his anger."

"Maybe I'm not sensitive enough for it to matter. After all, I'm not a poet."

How he hated that word. He suspected that it had been invented for the specific purpose of being applied to those whom it would trap. Cindy read his poetry, and now also Kevin. "It's good, Dad. It's real."

Cindy might add: "Couldn't it be a bit less sad? What about the beauties of the world?"

"At Auschwitz Dr. Mengele used to issue what

he called 'standing orders.' He and his henchmen would stand on the chests of prisoners until they died."

"That isn't the answer I expected, at least I'll say that for it. What if they lay there looking at the sky, looking past the men destroying them? The sky is made for joy."

"Romantic nonsense."

"It's what I would have done."

"Fatuous. The agony was too great."

"Damn you, Bob, your ego's always in the way. That's the reason your poems don't get published, you're too proud of them, and it shows."

He threw his head back and stared into the sky. He imagined the feet on his chest, the boots slowly collapsing his ribs, the click of the man's lighter mesmerizing him, the glow of his cigarette against the pearl-blue evening of Auschwitz.

He stared up into the belly of a passing airliner, whose roar mingled with voices and the smack of eating mouths, and the cries of the animals.

Inevitably, he looked back at the wolf.

It had never stopped watching him. He decided that there is no such thing as a human being who is not terrified of the wild. His wife's body touched him. Her hand still lay in his. Their love was so profound that there was nothing to be said about it. Anything could transpire between them, any anger, any hate, any outrage, and it would not matter to this love, which was like blood, like breath, more a part of the body than of the mind. Sometimes he knelt before her at night, and she drew him down into her cavern. Once she had said, "You cannot survive without me. I have become myth for you."

The ecstasy of love is what transmits human

feelings. Without it children cannot be truly human. If Adam and Eve had not fallen in love after their first child, humanity would have ended with them, for Abel like his brother would have been a beast.

"Don't keep tilting your head back like that. You look like you're having a seizure of some kind."

"I want to look at the sky."

"The pigeons are aiming for your mouth."

"You hope. But the statistics are on my side."

"Come on, sit like an adult. I don't want people to think I'm married to an overgrown child."

"You are."

"You're going to hurt your neck."

"Pain is good for me. Pain means something."

Cindy muttered a reply. What was it? Fatuous? He hadn't heard, but he didn't care, either, because he saw clouds. Another jet passed, and beneath the clouds it was so small. He imagined the people and the books up there, the copies of *Time* and *Newsweek* in the laps of the travelers, and their unimaginable dreams. He visualized the stewardesses stowing the empty food trays, the pilots reading off vectors, pulling and pushing levers, wheels, buttons, and the fire in the engines, the white fire of JP-6 waiting there to fulfill its dream, the dream of all jet fuel, which is to burn its creators.

He would have to go down to Atlanta bright and early Monday morning, a guest of Apple Computer, to attend a two-day session about the Macintosh Office. Wonderful, crazy, impossible computer, the Mac. All the people from Apple would be smiling, everything calm and rich in the Westin Hotel, and at night, in their dark rooms, they would all be lying awake worrying about their jobs.

He did not want to fly to Atlanta. He did not want to attend the conference with the despairing computer salesmen. He did not want to lie in an oversize bed in the Westin, wishing he was home in Cindy's arms, listening to *A Sea Symphony* while the stars passed and the pacing in the apartment upstairs went on and on.

I'm a selfish man, he said in his mind. A brat.

He sat up straight, surprised.

What was happening to him?

If only there was some way to tell her how he was suffering, surely she would have compassion —she would fill with compassion—and let them go out into the streets, go to a movie, to a restaurant, home, anywhere but this damned zoo.

The wolf was still staring at him. Its ears were pricked forward, adding to the impression of almost supernatural concentration.

Wolf, or man-wolf?

It blinked its eyes as the sun emerged. The animal within Bob reacted: he felt a slow, intimate movement beneath his flesh. He recalled his wolf dream with the kind of insight that brings sudden and intense clarity. Raising a boy, loving a wife, writing poetry, selling, advising, flying, eating, waiting, he had driven himself insane. A wolf in the belly was not the fantasy of a sane man. Should he go into analysis? Expensive, and also the only psychiatrist he knew was Monica Goldman, who was Cindy's dearest friend and the only woman he had ever desired to distraction, but for Cindy herself.

At the Esopus Hunt Club one night Monica and Steve had come in, she flushed with pride at the pheasants she had taken, her gun on her arm, her birds at her waist, dangling and beautiful, her color high, her eyes sparkling. He had kissed her cheek, there had been wine and Steve's bobbing bald head in the light of the kerosene lantern, the group of them with the enormous old club building to themselves but for the Brickmans from California, the deaf, smiling, ancient Brickmans, and he had thought of Monica in the night. Over the course of the evening he had contrived a plan that would enable him to accomplish his object without shame, or so he imagined. He had rehearsed the words, the gestures, the casual laughter if his suggestion failed. "It's cold. Why don't we bunk up together, all four of us?"

A short silence. Steve's pate reddened. Monica crossed her legs, put her chin in her hand. He could practically hear the phrases of her profession wallowing about in her mind: penile insecurity, death wish, sublimation.

They all burst out laughing, so loudly that the Brickmans, who were sitting in armchairs reading *Reader's Digest* Condensed Books, nodded and smiled, and Mr. Brickman went "ha-ha, a good hunt!"

It was a night of false groping. For the longest time only Steve was potent. He and Cindy had coupled together with Monica sitting in a chair and Bob curled up under the covers at the bottom of the bed, praying to God it would end, but it was endless, on and on, booming through the night as if an artillery battery had opened up on his position.

At three o'clock in the morning Bob had waked up, his body quaking with lust, and made furious love to Monica.

Only at the end did he discover that the shadowy, grappling woman beneath him was Cindy. Monica and Steve had gone back to their own room hours before.

Should he now sit across a desk from Monica and say, "I had a hallucination that there was a wolf in my stomach?" Well, she wouldn't charge him too much. "A professional visit," she would say, "of course."

The wind blew, and Cindy's heavy thigh rested against him, and his son went on drawing the tapir. The crowd passed, a baby bobbing in a stroller, a couple with linked hands, a pale man who watched Cindy, his face in an agony of longing. Cindy's eyes followed him. She carried a terrible electric stunner in her purse. She would not hesitate to use it.

Something made Bob get up, made him stand full height. "Get me a Pepsi," Cindy said.

His mouth might as well have been sewed closed, for he could not even begin to answer. He found himself moving toward the wolf, threading through the crowd, or so he thought until he collided with a girl in shorts and a tie-dyed T-shirt, and smashed her orange drink against her naked midriff.

Her voice chopped at him, a wave smashing on rocks. Seeing that she could not make him hear her, she stamped her foot and stalked off. The wolf had watched Bob until he reached the cage. Then it began to pace back and forth, its dewlaps wet, its eyes glancing from side to side, its tongue lolling. He watched the tongue, the black lips, the yellow, weak teeth, the eyes. The animal's tail was down, and when it passed close to him, it growled.

Was that entirely an animal sound?

He realized that it was literally frantic to escape, that its problem, very simply, was boredom. It was made for the woods, this creature, it belonged in secret and limitless spaces. But where were they? The woods that weren't being logged out were dying of acid rain. It belonged nowhere, this North American timber wolf. The animal was part of the past. Its last place was a cage in the middle of a zoo in the middle of a city totally beyond its understanding.

What *did* it understand? It understood how to snatch trout from streams, how to eat voles and gophers, how to bring down deer and moose. Did it also understand how to turn a key?

There was something about this creature, though, that Bob knew with crystal certainty could not be destroyed.

"It's beautiful," Cindy said. She had come beside him. He felt what Monica would call "inadequate."

"I wish I was some kind of an activist. I'd like to come in here and free all of these animals."

"Kill them, you mean?"

"Free them."

"To release them into the city is the same thing as killing them. Even in the wild, most of these animals would die."

The wolf remembers, though, the long shadows of evening and the darting movements of the muskrat. "You're so controlled. I think you're overcontrolled. What if they made it, all of them, even the sloth and the anteater."

"The anteater's cage is empty. I guess it's dead."

"What about giraffes? What if I found them all an apartment? They could live in comfort then, no crowds, no cages."

"Who'd pay the rent?"

"A secret zoo. Admission fifty dollars. Worth it to see a hippo cooking breakfast and a full-grown moose grazing the shag rug in the bedroom."

"I want to be together later. When Celeste takes Kevin and Joseph to the movies."

"I thought he and Joey were fighting."

"No. Now Dashiel and Kim are fighting. The rest of the class has suspended hostilities, pending the outcome."

The wolf turned and stood directly before Bob, lowering its head as if it wished it could ram itself into his belly. It growled—not a little, throaty sound, but a big noise.

It was magnificent, it had the whole wild in it.

Down the row of cages the baboon sat, its mouth lolling opened, its head resting against the bars, its eyes in Africa. The wolf paced and barked, and Bob knew that it was begging for freedom.

No, begging for forgiveness. "It's just their fate," Cindy said, trying to be kind to him, "they ended up here."

Bob thought, What if it isn't that way at all? The man-wolf knows. . . ."I'm no good today," he said aloud. "I didn't sleep. I don't want to go to Atlanta."

She was hugging her shoulders, watching the wolf. "It *is* us it's reacting to. There's no doubt about it."

"I'm scared. Maybe it's telling me not to fly. It's a portent."

She shook her head as if trying to dislodge a gnat from her ear. "No, it—" The wolf threw itself against the bars, growling and yapping, dragging its teeth on the iron with a clacking sound. Cindy stepped back. Bob's impulse was to throw his arms around the wolf, to kiss it, to caress it. He had kissed his dog Moe when he was a boy, had put his arms around Moe, and he remembered Moe's smell, that musty dogginess, the fetor of his breath. Moe had been ground to wreckage beneath the wheels of the school bus. The bus had let Bob off. As it pulled out, there had been a crunch, a thud, a canine scream, and the bus had rumbled away with Moe's tail fluttering out from under the fender. Bob had been left with his dog, its jaw torn back, gabbling against the street, making noises like wet paper being dropped from a height. Moe was a pulsating shambles, save for one rear leg, which was running furiously. There was nobody around, it was a block to home, and Moe was dying. Bob had screamed while Moe popped and spluttered.

Bob ran through the lush neighborhood, which had become a moonscape of empty houses and houses that would not answer the door. He had gotten home to find his own house also empty. He had called his father at the office. "Moe can't live, Bobby," his father had said. "You take my shotgun down and help him out of his misery."

Then there was a twelve-year-old boy, his eyes soaked with tears, rushing down the hot, empty street with a big old Remington held at port arms, who aimed the gun at the flapping puddle on the street, and shot, sending up a great splash of blood from the body of his beloved. The boy then turned the shotgun on himself, only to find that his toe could not—by an act of the goodness of God—reach the trigger. He looked down the smoking barrel into his deepest, truest wish. At last, dragging the gun, he made his way home.

The agony of that experience reasserted itself. Was the wolf rabid, sick, would it be taken up to the pound and gassed, ending its life in the ultimate prison, a chamber so small it would have to be stuffed in, with the gas hissing from the jet in the back? "Cindy, I am leaving this zoo. If you and Kevin want to stay, you can."

She knew him too well to abandon him. "Let's go to a coffee shop and get some lunch," she said.

Their son was not unwilling to leave. Bob usually did not dare to look at his drawings, and yet these were the very opposite of violent. He had rendered a portrait not of the tapir but of the wolf, a full face, eerie with knowing. "It practically posed. It was staring at you, Dad. Do you think it knows you love wolves?"

"I don't know."

Kevin took his father's and mother's hands, and they went out into the streets of the strange old city. "I wish we were in the country," Kevin said.

"Not when your dad has to travel on Sunday night. It makes things too hectic for him."

He thought of their rented house up in Ulster County, of Mount Tucker jutting up behind it, and the loons calling on the lake and the doves, and the occasional scream when something captured something on the mountainside.

Once he had watched a fox eating a small rabbit. The fox had torn out its bowels and was lapping at them while the rabbit shrieked. Or, another time, he had seen a rat taken by a red hawk. The rat knew what it was to be torn to pieces while being lifted into the happy sky.

Sometimes, warm in bed in his apartment, his wife sleeping beside him, his son in the next room, he thought he was close to a secret of incredible

importance, the secret of why life was so involved
with suffering, the secret the north wind said when
it roared through the snowy pines, the secret of the
fire in the plains, burning because it had to burn,
the dog dying because it had tried to bite a rolling
wheel, or the secret the great timber wolf had
dreamed as it succumbed to the zoo hunter's
numbing dart. But then something would happen,
his own body would go urgent or something, and
thoughts of secrets would come to an end.

"Would you like a hamburger, Kevin?"

"Fine, Mom."

Bob didn't want hamburgers. He wanted to take
his family to the Plaza, and dine in the Palm
Court on finger sandwiches, followed by enormous slices of cake and strong, black coffee. He
wanted to do this while listening to a Vivaldi
concerto played by the Palm Court String Quartet.
And perhaps to start with, a champagne cocktail.
Furthermore he wanted to spend the rest of the
afternoon in a movie, any movie as long as it was
gaudy and loud, and he also wanted to float out of
himself across the sky of the city, to float above
the towers, off farther and farther, until the last
sound from below whimpered out, and he could
see stars in the middle of the day.

He would let go the mystic chain, and fall then.
But he would not end up back on Fifth Avenue,
not at all. He would not fall back into the world
but out of it. He would fall past the moon, past
Neptune, past Arcturus and the Milky Way, fall
past stars and galaxies with names like NC-2376,
and past those without names, past them all, until
he thudded softly against the purple velvet side of
the universe.

Then what would he do? Dig through? Maybe
that was not such a good idea. Perhaps there was
another universe on the other side, maybe worse
than this one, a universe where no truth is real,
where the child's ball on the grass is a killing
boulder, or all of fate is concealed in the toe of a
shoe.

Maybe that's what the quasars that stand senti-
nel at the end of the universe are all about—they
are the spots where people like Socrates and
Christ dug through; they are windows into bright
and terrible wisdom. They are warnings.

Sometimes Bob agreed with the quantum theo-
rists, that the world was a knack of chosen possi-
bilities, nothing more substantial than that. Man's
true model was not Macbeth, not Othello, not
even Gregor Samsa, but rather Puck the fairy,
magical and insubstantial and so dangerous.

"Bob—watch out! Honest to God, I never saw
anybody so willing to walk in front of buses. What
do you think the bus drivers are—gods? One of
these days one of them'll be blinking and he won't
see you in time to put on his brakes."

"Let's not go to a coffee shop. Let's go to the
Palm Court."

"I'm wearing sandals, Bob."

"Champagne cocktails. Dancing to the music of
Vivaldi."

"We can't afford it. The American Express bill
remains unpaid."

"Let's have some fun for once."

She never let him down about things like this.
The Palm Court it was, and Kevin got a Roy
Rogers, she got white wine, and Bob finally settled
on a Vodka Sunrise. He assembled a banquet for

himself, managing to find goose with fresh snow peas, but no broiled wolf, frog legs, though, but no dog.

The music was gentle, persistently civilized, and Bob managed to sustain the illusions you need to enjoy food. You cannot think of the way hogs knock against the walls of the slaughterhouses, or of the chickens scrabbling down chutes lined with knives. As he ate he thought he could feel the world turning, exposing each part of itself to the sun, so that the light could sustain it. The engine of life labors so hard, but why? Nothing survives, yet everything tries. Worms on the end of fishing lines struggle through hells beyond imagination, slowly drowning, impaled, while monsters loom at them. Fish in creels take hours and hours to die, and you make them live a little longer so that they'll be good and fresh at the end of the day, a cheerful sight frying in the skillet.

What eats us? We can't understand it any more than the chicken can understand Frank Perdue. There is something out there.

"Coffee, sir?"

"I'd like to see the dessert cart."

Cindy luxuriated. Kevin's eyes lit up when the glorious tray was brought over, its perfections of sugar and flour and cream enough to make any boy feel suddenly quite cheerful.

When they came out of the Palm Court, it was nearly three o'clock. The sky had changed. Long, dark clouds rushed down from the north.

Cindy called Celeste. They would not go home, they would go to a movie and take Kevin with them.

The Ambassadors, a Merchant-Ivory picture based on the James novel, was playing at the Plaza

Theater. In the dark of that theater, Bob felt delicious, immense relief. He closed his eyes and listened to the music, and made the words part of the music, and imagined that he was Henry James, and had succeeded in his creative life.

That night Cindy asked him to come to bed naked, and she caressed him expertly, her fingers very slow. Even after all these years, the intimacy of her touch still made him shudder with embarrassed delight. He had not had many lovers before her, just one, as a matter of fact, with whom he had slept four times when he lived in London. There was another who had shared a single bed with him for a year, but without making love. It was the Catholic boyhood that had ruined his fun. When he made love, he still sometimes smelled the smoke of Father O'Reilly's cigar drifting through the confessional screen.

When he slept, draped across her, his chest half on her lap, while she read propped up against the head of the bed, he dreamed of a wide, empty walk. There were pizza crusts and popcorn boxes blowing, and on both sides of the walk there were cages, most of them alive with movement. A gibbon brachiated endlessly back and forth across a thirty-foot span, leopards paced, deer snorted, a weasel moved sinuously about, chimpanzees stared into the dark. The wolf watched him.

If you listened when the wind blew through its hair, you could hear the rustling of the whole forest. It came soundlessly out of its cage, drifting between the bars like fog. Bob didn't have to wait for instructions, he was familiar enough with the logic of dreams to start running at once.

Inwardly he was calm. He knew that this was a dream. He was not running through Central Park being chased by a breeze that had become a wolf. He was in bed.

The trees swept past him, their great trunks dimly lit by the antique pathside lamps. As he ran he found that he was moving along just above the surface of the path, almost as if he was about to fly like the wolf of his childhood dream.

There was nothing behind him now, nothing but the long expanse of the Literary Walk, so elegant at night, as if waiting for the return of the civilization that had created it. It was a windy night and the trees sighed and tossed their heads. No voice sounded, no radio blared. The park was empty.

The fear had left the dream, to be replaced by a sense of wonder. He had never been in the park in the middle of the night. Being here now filled him with sweet unease. Anybody he met would be dangerous, and yet it was also dark and he could hide. He could be the wraith in the shadows, the one who stalked the midnight lovers, the predator. He could be the one they all feared, the one who kept the park empty at this hour.

He slowed down. The wolf was gone. The dream became a stroll between dark pillars of trees. One part of him was searching for symbols; he sought the sense of his dream. Its landscape seemed connected to some obscure inner resurrection.

The wolf burst upon him, its paws outstretched, its teeth bared, its eyes dark beneath the hood of its brows. He fell back, hands out, kicking, pushing, and was swept along as if in water. He tumbled between the trunks of two trees. Then he gathered himself up, feeling the wolf right at his heels. Somewhere in his mind the voice of Walter Cronkite explained that wolves are shy and do not generally harm human beings. But the voice did not connect with the empirical reality. He tried to run but now he could not. He blew instead as a detached leaf blows, soaring past the crowns of the trees, high into the sky. Around the park the buildings glimmered, a wall of gleaming fortresses. Below and behind him the wolf rose amid flashes, as if its claws sparked against the air.

The higher he flew, the harder it got to continue. Finally he felt himself begin to fall. He did not fall fast—in fact he could control it enough to avoid trees. The wolf, though, had not lost control of itself at all. Its whole attention was fixed on Bob, who lusted to reach the ground where he could run again. But he fell as softly as a bit of thread on the whipping air. Growing increasingly desperate, he kicked like a swimmer. He felt the breath of the wolf on his back, heard its urgent little cries as it closed the distance between them.

Then his feet touched the ground. He was in the Sheep Meadow, running as fast as he could. A woman was running beside him, Cindy, calling to him in a shrill voice. He could not quite hear her, but he had the impression that if he could, her words would help.

The wolf snapped. A flash of white shot through Bob's brain and he tripped, falling head over heels in the rich grass. Then the wolf was upon him. Its claws melted his flesh with a puff of blue smoke and a hiss.

Then the jaws opened, and began to work the flesh off his bones. He became a mass of conscious agony. He could see the red, pulsating walls of the wolf's esophagus, could feel the sizzling acid of its stomach. He commenced a grim kneading suffocation. Then he began to dissolve. He became softer and softer until he seeped through the walls of the wolf's organs and began to race through its body, his blood screaming in its hot, quiet blood. He was the living victim of the night, sacrificed to the life of another.

Then he was seeing through the wolf's eyes, hearing the great rustling, banging, honking, shouting, roaring city all around, and smelling waves of odors that were like bridges of leaves and memories, the smell of dark, sick gardens, and most of all the smell of people and metal bars.

He was moving through the night in the body of the wolf when Cindy came into the center of his dream, her face streaked with tears, her hands on his wolf head, her voice begging, and this time the words made sense.

"Oh, God, honey, please wake up!"

By degrees, he obeyed the words. His wolf body fell away, smells turned back into sights, then the whole park seemed to melt. The trees flowed down like great candles, the grass shriveled into a pale Canon sheet, the cliffs of buildings became a cliff of pillows. Cynthia sat with his head cradled in her lap. He could smell sweat, his and hers. The bedroom light shone softly in his eyes.

"Cindy?"

"Thank God! Honey, it's all right. It's me. You're all right."

He grunted; his throat was so sore he could barely talk. "I'm sorry," was all he managed to say. There was terror in her eyes. He reached up, caressed her face, feeling her warm, tear-wet cheek.

"I couldn't wake you up!"

"I'm sorry. Truly, Cindy. I wanted to wake up, believe me I did."

He got up and on wobbly legs went into the bathroom. When he drank he felt a thirst like fire and drank more. Again and again he drank. Finally, gasping, he leaned over the sink and splashed his face with more water. He coughed. Cindy came in and put her arm around him.

The thing was, he could still feel himself inside the wolf. Somewhere in the night they were running together. Maybe they would always be together, running like this, running for the end of the universe.

Cindy turned him around and enfolded him in her arms. He kissed her, and her response was hungry at first. Then she sighed. She caressed him, a sad, almost apologetic gesture. "It's three o'clock in the morning," she said. "Let's try and get some sleep."

CHAPTER TWO

SOME YEARS BEFORE, ROBERT AND CINDY DUKE HAD tried to vacation on an island in the Carribbean. It was a beautiful island, its interior lush with waterfalls and orchids, its beaches chalk white, its lagoons as clear as air and swarming with colorful fish.

The only difficulty with this island was and is that the best beach is located at the end of the airport's one runway. The Dukes had just gotten to the island that morning, and having no time to discover its smaller hidden beaches—the pockets of sand secreted along its rocky harbors and lagoons—they were at this beach.

Bob watched an airliner bank over the ocean, then aim for the airport. Fortunately the planes today were landing from the west, so all the beach had to endure was a roar and a blast of sweet, warm fumes when one came to the end of the

runway and turned around. Otherwise they would
be thundering overhead at an altitude of fifty feet.

Dropping, the airliner disappeared below the
edge of the dunes. A few moments passed. Bob
heard a much louder roar than he had on previous
landings. Then there was a dull thud and a cracking sound. Then silence, but for the bouncing of
an enormous wheel, which bounded down the
dunes, across the beach and splashed into the sea.
People sat or stood, all turning toward the dunes,
all freezing when they saw the nose of the airplane
sitting there like a sculpture, not two hundred feet
away. Bob was locked in a kind of silence. Two
men in blue uniforms clambered out of the top of
the plane and jumped down, disappearing among
the dunes.

Bob began to run. When he reached the top of
the dunes, he found himself overlooking a scene of
astonishing destruction. A huge jetliner lay in at
least four pieces, festooned with wires and smoking tubes. Jet fuel poured out of half a dozen
places, making foaming pools in the sand beneath
the shattered plane. A man and a woman jumped
off one of the sections of the plane and, arm in
arm, began making their way back toward the
airport. The pilots climbed up into another section, the main section, and started shouting into
the jumble of detached seats and people.

There was a soft rush of sound as the jet fuel
under one section ignited. Bob could see the
people inside struggling frantically, then they were
obscured by thick, black smoke. The two pilots
had begun dropping people out of the main section. Bob ran over and began leading them away
from the plane. There were terrible screams coming from the burning part of the plane. A burning

woman leaped out of the smoke and began to dance, her arms flailing as she slapped at herself with her flaming purse.

Then the main section of the plane caught. The fire was for the moment confined to the rear. People kept jumping out of the front. The pilots and a stewardess could be heard inside, shrieking at them to hurry up.

Fire burst into the cabin from a thousand different directions, swirling in a vortex. One of the pilots rushed forward, leaped down, and ran away, his face black, his hair smoking. The other one could be seen in the fire, throwing seats, pushing people toward the gaping hole at the front.

Bob sat in his seat in the plane to Atlanta, reliving as he always did that afternoon on the Island of Escape. The Island of Dreams. Piña colada, limbo, snorkel. The Island of Coral Bedrooms.

"Will you be having dinner with us, sir?"

He nodded.

"Steak or chicken?"

Always the same two meals.

"I'll have the duck à l'orange and a half bottle of Chablis. Maybe the saffron soufflé for dessert."

"That sounds like the chicken."

"It's the chicken."

The flight attendant made a note on her little list and went away. This year he had earned over a hundred thousand miles on Delta. Soon he'd be able to cash his mileage in for a free trip somewhere. Maybe the Caribbees, maybe hell.

For once he wasn't lugging along boxes and boxes of seminar materials. Instead it was simply a matter of coming, listening, and going home again. The Apple Computer people were the ones with the boxes of junk.

He tried to let his mind drift. Last night's nightmare was still close to the surface, though, and when he drifted, he at once smelled its fearful scents: wolf breath, wet grass, and his own blood. The dream wasn't really over, that was the trouble. Cindy shouldn't have waked him up, as terrifying as it must have been to see him toward the end howling and snapping. She should have let the dream resolve. Now it persisted in him, lingering at the edge of memory, jumping for a split second into his vision.

To quell it he forced his attention to the face of his watch. Nine P.M. She would just be turning off *Masterpiece Theatre* and probably fixing herself a cup of herb tea. Kevin would be asleep, the cats at the foot of his bed. When Cindy lay down they would come to her, their habit being to share the society of sleep between the two beds in the household. He wished that she was sitting in the seat beside him, Kevin in the window seat.

If the plane was going to crash, though, better he be alone.

When Kevin had been a baby, Bob had taken great pains to preserve his own life. He did not want to leave such a vulnerable little creature. When there was someone in the world whose eyes literally shone when they regarded you, how could you bear to die? Kevin had needed a male image, had adored Bob in a way he had not known was possible, had so relished his every attention. But now Kevin was twelve, and he could grow up without a father, if necessary. Or Cindy could remarry. Bob could be replaced.

While these morbid thoughts passed through

his mind, the stewardess dropped his meal on his tray. He nibbled at the chicken breast, ate the parsley, ate the half of a cherry tomato that was on the salad. He drank the club soda and ate a bite of the dense brownie. He had brought Max Brod's book about Kafka. If he was going to keep up with his son, he was going to have to gain some sort of insight into Kafka. What were the parables about? And the "Penal Colony"—or, for God's sake, the *Metamorphosis*? This morning, while Bob was looking through the Amusement Section of the *Times* for notices about ballroom dancing, Kevin had suddenly asked, "Where's Away From Here? Is it away from here, or away from where Kafka was when he wrote the parable?" He had seen the mirth in his son's eyes, and decided that he had to learn more about Kafka.

He just stared at the pages, though. Half of his mind was waiting for the plane to fall out of the sky, waiting for the dreadful roar that would announce the explosion of a terrorist bomb, or the thuttering oscillations that would precede the separation of a wing.

Why should I read about Kafka? I'm living in Kafka. I'm a Hunger Artist on trial in the Penal Colony. There isn't any escape. Even death is no escape, not if there is reincarnation. Oh, God, what if I come back in Bangladesh or as a Shiite fanatic, or a Chinese peasant? What's going on, how does it all work, why do I keep thinking I've lost my keys when I haven't?

I'm in the middle of the woods and I suddenly realize that I can't get out. The wolf is no help, the wolf is only chasing me deeper.

A cold hand covers mine. A face, rusty around the edges, skin as tight as that of a mummy, hair too blond, voice older than the polished nails, the pearl-hard face-lift. "Jesus will comfort you," says the mask.

Bob realized that he had been crying, his tears raining down on the chicken and Max Brod.

"Jesus—"

"Pray with me. It'll help."

"I don't go to church." He thought: O'Reilly. Cigar. Communion. Then: Altar Society, mother picking up the lilies at Anne Warner's house. Benediction, Mass, the Last Sacraments.

"It doesn't matter whether you believe or not. Jesus doesn't mind."

Where was Father O'Reilly now? The Oblate Seminary, perhaps, teaching the dwindling few seminarians their truth and calling: "Don't drink after midnight or before five o'clock in the morning. Beware of female converts, they are all after your tail. Remember that most questions cannot be answered. Remember that most sins cannot be understood. Nuns expect terrible penances. That is what their lives are about. The church is dying, this is the key truth of our time. Trust in God. Judging from the amount of notice He takes of us, He isn't too concerned. Follow His example, He has perfect knowledge."

All things grow old. The girls of spring get face-lifts. Bob wondered how much skin the lady beside him had lost over the years, how much experience she had hidden in her waxed looks. Where was the skin? Incinerated, or lying in a bottle of formaldehyde in some plastic surgeon's private museum? What would he have there— removed scars pinned to cards like butterflies, septums, big lips, bits of eye sockets and breasts? And, floating in formaldehyde, the discarded cheeks, jowls, and chins of his best customers?

"Pray with me. You might find it helpful."

Her intrusion made him feel mean. "Play?"

"No, pray!"

"You said play."

"Well, hardly that. Play—I mean, oh dear, *pray* with me."

"Freudian slip. I don't remember any prayers except the Hail Mary."

"I don't believe in Freud. He knew nothing of Jesus. What is the Hail Mary? I don't know that prayer."

"Moslem."

"Oh."

She began leafing through the Airline Gift Guide. If you fill out the card—say, order a friend some golf shoes with retractable cleats—and the plane crashes and they find the card, do they mail it for you and take the charge out of your estate? Is there an airline policy covering this matter?

Until the island Bob had always assumed that people were just pulverized in jet crashes. But they had all been alive, broken arms and legs no doubt in the twisted jumble of seats, but alive. Twelve got out.

He imagined being twisted practically in two, the seat on top of him, his face against the floor, and the floor getting hotter and hotter and he cannot get free.

"Please fasten your seat belts, ladies and gentlemen. Captain Garner has begun our final approach into Atlanta's Hartsfield International Airport."

The flight attendant hurried along collecting the last of the meal trays and plastic cups. The landing was completely normal. Bob moved past the smiling crew members and out into Hartsfield's silly vastness without any difficulties. Maybe he only imagined that his life was running out. Perhaps this was an illusion, there to mask the far more horrible reality that he was going to live a long, long, long time.

My problem is, I'm in a panic state. I'm panicked about death. Over death. Death and going broke. At the moment I have no accounts receivable. I've got to drum up some new business. Dying and going broke are similar, except death is less embarrassing. He hurried along a moving sidewalk. But what do I do? How do I drum up business if I'm not sure what it is I do?

Maybe the Apple people would have some ideas. Maybe he ought to start advocating the Macintosh Office after all. A point of difference. "Spend your money with me. I advocate the Macintosh Office."

"Excuse me?"

"Nothing." The man beside him had responded to his thoughts, not because he could read minds but because he had obviously spoken out loud. All right, so you pass age forty and you start talking to yourself.

Nose, ears, and penis all continue to grow, even as your overall body mass starts to decline. Short-term memory is going. And now you mutter.

Silently, over the past year, Bob had begun to engage in the battle of the nose hair. You couldn't very well just leave it to grow longer and longer, curly and gray, like smoke flowing out your nostrils. You had to cut it. Bob used nail clippers, and the process made him sneeze. The more he cut it, the stiffer the hair became. Maybe he was one of those unlucky men whose beards grew inside their noses.

He would have drunk, but he had swallowed so many gallons of alcohol in his youth that he was almost unable to stimulate himself. He didn't smoke, drink, or chew gum.

He was nostalgic for the time in London he had been given some brownies laced with hash by a lush daughter of the nobility—possibly the only lush noble daughter—and had wound up writing a seventy-page epic poem about the death of Nebuchadnezzar.

This part of any trip was the worst, the cab ride from the airport to the hotel. You were alone and you were angry and you were bored. Stone bored watching the passing exit signs, the cars, a Camaro driven by a blonde so enormous she might be a depilated man. Maybe she was. What would *that* be like? A violation, thrilling . . . or depressing, a sexless struggle with someone too strong to escape.

The dull, steamy thoughts of the traveler. Already 10:35. Get checked in, for God's sake, you can't call Cindy after eleven. That's the rule, that way you don't inconvenience anybody. Too bad he couldn't afford a portable phone.

The cab hurtled around a corner and he finally accepted the feeling that the world was ending, or rather, he was ending. "It felt like I died and the whole world died with me," a man had once said upon awakening from a particularly severe auto accident.

"May I take your bag, sir?"

God, I wish you would! "No, that's all right." Check in: the people ahead have no reservations. Then they have a credit card on the Bank of Pakistan. They speak little English. Bob would carry them on his back to their room if it would hurry things up. The lobby smells faintly of cigarette smoke and food. Liquor. Steak. Later, he'll come down to the bar with all the other lonely men and sit staring around, looking for the Woman Who Is Not There.

He's being processed now. Credit card. Guest of Apple. Oh, that'll be the fourth floor. She says it like it's the bomb shelter. Go right up, you're already checked in, Mr. Drake.

Duke.

Okay.

Fourth floor: a woman of twenty in a tan suit with the Apple logo on her pocket comes forward. "May I take your bag, Mr. Drake?"

"Duke. No thanks."

"Let's see, you're in 403. Lucky you, you'll have a view down Peachtree Street."

Oh, how wonderful! What luck!

The room is very nicely packaged. Little soaps and creams and things, and a shoeshine rag that doesn't quite work, the bed turned down with a mint on the pillow. A bowl of apples and a lot of literature. A Macintosh on the desk to play with. Very posh. Apple wants to win.

Brochure: *Apple and Your Corporate Clients*. Oh, God, I haven't got any corporate clients. I've got to make some calls, but I hate to make calls. "Hello, may I speak to the president of the company? Hello, my name is Robert Drake—I mean Duke—I'd like to send you some information about—hello, yes, this is Robert Hack, I'd like to send you—this is who—oh, no, I need to speak to your podiatrist—or president. Well, good-bye."

That's called a line of gab.

Look at you, strutting around in the dreary room, proud and scared, an ego on a stick, signifying nothing. The girl left abruptly with a reminder that he was due for breakfast at 8:30 in the Dorset Room. Dorset Room. Breakfast. Okay, Mr. Drake will be there. Why not Mr. Mallard, it's similar but more interesting. Midlife crisis cliché. But I had my midlife crisis when I was thirty-eight. Working for Merril Witch, flacking bonds, all of a sudden you get up from your desk and go stomping off like a golem. You reach the elevator. You leave the building. A day passes, your boss Luke Skywalker finally calls. "Hi, Bill," he says.

"It's Bob."

"Yeah, that's right. You okay, Bob?"

"Am I?"

"Well, I'll tell you, Bill, I thought you were sick or something, looking at your numbers. Real sick! You can't get the business. Sure, you rush around with goddamn cups of coffee in your hand, but that's it. For you, that's the whole job. I've been watching you, Bill—"

"Bob."

"Rob, Bob, Bill, goddamn Irving! Your severance check is in the toilet!"

A factual story: A very hot man was once hired by a small but very hot brokerage firm but did not do the volume expected of him. The trouble was, he had gone there on a five-year contract with a five-year salary in addition to commissions. This was a man who could not work unless he was desperate. Mr. Float, they called him at Wrexler, where he had originally been employed. Soon the boss of the very hot brokerage firm wanted to get rid of Mr. Float. But how, with a five-year con-

tract? One morning Mr. Float walked in to find
that his entire office had been moved into the
men's room.

He remained in that office, reading comic
books, for the full five years.

Some say that is where the expression "taking a
floater," got its start.

Hanging up his spare suit, Bob thought: Now,
why in hell did I tell myself that story? Why don't
I go down to the bar and tell some broad that
hilarious story? This very night I may fondle
strange breasts.

That thought led to a frantic check of the watch.
Eleven-two. No. Grab the phone, *click*, dial, *click
click. Ring. Clunk.* "Hello."

"Honey—sorry I'm late."

Laughter. "I was reading. I knew you'd be late. I
was hoping you'd call."

Am I a self-absorbed by-product of a dying
culture? "I'm glad you're still up. How was *Masterpiece*?"

"I slept through it. Kevin watched it, though.
He says it's very well acted. Apparently some of
the period detail is wrong, though. Something
about the men's collar styles."

"I miss you."

"You know what I want to do to you."

"Oh, God, Cindy, I wish you could."

"Have a good night's sleep, darling."

"The dream—"

"What dream?"

"God, don't you remember? Last night I
dreamed I got eaten by a wolf? It's still in my
mind, I can't get rid of it. It's terrifying, Cindy. I
wish to hell I'd canceled out on this."

"You might make some good contacts. Now, I

want you to take a nice, warm shower and settle down with a good book. What did you take with you?"

"Max Brod on Kafka."

"Dear God. That's Kevin's influence. Let him deal with Kafka, you need to have some fun when you read. A good historical, Michener or John Jakes. Something that'll take your mind away from itself. Kafka's not for you, you're too old and overwrought to stand it."

"He stood it. He had to, he was in himself and couldn't get out."

"Didn't he cut off his ear?"

"That was Van Gogh, the painter."

"Yes, well, his skies are Kafka's words. They all ended badly, those men. You can't get on that road. It'll kill you, there are secrets down there we shouldn't know. I'm telling you, Bob, you've got to stick to the real. Throw yourself heart and soul into the conference. Learn, make friends, really work at it. Bob, you might lose your way, honey, a lot of people like you do."

He yearned toward her voice, wished he could flow through the phone and into her body, could swarm into every cell of her, the wet, the jittering electric places, and possess her and be possessed by her, to be her ghost, her aura.

"I'll do like you say, I'll go down to the newsstand and get some light reading."

"An author you like. Don't pick up someone who annoys you. Someone somewhat literate."

That's me baby, someone somewhat literate. I'm a man who happened wrong. I should be a writer, for God's sake, but I hear it's an awful profession. They're always going broke. It's a brutal, exploitative field. Oh, God, I've missed my life.

"Good-bye, Cindy, I love you."

Click. We're off. He hangs up the phone thinking that she is an awesomely decent woman. She's a priest, a shaman, Dante. Some people are here to lead the others through life, to succor and to guide. Does she not, in her blond and voluptuous ease, even in her perfection, the calm creator of Kevin and beneficent sustainer of me, does she not deserve my loyalty?

Somewhere in this hotel, right now, there is a woman who will sleep with me. Oh, yes, not Cindy but one of her allies. I will have to go home and go to confession in our pink bedroom, and my penance will be more serious than "say the Our Father three times my son, and keep your hands out from under the covers."

He heard distant howling, as if of a wolf.

It was feeling, it was sensation, his body quaking, bending over, hands clutching the center of his gut, eyes screwed closed, and he was aware of another Atlanta, a ghost Atlanta, when it was all forest, and the things of the earth swept and swished, trotted and crawled here. On the hill where the Westin now stood—which had been completely removed for the hotel, a million-year-old hill—a wolf had howled, a bigger, heavier creature than today's wolves, and his howl had carried up and down the river, and high, high into the night, where it had echoed against the fat rising moon. The howl still lived, domiciled in the hotel's bones.

When Bob was a boy in Texas, he used to imagine that if he ran fast enough, was secret enough, clever enough, he could step off the edge of Texas and onto the full moon. On the moon lived the ghosts of ten million Indians, and he also belonged there. The Comanches and the Tejas, the Apaches and the Kiowa, the Blackfeet and the Iroquois, the Pueblo and the Mixtec, all would greet him and call him brother, and he would go down the river of heaven in a bark canoe.

Reality: The sun of his youth came up like a big hubcap and Texas kept right on happening. San Antonio grew, row upon row of houses marching out into land so ancient and untouched that fossils lay on the surface, land so delicate that any footfall was permanent. And the power lines marched and the drive-in banks, and the Great Atlantic and Pacific Tea Company, and the kids, and the cars, and the law offices.

Bob had gotten himself into a very bad mental state by the time he arrived in the bar. It didn't matter much, there wasn't a woman in the place except for the waitress, who was spreading the vodka tonics and white wines in full armor, visor down. What can you do? Ishtar opens her legs and all the corn of Babylon flowers. When she closes them, the man who was involved gets his head cut off.

"Stoly on the rocks."

"You thought you were getting somewhere but you're not. Am I right?" A guy had edged in beside him, a used-car shill in a bleak checked suit. "Whatever you want, you end up with something else. Is that right or is it right? A guy like you, like me, we get tied up, we can't get away. Well, you have to go for the gold. I always tell people who come to me for advice, buddy, I tell them, go for the gold. You think you have a home but you

haven't got a home. You have a mortgage. This is
not a home, excuse me, a home would be your
own. The four walls belong to the bank, the paper
is what belongs to you. We have to get these things
straight. The trouble with you, with me, is we
cannot get these things straight. We own nothing,
have everything. It's all an illusion, complete and
total. Am I right? I'm asking you, I'm serious, am I
right? Here's a guy, asks you am I right, and you
can't get a word in, this guy's not a genius, he's not
a guru, he's not even a salesman, he's a compulsive
talker in a goddamn bar. Look, you want a decent
home for your wife and kids, that's why you're
here in this bar. That's why we're all here. We're
knights on the journey to the grail, every one of us,
even the old fart over there with the stogie, that
old pushbelly's Sir Goddamn Lancelot, am I
right? Look at this place. Not a skirt in sight. Even
the gigged-out old rejects leave places like this
alone. Where are the hookers? They are in the
places of youth. Not even hookers want us, we are
reject johns. Hookers won't bother with a bunch
of weepy fifty-dollar tricks. Nowadays even the
ugly whores and the sex changes make big bread,
you know how they do it? How the hell do they do
it, why can't we get them into the salesman bars
anymore? It's S&M ruined us. There was an old
war-horse used to come in here to drink and turn a
few. Now she's got a posh suite up in the Bonaven-
ture and she's bought herself some whips and a
pair of leather gloves. There are guys'll pay a
fortune even to them plug uglies to go after them
with a whip. Am I right? I miss that damn old
rotten whore. They're all the goddamn Blessed
Virgin Mary, that's our problem. Blaspheme, blaspheme, etcetera. Excuse me, ma'am—could you

bring me another couple of double bourbons?"

The waitress huffed off. Bob, who wanted desperately to get away from this man, but who was also curious about him, had to get rid of a bothersome question. "Is this a pitch for some kind of self-improvement seminar?"

"You ask that?"

"I don't want any more pitches for Jesus. I get Jesus pitches every time I get on a plane."

"That isn't a real question. Who am I, what do I want, those are real questions. You think you have a life but you don't. You do not have ownership, you have debt."

"My car is paid for."

"Wha—well, good goddamn, aren't we wonderful! Oh, may I touch the hem of the garment— well, let me look at you! Your car is paid for! Good goddamn. Well, hell. Isn't that wonderful. I'm so proud of my friend! Here's a guy can fuck the best part of your whole goddamn carefully rehearsed speech! We better be careful, this guy here with the plastic nerdpack in his shirt pocket might be president someday. He drives a car that is *his own*. Now, looky here, Mr. Smartass. You think your car is paid for, but you're wrong. You don't have the fucking holy grail just yet, Sir Gawain, my brother. Your kids' educations, are they paid for? Is your house paid for? And what about your business, your goddamn swimming pool, your time-share, your TV, your VCR, your home computer? Your car is paid for—what a lie. Unless everything is paid for, nothing is paid for. Your debt is just arranged differently. Look, what I'm leading up to is, you need something that is your own, and that nobody can take away from you. You need a stake in the earth. You need land.

Land, man! I know a lot about land. Specifically, I know about the sweetest little piece of eastern Canada ever was. The very sweetest."

Bob thought, Oh, lord, a real-estate salesman.

The pitch drummed on. He was like a penitent before the altar of the hustle. Kneeling at a bulging vest, not reading the contract, the haze of fine print, take the pen, hit it right here, thank you, you have just bought another American dream.

—But it's not paid for either.

Slam, bam, thank you, ma'am. Phrase that became current in Dodge City during the cattle drives, to describe encounters between prostitutes and teenage cowboys who had not seen a woman in years. What is a man like who comes in after two years on the range eating sowbelly and beans, working seven days a week twenty hours a day? Put him in the middle of the biggest, richest city he has ever seen, with three hundred dollars in his pocket, and also give him a gun. That's the American dream, although few of those young men lived to tell about it.

No, they bought real estate with their three hundred dollars and then went out to see their land. Slam, bam, thank you, ma'am. Goin' to Canada to see mah swamp.

Bob signed the contract "Ronald Woodrow Wilson Reagan."

"My God, you have a long name—like a Negro."

"I am a Negro."

"But you look—ah, hell!"

"Sorry."

"I can't sell this stuff to you on time. You've got to pay cash."

"Don't have it."

The real-estate hustler got up and went to the far end of the bar. Bob, for his part, left ten dollars on the table and slunk out.

He wished, how he wished, that there would come a knock at his door and that tall, beautiful blonde from the Camaro would be standing there, but no knock came. The air-conditioning hissed. He threw off his clothes, ate the mint on his pillow, and then brushed his teeth. He climbed into the bed.

The claws of sleep grabbed him, and he was dragged screaming down the nightmare escalator that never quite gets to the grail.

CHAPTER THREE

YOU LIE ON A BED IN A HOTEL ROOM. YOU ARE NAKED, you are rigid. Nobody cares, nobody will help you. Therefore you go to sleep.

The effect was as sudden and devastating as mainlining gasoline. His breath came in shattering barks, his hands fluttered, his legs kicked, his whole bones twisted in the elastic prison of his muscles. Air swooped in his lungs. Then his nose bloomed with odors, the plastic stench of the drapes, fungus from the air-conditioner filter, the body-ridden bed. This room seemed no longer slick and clean, but rather a dark, thick den swarming with the leftover flakes of a thousand lonely men.

His hands worked at the air. His fingers seemed dull and stubbed, and he felt streaming out behind him a hot dagger of nerves. He tried to touch his face—awful thick nails came up. He groaned,

which was a coarse inarticulation. He was full of
aches and newness. A leg trampled air, and when
he attempted rising, he fluttered and fell in the
bed, unable to make himself work right.

His legs skittered in the sheets. Oddly, his hands
wanted to work with them. What was he trying to
do, crawl?

In his extremity he cried aloud, a sound as high
as the air brakes on a truck.

Jesus, was this a stroke?

Get it together!

He scrabbled, he flopped—what the hell was
happening!

He was out of control here. With every muscle,
with every ounce of his strength he strove to quiet
his heaving body.

This was grotesque!

He struggled at least for order, for power over
the wild, twisting gyrations.

But his struggles didn't help. As if powered by
another soul, his body leaped up, jumping farther
than he had ever jumped before, soaring all the
way from the bed to the window. He hit the ceiling
and fell, grabbing at the curtains, which collapsed
around him.

He crouched in their folds. Burning in his mind
was an image he had seen as he leaped, a great
beast in the mirror, its front paws outstretched, its
tail soaring behind it. Experimentally, he tried to
feel for the tail. No luck, his arms didn't go back
that far anymore. All right. He tried a little hip
action. Behind him he heard the thud, thud of
something hitting the floor. He felt the weight of
it, and the air tickling its fur.

Do not move. This could only be one of two

things: complete psychosis or a really bizarre stroke.

What if he was one of those stroke victims who just sit and stare, saying nothing, locked forever in deep universes of fantasy? Or he might be the kind of psychotic who is so unruly he must be abandoned to the violent ward. He is the one so out of it that his care packages from home will always be stolen by the orderlies.

It was damn sad. He started to cry again, but stifled himself when he heard the whines. How could he even talk to Cindy? How could he discuss Kafka with his son, or play chess and Stratego with him, given the apparent presence of paws? Could he even think anymore? This room smelled like cigars, cigarettes, pipe tobacco, perfume, and human sweat.

He raised his head. Something was slipping through the brush nearby.

His immediate reaction was immense relief. If there was brush nearby, this must be a dream after all, because there was no brush in hotel bedrooms.

All right, then let it roll. A man was coming through the brush. Bob cocked his ears, heard the man breathing, heard him muttering, smelled alcohol on his breath. He did not smell the steel of a gun, only leather and cloth and sodden skin. The man was singing to himself as he put up plastic markers in the sodden ground. Clouds of mosquitoes swarmed around him, and from time to time he groaned and made a swipe with his arm. He was the real-estate salesman from the bar, and this was the land he was selling. The plastic markers went flying as he made a lunge at the mosquitoes. He took out a can of insect repellent and sprayed the bugs. "All right, you bastards, live with yourselves!"

I am not in eastern Canada and I don't have the ability to smell the vodka and the tonic separately on a man's breath. No, I am alone in a hotel room. I am not in the woods with this repellent old salesman. I do not have long teeth, Granny, I do not have big eyes. This isn't stroke or psychosis, it is one mega-dream.

I am in the Westin Hotel in Atlanta, Georgia, Room 403. I have a view down Peachtree Street which I cannot see because no matter how my dream makes them look, the curtains are in fact closed.

He heard the air conditioner hissing, felt the air brushing his fur. A sound in the hall made him snort.

From the doorway there came a knock. Another. Then the door made a clicking sound. A woman hurried into the room, elderly, in a gray uniform with a white apron. "Turndown service. Sir?" A grunt. The lights went full on. "Wha—the curtains!"

In the mirror that covered the wall behind the dresser Bob saw a large dog or wolf standing on the bed staring at the mirror. Startled, he cried aloud. The animal reared back, its barking filling the room, its hackles raised, its teeth bared.

"Oh, no! No pets allowed!" The maid threw all of her mints in the air and jumped back, falling over her cart full of sheets and towels and little bottles of body shampoo.

Bob's difficulty was that he could not find himself in the mirror. Did nightmares have reflections? This had to end soon. Dream or not, he could still see the mints on the floor.

Since he was not a wolf, what had she seen and run off to report? Had he exposed himself to her? Would the vice squad soon be here, ready to take him in, scare him good, and send him home to a furious wife? "Really, Bob, if you want to try it with strangers, why not just call an escort service?" Then the diminished relationship. Fifteen years of loyalty lost to a bad dream.

The maid had left her cart overturned in the hall. Bob, moving awkwardly, trying to keep all four limbs coordinated, went out and sniffed one of the slowly turning wheels. There was a click behind him. He didn't need to look. Of course the unseen hand of nightmare had closed the door.

He sniffed the handle, smelling a strong odor of the maid's hand, mixed of sour skin smell, cigarettes, mints, and body shampoo. He shrank back, thinking that he really couldn't handle sniffing a doorknob. It was part of the perfection of the illusion that he had just automatically done that instead of trying to open the door.

He thought: Probably I only *feel* like this. What I actually look like is a naked man sniffing a doorknob and I've got to stifle this peculiar behavior!

I'll be calm, straightforward. I was going for the shower and took a wrong turn. Honest mistake. No big deal. Just please God don't let me start barking again!

The worst thing about this experience was that it didn't have the logic of dream or hallucination at all, it had the logic of life. He wished to God for Cindy.

When he heard the elevator bell ring and the doors roll open, a powerful and unexpected instinct asserted itself. He cowered back down the hall, seeking some darkness. Excited voices came toward him. "I swear it's the biggest dog I ever seen." What was this? Was the maid part of the dream, after all, or was he shifting the sense of her words into his own delusional system?

"How he git it into de hotel, dat what I got to know."

"Ask the guest. He must have smuggled it in."

They came around the corner and stopped dead. "Aw, God. It got out." Bob looked up at them. A wave of sensation made him shudder, almost as if there were tiny creatures running on his skin. He felt frightened and dismal. He certainly seemed to be naked on all fours in the hallway of a hotel.

"Its creepin' along, look out."

"We gotta get the police, I ain't gonna touch nothin' that big." Hearing this, Bob cracked. Terror whipped him. He screamed and ran for the fire stairs. "Holy shit, it done got some speed on it!" Bob raced down the corridor, his claws catching on the rug.

"We can't let that thing out in the hotel, they'll fire us both!"

"Come on, woman, help me! We can head it off."

The yellow lights glaring down, the beige elevator doors, the confusing twists and turns of the halls, Bob might be in a maze of some kind, the lights too bright, the ceilings too high, the smells all wrong.

He saw writing on a door: EXIT. He threw himself against the bar until the door gave way into the fire stairs.

"That thing's got a mind of its own, it just opened that door."

Down, up, which way to go? Bob heard himself whimpering. He made a solemn vow: When I get home, if I ever do, I will call Monica and make an appointment. I will do this no matter how good I feel at the time. Frantically, he sought reasons for his predicament. Was it the salesman in the bar? Some kind of drug in his drink to make him a more pliant buyer? When he was selling, he had often wished for drugs of some kind. Just a nice little powder in the damn fool's steak sauce, and he becomes silly enough to buy the damn bonds. "Go out among the people, young man, and rape them." Fatherly advice from Charlie Decker, his boss in the bond office. Charles Decker: killed himself with a fingernail file.

Quite arbitrarily he started up instead of down. It was not long, though, before he heard voices behind him. "How high is it?" "Go up to fifteen. You're gonna head it off." "Come on, where's that elevator when you need it?"

Bob was having trouble working his body. If he thought about it, his back legs and his front legs stopped working together and he went to scrabbling. Trying to make his mind a blank, he moved up the stairs. His mind went back to Sister Eustacia, the music teacher at Sacred Heart. Sister Eustacia: playing the piano is a matter of mind over matter. Let your mind float free in the music, and your fingers will find their own way.

Mind, let go. Body, run. Door after door, smell of concrete dust and hot electric connections. Running, reduced to raw reality, no more thought, just the urge to escape, to get away from the embarrassment. The road to Cairo, *The Road to Rio.* Bob Hope, 1956, Ozzie and Harriet, *The Dinah Shore Show. The Honeymooners, Leave It to Beaver*. Ernie Kovaks, a station wagon going *boom boom* down into the ditch, Ernie Kovaks. 1956, remembering the dark side of the war. Yes, we went and found out what was behind the curtain, didn't we? The word "Hiroshima" even sounds like a soft explosion.

The last time you ran like this was in 1956. You were twelve years old. You and Roxanne de LaPlane rolled naked down the hill behind her house, and found yourselves at her father's feet. You rose up and you certainly did run, a naked kid in the evening.

Ahead, a door! God save me, it's the roof. They are still behind me, they have come forty floors. That security guard is made of strong stuff. Bob had to hang out his tongue, otherwise his mouth felt like somebody had stuffed a hot pillow in it. When he panted it got cold, spreading relief through his body.

He stood at the door jerking, twisting, pounding his tail against the floor. He tried to change back, straining and grunting. He hopped and yapped, hating the absurd sound of his voice. Poof, bang, abracadabra, hocus-pocus. *Hoc et corpus*, Father O'Reilly, Jesus. Mary Catherine Baker and Salvatore Allessio each completed ten thousand Hail Marys during Lent in the year 1957. Lent, sacrifice, passion of Christ: oh, Mother of God, intercede for me.

His prayers were idiotic yaps.

They brought, however, a curious relief. Someone heard the noises and came to the other side of the door. With a loud click a waiter in a red jacket opened it. Bob, aware only that this was the end of the line, knowing that the security guard was no more than a couple of floors below, rushed through.

Sights, sounds, and an overpowering mass of odors assailed him. His eyes could not understand, his nose could not sort out the chaos before him. He barked once loudly, and the face of every diner in the Starlight Restaurant turned toward him.

Damn that bark, without it he might have been able to slink past unnoticed. He was aware of his own nakedness, and sought to cover himself with his hands. The moment he did this, he toppled forward. When he recovered himself, he was confronting three waiters, one of them with a large silver tray in his hand which he used as a shield. A few of the diners had jumped from their seats. "It's a wolf," one of them shouted.

"How in hell—"

"Don't let it out onto the floor," a maître d' hissed. "You'll cause a riot."

The waiters skittered around. Bob's eyes went to the long corridor. At the far end he could see a glass door. Behind it would be the sky lobby. His own room seemed a million light-years away.

Oh, Cindy.

Remembering Sister Eustacia's instructions, Bob tried to concentrate his mind on the glass door and let his body do its own work. He shot forward with the power of four legs instead of two, moving faster than he ever had before. There was a blinding red flash and a shock of pain to his head. With a great shattering the doors became a rubble of glass pebbles. Bob rolled over and over across the sky lobby. As he rolled he moved through a jumble of smells, the glass, the sweat of his pursuers, his own fur and flying slobber.

Then he was on his feet. "Oh, God," he said. He staggered, his arms working like arms instead of forelegs. He was high off the ground and his nose was suddenly numb. The riot of odors had disappeared. He jabbed the elevator button with a normal finger. When it opened, three women in beehive hairdos and tight dresses burst into shrieks of hysterical laughter.

The nightmare of being a wolf had left him stranded on the fortieth floor, naked.

He dashed past the women into the closing elevator, hammered "four," and pressed himself against the back wall as the doors made a thumping sound.

The waiters, the maître d', the security guard, and about six male patrons were blasting down the corridor. Bob banged his fist against the "close door" button, but the elevator was at the top floor, and cycling on its own time. They reached the glass rubble and slowed down, picking their way to avoid getting their shoes cut open.

Not realizing that Bob was inside, the security guards ran right past the open elevator, heading for the fire stairs at the far end of this lobby. "It musta gone to the roof."

"It can't open doors, surely."

"I saw it open a door. That thing is smart."

Hail Mary full of grace, the Lord is with thee. Blessed art thou among women, and blessed is the fruit of thy womb, Jesus Christ.

"Hey, wha—lookit him—wait!"

The doors slid closed just as a man in a maroon polyester sports jacket and a string tie lunged toward them.

"There's a guy in there stark staring naked!"

"Dis a good hotel!"

Vroom, down he went, down to the fourth floor. Blessed be, don't make a stop on the way. No such luck, a stop is made.

Bob turned his back on the young man and woman in tan Apple Computer sports jackets, who entered the elevator. "Uh-oh," the woman said.

"Please, I was taking a shower," Bob replied, his face to the wall. "I was looking for my hair conditioner and next thing I knew I was in the hall. I couldn't make anybody hear me, so I tried to go for the security guards."

The couple remained silent. The doors opened on the fourth floor and Bob backed out, careful to avoid showing them his face. After the doors closed he heard a burst of laughter, the woman tinkling merrily, the man going haw-haw.

He raced around the corner and down the hall. Either the door would open or it wouldn't. He saw the overturned cart at the end of the hall, moved forward. He was praying as he walked, a breathy "Jesus, help me" at each step.

Somebody must have intervened, because he found his door unlocked. Given hands, it was blissfully easy to open. He rushed inside, grabbed clothes frantically, a pair of pants, his house shoes, a knit shirt. Dressed, dressed again, oh blessing divine. His mind twisted and turned. Go down to the bar. Forget the whole thing.

No. Foolish man. Your room will be full of cops when you return. A better idea: He went outside, heaped all of the maid's things on her cart and rolled it to the opposite end of the hall. There he overturned the cart and spread everything out at another door. Then he dashed back to his own room and replaced the curtains. If only he could have gotten into 422 and pulled the curtains down as well.

A shout came from outside. Very good. "Aw, damn—" Footsteps going in the opposite direction. Bob exited his room, stepping confidently toward the elevator bank as two security guards and a whole squadron of cops began hammering on the door to 422.

He remained in the nearly empty bar long enough to knock back two neat Stolys. Then, heavy with sleep, he returned to his room. Down the hall another computer consultant was talking frantically. He didn't have a dog, he had been asleep, he was from Houston, Texas, he was very quiet, yes, he had a driver's license, oh, Officer, there's no need to go down to the station.

Behind his own door, safe at last, Bob felt a giggly sort of relief. He took off his clothes and went into the bathroom. The mentally ill were often given Jacuzzis to calm them down, so Bob filled the tub and turned on the nozzles. Then he got two little bottles of Courvoisier from the room's fridge. He knocked one back almost immediately. When the tub was ready, he sank into it, floating the other bottle so it would get nice and warm. He watched it dance in the bubbles and he sang softly to himself, "You clever devil, you got away, got awaaay. . . ." He sipped from the second bottle, sipped the good fire. Like a man after battle he was suddenly seized with a need for sex, for the blood and passion of the life he had almost lost. He wanted sex, but he also wanted food. Maybe he would find an escort service. He would get to that. But first he decided to call room service and order a BLT and a bottle of beer. Dixie, if they had it; if not, a nice, cold Molson. Above the hissing of the tub and the foam of these pleasant thoughts, there intruded the frantic bleating of the poor sucker who had been sucked up by the security guards. His explanations must not have sufficed; they were on their way to the police station. Booking, indecent exposure, breaking down a door, bringing in a giant dog. Sent back to his wife in disgrace, there to be thoroughly punished. God help him, God grant that he deserves it for other sins.

He ordered his midnight snack over the phone in the bathroom, and was in the hotel's terrycloth robe watching *Midnight Blue* when it arrived, the cart being pushed by a fetching woman of perhaps forty, neat in her red dress and white blouse, as cheerfully efficient as a stewardess. As she swept the silver dome off his sandwich she glanced at the TV. He saw color come into her cheeks.

Now, Bob, by God, this is a definite chance. This is what you've been wanting, a stranger. She's no kid, but then neither am I. I need a woman who's had a little experience. She lingered, waiting for him to sign the chit. "Want to share it with me?" he asked.

She looked down at the chit he had handed her. "How?"

"I mean the sandwich."

"I don't want a sandwich."

What an asinine attempt. He should be ashamed of himself. She was between him and the door, turning to leave. "Wait," he said. He was trying to think but his mind was blank. He leaped across the bed and threw himself to his knees at her feet. She jumped back, her face registering surprise and annoyance.

"Ma'am, you must know the extraordinary

effect your beauty has had upon me. Seeing you
this moment, I must confess that I was stunned by
the intensity of my own reaction. You look angry,
but consider rather that you should be flattered.
I'm a decent enough man. My interest is in itself a
compliment. I give you my body, my soul, for an
hour's love or a lifetime."

"I—uh—ah—" She had no words, no reply.
He fancied that she realized any reply would be
fatal. Thus encouraged, he seized her hand and
kissed it, the first flesh not of Cindy he had kissed
in passion almost since he could remember.

She drew her hand away, but slowly, like she
was removing a luscious glove. "I can't just disappear into a room, I'll lose my job." His heart
started thundering. She was saying yes. This was
yes.

"When do you get off?"

"At three. It's an hour from now."

He kissed her hand again, then her red sleeve.
He rose and swept her up in his arms. "At three.
I'll be waiting for you."

She slipped out, he ate every scrap of his
sandwich and drank his beer.

The next thing he knew his phone was ringing.
"Hi, this is Amanda from Apple. Just calling to
make sure you'll be at the breakfast." What time
was it now? Seven-thirty. He ached from a night
spent half in dreams, half in hard, physical longing.

"I'll be there," he said. He put down the phone.
The world was so disappointing. It took more than
the real passion of a decent man to entice a
woman. Just not very good-looking, that was Bob.
His approach had been stupid. Sexual competents
didn't go down on their knees and blubber. No

macho. A wimp, to use an expression only wimps use nowadays.

He shaved, lathering his face with Trac II Shaving Cream and then using the Bic shaver the hotel had thoughtfully provided. He rubbed some Brylcreem into his hair, brushed his teeth, and dressed in a J. Press suit. None of this polyester junk for him. He liked to look Manhattan.

As he was leaving the room he saw a note at his feet. It had been slipped in under the door. "Sorry, a big ruckus in the hotel. No way I can get back after my shift without being noticed, security everywhere. Love ya, crazy guy, Alison."

For an instant he was delighted with the note, then he threw it down with an in-sucked cry. "A big ruckus in the hotel": reality. The engines of the impossible, still churning. He looked at the note again, then at the door. He was going to have to go out there and pretend ignorance of whatever it was he had done.

He couldn't hide, that would create suspicion. The thing to do was to attend the breakfast, maybe hit a seminar or demo session, then plead a business emergency and depart on the next plane. Do it smoothly, correctly. Do it well.

Still, he hesitated. There was always the possibility that the disturbance she referred to had nothing to do with him.

But of course it did. Last night he had assumed the structure of another kind of creature, perhaps a dog or wolf, and had gotten himself tangled up in a flickering, dangerous adventure in the halls. It remained in his memory, a thick storm of odors and sounds, odd, gray visions, confusion, people shouting, and then a queasy, naked escape back to his room. He remembered his eerie *other* body as a storm of rich sensations: the tickling joy of paws upon carpet and concrete stair, the movement of air through fur, the sounds and above all the smells of the restaurant, almost as palpable as the food itself. He caught himself sucking breath through distended nostrils, and thought of breakfast eggs, of coffee, of buttered toast, of the shifting, magical steam rising from a plate of food.

He left the room and strode down the hall. "Hi, Mr. Drake," said a young woman in an Apple blazer. "I'm Jane Poole, I'm your coordinator for the conference. Breakfast's just starting in Ballroom C on the mezzanine."

"I'm as hungry as a wolf."

Going down, in the elevator he was joined by two other conferees, named, according to their tags, "Hi, my name is Winston Jeal, Jealco Systems," and "Hi, my name is Harry Thomas, CompuTex." Bob's own name was "Hi, I'm Bob Drake, Drake Business Consultants." What had happened to Bob Duke? he wondered. Been canceled, apparently, at least as far as Apple was concerned.

Winston Jeal looked haggard. The Kaywoodie in his mouth was the only thing holding his face together. Without it he would collapse into twitches and snickering anger. Bob knew just exactly who he was. This was the remains of the man from 422, who had spent his night in a police station fielding accusations that must have sounded rather bizarre. "You brought a wolf into the hotel! You ran naked through the halls!"

"'Morning," Bob said.

"Hiya," Harry Thomas replied. "Hope you're hungry. I've been to these Apple dos before, and they really lay a table."

Jeal said nothing, only stared at the elevator doors, his pipe jutting from his mouth. There was a copy of Thomas Pynchon's *Gravity's Rainbow* in his jacket pocket. His glasses, in desperate need of cleaning, were held together by a couple of Band-Aids. The doors opened. There was also a conference of independent real-estate agents in the hotel, and they had gathered into boisterous, boasting knots in front of the elevator banks, preparing to go to their own breakfast in Ballroom A. "If those bastards try to sell you some damn land, sell them back with a damn computer," Jeal said. His voice was hollow and deep, resonant with bitter meaning.

Once in Ballroom C, he went down the row of steam tables loading his plate with eggs, bacon, and sausage, with the darkest toast in the pile, with slices of honeydew melon and tiny pastries, finally with a small croissant from a last pile at the end of the table. A sudden roar arose from the real-estate salesmen two ballrooms away. They were there to be set afire with greed by some blazing expert, to be whipped and massaged until they were virtual psychopaths of sales. The hunger upon them, they would rage out into the land, to sell its still-empty meadows, its forests, to people who might haul in trailers or put up A-frames, and drain their septic tanks into its arteries and veins.

Bob once saw stalking the night woods near his hunt club a ghost Indian whose face was so pocked with anger that it had festered. Black puss fell in globs from the rotted cheeks, and the eyes were bloodshot with rage. The Indian had walked right off into the sky, and Bob had heard a sound like a stone door closing.

He sat down now across from Jeal and tucked

into a forkful of wobbly scrambled eggs. They filled his head, his lungs, his esophagus with fluffy flavor. Through his mind there flowed images of chickens, clouds of chickens, laying eggs to *Eine Kleine Nachtmusick, ta ta ta bloof, dum dum dee. Bloof.* And the clerks at their computers, hen number 11893, laying rate 4, weight 2.2 kg, *cluck cluck* went the disk drive, and the sausage and the bacon, and the howling pigs in the slaughterhouse, the sows and the hogs, the shoats going down the chute, the screams of terror in processing, the automatic clubber smashing ten thousand skulls a day.

They evolved without hands, the pigs, but bearing meat that looks, tastes, and smells just like human. Poor pigs, condemned to be at once reviled and loved by man. Sometimes, eating bacon, you almost remember something. Then you don't, you can't.

"What?"

Bob looked up. It was Jeal; he had taken his pipe out of his mouth and spoken, raising his coffee to his lips.

"Excuse me?"

"You said something about a pig."

Bob smiled. "I was thinking about—I used to—I mean, my father once took me to a slaughterhouse." He barked out a laugh. "Sorry."

"You just blurt out gobbledygook about pigs because you're eating bacon? This industry needs more people like you." Bitter, enraged, his words sharp, his voice thick with anger.

"What's the matter?"

"I spent the night as a guest of the goddamn Atlanta police. And I never figured out why. Some crazy story about me letting a dog loose in the hotel. I don't have a dog. My sister has a Lhasa apso, and I had a bulldog named Jane when I was growing up. They say this dog that was allegedly in my room wrecked the goddamn restaurant. What is this, a police state?"

"They had the Wayne Williams thing here, remember. Child murderer. The Atlanta cops are pathological about anything strange."

"A guy sitting in a hotel room in his goddamn underpants watching Arsenio Hall is strange? Now I've heard it all." He attacked a poached egg, slicing through it so that the yolk ran and the white collapsed. He cut furiously for a time, until the egg was pale yellow pulp. Then he knocked back a glass of prune juice like it was a shot of Old Crow. "There isn't a goddamn thing you can do. All of a sudden the door flies open and here comes a maid and about six security guards and a dozen cops. 'He put the curtains back,' the maid screams. The damn cops grabbed me. I was so startled I almost swallowed my pipe. As it was I blew the fire through the bowl and set one of the cop's hair alight. He was using this inflammable Georgia Peach goo they've got down here, and it took them a while to get it out. So off I went, booked for assault by a furious five-hundred-pound policeman with a wet towel wrapped around his head." Leaning close to his plate, he shoveled in the rest of the pulped egg.

"You were actually booked?"

Jeal regarded him with suspicious interest. "If I'm talking to a reporter right now, I want to say something real simple. You print a word about this, and I will kill you." He started on his toast, tearing at it with a jerk of his head. Bob realized that the man wasn't exaggerating. He wondered if

Jeal had killed before. Vietnam, maybe. Bob had gone the professional student route to escape the war. Jeal did not seem the type to escape anything.

"Are you in any trouble?"

"Apple sorted it out. That coordinator honey was down at the precinct house the whole time. I don't think it amounts to much. It's just the goddamn abuse that gets me. I mean, a man is sitting in a hotel room minding his own business, and *bang.* Can you imagine what Apple thinks of me? How is this going to look once Miss Coordinator files her report? Beware of the kook from Houston. That's all they'll remember. I'm trying to feed a family just like every guy here. This is not going to help me. Hell, let's talk about something else. What we all want to talk about. You got pictures?"

Bob experienced the familiar delight, the ritual of showing his own fascinating pictures of Kevin, then politely observing his companion's boring ones of his own kids. You pretended interest in the other guy's pictures and he pretended interest in yours. That way you both got to say the names of your children and your wife.

As Jeal opened his wallet his photos slid into his coffee. His pipe jutting from his mouth, his teeth gritting with anger, he retrieved them, laid them on a napkin. "Damn! That one's the only one I have of my first wife, Ellen. She died in childbirth, it was just utterly fantastic. So sudden. Right in the middle of transition, her heart stopped. *Bam.* What remains of Ellen is this picture and Hillary. This is Hillary, damn, it's soaked worse than Ellen. She's twelve. This is Franklin, my son. I married his mother in '78. She gave me this boy."

Bob held out his pictures of Cindy and Kevin.

"He's our only one. My wife had toxemia and it's a risk for us to have more."

"Don't take any risks. It's damn foolish. You have a beautiful child, a beautiful wife. You are content."

God, if only this poor, beset man knew what it was to be *really* beset. Last night I roamed the halls. Last night I was another kind of being.

I, Robert Duke, roamed the halls.

CHAPTER FOUR

THE FAMILY SAT TO ITS DINNER, CYNTHIA AND BOB AND Kevin. They sat in the light of a Monday evening, with music chosen by Kevin. He had picked some Chopin Nocturnes he claimed that Kafka had loved. In his wallet he now kept a small photo of Kafka at the Prater Amusement Park in Vienna, sitting in a fake airplane with a straw hat on his head. Instead of throwing his arms around his father's waist when he returned from the journey to Atlanta, Kevin had showed him this picture.

Kevin was a large, slightly overweight boy, whose skin seemed unnaturally smooth because it was filled with fat. He was loving, dutiful, and unforgiving of falsity. He needed love, attention, money. His dream was to write, to paint perhaps, or to own his own airline. Sometimes Bob thought his son was going mad; others that he had been born mad. He loved his son.

They ate boiled cabbage, beef stew with pearl onions and green peppers, small new potatoes, and salad. They all drank an inexpensive Pinot Noir from Astor Wine and Liquors, a large store around the corner from their apartment building. Cindy had her usual single glass, exhaling through her mouth each time she took a swallow. Kevin had a quarter of a glass, which he drank off at once. Later he would creep out to the kitchen and knock back four or five shots of Stolichnaya neat, but not until long after his parents were asleep. Then he would watch *Midnight Blue* and count the number of times the escort-service ads were repeated. His interest was strictly clinical. Kevin's sex life hadn't yet started in earnest. There had been Ricky Riles, of course, and Ginny Starer, and Bobby and Sally Harper, and that group at Tim's slumber party—those, but no others. Such questions as hetero- and homosexuality never concerned him. He had grown up in a neighborhood that was at least a quarter homosexual. His parents had preached toleration, often expelling long, sententious speeches on the matter. Toleration of what? To Kevin homosexuality was no odder than air, and no more interesting.

What was interesting to him, and more than a little disturbing, was his father's condition. Kevin loved his dad with a great passion. In response Bob had poured himself into the relationship, had lavished his heart and soul on his son.

Kevin ate his cabbage, chewing without real interest, watching his father, trying to draw him into conversation. "I got a neat book about Kafka, Dad. Want to hear about it?"

"Kafka?"

"It's a photo album. *Kafka, Pictures of a Life.*

That's where I got the one in my wallet."

Bob stared at his son in a way that made Kevin extremely uncomfortable. He did not want the foundations of his life disturbed—it was a difficult enough life without this happening. But there was something in Dad's expression that Kevin did not like at all. The boy lapsed into silence and concentrated on his food. In his mind's eye he saw his father's burning gaze changing to a smile that got too bright, and stayed too bright. Then where would Dad go?

Cindy felt the luxury of herself, her ampling flesh, the warmth of her legs in her dress, the possible pleasures of the coming night. Would Bob notice her, or had the marriage slipped beyond that? Love, no matter how rich and wet, has dry, crinkled borders—and beyond was the sky through which lovers fell forever.

It had taken fifteen years of a good marriage for Cindy to become confident of her own beauty. As a girl she had thought of herself as too large. Loving her was a big job, there being acres of pale flesh to kiss, and a mouth she imagined able to swallow the heads of most boys. She had wanted for lovers, too proud to call the boys, waiting in her room, her imagination soaring in the steamy nights, when the breeze seemed to penetrate every crack in her body with warm, touching fingers. The trees tossed and there were words of magic in the air.

A siren rose in the street, fading quickly into the blaring of a radio and hard laughter. A window opened, a woman shouted at a boy gluing the flier advertising a rock club to the wall of a building. Cynthia turned away from the table, drawn by whatever more was in the world. "The wine's made me flush."

Bob wondered if now was the moment to relate his experiences. "I think I'd like to see Monica," he said instead. "Have a chat."

Kevin was toying with his food, his wife leaning back in her chair, shaking her long brown hair. Beyond the window the night was growing into a density of a yellow sodium-vapor light. The Columbia Hotel sign came on, and began to cast its shaking reflection against the ceiling of the dining room. The music poured out of the stereo.

"I have a story to tell," Bob finally managed to say. He drank the dregs of his wine, poured himself another glass. Kevin went for the bottle. "No. You've had yours." The boy stopped. He ate a morsel of cabbage.

"Was there any trouble, honey? Is that why you came home early?"

"I came home early because I had a disturbing dream that perhaps was not a dream. Not entirely. There were certain indications afterward that the dream, at least in some way, was real."

They were naturally eager to hear more. But he found he could not bring himself to tell more. The trouble was his son; the family always shared everything, but this was too much. He could not share this with his boy. To Kevin he was golden; his ego would not allow him to compromise that image.

"Dad, come on. That's got to be one of the classic lead-ins. You can't just say that and then stop."

He traded looks with Cynthia. She understood perfectly. "I don't think Dad actually remembers the dream."

"I thought I did but now I don't. It's just, as I

said, there was some sort of a disturbance in the hotel that happened to coincide with the dream. I do remember I left the room in my dream. And there had been a disturbance. Maybe I actually did leave the room. That's why I came home."

"Was anybody hurt?"

"No, son, not as far as I know." He remembered Jeal and the police. "People were inconvenienced, and a glass door was broken. That's about all."

"Wow, Dad." The boy smiled but it was obvious that he was scared. Bob was ashamed of himself.

"Eat," Cindy muttered, addressing them both. "I worked hard."

Bob loved cabbage; he ate eagerly. "It's a delicious dinner, hon." There came to him an impression which before the dream had been fuzzy, but which was now quite clear. His life seemed a series of paper cutouts, his own body merely a jointed thing, able to move only on command of some mystery that could neither be controlled nor ignored. When the music stopped, it was replaced by the sounds of eating, the clink of knives and forks, the working of jaws. Three ordinary people consumed an ordinary dinner deep in the flaring night of Manhattan, while the neon glared on the ceiling and the traffic crept past below, long lines of honking cars jamming Broadway.

The clock that had been in Cindy's family since before the Civil War chimed eight times. "Any more homework, son?"

"No, Mama. I want a tub bath tonight. I want to sit in the tub and read the *Metamorphosis*."

"As long as you're in bed by nine, this can be free time. What did you have for homework?"

"Do a book report on *The Penal Colony*. Do

some algebra problems. Write a poem about a subject of my choosing. The usual sort of thing."

"You're lucky you're in St. Anselm's. You could be at public school where you have to carry a knife in order to survive."

"Obviously I wouldn't survive, Dad. As you well know." Bob did not say it, but he thought bitterly that nobody survives. Nobody. There is a story of some strange tiles from a floor in Spain in which the faces of the dead have emerged, terrible, glazed horrors, apparently hellbound. And in Lake Ontario there is an island that looks from the air like George Bernard Shaw, and most of the views in the Catskills look like the profiles of Dutchmen and Indians, and there is a plateau on Mars that looks like an Egyptian, and then there's the man in the moon, that most haunting of natural faces. Maybe we get trapped in matter, some of us, condemned to contemplate the starry world forever, staring at sky or cloud, motionless. We discover, then, the simple truth that meditation—real meditation—is a stupefying bore. If you must do it forever, even contemplating the cosmos must get frightfully dull. God's probably bored silly. Look at God's sense of fun—see the fish, the birds. How can something with the glee to create them stand playing such a passive role?

Then again, maybe God is not passive, but coy. Shy. A coquette, or cocotte. A wallflower. A hermit. A zombie. A ghoul.

Life is movement; finally it is nothing more than random movement, any movement, the twitch of a hand in the dark, the hiss of legs beneath a sheet.

Kevin pushed back his chair and bounded off to

his bath, with his boat and his book. "He's so beautiful," Bob said as the boy ran down the long hallway to the bathroom. "Don't forget to come tell us good night," he called.

Perhaps there was no answer, or it might have been absorbed by the walls. Bob began helping Cindy clear the table. "Kevin hardly ate, Bob."

"I'm sorry. I shouldn't have brought it up." The boy's psyche was an eggshell. When Bob felt wrong, he involuntarily hunched his shoulders.

"Don't do that, I'm not attacking you. If you want to see Monica, see Monica. If you want to leave me, leave me."

The words settled as wet smoke in the air. Bob was wary now. He often worried that a day would come when Cindy became exhausted with him. His self-absorption was that of an artist, but he had not the glory. There was no reward for the waitressing Bob Duke demanded. Only her kindness sustained her; for her any reward had to be internal to herself. Bob did not see what she got out of the relationship, which worried him.

"Cindy, please, I didn't mean to imply anything like that. I need you. It's just that I also need professional help. I'm under a lot of stress."

"We're running out of money."

"I know that, don't hit me with it."

"How dare you say that? I'm not hitting you. I'm just telling you so you'll know."

Despite all the terror he had felt last night, the sense that the universe had ripped and he had been the one who fell through, there was also a sense of wonder. Once Kevin had commented that seeing even the most dreadful of supernatural manifestations, a disfigured ghost or a vampire, would make him happy because of everything else it implied about the persistence of the soul. Bob had not used the word "supernatural" in reference to his experience before, but it now occurred to him to do so.

He wished that he could impress Cindy with the seriousness of the situation. To do that, maybe he should express the wonder. For, despite everything, there was wonder. Even if it was all a complex, subtle dream, woven of lies and illusions, it was remarkable, ranking as a psychological phenomenon. And if there was any truth to it at all, *any* truth—

Good God.

How would she take the blank suggestion that he believed he had, for a period of about fifteen minutes last night, actually been another creature? He knew very well how she would take it: she would react in anger. And her outrage would have entire justice, for he had no right to place such a burden upon her. Cindy was not good at earning money. She was too bright for the jobs she could get. She annoyed people. As a brilliant, untrained woman she was a sort of economic defective. She had been fired from a dozen secretarial jobs; she had been fired even from a position as a school librarian which paid only five thousand dollars a year and was practically unfillable. In work situations she tended to be huffy and rebellious. And yet, as business manager of their personal firm she was superb. Her decisions were always correct. She could handle money. The trouble was, he did not bring in any money. She spent her time playing credit cards off against one another and working the float.

"Cindy, please forgive me." He opened his arms and she came to him.

"I can't live with all this Sturm und Drang, Bob. You're such an overdramatizer. I don't even want to know what happened in Atlanta, as long as you didn't do anything that's going to cause the police to come after you. I just want to accept you, and I'm doing my best. If you are having a problem, I'll do what I know how to do. I'll hold you, I'll listen to what I can bear to hear, I'll comfort you if that is in my power."

She was afraid, and that made him pity her. It did not stop him, though. "I've had an experience that will remain with me until the end of my days." He caught himself in the posturing, the destructive silliness, of that statement. So did she—he heard her soft moan.

People call it midlife crisis, male menopause, whatever. They laugh, they simplify, then when it happens to you and you're in trouble and afraid, what do you do? Where are the resources? He had shamed himself before her. "I think it was just a very bad dream," he said carefully. "It's nothing I can't handle. But please be straight with me. Do you have a problem with my seeing Monica about it?"

She touched her cheeks, her long fingers graceful against the gentle weight of her jowls. What a strange journey it was, the lasting marriage.

She remained silent for some moments. He raised his eyebrows: she owed him an answer to his question. She took a deep breath. "We aren't children. Monica is my friend, and I think I might even have suggested you see her. Now, when I think of her hearing my intimate details with you, I wonder if the friendship can take it. I don't have many friends, Bob. If I lose Monica, I'll be lonely."

"I understand. I can get Monica to refer me to somebody."

Cindy nodded. "On the other hand, she knows us both. She will be more help to you than a stranger. And she's very skilled; I've heard that from a lot of people. No, Bob, I think she's best for you. I think you should go to her."

"Your friendship?"

"We're old, old friends. I met Monica in grade school. We've shared so much—you and Scotty, that crazy night." She laughed a little. "We'll share this too. Who knows, maybe it'll have the opposite effect. It could make us closer."

"She'll separate the personal from the professional."

Cindy put a period to the conversation by announcing that the news had started. They told about a terrible series of murders in Calaveras County, California. Pictures of the concrete blockhouse where the crimes were committed were shown. Bob felt fascinated loathing at the sight of the thing. He wondered what had gone on inside.

Later he went into Kevin's room and talked to him about Kafka. Then he read the *Metamorphosis* and grew slightly sick. People assumed that the story of a man turning into an insect was metaphorical, but what if Kafka had taken it from life? What if it was a real experience?

Of course it wasn't real. How could he even think that, and so debase the literature of the piece?

Later he drank three Stolys and listened to Steve Reich's *Desert Music*. He ate some cold shrimp that were in the fridge and wished he was at Pascal Manoule's in New Orleans. Barbecued shrimp and a Dixie beer. God love it, perhaps the best meal in America.

This night passed without dreams.

When he woke up, there was thin, gray light coming in the window. He went through the ceremonies of the morning, the shave, the brushing of the hair, the dressing in the gray suit, the kissing of the schoolbound boy, the march out into the sun-drenched traffic, the subway, the jammed crowds of Thirty-fourth Street, the elevator, the office of Duke Data Consultants on the sixth floor of the Empire State Building. At the moment he could not afford a secretary, and his outer office contained nothing but a desk, an archaic Mac, and a telephone.

He took in the mail, which consisted of the usual pound or so of computer magazines, trade journals, and bills. There were no letters of inquiry, and none of his outstanding accounts had sent checks. The bills he piled up to take to Cindy.

He had not yet sat down when the phone began ringing. "This is Joe Tragliano, I want—"

Bob put down the phone in horror. Tragliano? Somebody from the landlord's office—but which landlord, home or this place?

He didn't want to call Cindy about it. The mere fact that landlords were beginning to phone would terrify her. Why didn't things ever come out right? The world is not made to come out right, the world is made to burn. And yet flowers, spring, glistening lakes, snowflakes, laughing children.

And yet—the phone ringing again. Bob jerked back and forth. God, God, it could be a client. Or—he answered.

"Tragliano. Look, we got a hot check here. We can't deposit it again, you gotta send us a new check. You understand that?"

"Yes."

"Okay, there's gonna be an eviction notice in your mailbox tomorrow. It's no big deal, don't get worried, just get the money to us, okay?"

"Okay." Oh, God. The apartment, sixteen hundred and fifty dollars a month. It hadn't seemed like much a year ago but now, God.

There was a pink envelope on the floor he hadn't seen before. Pushed under the outer door while he was on the phone. He opened it. A pink copy of his April office rent bill, a yellow copy of the May bill, a blue copy of the June bill, a white copy of the current bill.

They had been waiting for him to come in. Eyes had watched his entrance, feet had moved. Was somebody now hanging back in the hall, waiting to buttonhole him when he came out?

Please somebody—if there is a God—help me, help me get out of this mess.

He would go down to the coffee shop in the basement and coffee himself and read the latest issue of *MacWorld*. Maybe there'd be some useful tidbit in the computer-industry gossip columns, something he could make a few cold calls about. "Hi, Willard, I just heard a rumor that Compaq's coming out with an AT clone that's—"

What? Who cares. His "clients" didn't need him, they subscribed to computer magazines, too. Soon he heard the coffee bell in the hall. Never mind the shop in the basement. He shouldn't risk leaving his office, anyway. What if they changed the locks on him? But they were nice people here. He was nearly half a year behind and they hadn't even given him an eviction notice. Just these bills, and the feeling that he was being watched.

He went out and bought a cup of hot tea. When he returned to his desk, he noticed that there were tears streaming down his face. He worried that he was in imminent danger of becoming the first person to commit suicide by jumping out of a lower floor of the Empire State Building. He called Monica.

She took the call personally, bless her soul. "Bob?"

He had planned a big speech, but the sound of her voice washed it all out of his mind. "I need a little help." He hated the shaking tone, the whine behind it. "Monica, give me an appointment as soon as you can."

"Where are you, Bob?"

His throat was constricting. The dreadful memories, the sheer terror of what he had experienced in Atlanta now flooded in on him. "My office." His voice was a whisper. He jammed his teeth together to capture the sob that was about to follow the words.

"If you can get here by ten-thirty, I'll give you half an hour. We can meet again after five."

The even tone was like a handclasp right through the phone. As soon as he hung up, the phone rang again. This time it was American Express. "Mr. Duke, we must have a fifteen-hundred-dollar payment at one of our offices by the close of business today, or we'll be forced—"

He put the phone down, a fussy, frightened gesture. Fear made him feel so careful that he thought he must look prissy. Did pilots in crashing planes become fascinated by bug splotches on the windshield as the ground rushed up?

He tried to swallow his tea and leave, but the tea seared his throat and he gagged, spitting it all over the pile of bills and computer magazines. Oh, so what? His lips, his tongue burning, he stalked out into the silent hallway.

He no longer cared if the Empire State Building was watching him. Better to be outside than in here with all these miserable creditors and the spilled tea. Who knew, maybe something good would happen. He might find a dime on the sidewalk, for example, or be run over by a bus.

As he moved through the streets of the city he experienced a radical change of mood. His spirits lifted. Hard, white sunlight was flooding the world. He went up Fifth Avenue past the corpse of Altman's and still-moving Lord and Taylor's. The people who passed him were shining with what he told himself was the light of the soul. For a moment, reveling in the secret understanding that there was something beautiful here, he loved the faded plastic sushi in the window of a Japanese restaurant, the roaring buses, the sweating Con Ed workers at the corner of Fortieth and Fifth, the new Republic National Bank building, the library with its bright lions and its grand facade.

He was in essence a family man, he decided, and trudged on to the Olympic Tower, where Monica's office overlooked all of mid and lower Manhattan. The waiting room was full of teak and zebrawood furniture, rich, dark paneling, and floor-to-ceiling windows. An elderly, beautifully dressed woman sat behind the reception desk and a man of perhaps thirty in one of the chairs. Far below, St. Patrick's Cathedral spread like a stone beast.

"You can go right in, Mr. Duke," the woman at the desk said. Monica was so successful, so rich. Look at all this. Somehow it enabled him to regain his composure. "Look at all this," he said as he went in. "It's a long way from a psychiatric residency at Bellevue." Bob remembered her as she had been then, a laughing girl so blond she might have been an angel.

He sat down gratefully in the heavy chair she indicated with a gesture. She came beside him and sat in a higher, stiffer chair.

"Go ahead," she said, touching his hand.

"I was in Atlanta at a conference. Business. I went to sleep—no, it begins before. It started on Saturday. We were at the zoo. The wolf stared at me. Later I had a strange dream, that the wolf had eaten me, and I sort of filled its body. I animated it, like. That must have been Saturday night. Sunday I went to the conference, and I had another dream. Far worse."

"During the conference?"

"Well, at night. I was in my room. It was like I didn't even fall asleep, when suddenly I was not a human being anymore. I was this animal again."

"The wolf from the zoo?"

"An animal. Whatever animal. Probably a wolf, maybe a dog. I dreamed I went out of the room and got chased by a guard and ended up, for God's sake, in the hotel restaurant. I crashed through a door and made it back to my room. I became myself again in the elevator and I had to stand there with my face to the wall because I was totally naked. I have never felt so naked." He dropped to silence. That had not been as hard as he had thought it would be. The next part, though, he wondered if he could utter.

"Yes?" She touched his hand again. She had done that ever since he had known her. Surely she understood how provocative it was. He wished for perhaps the hundred-thousandth time that he had made her that night in the Catskills.

"Monica, I think some part of this dream was real. The next morning I got up and everybody at the conference was talking about how this giant dog had gotten into the restaurant and broken down the glass doors, and escaped into an elevator."

She did not do what he had thought she would, which was to cry out in amazed disbelief. "So you integrated this into your previous night's dreaming."

"Integrated—Monica, you don't understand. It *was* my dream. My dream was true. I became something else, something wild. I remember how it was to be that creature. Exactly how it was."

"Yes?"

Could he talk about it? It was almost as if the part of him which contained those memories had not the best grasp of the English language. Or was that true? Maybe he could do as she asked, maybe he had language enough. He had planned to talk about what he did, and how it was all real, not a dream, but some baroque effect of a deteriorating mind—the emergence of the wild. But how it *felt*—well, how had it felt?

"I was lying on my bed in the room. I was naked."

"Lying how, on your back?"

"On my back. I was aroused."

"Meaning?"

"I had desire. Intense desire and there was nobody there. I don't fool around on Cindy, but right then I wanted to. I was in a state of intense excitement, and I was alone."

"Did you do anything at all about it?"

"I rarely do that—you're referring to—"

"Bob, try to relax. If you can't talk comfortably with me, I can certainly recommend somebody else."

"No, Monica, I love you—" How in the world had he come to say that? This wasn't going to come out right. "You to help me."

"Bob, I'm a mother figure for you, as much as you may think you desire me sexually."

"I never had much of a relationship with my mother. When I got in her lap, she used to say I was too bony and put me out. Or she'd say she didn't like to be touched when it was hot, her skin was clammy. It was always hot, and her skin was always clammy. When I say that, I feel a hideous, upsetting sexual stirring. I remember when I used to get punished, my sister would watch. It was horrible."

"How were you punished?"

"The old-fashioned way. I was spanked. Viciously, at times. It happened constantly, but I only remember one or two specific occasions."

"Do you think that this is where your masochism started?"

"Masochism?"

"You tell me."

"I want to tell you about my experience. What brought me in here. I have to, it's terribly important. I think that I may be the victim of a rare psychophysical effect. My mind and my body are working together in some mysterious manner—oh, God, Monica, I've got to get this through to you: I *was* that animal. I turned into something that everybody else in the hotel, the maid who first saw me, the security guards, the people in the restaurant, they all thought it was a big dog or a wolf. And Monica, I felt like a wolf. I did not feel like a human being."

"Did you want to eat them?"

"No no no, that's totally off the point. You're not understanding me. My whole frame of reference changed. Sense of smell, hearing. For God's sake, I could hear people breathing at the far end of a long hall. I could smell all the components of their sweat, their perfume as seven or eight different odors, even the difference between the smell of their hands and the smell of their faces. And I saw it all in vague, muted colors. The point is, what I did in the dream is what people in the hotel saw this big animal do. And I dreamed I was that animal."

"Bob, I want you to listen to me for a moment. Our half hour is up and I'm going to run late with all my patients until lunchtime. I'm going to write you a prescription for something that will calm you down. You'll feel much better. I want you to take it and have a good lunch and then do something you enjoy. Go to a movie. Afterward come back here. I'm finished at five-thirty and I can spend a couple of hours with you. Does that sound like a good plan?"

He nodded and she wrote something on a prescription form. He didn't read it and didn't intend to. He was so grateful that she had instructions for him to follow that he would have followed them into a fire, had that been demanded of him. On the way out of the office he had quite a surprise.

"Mr. Duke, that's a hundred and fifty dollars," the receptionist said with a smile.

"Excuse me?"

"Your bill. We prefer payment by visit. The fee

is three hundred dollars an hour. The doctor said you should pay for this visit now, and be sure and bring another check tonight."

For a moment Bob felt anger, then disappointment. Then it occurred to him that she was doing the professionally correct thing. The relationship was being established for what it was, being separated by the check from the friendship. As he wrote he felt a little sick, thinking of the astounding dwindling of the money. Another hot check. How would she take it, when she discovered that he was a deadbeat?

It hit him that he could spend the next few hours productively by writing an ad for the Consultants Market of the Tuesday Science Section of the *Times*. That made sense. He could run it for a month and maybe something would happen that would spare him the hopelessness of letters and the indignity of calls. Or he could go over to the library and look through the Standard Rate and Data Catalog of Mailing Lists. A new SRDC was out; maybe this month's edition would show some relevant mailing lists he hadn't tried. Or better, he could get some lists of people in computer-intensive industries like accounting, and send them letters. Lists of known computer users weren't worth a damn. Consultants had a bad rep with those people. Too many fast-buck operators in the business who turned out to know less than their clients.

After all, it wasn't entirely hopeless. He did have a few miserable assets. Last week he had found some useful changes to the WordPerfect word processing program in an obscure freeware database. Those were worth money. They sped up the program and removed many of its minor annoyances. He could look like a hero to companies that used WordPerfect as their word processor. Surely he could find someone, somewhere willing and able to pay him a few thousand dollars for increasing the efficiency of their secretarial pool by twenty percent. Surely he could. For the love of God, Monica got three hundred dollars an hour. He was more poorly paid than a private detective in a Raymond Chandler novel. He was lucky if he was paid at all.

As he walked he read the prescription. Elavin. What would it do? He had no idea, but it was an immense relief to consider using it. He would place himself in Monica's capable hands. Let her make the decisions. Let her reorder his life. Give up every dignity to her: take the pills she prescribed, let her alter his brain.

He went down to the Duane Reade Drugstore on Madison and Forty-first and filled the prescription. Like a skulking thief he continued on the avenue, half expecting to find his office rekeyed when he came back.

And what about the apartment? Would they start eviction? How long did it take? Could they keep their furniture, and would there be anyplace to go?

Back in his office he took the dose, two pills, with a cup of water from the men's room. His water cooler had run out last month and they had not showed up to replenish it, not with their bill unpaid for six months. It was autumn. His last good month had been April.

The disturbing thought occurred to him that the Elavin might trigger the reaction. He looked down at his hands, took them to his face, and inhaled the familiar smell of his own skin. There hadn't been any sensation when the change took place in Atlanta. He had been assuming that it was instantaneous. Was that true? Maybe he had been lying there for some time, oozing and twisting. There really wasn't any way to tell.

Therefore he would have no warning if it was going to happen again. They said that a strange disquiet often preceded a stroke. And there was a moment of melancholy, he had heard, prior to a grand mal seizure. There was nothing now, just the silence of an office, the faint hissing of the air-conditioning, a man sitting at a desk waiting. It was possible to believe that he was alone in this office and in the world. He could look down six stories to the street and see the cars, the passing people, the rich human activity of Thirty-fourth Street and Fifth Avenue. He could enjoy the faint art deco quality of his office, and dream of sunny days long ago, the late forties perhaps, some magic time when New York was right.

Then again, he had the habit of walking up to the Strand Bookstore and looking through the collections of Weegee's searing photographs of tragedies of city life, most of them taken in the forties. Maybe New York was never right.

Something deep within, a sort of turning of his gut, made him sit up rigid. His heart started pounding. "I won't run, I'll just stay in here until it passes." Footsteps came and went beyond the door; female laughter went by. Something tickled his cheek, a tear. He brushed it away. Should he call Monica? Was that allowed? Maybe Cindy, but Cindy couldn't handle this, she had said as much. He sucked a breath through his teeth. The churning in his guts grew more intense. He imagined some great hand within him, remixing his body.

"No." He took a deep, slow breath, shut his eyes. At once he realized that he wasn't really alone here. There was a presence staring at him much as the wolf at the zoo had stared, glaring into his heart. It was formless, you couldn't make out a face or even eyes, and it was full of furtive eagerness, like a thief. "Who are you?"

Outside, the bell tinkled for afternoon coffee. Doors opened and shut, voices filled the hall. What of them, the people in the other offices? They never seemed to have such moments as this; they were not like him. But they were. In his heart he knew that he was a more or less ordinary man, living the common desperation.

His breath left him with a whoosh, and when he gasped back his air, it was through a nose able to tell the difference between the smell of his own sharp and frightened sweat and the succulent damp of the secretaries in the hall.

He had to feel his face. He had to know. His hands were trembling so much that he could barely control them. It was a struggle to raise them. They were clutching human hands, not paws, the fingers a blur of jitters, like the legs of a scorpion running in a ring of fire.

They touched a human face. He heard a loud sound, identified it as a sob. His own sob. He sat there shaking, weeping. An almost overwhelming sense of tragedy possessed him. He wanted to feel his boy's arms around him, to hear Cindy's comforting, familiar voice.

He remembered his mother when he was very little, her powdered mask of a face looming down into his world of toy cars and tunnels in the sandpile, the way she smelled, the way she looked, the dark eyes in the pallor, the bright, unlikely smile and those fingers on his cheek, too freezing cold to be real.

Then he would be alone, as he was now alone. Monica's advice returned to mind: see a movie.

He went out into the bright, rushing afternoon, haggard, his eyes full of memories, his hands stuffed in the pockets of his suit. Nobody noticed him, nobody cared, for nobody in the world but he himself knew the truth, that a wolf was awakening in his belly.

CHAPTER FIVE

BOB HAD TROUBLE KEEPING HIS FEET ON THE SIDE-walk. He was slipping and sliding along, the victim of frustrating air currents. It was as if he was coming unmade in himself, his body not changing shape but losing all shape. His mind was fine, but his body was falling off some kind of edge. "Monica, it really is physical, that's what you just would not believe." The pills were making it worse. They provided the lubrication: if he didn't walk like a man of glass, his hands might drop off, his knees go rolling up under the shish-kebab stand on the corner, his head topple into the goo of wet cigarette butts that floated in the gutter.

Easy does it, fella, this is serious. You are out in the middle of the street. But was he walking, flying, or being blown like a leaf? And where was he going? A bus leaped at him, its driver leering down, chewing gum furiously. Someone had him

by the hand, was drawing him farther and farther
—no, he was still in front of the bus, it was his
arm that was getting longer and longer. He stared
down the immense stretch of his sleeve into the
real world. There was a man out there, holding
hands with him. Dance?

"Can't you cross a goddamn street?"

Bob ran around in the garden, gathering flowers, and each flower was a word of a part of a
word. "Oh," snapdragon. "I'm," daffodil. "Sorry," Easter lily. "I," Queen Anne's lace.
"Slipped," Mountain laurel.

"Holy Christ, leggo my hand. Goddamn pan-
sy." The man shook Bob off and hustled away.
"Geek," he cried over his shoulder.

Bob was struck dumb with wonder to find
himself at the corner of Fifth Avenue and Sixtieth
Street. The zoo stood just across the street, a
damnation of cages. He saw it not as a place but as
a state of being. It was as ideological an institution
as mankind has produced, a place of total and
perfect injustice, where innocents were confined
in hell for the amusement of the curious.

Oh, getting sentimental about the animals
again, Bob? What about people, what about
Auschwitz, Rudi Mengele standing on Sonja
Teitelbaum's chest? Did that happen because
Sonja went to too many movies, or smoked on the
street? And why is the wolf here? He ate living
flesh, and so is no more innocent than his captors.

Here we have it: To survive is to be guilty. To die
is to be more guilty still. That's the point of
Kafka's *Trial*, isn't it: guilt is the central quanta of
life. The trial is itself the sentence. The accusation
proves the guilt of the accused, okay? And the
wolf? Well, he was tried in the court of the

tranquilizer dart, and in that court the sentence is always the same: life behind bars, thank you very much.

Once upon a time Bob had known a man who had suffered from a tic so extreme that it made him look as if his face was a wobbling gelatin sculpture. He was a bond salesman and his life depended on the impression he made on people. He had a pipe, which he would grasp in his teeth, surround with his lips, and struggle to hold. He never lit it. The pipe was his anchor. And the guy in Atlanta—Jeal—had used his the same way.

The pipe—Bob needed its equivalent on this terrible pilgrimage to the lair of the wolf. He needed something totally ordinary that would contain his urge to flutter, to run, to skitter along under the benches.

"Popcorn," he gasped, the prospector dying in the desert, calling to his last mirage.

"A dollar."

He took the bag of warm popcorn, gratitude humming in him. The world made nice things. He could remember the six-to-sixty matinee at the Broadway Theater in San Antonio—oh, to just once hear the faint cataract of fresh popcorn being expelled during the love scene, and you could go out to the lobby and for a dime actually buy a red-and-white-striped box of that wonderful smell.

There is no six-to-sixty matinee anymore, because there are no children. Childhood was invented by Lewis Carroll as the private amusement of a master of paradox. Carroll's brilliant artifice was destroyed by the twentieth century.

But there is still popcorn, and walking along the rows of cages to the cage of the God, Bob looked just like any other lost man ambling through the forest that never ends. "Hey, tapir, I know somebody who might like to free you. And you, kinkajou, let's set you up in my secret zoo." He elaborated on that theme. Manhattan is a place of secret clubs, even a secret coffee shop on Lexington Avenue, a place where they serve perfectly ordinary coffee and danish and make a decent egg cream, all ordinary and nice, except it is a secret, and because it is a secret, is fought over by the endless stream of the newly famous who make the city at once so sad and so hilarious.

The popcorn was good. Overhead the trees, swept by afternoon wind, hissed with a voice too subtle to be understood, too important to be ignored. Bob looked up and almost wept with the grandeur he beheld, the leaves dancing, the clouds sailing past angels on their indifferent ways.

In his preoccupied state it took him some little time to understand that the zoo had gone into pandemonium, more or less coincident with his arrival. He realized it only when a condor began beating its wings against its bars and huffing as he passed. He noticed that keepers were running back and forth, one a young woman in tears, sobbing words of comfort to a cage full of bellowing, eye-bulging monkeys. The tiger dragged its flab around, rippling as it waddled. Its eyes stared into Punjab.

The ring-tailed cats were screaming and hissing, slashing at the air, which was itself in turmoil, the wind whipping women's dresses, grabbing a baby carriage and sailing it off, its au pair frantic and far behind, shrieking in Swedish. A tiny hand waved from the carriage.

The mountain goats were leaping toward the

top of their enclosure, the gorillas were roaring, the gibbon was laughing, its teeth bared.

Still the wind came on, sharp and cold, sudden black hands of cloud chasing the fluffy angels, stinging flecks of rain and squadrons of leaves sweeping down the paths, catching in Bob's popcorn, swarming, swirling, and the clanging of the little Indian elephant as she tortured her bars.

Just then three keepers rushed past carrying between them a huge slack snake with an oblong bulge in its middle. "For God's sake she swallowed a purse," one of them wailed. "Maggie swallowed a damn lizard purse!"

Behind them came a well-dressed woman of perhaps fifty, her black face tragic, her makeup running. "I never seen no snake that big strike," she said to Bob. "They think she's gonna die because of my purse!" The last word came out as a crackling moan. Then the woman hurried on, presumably to claim her belongings after the vet operated on Maggie.

Bob let his popcorn fall away. He was drawing close to the cage of the wolf. There was only one word to describe his feelings, and that was awe, for he had seen the eyes. The wolf alone was not screaming, it alone was not gnawing or beating or pushing its bars. Bob was overcome by emotion. He could not look into the face of the great forest beast, but rather looked down. He felt its gaze, as implacable as diamond, a radiant fire. Now the God reveals itself, he thought. It has hidden long enough in the folds of the animal.

He went to his knees, crouching, and felt himself raise his right hand, press it closer and closer to the jaws of the cage, spread it wide, and slip it through. The wolf sniffed Bob's fingers.

It snarled. Then it took his hand roughly, shaking its head from side to side. Bob could almost see as if through the tips of his fingers the crusted old teeth, the cracked and yellowing tongue. The wolf shook him once and let him go, then raised his own paw. Bob looked up. The animal's ears were back, his eyes gleaming like taxidermist's glass. Bob sensed within himself a great animal awakening and flexing.

He knew with a clear and sickening certainty that he was going to change. Right here, right now, he was going to become body with body, this wolf. His insides bubbled. He was melting, being reformed by powerful, hidden hands. His mind struggled with the matter—he was out in public now, people were bound to see. His clothes would be lost, he would be naked. And what about his wallet? There came a great spasm and his back went as straight as a rail. Frantically, he put his hand over his wallet pocket.

Then there were strong hands. "Hey, buddy, you okay?" He was lifted and he saw a flash of brass and blue. A cop was bending over him, lifting his head in a big palm. "You okay?"

"I—I—"

"Have you taken anything? Do you need a stomach pump?"

Would that get it out—he thought not. He lay with his head on the cop's knee, gazing up the powerful lines of the cage bars behind him, and high above he could see the nose of the wolf poking through, and one fang. Ever so carefully, the wolf was gnawing at his cage.

The rest of the zoo was growing quieter. "I'll be all right," Bob said through a thickness of tongue he had never felt before. A shudder racked him.

A policewoman bent over him, her face pinched. "Don't let him swallow his tongue."

"Mary, what the hell's the matter with him? I can feel his bones, he's shaped funny."

"Sim, it's a fit. The guy is a cripple and an epileptic." Her face softened. She was a mere child, probably not much past twenty. "Grand mal seizure," she said. "We've got to keep him from swallowing his tongue."

He could not speak, especially not when she stuffed a pocket comb redolent of her styling mousse in his mouth.

"It's not drunk or drugs?"

"Nah. Don't haul him in on a substances charge. We'll look like jerks."

"Thanks, Mary. I don't want an arrest. I don't want to lose lunch break."

Their hands holding him, the sweat of their presence, the faint scent of deodorant and cologne and gunmetal had brought Bob back to the world of fingers and eyes that see in color. It hurt a little: some sort of magic was leaving him, and that was sad.

The comb was bothering him, held firmly in his mouth by Officer Mary. He began to work it with his tongue, which only made her hold it more firmly at first. "Wiiff—pibb—" Finally she removed it. She smiled. "Welcome back. See, we're gonna be fine, aren't we?"

He tried to sit up, but the cops restrained him. "Just a minute. Catch your breath."

"I'm okay."

"You sure?"

He hoped that his expression wouldn't betray him. "Yeah," he said.

The male cop suddenly ran his hands along

Bob's chest. He was frowning. "You're—you were—"

"I'm okay."

"You sure are!"

They didn't prevent Bob from getting up when he tried again. The male cop was staring hard at him as he stood.

"Thank you, Officers."

The cop stood with him, looked him up and down. "Jesus!"

Bob could only turn and hurry away. Behind him he could feel the raging presence in the cage, the very wild itself straining at the toils of rusted steel.

Behind him, he heard the cops talking. "He was all bent up, Mary." There was an edge of panic in the man's voice.

"It was the seizure."

"I felt twisted bones! I felt them straighten out!"

Bob kept moving. He hardly glanced to the left and right, ignoring the remains of the pandemonium, the gorilla curled into a giant ball of fur and clutching hands, the monkeys piled in the back of their cage, still and silent, the condor staring, its beak agape.

The cop's voice rose in the distance, high, full of scream. "That man was crippled, I felt his body. I felt his *bones*!"

An energy had definitely departed. Even the wind had ceased to blow. The light in the streets had lost all magic. Buses and taxis went screaming madly down Fifth Avenue, people dashed back and forth, lovers walked hand in hand, women in furs gazed at the windows of Bergdorf Goodman, limousines lurked before the Plaza. A bag man leaned against the wall that separated Central

Park from Fifty-ninth Street. He was totally inert.

Bob felt as he had when he was a teenager, after some immense act of sex, drained, emptied of all spark, of all friction, a dreg.

The policeman's attentions had interrupted the process. But the cop had *felt* his bones. He had been in the process of actually turning into something physically *else*!

By the time he entered Monica's office, he was wondering why he had ever bothered to call her. No psychiatrist could help a man who was melting.

She was cheerful, still dapper in her blue double-breasted suit, her eyes wide and bright, so innocent that they stopped the heart, so knowing that they made him humble. "Well," she said in a confident tone, "how are we this afternoon?"

He could only lie into her broadside of supportive signals. "I feel better."

"Elavin is a good drug. There's nothing like it when somebody's feeling a little panic."

Panic. Yes, that was a good word. But it was not bad panic. Grand panic. Exotic panic. Magical panic.

"At first I thought the pills had made it worse. I got into a really horrendous state."

"How so?"

He related his story, ending it with the kindness of the two cops.

"The zoo animals we can discount. If there really was a disturbance, it was coincidental. It might even have been what induced your attack."

"I was having trouble before I got to the zoo."

"No doubt you were. But we can't trust our own perceptual memory, can we?"

"Monica, I can only repeat that it was a physical

thing. One of the cops that helped me out at the zoo thought I was crippled. He was practically screaming when I walked away, because he obviously didn't understand how a person that twisted could just get up and stroll off."

"Well, this is your perception."

"I had a seizure."

"I grant that—but only that. A seizure I can deal with, hallucinations I can deal with, panic I can help you with. But we have to have a basic understanding that these perceptions of yours are not real. Otherwise, Bob—well—"

"I'm psychotic."

"That would be one diagnosis." Her voice was soft and even, but the sharpness in her eyes betrayed her.

"You think I'm going around the bend."

"I think I can help you."

"Then it's Cindy. You're worrying about her."

"Of course. She is my dear friend. I've known her for more than twenty years. And I know how much she loves you. She treasures you."

"Why would anybody do that?"

"I am not in the profession of analyzing love. I'd be a fool to try."

"Implying that you cannot imagine why she loves me. Well, neither can I. I'm a lot of trouble and not much good."

"You've made her happy." There was an edge in Monica's voice.

"Am I leaving my marriage behind? Is that what this is all about?"

"What do you think?"

"I don't know! That's why I asked. You're the expensive psychiatrist. You tell me."

"I'm not a Miss Lonelyhearts. My profession is

to guide you toward insight."

He remembered the wolf sucking at his hand. He could feel the tongue, the teeth, could see those glaring, empty eyes. They looked like glass because the soul behind them had been burned away. That wolf was already dead. It wasn't responsible for what was happening, it was just a mechanism.

There was an impression of somebody so huge that they contained the whole earth. He thought of the Catholic image of the Blessed Virgin Mary standing astride the world, and was for a moment deeply comforted. "Officer Mary."

"Excuse me?"

"Did I say something?"

"Something. I couldn't hear you. What were you thinking about?"

There was no way to say it, because the image was so strange and private. His mother must have held him newborn thus, a magical being cradling an infant who trailed in his soul the whole world.

"We underestimate ourselves, Monica. Human beings don't know what they are."

"I've often thought that." A smile almost captured her face, but it got away.

There was something startling here—this woman was not at all wise. She wasn't even a good questioner. Her mind wandered about. She occasionally repeated something you said, agreed, tried to make you expand. But she was not concentrating. For all her well-groomed beauty, the perfect blue of her eyeshadow, the colorful humidity of her lips, her heartbreaking almond eyes, her radiant blond hair—for all of that—she was just not here.

Bob was here, totally. Maybe that was his problem. He had come awake to a life which is normally meant for a sort of sleep. A soul might be like this in heaven, but when it was born, it would forget everything it had learned in the airy libraries of the angels.

"What are you really, truly thinking about right now, Monica?"

"Why do you ask?"

"Monica, please. Forget the session. Forget the questions. *What are you thinking about?*"

"What should I be thinking about?"

He noticed that there was nothing near the patient that could be thrown, no ashtrays, no fat little statuettes of Buddha like in the rest of the office.

"I could get a computer that would ask me these parroting questions."

"Would that satisfy you?"

A tingling iron was thrust directly into his groin by an unseen hand. His penis sprang up. Sweat flowed from his every pore. Her skin was alight, pale and smooth, her fingers tapering, her breast a milky stillness. The fire in him almost cracked him open. He thought for a moment that he would split in two and his organs would fall out, a stoke of blazing coals.

She laughed a little, leaning forward, her chin on one of those long, soft hands he wished to God would touch him. "Bob?"

"I'm remembering the Catskills." It wasn't true, it was more than that. He wasn't remembering anything and it wasn't her in particular. His desire went flying right out the window, and in an instant included everybody in the world, good, big, little, bad, old, new, every sweat and softness, hair in the sun, sweet skin in the dark.

Singing came from the reception room. Monica

turned her head sharply. "Katie, are you still there?"

"I'm leaving now, Monica. Is that okay?"

"Sure, Kate." She got up, a glory of whispering movement. In a low voice she spoke to her assistant. "You don't need to stay for this one. He's a little overwrought, but he's harmless. I've known him for years."

The kiss they traded, made to look casual, seemed to Bob like two molten cymbals crashing, a thing of fury hidden behind a thousand curtains, and on each curtain was another deceiving word. It was not casual. It meant that their hidden souls were in deep and abiding love. They should share their bodies, their very blood. That they did not know this, or ignored it, made them sinners.

She closed the door firmly and came around her big desk. She stood before Bob, her arms folded. "That night haunts you, doesn't it?"

"I want you."

"We could put all that to rest, you know. I'm speaking as a friend. You don't want me, you want your image of me. If I satisfied your curiosity, maybe we could get on with the analysis."

Her words shuddered, and Bob saw that she was shaking. Behind the folded arms, her hands were clenched fists. He felt sorry for her, because he had discovered her secret. She had tried so hard to hide her failure. The reality was before him, though. She had no idea what she was doing: her profession was exactly what it seemed—a superficial fraud clinging to a deeper truth.

There came to him an insight. His path had diverted from common reality and entered uncommon reality. He might be off in this fog, lost here at least for a time, but it was a grand fog.

Within it there were fearsome discoveries to be made, but also he was closer to the old immortalities. Saints and the innocent of God had been here, the geniuses of the surreal like Francis of Assisi and friend Kafka.

He had to break the tension between himself and Monica. His passion would not be satisfied by some hurried roll on her rug, indeed not by any physical thing. It was too deeply of the body to be appeased by the decorative rituals that have grown up around the act of procreation. Maybe giving her a child would wet his fires a little, but he did not want his fires wetted. He had to see this through.

A new experience had claimed him.

She, though, still assumed him to be part of the old reality. Her eyes were wet, her lips parted. Her fingers took his cheeks and guided his mouth to her mouth. He turned away and her kiss came to his cheek.

"Bob?"

"Monica, this is not—"

"Hush. Don't say it." She dropped her eyes, her head, knelt, then crouched before him like an Egyptian at the feet of Pharaoh. He heard constricted sobs. But the constriction began failing, the sobs growing louder. She had come to her own darkness, here in this lovely room, with the late sun bathing the cathedral below the windows. She was seeing full how close she was to the mysteries that her ancient sisters in magic had celebrated with potions and flying ointment and broomsticks. So close, and yet denied. Her science, in seeking to penetrate the heart, locked the heart.

He felt sure that she had just at this moment discovered her own fraud. As softly, as gently as he could, Bob rose. He stepped over Monica's crouching form. He left this soul to the privacy of its discovery.

There was no point in trying any longer to escape. Not Monica, not her pills, nothing could help him. If there was a guide, he would find it in the black letters of the past, the *Mabinogion,* the *Little Flowers of St. Francis,* the *Metamorphosis.*

Bob Duke had come to the center of the forest. There was no sound, not even wind. The path was not marked by moon or stars or prior passage. All around him the eyes, the fangs, the claws of another world—the wild and true world— gathered themselves.

As evening settled over New York St. Patrick's Cathedral raised its bells. He started off through their glassine clamor and at the same time through this silent forest in his soul. Now he was alone.

CHAPTER SIX

THE ENCOUNTER LEFT BOB DESPERATE FOR TYLENOL, and he was glad when he was finally riding the old elevator up to his own apartment. Lupe drove it, one-eyed, silent Lupe who had been here since this building was called "The Montague House" and dressed its doormen and elevator operators in tan uniforms with gold braid. Now there was only Lupe, and he rarely wore his shaggy formals. They were reserved for Christmas, or if there was a wedding party in the building, or a wake.

Lupe never talked. He had stopped talking, the old-timers said, back when the Dodgers had left Brooklyn. Mrs. Trask in 14C remembered Lupe's last words: "Too sad."

Lupe's last words, Mrs. Trask . . . the life and history of the building. Mrs. Trask also remembered when your maid piled your dirty sheets on the dumbwaiter and sent them down to the laundry, which was staffed by six Chinese. "At Christmas we gave twenty-eight tip envelopes, a dollar each. Our rent was forty-one dollars a month. Let me tell you, young man, this place was class with a capital K."

Lupe pulled back the rattling brass cage. "Thanks, Lupe." Bob heard, and disliked, the superior drone in his own voice. "I need about twelve Tylenols," he said as he went through the door into his dark, silent apartment. "Hello?"

There was a scrabbling sound from the bedroom.

He went down the hall. "Cindy?"

She was sitting cross-legged on the bed in the dark, smoking. He was stunned. To his knowledge, she had never smoked. "What's the matter?"

"We have thirty days to go in this apartment. Jennie called from the bank, we're eight hundred dollars overdrawn. I spent all afternoon at the welfare office trying to get food stamps, and we can't get them because we've already made too much money this year. So I bought a pack of Salems and I've been sitting here ever since smoking them and get me some money or leave me alone!"

He stepped back as if a snake had lashed its head in his direction. Her breath hissed between her teeth.

She was hurting, and he loved her, but he could not comfort her. The source could not melt the pain. Still, there must be something to say.

"We—"

"No, Bob."

He held out his arms. She looked at him, and for

a moment she seemed to be gazing at him through the bars of a cage. Gazing in. Her beauty flowed in the dark.

"Don't come any closer, Bob, unless you've got money."

"I went to Monica. She made me take pills—"

"We need money more than we need you sane! Why didn't you rob a bank and then go to Monica?"

"They rape you in prison."

"Forty-year-old men with Jell-O around the middle? I hardly think so."

"I've forgotten how to make money. Why don't you work?"

"Doing what? Taking in wash? Pumping gas? Scrubbing floors for our friends? I'm equipped for nothing. A drone. A victim of the culture." She laughed silently, mirthlessly, her cigarette bobbing like a little red lantern. "I've been paying for being a woman all my life, and now I'm really going to pay, I guess." The bobbing stopped. "That's what being a woman's all about. You're born, therefore you pay."

What did she mean? Was she referring to pregnancy? They had used the Lamaze Method for Kevin, working as a team, two shouting, screaming people in the University Hospital birthing ward, and afterward she said it hadn't been so bad.

She stubbed her cigarette out on the bottom of her sandal and aimed the butt at the trash can. "Bob, I've loved you so much. More than I ever thought I'd love anybody. You have a decency about you, honey, that's just so sweet. You're the only thoroughly good person I've ever met. You wouldn't hurt anything. I don't think you've ever even killed a fly." She sobbed. "Is that why you're such a failure? Why we're always broke?"

"Actually, I think I might have something with the Macintosh Office concept. I'm planning on hitting my old client list, making some cold calls——"

"Shh! Honey, don't belabor the absurd. Just leave it alone. We have no money. This is who we are. We are the We Have No Moneys. 'Hello, this is Mrs. We Have No Money. I'd like to get a credit line, please.'"

"We have MasterCard. Gold American Express——"

"Used up, used up."

"Maybe the bank——"

"They don't have time to assist the indigent."

"Something will turn up." He smiled at her, giving it his biggest, his brightest. Maybe somebody would take the apartment, maybe they wouldn't even be able to get food, but this love they had was bigger than a roof over your head or a meal.

Or, actually, maybe that was taking it a little too far. The love was big. But food and shelter were also big.

"I was poor as a kid and poor when we first married. The rest of the time I've worked the float. Just for one month, for one week, I'd like to have enough money. Get it. Get it now!" She grappled with another cigarette, lit it, and smoked with amateur fury. White streams roared out her nose.

He took all he had out of his wallet and laid the three one-dollar bills on the bed before her.

"Wonderful. Kevin and I can go out and share a Coke and a burger at the Greek's."

The numbers on that didn't quite work, but Bob

thought it better not to mention it. They could get a grilled cheese sandwich in lieu of the hamburger and still have enough change for dessert from the Muscular Dystrophy gum machine beside the cashier's counter.

Bob's body seemed to churn and boil, as if he was turning under his skin to the consistency of a milkshake.

He was changing right here in the bedroom! He had to get out of here. "Isn't that music?" he asked, desperate to conceal his inner turmoil.

She sighed. It must be obvious to her that his voice was not right, and she probably knew why. "Kevin's got a friend over."

"I think I'll go say hello." He took a long step back. He quivered, goo in a sack of skin.

"Bob?"

"Yes?"

"Is that a dance you're doing or what?"

"The music—"

"You don't do the frug to the 'Blue Danube.'" Backing away from Cindy was an evasion, of course. He should go to her, and let her spend her rage on him and then ask her for the blessings of the night, but he had not the courage. Over the years of their marriage she had remade herself in an image he preferred, but now that he couldn't pay her way anymore she was back to her old self, the real Cindy—a stranger he had from time to time glimpsed in moments of rage or passion. There were jets of rebellion flaring.

And yet—and this was the most awful part— the strangeness of her anger was what was making her attractive. Her rage was a fierce aphrodisiac.

All the rules were changed; reality had come unstuck, danger and the unexpected now reigned.

His bones shifted, scuttling beneath his skin. Step-by-step he backed down the hall. Cindy snorted, a derisive, cutting noise. The light streaming from under Kevin's door was yellow and rich.

He had to hide, to get away, to save his family from this absurd horror—

His bones were oozing in his skin, his muscles bubbling as if they were carbonated glue.

He stumbled, fell against Kevin's door, lurched into the room.

The whole place was done up in blue construction paper. From Kevin's record player there blared the "Blue Danube." He was waltzing around and around with a girl in his arms.

"Dad!" They stopped waltzing.

The girl held out a soft, child-fat hand, smiled around a bucking reef of teeth. "Pleased to meetcha."

To take the hand Bob had to concentrate all of his attention on his own arm, force it forward, scream in his head for his fingers to open. Then he had to draw his hand back, which was like pulling against a cold river. The arm wanted to go straight out before him, the hand to crunch and twist itself into a new form.

This must not be allowed to happen, not here, not now. But he *wanted to,* his body *wanted to,* it had wanted to all day, to just burst its old skin and become the new, magic self that belonged to the wild.

Both children looked at him, the little girl's face flickering fear, Kevin's a mix of amusement and concern.

"Dad, have you got a sore throat?"

"Rrr—no!"

"Then why do you keep growling?"

"Your dad is really weird."

He finally managed to lurch out, caught himself leaning forward toward all fours, scuttled into the living room, and hit the phone. He fluttered through Cindy's directory, a pretty cream-colored book with roses pressed in the Lucite cover that Kevin had made last summer at camp. Here was Monica's home number. Thank God, what a convenience when your wife and your psychiatrist are such good friends, no need to gabble to some gum cracker at an answering service. *Ring.* Please. *Ring.* Oh, please. *Ring.* "Monica, thank God you're home."

"Who is this?"

"Bob; I need help."

"Are you hurt?"

"No, Monica, I'm changing. I swear."

"You sound like you've got a mouthful of Brillo or something."

"I swear, my whole body—Monica, it isn't a psychological problem, it's real. I've got to have help."

"Can you come to my office?"

"Please, I don't think I can get out of the apartment."

"Is Cindy there?"

"They're both here. And a little friend of Kevin's."

"Give me ten minutes, Bob." She hung up. He slumped over the phone, breathing deeply, trying for control, clutching his chest, huddling in on himself. Evening light gathered to waltz time from Kevin's room. Bob crept into the darkest corner he could find, the coat closet.

His body gave itself to its rebirth. He wrenched

and quivered, saw waves passing through his muscles, felt the grinding reorganization of his bones. His organs seemed to have become detached from their moorings. They swooped on cold comet tracks down new paths inside him, freezing and burning at the same time, while he gasped and gargled, trying not to scream.

"Tales from the Vienna Woods" gave way to the "Acceleration Waltz," and the *pop* of a bottle of fizzy apple juice. Bob stared at the faint light coming under the door of the coat closet. He darted his ears toward the rustling sound of movement—Cindy was coming down the hall. Now she was in the living room. "Bob?"

He pressed back against the wall. The smell of overcoats filled his nose: his own coat smelled of moldy money. Perhaps that ten dollars he had lost had worked its way down into the lining. There was a faint aroma of Paco Rabanne coming from Cindy's coat. Either she had taken to using it or had walked arm in arm with a man who did.

Didn't Monica's husband use it? That, or Aramis. Bob did not care for fragrances on his own body. His ears followed Cindy as she came to the center of the room. The light increased. She had turned on the lamp over by the TV. "Bob?"

The downstairs buzzer sounded, blasting the silence in the closet, making Bob chortle out an involuntary growl of surprise. Cindy came across the room, lifted the receiver of the intercom. "Yes?"

"Cyn, it's me."

"Oh, Monica, come in."

A few moments later they embraced with swishes and a ripple of ginger kissing. "Why did you come?"

"He phoned. Where is he?"

"I think he went out."

Light burst into his eyes. There stood Cindy holding Monica's airy mink. She dropped the coat. "Bob, my God."

Monica appeared, a dark mask before the light. She squatted down, reached in and took his face in warm, firm hands. She drew him out into the blinking light. The waltz music had stopped. Briefly his eyes met his son's, the boy standing at the far end of the room. "Is this for real?" his playmate asked.

"Kafka," Kevin said, "the *Metamorphosis*."

"Look at his teeth." Cindy's voice was analytical, the tone of someone so fascinated that for a moment they have forgotten to be upset. Then she fully realized what she was seeing, signified by the fact that her skin went corpse gray.

He tried to raise his arm, to touch what he sensed as a numb disfigurement of his lower face. His right arm shot out before him. It was short, the sleeve of his shirt drooping around it. The fist at the end of it was so tight it felt like it had been strapped to itself with cord. His palm was hot, his finger joints oozing red pain.

"It's a hysterical reaction," Monica said crisply. "Get him down on the floor. Get his clothes off. We've got to massage those limbs before he loses his circulation."

"What do you mean, a hysterical reaction? Look at him, he's—oh, Bob, oh, my baby!"

"The body can do wonders. You wouldn't believe what some patients look like. Especially from the East. Indians. You'd swear they'd half turned into monkeys, the way they contort themselves. It's nothing that modern psychiatry can't handle, of that much I can assure you. A few months on a Thorazine drip, a course of electroshock, and he'll seem fine."

"Months! Monica, we have no money. He can't go into the hospital, he has to work."

"I'm sorry. This is a classic case of avoidance. He can't handle his problems, can't face his responsibilities. It's a fortress mentality."

"Mother, his teeth are actually growing."

He heard all of this with absolute clarity as Monica and Cynthia undressed him. Through eyes that had gone to vague colors and shades of gray he watched his son and the little girl standing hand in hand at his feet. "Don't cry, Kevin, I'm gonna—"

Kevin clapped his hands over his ears. "He sounds like a dog!"

"Rub, Cindy." Their fingers raced along his arms and legs, raced and kneaded. Within his limbs there was a continuous churning, and it was getting worse. He delivered himself to their efforts but it was no good, not really. He was slipping, sliding through their fingers. His wife's hands were soft and cool and dry, Monica's damp and warm. Their manipulations were beautiful agony.

It faded like rain fades, and the rubbing of skin against skin was replaced by the whisper of fingers in fur.

"Oh, God, Monica, what's the matter with him!"

Monica lifted her hands as if she was being burned. A rictus twisted her face, her teeth gleaming behind tight lips, her eyes beaded to amber chips. Then a great force seemed to descend upon her and she controlled her face. Her lips were a line of wire. Young Kevin had moved away. His girlfriend was huddling in a ball beside the TV. Kevin's tape had recycled and the "Blue Danube" now filled the room.

A passing fire truck wailed. Bob, lying on his back, slowly windmilling arms and legs that no longer worked right, heard a voice from the street call out, "Artie, don't forget . . ." Then again, "They'll kill you if you do . . ." Somebody laughed. High in a window a pale star shone down.

Bob wished he could fly out into the wild emptiness between here and that star. His heart almost burst with longing and he cried aloud. A sound drowned the waltz, making Kevin cover his ears and stare with stricken eyes, making Cindy beat her fists against his chest, making Monica gather him in her arms and press her warm, soft cheek against the cold wall of teeth that half formed his new face.

The sound he made felt in his chest like flying, it was so high and rich and full. He would have thought such a voice would reach the stars, but when his breath ran out, the world was still exactly the same. Or, not quite. The little girl had gone to her knees facing the wall, and was loudly praying the Confetior.

"Bob," Monica whispered, "Bob, it's all right. I know you're still in there. I must tell you that I don't know exactly what's happening here but there must be some rational, perfectly sensible reason that explains this. I want you to know that you are not alone. I am with you. I will help you."

"Dad, can you talk?"

He wanted to talk. Very badly. He wanted to tell them to go, to leave him alone.

The world and the dark beckoned to him, the

long paths and shadowy leaves, the barking of the pack, the high wind at night.

"Bob, please, if you can talk, say something."

Of course he could talk. "Lorr." No, not quite right. "Bwaorr." It was an awful moment. "Urraoo." The walls seemed to come closer. He heard his own frightened panting.

Kevin burst into open tears. Monica's drone started again, and Cindy's sobs were in waltz time, unconsciously keyed to the sway of the "Blue Danube." In the corner the Confetior had given way to the Apostles' Creed. This little girl was a full-scale Catholic.

Bob wanted to comfort his son, to take his wife in his arms. He was sad, now. His initial fear was evaporating. Beneath the sadness there was something new, an interest in the dark beyond the window. He knew that there was nothing out there but Washington Square Park, New York University's private drugstore, jammed with dealers and students. He could hear the trees, though, speaking in soft night voices, and the glittering rattle of crickets.

Clumsily, he got to his feet. There was a general outcry in the room. Even Monica shouted. "What's he wearing?" shrieked Kevin's poor playmate.

"Get her out of here," Cindy said. "Take her home, Kevin. Your dad is sick."

"He's metamorphosed. Kafka's story isn't fiction anymore. In 1990 it's a medical text."

"How can you be so supercilious! Look, Jodie, he's wearing a wolf rug we bought last year in Alaska. He's having a nervous breakdown, that's all, do you understand?"

"No."

"What do you mean no—oh, God, Monica, can't you see what this will do? This kid'll tell her parents. Before we know it, everybody at St. Anselm's will know. What will happen to our reputation?"

Bob tried once again to talk. "Mwee, mwee. Eooo." It was horrible. His mind was swarming with thoughts, with explanations, answers, above all with the reassuring notion that it had worn off that night in the hotel, and it would wear off again.

Then he heard the wind again. He wanted to go out and run the night.

His nose came to life. This was nothing like the hotel. He was so startled by the change that he reared back, growling involuntarily, causing a renewed outburst of woe from those around him. Smells in hundreds and thousands and millions burst alive. He was instantly overwhelmed. The floor, the remains of his clothes, Monica's sweat, Cindy's soap, Cindy's sweat, her intimate odors, Kevin's child-sourness and Jodie's child-sweetness, the hot electronics of Kevin's record player in the next room—a smell like a Formica countertop with a hot pot on it—and the outdoor odors, the leaves, the bark of the trees, the squirrels sleeping among the branches, the brown odor of the crickets on the leaves, the chlorine-sourness of cocaine and the smoky, pungent aroma of the drug dealers, a complex of sweat and cigarettes, and the smells of marijuana and tobacco, of the concrete in the sidewalks and the rubber on the tires of passing cars, of gasoline and nitric acid from exhausts, the smell of garbage and hot food, garlic, beef, broccoli, and the faint, distinct odor of their bedroom, powder and the oils of human bodies, and a musky whiff of the spermicide

Cindy used with her diaphragm.

He jerked his head back, gobbling out twisted cries, his brain overwhelmed by the sudden plunge from the universe of seeing to that of smelling. The warm room, the lights, the furniture, the people, were in an instant ripped from their moorings in sighted life and plunged into a madhouse of radiant odors.

The world, as he saw it, was mostly gray. Red he could see, and green, and shades of brown. Would the blue sky be gone forever, and what of the beautiful smooth whiteness of Cindy's breast? He experienced as deep a pang of yearning as he had ever known. He bowed his head and covered his eyes with his hands.

The moment he tried to do so he fell painfully on his chin. "He's trying to use his hands," Cindy cried. "Look at him, oh, *look at him*!"

"Cindy, we have to stitch ourselves together. Remember this. It's very, very important. *This is not a miracle!* No, not a miracle. No. Somewhere, there is some quite, quite rational, clear, and understandable scientific explanation—"

"Oh, shut up, Monica. You're repeating yourself because it *is* a miracle and you're scared. You're terrified."

"I admit I'm uneasy. This is a very unusual case and it's appropriate for me to feel uneasy."

"Oh, yeah, I'd agree with that. Uneasy."

Bob was catching and then losing the thread of words. He was so disoriented by his changed senses that he couldn't pay attention, no matter how hard he tried. It was as if his mind was going blind.

The room, he realized, stank. The odor was salty and like cold, wet hair. It was cloying, as if made of oils, and lingered in his nose. A shiver coursed through his body. He felt cool air against the skin on the back of his neck.

"Look at him now. His hair's standing on end."

"Is he mad? What's happening?"

"Bob—"

He could not speak to them, could not tell them that their own fear was infecting him, that he was helpless before the odor of emotions that they couldn't smell. Every nuance of feeling created a change in odor that shafted at once to the depths of his soul. He had no way to defend himself from this assault, and could only suffer it, the raw march of feeling among those he loved.

"May I go?" A tiny little voice coming from Jodie. She was knotting her hands.

Cindy knelt to her level. "Honey, of course you can go. Monica will take you home, there's no need to call your parents to come get you. Just as long as you understand that this is all . . ." Her voice whispered away, and was replaced by a keening as of stressed wire. Bob longed to embrace her. He knew the sound of Cindy in abject sorrow.

Monica took the girl by the hand and left, promising to come back as soon as she had delivered the child.

"All a game!" Cindy shrieked as they left.

Not fifteen minutes had passed before the phone rang. Cindy snatched it up. "Hello—oh, hello Mrs. O'Neill. Yes, I'm glad she had a good time. Bob? Oh, he's a little indisposed, you can't talk to him. You want to do what? Oh, sure. I guess—well, of course." She hung up. "How nice. How goddamn nice! The woman's going to bring us a covered-dish supper. She acts like we had a death in the family."

Bob wanted to say just four precious words: "It wore off before." But he could not speak and despised the sound of his own efforts too much to try again. He sat on his haunches and stared helplessly at his wife.

Not long after, Monica returned. She and Cindy and Kevin sat together on the couch. None of them spoke. Bob sank deeper and deeper into despair. The emotion he was feeling now was loneliness. He was not a wolf, but rather a profoundly deformed man. He was the victim of some odd psychophysical disorder, that must be it.

And yet, in him there was something triumphant and free. He remembered the wolf in the Central Park Zoo. What of that wolf, what was it doing right now? Was it sleeping, dreaming only of the wild?

His own childhood dream of becoming a wolf had obviously been a true experience. He had swept through the backyards as a wolf. There *were* grass stains on his pajamas. There *were* those memories, so perfect, of a wolf's movements and ways.

Shape-shifting . . . it was said that witches could turn themselves into owls and rats and hares. And the Indians—didn't they have legends about it, too?

Was that poor old wolf still in its cage, or had it died and the two of them somehow come to inhabit this same flesh?

It had looked at him, looked into him—yes, actually entered him with its eyes.

That was the secret, the wolf had done it, had entered him with its eyes. And it had happened before, yes, it had, back at the San Antonio Zoo in the summer of 1957, he remembered it vividly now. There had been a wolf there, a sleepy, dejected old Texas red wolf and it had *looked* at him and then . . .

Then had come his dream.

"Could I watch *M*A*S*H*?" Kevin asked.

"No! No TV." His wife's voice was so lovely, full of melodies he had never heard before. He went to her and stood before her, looking into the creamy miracle of her face, the blue, wide eyes, the dramatic, perfectly proportioned nose, the lips that seemed always to conceal, as their deepest secret, laughter.

By degrees she raised her hands. "If I touch him, will it help?"

"I can't answer that."

Kevin, sobbing softly to himself, leaned against his mother's shoulder. Cindy seemed to Bob small and weak and vulnerable. For fifteen years he had been taking this woman in his arms.

Now all he could do was to nuzzle her with his big jaw, trying to avoid letting the tongue—which felt like a mouthful of belting leather—get in the way. As he got closer her scent became stronger. It was nostalgic, familiar in ways he had never before understood.

Oh, Cindy, fifteen years. I knew you as a girl and I knew you as a woman. I'd been so looking forward to gentle old age together. Pressing his nose up against her neck, into the place under her ear he had kissed a thousand times, he inhaled.

The odor stunned him. To call it an odor, even, was to diminish it terribly. Voices, songs, high summer days, blue sky in the Catskills, the warm of winter fires, snatches of love talk, the hot and the wet of bed night, the first halting glances and the settled looks of the marriage, her body big with Kevin, so much more. He realized that every good thing that time takes from us lingers in our odors—and we have lost the sense of smell.

Her hand came up, shaking, and she pressed her palm against his cheek.

To truly find her love, he had become a prisoner from her. He lay against the touch of her hand, and heard the final establishment of the night outside, the course of the stars against the restless sky. A leaf tapped the window, dropping silently past the light.

PART TWO
THE JOURNEY
TO THE WEST

A man without anything, alone on the road
long after midnight,

is told by the choking street light
morning will not come.
He jams his hands in his pockets, walks on.

   —Robert Duke,
     "In the Matter of the Night," (1983)

CHAPTER SEVEN

ROBERT DUKE HAD A NEW BODY TO LEARN. BREATHING through the long snout, and seeing around it, were difficult. He had lost the power of speech and what he now saw as the great privilege of hands. He was fallen from the human state, there was no other way to look at it.

His wife and son stared at him, stricken but also fascinated. Monica sat in the blue upholstered chair, watching him through quizzical eyes. "I need to do a little research," she said. "I'd better get up to the library at the hospital."

"At eight o'clock at night?" How Cindy's voice pierced! He was standing at her feet. When their eyes met, she reacted as if struck a blow, and looked away.

"The library's open till midnight. It's a teaching hospital."

Why did she need a library? Didn't she realize

she could use his computer to access Medline? She could do whatever research she needed from the next room.

"I wish you didn't have to leave. I'm so scared."

"Don't be scared, Mama." The bright edge was gone from Kevin's voice. His own fear rose to a stench like acid wax when he looked at Bob. "He'll change back any minute now."

Bob's impulse was to comfort his boy. He turned his head, only to see him shrink away from eye contact. It hurt Bob, and he humiliated himself by quite involuntarily making a high keening noise.

Cindy clapped her hands over her ears. "Don't do that, please!" She looked at Monica. "He can only make animal sounds." Another wave of fear poured from her body, that strange tart-musty odor that made Bob's heart beat harder and the hair at the back of his neck thrill.

Monica came down to his level, pressing her face into his. "Can you understand?" she said in a loud voice.

He was having trouble dealing with the cascade of odors that were now pouring from their bodies. Their emotions seemed to run in waves, bursting forth for a few moments, then subsiding, then coming out again. And each time they came forth they were stronger. Their fear was rising, and soon it would break them. Inside himself Bob was in turmoil. He felt so odd that he could barely walk. It was a tremendous effort to coordinate four legs, to see through these shape-sharpened, color-dulled eyes, to sort out the smells and sounds that shoved and swarmed at him from all sides.

What's more, the presence of the night was oppressing him. The walls of the room seemed almost alive, like malevolent flesh keeping him from the freedom of the woods.

He moaned again, he couldn't help it. Cindy clapped her hands over her ears. "Bob, are you in pain?"

"Bob—" Monica took his face in her hands. "We have to communicate with you. We have to have some means of knowing how you feel and what you want. Now, please, try to listen to me. Tap the floor if you hear me."

Tap the floor. Was that all that was left to him?

"He tapped! Dad, Dad, tap once if you're in pain, twice if you're okay."

What could he do? He was not in pain. Anguish is not pain. Desperation is not pain. He tapped twice.

"He's not in pain!"

A barrage of questions followed. Bob heard the fluttering of wings outside the window. When he cocked his ears, he could also hear the alien breathing of a large bird. He was astonished to know that there were owls in the city. He could imagine the bird skimming over the buildings, searching out the dark places for mice. From the rapidity of its breath, its busy fluttering of feathers, it was working hard, and full of excitement. Then it flew on, after a faint scuttling sound that came from the edge of the cornice.

There was a secret world out there.

"Don't even think about it," Cindy yelled. She put her arms around his neck. "It's a six-story drop, don't you remember?"

"Close the windows. There's not much he can do but jump."

He tapped once, sharply. "Once is no," Kevin said.

"Yes, yes, we will close the windows. Bob, this is all going to be over soon. You'll get back to normal. You'll be all right. Monica's going to do some research and find out what's wrong with you and she's going to fix it, isn't that right, Monica?"

"That's right."

Didn't they realize what had happened here? A great reordering in the world had caused this. The petty ministrations of a doctor weren't going to undo something so enormous.

But if he didn't change back, what would he do? He couldn't spend the rest of his life in this apartment. Not the least reason was that they were due to be evicted. What was Cindy going to do? She was desperate for money. Now how would she get it?

The wind whispered, the wind called. It was seductive, it was insistent. And now the wind rattled the windowpanes a little bit, tapping for him to come. He saw himself running across the top of the wind, escaping from the maze of prisons that was this city.

He might have wished for wings, but thought perhaps he'd better not.

He watched Monica and Cindy frantically locking the windows. He climbed up and dragged his paws against the glass. "Down," Cindy commanded. "Down, Bob!"

How dare she talk to him like he was a dog. He wanted to tell her, to scream it out: I am a human being in here. I am a human being! All that escaped, though, was a very unpleasant snarl.

He had bared his teeth at her, he had raised his hackles. Terrified, she was backing away. "Now, now, Bob. Nice Bob." Oh, good Lord, how stupid.

Kevin came up to him. "Dad, I know you can

understand everything. Look, they don't want you near the windows, okay? So let's compromise. Let's say you stay away from the windows and I'll get Mom to leave them open."

Bob tapped twice on the floor.

"Hear that, Mom? He *does* understand. Is it a deal?"

"You won't go near the windows, Bob." Again he tapped. He was a little bit in control at least.

Then Monica went to Cindy and whispered in her ear, a whisper that Bob could hear clearly. "Don't open the windows. He could be suicidal."

"How can we be sure? He's always been fascinated by wolves. Maybe he's having a good time. At least he doesn't have to get out and earn a living."

"Look, Monica, how would you feel if this—this—fantastic catastrophe happened to you?"

They both regarded Bob, Monica with a weak smile, Cindy sadly. "I want to turn on the air conditioners," she said. "It's too close in here."

Lacking voice, lacking hands, all Bob could do was watch as she defied him.

A moment later the downstairs buzzer sounded. Monica picked up the handset, spoke for a moment, then let somebody in. She turned a shocked face to the others. "It's Jodie O'Neill and her mother. They've got the covered-dish supper."

Cindy rushed to the door. "I don't believe it. We can't—" The doorbell rang. "Monica!"

"What can we do—tell them to leave it on the stoop?"

"Say anything, say he's got AIDS. No, don't say that. All hell will break loose at the school."

"Cindy, as far as this woman is concerned, Bob's been taken to the hospital. You have a big dog, that's all. It's simple enough." Monica opened the door.

The O'Neills were all there, the mother and father, the daughter, the teenage son. They came right in, bearing sweating Tupperware dishes. "Hi, Cyn," Betty O'Neill said.

"Is that him?" the son asked. So much for Monica's subterfuge. Jodie had obviously told her family everything. And why not, she had witnessed the whole transformation.

"Now, this is truly amazing," said Mr. O'Neill, a flat-faced man with a pencil moustache. "He looks every inch a wolf."

"That's no wolf," Cindy shouted. "That's our dog."

"Jodie said—"

"She was confused. The dog bit Bob. He went to St. Vincent's to get a shot and some stitches."

"I hate to be nosy, but if a dog's biting its own master, shouldn't it be destroyed?" Mrs. O'Neill's words were almost snide.

"Oh, God, no!" Cindy put her hands to her cheeks. "No."

"At least take it to a vet," Mrs. O'Neill put in.

Bob saw Monica blink. She said nothing, but he didn't care for the look that had come into her eyes.

"We brought baked beans and ham, pea soup, and broccoli with hollandaise."

"Oh, that's very kind," Cindy said. "You needn't have done it."

"No trouble. It's left over from a wake a couple of weeks ago. The only work we had to do was to turn on the microwave." She laughed. "We have a huge family, and a lot of them are old. I keep this sort of thing ready all the time."

Bob hardly heard her stupid nattering. His skin felt hot, he began to hear and smell with even greater clarity than was now his exquisite norm. His whole body tingled, his muscles became like compressed steel. His breath got long and low, and came through his throat in growls he could not control. He was furious. That nattering woman, the gaping children, the superior sneer in the father's face—he wanted to hit somebody. How dare they put ideas of vets into Monica's head! He was damned if he was going to submit to an examination by some animal doctor.

He was a human being. In here, yes, but still a human being, with the rights and lordship of a human being. They would not treat him worse than any degenerate junkie, and put him in a cage for observation, and shoot him with a tranquilizer dart, and examine him on some dirty table covered with dog hair.

"I think it would be a good idea to take him to the vet," Monica said. "We could get a full X-ray series. Find out what's going on."

Mr. O'Neill was sampling some of his wife's baked beans. "A Bud'd sure go good with this."

A Bud! The bastard, that's my last Bud in that damn fridge!

"Sure." Cindy spoke casually. Who cared anyway, Bob wouldn't be drinking any more beer, right?

He snarled when he heard the *pschtt* of the can. "Damn! That dog's skittish."

"It's not a dog," Jodie said. "It's their dad."

"Jodie, I don't want you to say that. It's too embarrassing."

"Well, it is."

Mrs. O'Neill looked at Cindy helplessly while

the father swilled Bob's beer.

The clock struck nine. "*Mystery's* on Channel Thirteen," Kevin sang out.

"We don't watch that highbrow dreck," O'Neill said.

Bob growled again, harder and not by accident. He wanted to watch *Mystery,* to sit on the couch between his wife and his son, with his damned Bud in his hand, and enjoy every minute of it.

"What do you do, Mr. O'Neill?" Cindy asked smoothly. "Are you in trucking or something?" Atta girl, atta girl, needle the moron!

"No, I teach philosophy, actually, at NYU."

Which philosophers did he teach? Bob wondered. Howard Cosell? Madonna?

Cindy gave up nothing. She simply shrugged. "Bob's an entrepreneur," she said smoothly. "He teaches big companies how to use small computers."

Wonderful woman! O'Neill squirmed. "I've always wanted to have my own business," he said, a whine entering his voice.

Bob decided to get rid of the O'Neills. He trotted over to the dining-room table, where O'Neill sat, beer in one hand, fork in the other, tasting the beans right out of the pot.

But when he tried to unleash a barrage of barking, all he could manage were silent gasps.

Was barking something canines learned, like walking on their hind legs? Surely it was instinctive.

He thought with horror: I don't *have* any canine instincts. I'm not a canine. I have no idea how to bark.

"Do you brush your dog's teeth?" O'Neill asked cheerfully.

"Why, no."

"Why does his breath smell of Crest, then?"

"Uh—maybe—he likes it! Yes, he eats it every chance he gets. Kevin! You must have left the top off the toothpaste again."

"No, Dad brushed his teeth right before—"

Kevin silenced himself, thank God, but the O'Neills all looked sharply at Bob.

"Their dad turned into a wolf," Jodie said again. "That's him."

"Oh, be quiet. Sometimes I think my daughter's a little addled," Mrs. O'Neill said.

"Merely intelligent and imaginative," the father said. "Unlike Spider here. Right, Spider?"

"Right, Dad. I'm fit only for basketball and then the grave."

If Bob couldn't bark—what other routines could dogs pull? Oh, yes, he vividly remembered a damnable Irish setter back when he was a kid. He knew exactly what to do.

Sitting down on his haunches, he prepared to wait. He stared up at O'Neill. Soon the man would get up out of the chair, and then Bob would do his deed. O'Neill was wearing a white cotton sweater and a nice pair of worsted pants. So much the better. Bob waited. When O'Neill met his eyes, he wagged his tail.

"Dog's a paraplegic, or what?"

"What do you mean? He's perfectly healthy."

"I've never seen an animal that bad at wagging its tail. He shakes his rear and just sort of hopes the tail will wiggle."

Cindy put her hand on his head. "I think he does very well, and he has a magnificent tail." Bob heard the sadness in her voice, and his heart was made very full. She was a real fighter, was this

Cynthia he had married.

There came a great shuffling and creaking from O'Neill. "Well, we'd better get going. Don't want to miss the ten o'clock news. Channel Five's got the best sports." He laughed. "Also, I've got some papers to grade, if the cat didn't piss on them again." Another laugh, chair pushed back, man standing.

Bob leaped up on him, planting his forepaws on his chest and dragging them down, shredding the sweater and tearing the pants in about four places.

"Oh, Bob, no!" Cindy came, grabbed him around the neck just as he was rising for another pass. "Bob, what in the world are you doing?"

O'Neill lashed out, kicking Bob hard in the chest. The blow hurt and Bob involuntarily bit at the foot that tormented him.

With all her strength Cindy pulled back.

"That dog is crazy," O'Neill snarled. "Look at my clothes—and look at this shoe. Oh, shit, I'm bleeding. Broke the skin."

"It's their dad. You made him mad. He doesn't like you."

"Shut her up, Betty! Look at what it did to my foot!"

"I'll get a Band-Aid, Mr. O'Neill."

"Band-Aid, the hell. Now I'm going over to St. Vincent's. I've got to get a stitch." He tried to walk, hobbled, nearly fell. "Two or three stitches right in the ball of my foot. Betty, where's the car?"

"This side of the street, halfway up the block."

"At least it's not over on goddamn Mercer." He glared at Cindy. "I think you'd better look over your liability policy, girl."

Cindy went gray with rage. She detested sexual diminutives.

"Oh, now, John, you won't be doing anything like that. Come on, children, let's help Daddy get over to the emergency room."

Bob saw Cindy's hands on the baked beans. The O'Neills began to leave. Bob cringed. He knew exactly what was about to happen. The O'Neills went into the foyer, began waiting for the elevator. At that moment Cindy snapped. "You can take your damned baked beans and shove them you know where, *boy*!" With that she poured them over O'Neill. They were followed by the soup and the broccoli and then the door was slammed on the howling, food-covered O'Neills.

"You're harboring a rabid dog, you've assaulted me," O'Neill roared. "There will be revenge, girlie, there will be sweet revenge." Then, in a lower tone: "Stop eating that broccoli, you fool."

"Sorry, Dad."

The elevator took the O'Neills away. "Well, I guess I can write Jodie off as a friend," Kevin commented absently. He turned up *Mystery,* which he had been watching with the volume off.

"Oh, hell, now I've got the whole damn foyer to clean up."

Monica put her arm around Cindy. "I've got some nice Melozine in my purse."

"Tranquilizers give me anxiety attacks. I keep waiting for the other shoe to drop."

The two women cleaned up the mess, assisted by Kevin. Bob could easily have helped them by eating the beans off the floor, but he was damned if he was going to act like an animal. He went over, lay down on the couch, and watched *Mystery* with his muzzle on his paws.

Monica came and sat beside him. "I want to talk to you alone for a moment, Bob. I'm assuming that you can understand what I'm saying. Your actions tonight make it clear that your mind is unchanged. You're as odd as ever. First, I have some sort of an idea of what you have done. It's called hypnagogic transformation. You, of course, have accomplished a miraculous hypnagogic transformation. Among American Indians it is called shape-shifting and at best involves a certain amount of straightforward contortion. What you have done staggers the scientific mind. I always knew that you were a repressed, undeveloped genius of some sort. That you would choose to express your genius in this particular direction is naturally a surprise. But I must say something to you. Now listen to me. You are causing your family great suffering by what you have done. You must shift back. You must leave this utterly fantastic contortion and return to the human form. You can do it, you're in complete control of the situation. You and I know this, even though you yourself may not be willing to admit it. Bob, I beg of you, for the sake of a marvelous woman and a lovely little boy, return to them. Accept reality. You are a failure in life. A complete failure. But you are also a wonderful, surprisingly charismatic man. Your wife loves you to distraction. And that little boy—he adores his father. Please, for them, come back to us."

Outside the wind blew, sending a rattle of leaves against the window. Autumn was here. Time for the running of the deer, time for the gathering of nuts and the making of nests. The wind was wild, the wind was rich, the wind went where it went.

Bob could see the high stars changing in their courses, could hear a rat scuttling along the roof across the street, could hear pigeons fluttering in their sleep. The owl that had been here earlier was now gone, but bats squeaked in the sky, dashing about after the last flies of summer.

He could not tell Monica how mistaken she was. His present form was as real and as immutable as his former one had been. Whatever had affected him had come and gone its merry way, leaving him as he now was.

"Am I reaching you, Bob?"

He tapped.

"Wait until you see what this absurd avoidance response is going to do to your family. You've sent a wonderful woman and a beautiful child to hell. So be it. I'm off to the hospital, where I intend to spend the rest of the night doing research. If I can find a way to force you out of this maneuver of yours, I'll do it. But I doubt that there's going to be a thing in the literature."

As she left, Bob disconsolately watched Lord Peter Wimsey dance through the intricacies of some mystery he couldn't identify.

"I'm going to bed, Mom."

"Good night, son. Maybe things will be better tomorrow."

"Tomorrow is another day, eh. That might not be entirely correct. Kafka—"

"Shut up about Kafka! I'm sick of hearing about Kafka."

"We're living the *Metamorphosis*."

"I don't care if we're living the *Niebelungenlied*, no more Kafka. At the moment I find it almost invincibly depressing. Now go to bed, I want to be alone with the remains of your father."

With a murmured "okay, Mom," he left the room. Soon the "Blue Danube" was drifting out his door.

"Turn it off! I never want to hear that again!" She sobbed, then rushed after him. "Oh, honey, I'm sorry. Please forgive your mother. It's been a pretty dismal day."

Bob could not cry. In fact, great emotion made him droop, loll his tongue, and stare. He watched as they prepared for bed.

"Can I stay with you, Mom?"

"Sure."

They climbed in bed together. They were beginning to respond to him just exactly as if he were a real dog. In a word, he was being ignored.

Cindy lay still, her mouth slightly open, Kevin in the crook of her arm.

Then the doorbell started. It was insistent, buzzing again and again.

Bob could do nothing but wait and watch. Cindy opened her eyes, gave a grunt of confusion, then turned over. The buzzer started up once more. She sat up in bed. "My God." With a hustle of covers she arose and went to the intercom. "Who? The *police*! Of course." She buzzed them in.

Bob paced, panting, which reduced his body heat—cold air across the tongue, a good, new sensation.

Then they were there, a whole foyer full of them, men smelling of cigarettes and oiled steel, of leather and sweat, tough men. "We got a dog complaint, ma'am."

"That bastard."

"He had twelve stitches. He lost a nerve in his foot. It'll be months before he walks. The dog's gotta go in for observation."

"No! That's completely impossible."

"Ma'am, the ASPCA truck is downstairs. It'll just be a week, he'll be treated well. You can visit him. It's no big deal."

"They're afraid of rabies?"

"Yes, ma'am."

"Doesn't the rabies test involve dissecting the head of the animal?"

Bob shrank back into the coat closet, staring wildly.

"Ma'am, it's a matter of observation first. It won't come to no tests."

"But if it does?"

"Well, the test terminates the life of the animal. But if he might have rabies—"

"He doesn't have it! The worst he has is a slight case of the sniffles!"

"Well, it's put him in a kind of a bad mood."

"You can't take him. I'll have my vet look at him."

"No, ma'am. There's been a complaint filed. We have to take the dog."

"Where's your warrant? You can't even come in here without a warrant!"

"I hate these pet schticks. We don't need a warrant, ma'am. I'm going to tell the ASPCA guys to come up." He spoke into a handheld radio. The other cops fanned out into the living room, their bulky bodies filling it, casting black shadows from the single light that was on, the lamp that hung over the dining table.

Bob was so horrified that he couldn't move. He stood watching Cindy lose her battle with the police. She literally wrung her hands as she talked, and then three more men came in, dressed in khaki overalls, carrying a large cage between them.

"Come on, boy," one of them said, opening his face at Bob in a most insincere approximation of a grin.

The smells, though, told him a great deal. When the man spoke to him, an odor of tooth decay and old bacon grease came across the air. Bob took a step forward and it blossomed with acid, a stench like boiling wax and onions. The man was afraid of him—terrified. And full of hate.

Bob could not go with these people. They would kill him, he knew it certainly.

"What the fuck," the man burst out. "This ain't a dog!" His voice was high, his odor grainy with fear. "You got a fuckin' wolf here."

One of the other men in khaki spoke up. "Why didn't you say this was a wolf, lady?"

"I—I—"

"People think these things are pets. They're crazy. This is a dangerous animal, my men aren't going near it."

Two of the policemen had their hands on their pistols.

"Go back to the truck," the flushed man said to one of the others. "Get the dart gun."

Cindy gave a little cry. A flash of panic made Bob growl. It was short and sharp, almost a bark.

The head cop took off his cap. "Lady, why are you keeping a wolf? Don't you know this is illegal?"

"He's a—he's just a big husky."

"Back out," the chief ASPCA man said, "these things can cut you to ribbons in a second. Where the fuck's Louie with that dart gun?" He grabbed one of the radios. "Louie, for God's sake, its hackles are up!"

The police had their pistols out now, all of them. Behind the clutch of blue and khaki the elevator door opened. Bob bolted, racing down the hall toward the bedroom.

"I'm calling my lawyer," Cindy shouted. Who? Bob wondered. Stanford Shadbold, whom they hadn't paid in a year?

"Okay, guys, break out the net. Block the corridor. I'm going in." As Cindy started her frantic phone calling Bob raced back and forth from bathroom to closet. The smells of fear and rage coming from the men drove him to panic, that and the knowledge of what was coming. From the bed there came a groan, then young Kevin was sitting up. He stared, stupefied, as a man in khaki, wearing a fencing mask and heavy quilting on his chest, arms and legs, advanced. In his hands was a neat plastic gun. Bob tried to rush past him at the last moment, his heart full of hopelessness, his body still determined to escape.

There was an awful, burning pain in his breast. He heard himself screaming, a doggy wail.

"Dad, Dad!"

"Shut up, kid. Okay, guys, he's going down."

The fire spread, an agony that turned him to wood. It hurt but he could neither move nor cry out. He lay on his side, stiff, while his wife yammered at answering services and the ASPCA team gathered him up in a stout nylon net.

They took Bob's burning, paralyzed body down the hall. His eyes had blurred but he could still smell the horrible odors of the men, the faint smells of other animals on the netting, the rancid butter of Cindy and Kevin's terror.

Shrieks followed him down the hall, their razor

agony penetrating even the tranquilizer. He could not even struggle to help Cindy, he could do nothing but listen to her at the far edge of panic, making a sound beyond grief.

"What about the Bill of Rights?" Kevin screamed, running along behind his father, wearing nothing but a pair of underpants. "What about due process? You can't just wrap my dad up in a net! You can't do it, this is America."

One of the policemen enclosed Kevin in a hug. "Gonna be okay, son. You wait and see."

"Don't you do that! Don't you grab my boy like that!"

Then Bob was in the elevator. The door rattled closed. Cindy's bellowing and Kevin's rising, frantic voice receded.

The world receded. There remained only the burning pain at the center of his chest, where the needle had been embedded. There was that, there was the blur of lights as the net was carried through the lobby. Then the back of the truck, thick with the scent of animal despair, a urinous, rotted stench. One of the men played a harmonica, some Spanish tune. Bob drifted helplessly away, and the world went silent, and odorless, and black.

CHAPTER EIGHT

TOTAL OBLIVION ONLY LASTED A FEW MINUTES. HE WAS still in the back of the truck when he became aware that they were fitting a wire and leather muzzle over his head. Vaguely he could feel them doing it, could hear them grunt when the truck lurched. His body seethed as if it was filled with insects. Try as he might, he could not move.

He understood, though, that he was in a cage in the back of the truck, and another cage had been fitted over his head.

"Man, this sucker is big."

"Just once I'd like to get it on a leash and go down Hundred and Thirty-Fifth. Nobody bother me then."

"Big boys bother you, little man?"

"Fuck you. Man, look at those eyes, just starin'."

"Starin' at you."

"We gonna gas 'im?"

"Dunno. Cage 'im tonight, in the morning, Tony know what to do."

"Look out, man, he might be comin' 'round. Give 'im another dart."

"No, man, what can he do? He's in the muzzle. Let him wake up. I want to see that sucker on his feet."

"Tear your throat right out."

"Yeah, man. Beautiful."

"You sick, man."

By the time they got to the pound Bob could lift his head enough to see. He could also scent things with great acuity, but the smells were meaningless to him—a jumble of startling new sensations. He could identify some of the odors: the stale fetor of sick breath, of tooth decay and smoker's mouth, the odor of other animals in the truck, the smell of the steel and the plastic and the gasoline. But there were other scents, far more subtle, that seemed elusively beautiful. He was in contact with the world in a new way, but he had no time to appreciate it, for the truck stopped and he was carried down a corridor into hell.

The sound hit him in flashes. He imagined that he was at the exploding muzzle of a machine gun. Then he saw walls of cages all filled with roaring dogs. Their barks were wild and furious, their eyes terrible. Close up, on direct terms with it, he could scarcely imagine the intensity of this passion. The dogs' voices were blasting with fear and savage hate.

They knew he was no wolf, they knew it at once. Quailing in their cages as he was carried past, screaming, their lips frothy, their eyes beyond the border of sanity, they leaped and clawed, trying to get away from the monster that was being deposited among them.

"Don' like the wolf," one of the men said.

"He a mean sucker. They knows it. He kill ten of 'em all at once."

"You wanna see 'im fight?"

"Shit, he'd never make it tonight. Tomorra night, though."

"You on tomorra night?"

"Yeah."

"I got fifty bucks says he'll go down against the three shepherds that're up for gassin' Friday."

"You got fifty bucks sayin' that wolf ain't gonna stand against three mangy, broke-down street mutts? I got fifty bucks sayin' you is wrong."

There were slapped hands, then the two men walked out, oblivious to the noise of the crazed dogs. Bob lay on the filthy floor of a large cage, surrounded by other large cages. To his left and right large dogs shrank away from him. Across the aisle a terrier yammered, glaring at him out of scared, dripping pop eyes.

Despite all the noise, the barking and the whining, Bob was overtaken by sleep. It came quite suddenly, a black sheath. Abruptly he was dreaming. It was May 1961: Junior Cotillion Night at the Country Club. He was taking Melissa Costers, driving Dad's enormous new Thunderbird. There was a scent of oleander blossom in the air. He gave Melissa a corsage of gardenias, and the two smells mingled. On the way to the cotillion they listened to Fats Domino on the radio, singing "Blueberry Hill." Bob fell in love with the softly smiling Melissa. He even liked the way she looked in her braces. At a light he asked very solemnly if he could give her a kiss. Their lips touched dryly, then a waiting hunger captured them both and the kiss grew more intimate and humid. Their braces clattered together but neither of them cared. The light changed to green, a car honked and finally came alongside. The driver asked if they needed help.

It was then that Bob discovered that their braces had become locked together. Receiving no answer to his question, the other driver huffed and went away.

Bob woke up, sweating out the hideous waiting for rescuer, the frantic bending and twisting of the braces, the amused stares of the police, the flashbulbs of the *Express* photographer.

He awoke snapping at his muzzle, and knew to his despair why he had been dreaming about braces. The iron bound him, the leather straps tasted of the saline gnaw of a thousand other canines. He got to his feet, glanced around for a water fountain. Then he realized that he had a hangover from the tranquilizer dart. He was sick in a corner of the cage.

Thirsty, and he smelled water. All he could see, though, was an encrusted dish attached to a feeder tube that automatically refilled when the dish was empty. There was something floating in the water, possibly the previous occupant's spittle. The dish was slick with the licking of thousands of tongues. Bob was revolted, and crept to the far side of the cage.

Presently a small man came hurrying along, pushing a cart stacked with bowls. He thrust one into each cage through a spring-loaded door. The dogs commenced eating at once, gobbling down the appalling mess with gusto.

They were a dull group of creatures, these dogs. They were tired and broken, most of them, standing in these cages awaiting their turn in the gas chamber, which was a little black hutch at the far end of the room. Bob tried to remember how long animals were kept here before being destroyed. Five days, wasn't it?

Surely Cindy would manage something.

But time passed, and he remained in his cage. The light coming in the high, barred windows changed, grew thin. Bob yearned toward that light. His initial despair had given over to fury. Most of all he was furious at science for giving him no hint at all that this could happen. He had grown up in the illusion that there is something fundamentally stable about the universe. But that was a lie. It was only stable for those who believed it to be stable. If you did not so believe, you risked personal catastrophe. How many others had ended up like him, stuck in the bodies of creatures that had interested, inspired, or obsessed them?

He walked over and stared at the drying glop in the bowl. It was so damn stupid. He had to get out of this mess. The thing was, he hadn't felt any control over his transformation. So how could he hope to change himself back?

He searched his mind, trying to understand how this had happened to him. All of his life he had been fascinated by wolves. He had tried to observe them in the wild in Minnesota, but had gotten only a few glimpses. They were the devil to track. Hunters flushed them into clearings and shot them from helicopters. Bob had used years of tracking skills, gained from the Boy Scouts, from books, from professional guides. Still, the wolves had eluded him.

All but one. This was a she-wolf, young, weighing no more than eighty pounds. He had been crawling down a brush-choked ridge to a little stream when he had encountered a thatch of gray-brown fur. He had felt ahead and discovered the animal. She had been so frightened by his approach that she had become like a thing of rubber. There had been a brief moment between them. Her eyes had met his. He had thought himself the possessor of a great secret, to stare into the enigmatic, panic-clouded eyes of this alien creature, to see her as she was in her own world, a place intended to be hidden from human eyes.

Had that done it—had something of her somehow stuck to him all these years, some strange seed . . . ?

But this was a matter of the flesh, of the real, immutable body, of blood and bone and skin. There had been some kind of dance of atoms, for they had reordered themselves. Wouldn't there have been a discharge of energy as the molecules of his old body broke their borders and sought new ones? And why had he first melted, then re-formed?

It was all completely impossible. And yet here he was in this cage with a bowl of dog food to eat. Not a very high quality brand, either, judging from the fatty bits and the chunks of what looked like organ meat suspended in the dissolved cereals. He sniffed at it. Most unappetizing. He wanted eggs, bacon, orange juice, and coffee. He wanted toast, dammit, butter, a bit of strawberry jelly. He wanted the *Times* and maybe another cup of coffee. He wanted all of these things at the Elephant and Castle restaurant on Prince Street, with Cindy sitting across from him with her croissant and cappuccino.

He wanted them now!

When the echo died away, he realized that he had somehow learned to bark. He had rattled away like the worst of them, yammering at the top of his lungs.

What a foul degeneration. He was now a coarse beast, he couldn't say a word, he couldn't turn a key, he had no clothes and had only garbage to eat. There was a gas chamber right out in the middle of the room and they were soon going to put him in it, and this terrible mystery was going to die. A human being who had gone through the mirror was going to come to a choking end, pitiful, terrified, claustrophobic.

All around him dogs licked bowls, paced, slept, barked, whined, defecated, urinated. The air was a fog of canine odors. When the door to the front of the building opened, expectant noses twitched, eyes followed the coming of the men with the big plastic garbage bags. They opened a cage and took a scrabbling animal down to the gas chamber. In a moment it was locked inside. The others paced and panted, then a buzzer rang and the inert form was pulled out and stuffed into a bag. Another dog, this one screaming and running, was processed. Then another, and another and another. The cages were disinfected.

Didn't these people realize that the dogs knew what was being done here? They all knew it was a charnel house. But they could not make the leap of consciousness to see that they themselves would be victims in a few days. They could not see this. When the men went away with their bags of cadavers, the other dogs settled down to an afternoon of licking themselves, pacing, barking, and sleeping.

Bob was alone. He could not befriend one of

these creatures, for they had not his intelligence. He could not tap out signals or share noble thoughts in this filth.

During the day new dogs were brought to fill the cages of the old, most of them scruffy, terrible creatures, things of the streets. One was so emaciated that all it did was lie on its side. When a keeper offered it food, it gently licked the man's hand and closed its eyes.

Whenever a new beast was brought in, the other dogs barked. For Bob there could not be any real rest or even contemplation—much less sleep— with the cacophony. He kept wanting to believe that it was mindless, but the more he listened, the more he heard something new in it.

He heard a song, built on a very definite, very unhuman esthetic, but certainly a song. When dogs barked they expressed excitement or fear or rage, but they also expressed a beauty, something in its way as subtle as the luster of an aria. An aria, or was it a prayer? There was joy in it, even from these trapped beasts, and when one of them went to the gas chamber and the others barked, it seemed to Bob that the unseen world shifted and fluttered in sympathy.

"It isn't eating. It hasn't touched a thing through three feedings."

"Shit, I got fifty bucks on it. I hope it ain't sick."

"The pool's seventeen hundred dollars, you aren't the only one who doesn't want it to be sick. I've got some money on it myself. It's an exceptional wolf. Must weigh in at a hundred and sixty pounds, maybe a little better."

"It jus' look at you. You think it wants to eat us?"

"Don't take the muzzle off before the fight. If

that's what's keeping it from its food, it can wait a little longer."

"That lady been by. We say we ship it up to Queens."

"I've got a buyer already. Movie guy."

"That lady done los' her a wolf!"

The man in khaki and the one in the soiled white coat left. Bob followed them with his eyes, hungering for their freedom, their voices, their beautiful hands.

The implications of their conversation were so unfortunate that it was a few minutes before Bob fully realized what had been said. Then it hit him a solar blow: he ran back and forth in the squeeze; he panted and snapped at his muzzle; he butted his head against the cage, finally stared in fury and frustration at the rusty padlock. Given the muzzle, he couldn't even chew it—not that he'd have a prayer of chewing it through.

They were stealing him, if they didn't kill him first. Made to fight to the death, then sold to some movie producer for God knew how much money —it was outrageous, criminal.

He raised his head and found that he could howl, and it felt good to howl out the misery of his situation. God, though, was as silent as ever He had been when Bob used to pray the Our Father and the Hail Mary. He hadn't been really Catholic since he was twelve, but now the nobility of the old prayers returned to his mind. He saw his religion as a grand and rather pitiful human attempt to somehow speak back to the mute wonder of creation. He had prayed just now, with his howl.

The dogs had fallen silent. Many of them were staring at him, and in their faces he could see reproach. He knew why: he had interrupted the song of the barks with a noise that did not fit. One little Shih Tzu in a tiny cage yapped. Then a terrier, then a mutt, and another mutt, and a burned mutt and a starved mutt, and two shepherds and some other nameless breeds, and then like a night full of crickets they were going at it again, deep in their esthetic.

It came to him with great force that he was the only creature here who was not already in heaven. Nothing could happen to these dogs that really mattered to them. They were all lovers, they had all seen God many times in the human form, and theirs was the celebration of the heavenbound.

He yapped, but it was wrong, a sullen little note in these symphonics. He brought the habit of concept, of memory and forethought with him from the human world. That was why he was so much less than the dogs, why his voice lacked timbre and resonance. He had the past to savor, the future to fear, the present to endure. The dogs had only their barking. They strove to make it fine and exciting and fun. It was prayer, yes, but also entertainment: they were singing a song of dog-affirming.

This was not an unhappy place. Dogs suffered terribly here, yes, but the suffering only reached so deep. The gay tails, the flags on the jumping bodies of the condemned, attested to the persistence of life and the triumph of dogdom in a way that nothing in human experience could, save perhaps the singing that came from the gas chambers of World War II, when briefly man had experimented with treating himself as he did the animals.

He longed to ask these dogs: "How does it feel

to love a master, to live with and see and smell a God?" And how does it feel to be deprived of this love? Each dog was a detailed, complex tragedy. Lost, given away, abandoned, forgotten. They knew what it was to be discarded by someone they adored. Why then were they not lovelorn, and what was this strange humor in the barking? Did they see themselves as absurd? Were they capable of sensing the ridiculousness of being a dog?

When once a woman came looking for a dog to take home, the whole place filled with a smell as if of hope, and dog after dog shambled to the edge of its bars, dancing and panting its friendliness.

"That one you can't have," the vet said to the woman, a girl of perhaps twenty, with clear, hard eyes and the heart-stopping skin of the just-formed.

"Is he a husky?"

"He's a wolf."

"You're kidding!"

"No, ma'am, that's a full-blooded male timber wolf in the prime of life."

"What's he doing here?"

"Bit a guy's foot off. Cops confiscated him as an illegal pet."

"I don't want any problems like that!"

"No, ma'am. Now, let me show you this little husky over here. Name's Rindy. Got him in two days ago."

"Hello, Rindy. Rindy?"

A wave of ambrosial odor poured from the dog at the sound of its name. It wagged its tail, it shot gladness and welcome from its eyes.

The whole pound awaited the decision of the human goddess, who turned with a murmured instruction to call her when a female husky came in. When he saw she was leaving, Rindy circled his tail, climbed his cage, panted, yapped, licked at the withdrawing hand. This was blood-love, this feeling the dogs had for humankind. They were not capable of hating people, only of fearing them.

The pound was silent for a time after the young woman left. Then the barking started again, a rhythmic mystery.

CHAPTER NINE

CINDY FELT LIKE SHE WAS TUMBLING DOWN A SCREAM-
ing well when she saw poor, netted Bob disappear
into the elevator in the hands of a bunch of near
thugs. Blotches of fur stuck through gaps in the
net.

It was more than she could bear. A curious
silence enveloped her. Little Kevin hopped
around like a frenzied dwarf, trying to break
through to her. She watched him, heard him
calling her name. Or was that all a dream?

Eventually he gave up, lay down on the couch,
and slept a miserable sleep. Cindy stared at a
corner of the rug.

A long time later the door buzzer rang. It was
now nearly three o'clock in the morning. The
buzzer rang and rang. Cindy heard it as a voice
calling from the top of the well. It didn't seem very

important. Then she heard Kevin, saw his stricken face. "Monica is here," he said.

Monica, Monica, the ocean whispered. Monica, the ocean said. Monica, Monica.

Monica soon appeared beside Kevin. Something tickled Cindy's face. Monica's hands were holding Cindy's cheeks. It felt nice.

A blow followed, sharp and colored red. It exploded the numbness. "Kevin," Monica said, "that sort of thing is unwise!"

"It worked."

Her son had struck her.

"Can you feel your body?"

It was as if she was enclosed in a cotton wool. "Sort of."

"Hysteria. Under the circumstances, an appropriate reaction."

Kevin's voice cracked. "She was like a wax statue, just sitting there. I couldn't get through to her! Monica, I was scared."

Cindy realized she had frightened her dear man-boy. She had to pull herself together, she was a mother. He lay against her chest, and she stroked his trembling body. "It's going to be all right, Kevin. You'll see."

He drew back from her. "Please don't act like I'm eight, Mother. I'm twelve, remember. I know what's going on." He looked at Monica. "They took him away. He bit Jodie's dad. The police saw he was a wolf—" Kevin stopped, became the little boy again. His body shook and he stifled his cracked sobs into his mother's breast. It was all she could do not to cry with him.

"The police?" Monica's eyes implored for more.

Cindy told how they had taken him. Still listening, Monica bustled across to the kitchen and ground some coffee. In the middle of it she stopped. "Get a lawyer." Cindy did not like to hear tremor in that voice. Monica had to be strength.

"I thought of that. What do I do? Call Stanford and tell him he's got to get Bob out of the pound?" Saying it, she was suddenly convulsed with a fit of laughter. Monica watched her, appraisal in her eyes. When it ended, she went back to preparing the coffee.

Kevin became furious. "Don't you dare laugh! This is the worst thing that's ever happened to anybody just about. It's horrible." His hands had become fists, his face pasty gray.

"I'm sorry. Monica's right, I'm in a state of hysteria."

The pot whistled and Monica poured the coffee.

Sipping from her mug, feeling a little stronger, Cindy began to wonder what Monica had found at the library. She was unsure about asking, though. She did not want to hear a hopeless prognosis.

"It is a disease, isn't it?" Kevin did not share Cindy's hesitancy.

"Kevin, I don't know for sure."

Cindy felt cold within. "Is there anything, any information?"

"Cindy, I'm afraid it's a genuine medical miracle."

"A miracle? Gee, thanks, God, thank you so much! How about more miracles? Turn me into a frog, Kevin into a sheep! Miracles are supposed to be good!"

"The whole event defies physics, biology, all understanding."

"No, ma'am," Kevin said. "Not quantum physics, not if you assume subjective reality. Or if the Many Worlds theory is an accurate reflection of the actual situation, then you could even argue that this was inevitable, in one or another universe. Given many worlds, everything that might happen will happen, and each possibility will create its own universe."

Cindy looked at her son, hurting with pride and love. "What actual material did you find, Monica? Anything?"

Monica might have understood Kevin better, because she ignored Cindy's question and flared up at him. "What the devil are you getting at? You're saying that princes *do* turn into frogs?"

"I'm saying that they could. It might be that we've only recently—say, in the past ten thousand years or so—gained enough imaginative stability to prevent our dreams from coming true. One of the greatest achievements of civilization might well be that it has contained the mind and shorn it of its ability to project into physical reality."

Monica rocked back on her heels, her eyes wide at Kevin's unexpected brilliance. "All I found was folklore. Grimms' fairy tales, Apuleius's account of the wolfman, and medieval superstition. Nothing modern. A couple of movie scripts."

He began noisily sucking the dregs of a box of Hawaiian Punch through the little straw that came with it.

"No scraping bottom," Cindy said automatically.

"If what you say is true, why don't we have more recent incidents?"

He looked at Monica over his box. "Who's to say we don't? The thing is, once people change, they're gone. Maybe there are a lot of them, changed into what they loathed or loved—whatever fascinated them enough. The people that do it might be genetic throwbacks or something."

"They never come back?" Monica winced at her slip even as she asked the cruel question. Kevin and Cindy clung to one another.

"There are no stories," Kevin said quietly.

Monica had to remind herself that this was not speculative. She had seen Robert Duke change. She had seen the slow alteration of the body, had massaged him with her own hands as his skin became soft and dry and fur emerged in clumps and sprays. She had to ask herself the fantastic question, were there others out there like Bob?

It was a fearful thing even to be in the room where it had happened. The event challenged her most fundamental assumptions about the nature of thought and the boundaries of the mind. What is a concept, or a fantasy? Are there universes filled with the tatters of our fantasies and nightmares, places where we *become* the shape in the dark?

"You came back to tell us you hadn't found a thing!"

"A lot of people wouldn't have come back at all, not after what I saw. I *know* what happened here. But I am back."

"Without any idea of how to help."

The bitterness in Cindy's voice gave Monica a brief rattle of anger. She made sure it had subsided, though, before she spoke again. "I cannot offer a cure—not a magic bullet. What I can offer, and I am willing to try this, is theraputic support—"

"Monica, you can't expect him to sit down and

have a session with you? Surely, you must see the joke."

"I'm willing to try. Maybe we can get him back to the real world."

"He's in the real world. An uncommon version of it. Isn't that the gist of what you're saying, Kevin?"

"Yes, Mother."

"Well, then maybe I can help him get back into a common version of it."

Tomorrow morning Cindy intended to march up to that pound and extract him by sheer force of argument. Kevin's analysis had helped her immensely, in the sense that it sounded sensible enough to enable her to rest. In what he said there was a thread, however thin, to the understandable.

It was a matter of fighting idea with idea. If she could conceive of a successful outcome, she could move toward it.

"Why don't we call Stanford in the morning," Kevin said, "and tell him that it's a pet they've taken and we want it back? Don't tell him the whole truth."

Monica stroked Cindy's cheek. "Your color's coming back. I like to see that. Do you think you'd like a little something to help you sleep?"

"No. Absolutely not."

"But you will sleep. It's three-thirty, and there's nothing more to be done until morning."

A weariness was there, waiting to receive her. Cindy went back into her own dark bedroom. Was this how widows confronted the first night, looking across the sea of perfect sheets? No, not perfect. There were wrinkles in the middle where she had sat waiting for him earlier, sat like a spider.

She had lashed out at him, struck him. But they had no money. She had to do it, to inject him into the real world, to *make* him earn something.

How stupid, how arrogant. Now what would she do? Abandon his office and everything in it, for starters. She dropped onto the bed fully clothed. What about money? What about breakfast? And would Stanford work without payment? Didn't they owe him, too?

So many questions.

"Mom, can I stay with you?"

"Sure. There's room—" She had been about to add "on Dad's side," but the words did not come.

She lay in the dark, the huddled form of their child beside her, the talisman. Monica came in and silently held her hand for a time.

She plunged into black, empty sleep.

The ringing of the telephone woke her. At first she thought it was the alarm clock, time to get Kevin off to school. The rhythm of it was what made her come to full attention. Then Kevin was standing with the receiver in his hand, holding it out to her.

"Hello?"

It was a moment, listening to the snide young voice on the other end of the line, before she understood that she was talking to a newspaper reporter. "We understood that you are the owner of a wolf that attacked a Mr. John O'Neill. Would you care to make a comment?"

Her mind cast wildly for something to say. From somewhere she recalled the ritual formula. "No comment."

"I'll be writing that you harbored this wild animal, is that correct?"

"No." Now that she fully understood the implications of this call she was grim with fear. What would happen to Bob now?

"Look, Mrs. Duke, you can save that stuff for the movies."

"Please leave me alone. Don't hurt us."

"I'm just trying to get a story."

"Don't hurt us!"

"Your wolf hurt a man pretty badly. Don't you think that entitles the public to know, at least how long you've had the wolf? And what's its name?"

"We found it on the street," she said miserably. "A week ago."

"Is that all? What street?"

"Fifth Avenue."

"You're kidding, a wolf just walking down Fifth? How did you capture it?"

"We fed it a ham-and-cheese croissant. It was starving." A lump of coldest ice had settled in her gut. This was only going to lead to more trouble. "We didn't know it was a wolf until the police came. We had no idea."

Without so much as a good-bye, the reporter hung up. Why not, he had what he wanted. To him other human beings must be no more important that dumb animals.

It was too early to call Stanford, so she contented herself with making a breakfast of oatmeal, orange juice, and tea. Kevin came in and ate. Monica, who had stayed on the couch, stretched and rose, and drank some coffee. In a dull voice Cindy told her about the reporter.

"That's all we need."

"God, what'll it lead to? Poor Bob's going to become a cause célèbre."

"We've got to get him out before the story breaks. Have you called your lawyer?"

Cindy glanced at the kitchen clock. She tried his number, although she didn't have much hope at 8:40 in the morning. He surprised her, though, by both being there and answering his own phone.

"Cynthia. How long has it been? A year at least."

"At least that, Stanford. Stanford, we have a problem."

He remained silent.

"We've had our pet wolf confiscated by the city."

The sound that came over the line was like that a man might make on discovering a spider has gotten into his trousers at a funeral: a politely constricted whinny.

"It's in the pound. We want it back."

"A wolf-dog? A breed of dog?"

"No, an actual wolf."

"It's an illegal pet? No permit?"

"We didn't know we needed one. We found it on a street corner."

"You found it, or Bob?"

"Bob."

"Ah, now this begins to make some sense. Bob brought home a wolf and it has been taken away. You want me to have the animal released to your recognizance. But not, I presume, to Bob's."

"Bob is my husband. To both of us."

"Cynthia, do yourself a favor and keep Bob well in the background. Don't let him talk to the police or go to the pound. If anybody asks why, tell them he's indisposed."

Bob had been Stanford's client for many years. He had been in the middle of some unusual capers, such as the matter of the automatic theater seats that folded up around their victims, and that of the blue bread made from seaweed. He had also helped Bob with the FBI when he had tried to set up a series of computer conferences in Bulgaria. It had not occurred to him that the computers he had shipped out ahead of his own departure were proscribed, and that the Bulgarians had agreed to his project simply in order to get them. He wound up losing thirty-one thousand dollar's worth of equipment and narrowly escaping criminal charges. "Don't tell them he's eccentric," Stanford said. "Tell them to call me. I'll explain Bob."

"Bob won't be involved."

"Good. I'll have to look up the ordinance on dangerous pets to see if it's changed, but back a few years ago I had a client who had some trouble about importing a jaguar. As I recall, it was a pretty straightforward matter. The city wouldn't allow it in. New York takes a dim view of dangerous pets. Too crowded."

That sounded bad. She strove to keep the wild rising panic out of her voice. "Could they ship the wolf to another city and let us take possession of it there?"

"Well, we'll see. I'll give the law a look and telephone you back."

"When?"

"Oh, soon. Why?" Suspicion was creeping into his voice. He knew perfectly well that there was more to the story.

"We're afraid they'll hurt him. He's a wonderful creature. We all love him terribly."

"People and their pets. I have my cats. If they were impounded, I'd be beside myself. I'll get to it right away."

Monica had made some instant oatmeal. They ate in silence, drank orange juice and more coffee.

It was agreed that Kevin would not go to school during the family emergency. Cindy ate because she knew she needed strength. She was not hungry.

The telephone rang again. "Is this the home of the wolf lady?"

"No." She hung up. "Another reporter."

It rang yet again. "My name is Rebecca Fontinworth. I represent the Animal Rights League, and I'd like to ask you if you realize just how evil—"

Cindy hung up again. "Stanford, please hurry up!"

His was the next call, and it broke her heart. "As long as the wolf hasn't hurt anybody, I don't see a problem."

"And if it has hurt somebody?"

"Big problem. They'll want to test it for rabies. They'll keep it in quarantine, probably donate it to a zoo. And you'll get a fine, not to mention the inevitable lawsuit. Cynthia?" She could not speak. "Hello? Tell me this isn't the situation. Cynthia?"

"He bit a man."

"Badly?"

"In the foot. Plus the papers are calling."

A sigh. "All right, then we have a problem. I am going to do what I can. You cannot expect me to get the wolf returned to you. The best we can hope for is a nice berth in the zoo. I will try to prevent the animal's being destroyed."

It was hideous. She threw the phone as if the instrument had gotten hot. The man was talking about Bob, about Bob's *life*! She could hardly breathe, couldn't do more than make an awful sound—"eh, eh, eh"—as her blood thundered and her breath came in raw stutters.

Monica took up the phone. "I'm their psychiatrist."

"You live with them?"

"When I must. And right now I must. I'm camped out in the living room."

"The one I'm most worried about is Bob. Don't let him get involved in this. God knows what will happen."

"Maybe God knows and maybe God doesn't. Try to get the wolf out. As their psychiatric adviser, I'm telling you that this is the best course."

"I can't possibly get it out."

"Try. Do anything. It is important to their sanity, to their very survival." She put down the phone.

"Thank you, Monica. But it's hopeless. I know it's hopeless. He's going to die this insane, stupid, impossible death. Oh, how stupid, how stupid!"

"Mama, we're going to get him out. If we have to spring him, we're going to do it. We can't let Dad just die!"

She thought of last Saturday at the zoo. Was that when it had all started, when that strange wolf had been staring at Bob? He had wanted to leave there, as if he already sensed that something was wrong. And what of the wolf, what had it known? Maybe that wolf—maybe it was somebody, too, and it knew the signs, had seen them in Bob. "The world isn't what we thought," she blurted. "It's completely different!"

"Well, I have to agree now." But Monica looked personally insulted. "Science is a limited view of things."

"Every view is limited. The occult is limited."

Kevin spoke up. "The occult isn't a limited

view. It doesn't reject phenomena like science. The trouble with the occult is that it misinterprets everything. Demons, ghosts—"

Monica slammed her hand against the table. "How do we know! At least one thing is true for the three of us. We have had the veils lifted from our eyes, and that is not bad. We *know* for certain that things are not as they seem. We *know* that this world is full of dangerous and mysterious powers. That gives us an advantage. And I'll tell you another advantage we have. We know that Bob is inside that creature. He understands English and he has the mind of a human being. If we can get to him, we might be able to spring him."

"We're no SWAT team. How do we get into the place? What do we do?"

"We're both pretty."

Cindy was thunderstruck. "We use—"

"Sex, of course. We seduce."

"You saw those goons?"

"They'll seduce, believe me."

Kevin, who was as prudish as his father, had gone still. He was clutching his spoon, his knuckles streaked red. Cindy reached toward him. For all his brilliance, her son was the most vulnerable human being she had ever known—next to Bob. At least Kevin had inherited his mother's temper, and could use it. Bob had no temper, little anger, no guile.

Sometimes, though, he could see beyond the mountains.

CHAPTER TEN

THE DOG SLOP BECAME INTERESTING TO BOB AT ABOUT noon. He could well imagine what must be in it—possibly even the remains of animals that had been gassed. His impression of the Animal Control Foundation was not a bad one. Obviously there were employee abuses here, but the basic situation wasn't intolerable. Too bad young Kevin had never wanted a dog. Had there been dog food in the house, Bob might have been able to identify this by brand—if, indeed, it was a brand and not something made here. Nutrition concerned him. He would have known the cereal, ash and waste content, and the food value.

He sniffed it, and was surprised to discover that his nose could tell him a great deal about what was before him. There was a thick, oozing odor that seemed to congeal in his muzzle: perhaps that was fat. Another odor, slightly gray, almost like wet cement—that was ash. There was some cereal, not much. Then a faint but piercing scent that made his stomach tighten with need. This was the meat, the real food. Then there was bone, and the dense smell of organs. What had they done, dropped dead animals into a hopper and ground them up, then thickened the whole mess with ashes? Was that all there was to making cheap dog food?

He returned to the question of the source of the meat. Certainly it wasn't steak. Dog was probably a good guess. Or maybe bulls, roosters. What if unscrupulous zoos sold their cadavers to dog-food manufacturers? This could be anything. Gorilla. Python.

The smell of the meat went deep into his brain, into lusty new centers. This new, inner self must be the instinct of the wolf he had become. He turned to it, and found confidence mixed with churning fury, a questing, probing mind that was designed to compare and make sense of millions of odors. If he quieted his chattering human thoughts, he was at once connected to this spirit. His nose made sense for him then, and the few odors he could verbally identify expanded by a thousandfold into a nonverbal catalog of great richness.

That wasn't good enough, though. He was a man, and verbal. To use the powers of this new body, he had to break the boundary that existed between its instincts and his familiar mind. He could not abandon his human self to the wolf. And yet there were things in the smells—living, twisting things—that were not connected to human words at all. Call them memories, call them longings, they shot through his body like the very words of creation.

His wolf sense knew there was food value in the slop. But the man Robert Duke was not about to taste it.

At one o'clock his gut knotted. In the distance he heard Paul Simon singing "Graceland," and they hauled four more dogs down the hall. The slop, drying and lined with flies, said, "I am life."

Two o'clock. The keepers muttered. A man came, smelling of coffee dregs, sauerkraut and hot dogs, and took pictures of him through the bars. When the keepers retreated, the man pulled a monopod out of his camera case and tried to prod Bob. "C'mon, you sucker, get mad." He laughed, a cruel, nervous man with a nose like a knife, a man with eyes glazed by what Bob saw was a habit of sadness. "Heyah! C'mon, sucker, give me a snarl!" He lit a Bic and thrust it at Bob, flame full on.

With a blubbery flap of tongue and lips, Bob blew it out.

"Holy moly."

The man then met his eyes. A terrified, screaming mutt was slammed into a cage. Barking erupted, the flip-flop rhythm of doghood.

The man looked away. "What the fuck are you?" he said in a hoarse voice. He started to raise his camera, then dropped it and grabbed the monopod. "You bastard!" He jabbed it at Bob, who pressed himself against the far bars. He jabbed again, and Bob felt the monopod against his skin. Again, and it seared a rib. The man was sweating, grimacing. "Fight, baby! C'mon, you aren't gonna fucking eat me! Fight, you bastard!"

Then the camera, *click click click*. Bob tried to create an expression of utter peace, deep, soft, calm. With a curse the man ran off. Soon he was back, one of the keepers in tow. "Look, get behind

the cage. Get the damn thing's tail and give it a
pull. I gotta have it growling. I'll get page one if
this sucker looks dangerous enough."

"I ain't doin' that. It ain't right."

"Ten bucks says different."

"Ten bucks, man, I can't buy shit with ten
bucks."

"A double saw, then."

"Double, you got yourself a man." The keeper
headed around to the back of the cages. Bob stood
in the middle of his space, his tail curled way up
under his legs. "C'mon, c'mon— Jeez, how you
know I'se after your tail?"

"It's weird. You shoulda seen it a minute ago, it
blew out my lighter. Sorta slobbered it out. I
dunno."

Fingers came in and closed around Bob's tail.
He felt stabs of agony right up his spine and he
cried out.

Almost at once the pain stopped. "Christ!" The
keeper was out from behind the cage. "You hear
that? You hear what it sounded like?"

"What of it?"

"I been around dogs for fifteen years. Wolves, I
seen a dozen wolves. We get 'em in here once in a
while. They jus' big, quiet dogs. They don' make
no sound like that." He was staring at Bob. "We
oughta gas that thing right now. I don' know what
that is."

"I still didn't get my picture."

"You can keep your fuckin' picture! I don't want
your money. Thas' a voodoo in there."

"Oh, Christ, do you believe in that stuff?"

"I'm from Brooklyn, turkey. But there ain't no
wolf that screams like a man. Ain't no wolf."

The keeper retreated, his footsteps echoing on

the damp concrete floor. The newspaperman took a final picture. "Thanks a lot, Voodoo Wolf," he said. With a last jab from his monopod he also left.

Silence brought boredom, the curse of all the creatures here. Boredom intensified hunger. Bob imagined a nice array of sushi: *tekka maki, taro, ikura,* sparked by a pyramid of green Japanese horseradish, freshened by delightful slivers of fresh ginger, the whole deliciousness washed down by a rich Sapporo beer. Then he would have *yokan,* sweet red bean paste, as dessert. Not this flyblown bowl of garbage that so tempted the wolf.

Left alone, he had plenty of time to consider the significance of a newspaper photographer. Maybe there would be a public outcry against his imprisonment. But no, on reflection he suspected it would go the other way. Man fears the wolf, that is in the nature of things. Newspaper people would have one objective: excite that fear in order to sell papers.

Water dripped, a dog whined, four more animals were gassed together, their frantic, muffled barking sending thrills of fear through the little colony. More strangers were brought in, to fill the cages of the dead. Doors clanged, slop was poured, a vet forced something down the throat of a dog with diarrhea. Another dog vomited worms and was gassed at once, and his cage swabbed down by a tired-looking keeper.

Pigeons, sitting on the sills of the high windows, gobbled and cooed. Bob looked up, as millions of men and others have looked up from cages and jails, and longed after the wings, and saw a thread of sky. He could have wept but he had no tears. Then he leaned swiftly down and ate his slop.

His cage was thrown open, and before he could so much as growl, a net came and he was being carried down the hall. The black gas box stood before him, open, its wooden interior scored by a legion of digging dogs. He could see where they had chewed frantically on blocks and joints, and he could see the grille at the back where the gas came through.

He screamed, it was his only hope, apparently all he had left from humanity. Their faces went wide with surprise, but they kept at their work. He wallowed in the net as they stuffed him down into the box. Then the door closed. It was tight. His legs were twisted under him, his muzzle jammed against the wood. The oldest and worst of all terrors burst up within him. Monster though he had become, he wanted to live. A windy night, a bucking deer, blood beneath the moon; starlight in Manhattan, dancing at 3:00 A.M. Slow love, the jumping of cubs in the spring, watching Kevin sleep the sleep of an angel.

A valve creaked, the gas hissed. He smelled its choking must, a powerful, ugly note of ether in it that marched him off to sleep.

An angel stood before him in a seersucker suit, his white wings glancing sunlight. He was laughing and waving a red lantern. When their eyes met, the library of the universe was opened to Bob, and he received rich, sustaining knowledge: he, too, was known, Robert Duke, and his fate was understood, and he was loved.

Then he was strapped to a table and there was another strap so tight around his jaw that his muzzle whistled when he breathed. His side was partly shaved, he could feel the cool air. And his head was thundering. They had only half killed him, had stunned him.

"Weight's a hundred and sixty-one pounds. That makes him one of the largest wolves ever found. He has a most unusual voice, and he has green eyes, another unusual feature. His coat is richly colored, displaying seven distinct shades, browns, grays, tans, white, and black. The overall effect is to give him an extraordinary glow. His teeth are healthy, and his skeleton is massive. Until we have done detailed X rays or dissected him, we cannot determine the laryngeal features that give him his voice. Our present theory is that he is a highly unusual breed of wolf, perhaps Russian or Chinese in origin, possibly imported to serve a ritual purpose within the voodoo community. When he wakes up fully, we will display him in the rear courtyard, at which time you may take pictures."

Bob watched a stuffy man with the bald head fold his papers and clear his throat. Then the net floated down and he was carried away again. As two of the keepers were putting him in his cage he heard a number whispered in awe: "fifteen grand."

"You kiddin.' In the pool?"

"Sure enough. This a voodoo wolf. They gonna be a doc to bleed 'im. They gonna be a mama-san. He gonna eat them shepherds up. I glad I ain't got my money on 'em."

"It a bad scene, man, you gonna get some demon outta that thing. I dun hear it screamin' in the gas, it's some kinda banshee or somethin.' Gonna let Roy hold my marker for the pool."

"What make you think Roy so brave, if you not? Who gonna run the fight, the mama-san?"

"They gonna ring the whole courtyard with the

Fierce Water of Johnny Blood."

"Then it safe."

"I ain't so sure. Them voodoos always get all mix up. You never know what's gonna go down, they start playin' with the demons."

"Where your faith my man, Papajesu gonna protect you."

"Papajesu, shit. I ain't goin'."

Later Bob was brought to the courtyard. For a time the air was brilliant with flashbulbs. In the green, glowing haze they left in his eyes, he saw a single pale face and his whole body ached with longing. He stared straight at her, he devoured her with his eyes, he tried to coordinate his tail enough to wag it. Cindy shone in his glance. She stood familiarly beside the vet who had examined him, seemed to speak to him easily, and even touched his arm from time to time with the tips of her fingers.

That gave Bob hope. If he understood what she was attempting, it was a good idea. She might be able to accomplish it. When he was returned to his cage, he found there a bowl of chopped steak. He gobbled it; this body did not easily bear hunger. Cindy had somehow been responsible for this food, he was sure of it.

As night slipped in the high windows, he became less sure. Finally there was a stirring among the dogs. His heart raced. He expected to see her with keys.

Instead there came a strange procession. He had always heard that there was voodoo in New York City, but this man was more elaborately dressed than the cardinal on Easter Sunday morning. He wore long white robes embroidered with a collar of dancing skeletons. There was a red cross on his

back and a black pentacle on his breast. He wore a
top hat and carried a cane. Over the robe was the
tattered tailcoat of an ancient morning suit. His
fingers were all ringed with skulls and such, and
his feet were shod in doeskin shoes. He smelled of
oil of cloves and dried blood, molasses, and thick,
decayed breath. A drum beat in his shadowy
entourage, and many of the dogs barked with fear.
Straining on leads, their collars worked with dai-
sies and spray-painted purple carnations, came
four powerful young German shepherds. They
were snarling and eager. Bob had seen them
before, waiting in the front cages where the keepers took prospective owners and claimants. You
could get a mutt here free, but one of these
animals would cost. They were fine and brushed,
and the keepers exercised them daily.

As they passed Bob they set off a poundwide
round of nervous barking.

He listened to the rhythm of drums and the
bleating of a trumpet, and saw flames flicker up
from time to time in the dark outside. There were
chants. The old priest pranced past the door, his
top hat shining in the torchlight, a cigar clenched
between his teeth.

Bob kept watching the corridor, hoping that
Cindy would come through it, having somehow
struck whatever deal she was making with the vet.
But she didn't come, and the ritual that had
formed around the betting pool grew louder.

Incense, cigar smoke, the sharp scent of hashish
all wafted in, borne on a heavier layer of oils: rose,
clove, pepper. The worshipers danced past, their
faces alight in the torches, saying words he could
not understand in the pidgin of the islands. When
they put their hands on him, he let forth the

scream that had terrified them before. If it frightened them now, they gave no sign. He was carried out into the courtyard and left there with the four shepherds, who had been worried during the ritual to a pitch of rage.

He could smell their anger and their hurt. These dogs had loved man. Human enmity made them feel bad about themselves.

Their thick, angry odor gave over to the hot pitch of breath when they barked at him. To be with him in unbarred surroundings terrified them. He was more afraid, though, and he clawed desperately at the door, trying to somehow get away. At all of the high windows there were faces peering down, and over the back wall they also peered.

Bob didn't know what to do. He couldn't talk to these dogs, he had no arm to parry with when they attacked. All he could hope to do would be to bite back. But he'd never bitten. He didn't know how to bite.

The dogs hammered out their barks, their ears back. In Bob the wolf stirred.

They rushed him, all four of them at once, their bodies slamming into him one after another. The first came in under his throat, the second right beside it. They knocked him off his feet. The other two buried themselves in his soft belly. He felt an awful pain, kicked, squirmed, and was surprised to notice within himself a confident undulation. He rose and his jaw went off like a spring mechanism.

One of the dogs was on three legs, screaming dog screams, and the crowd went wild. Then the fury of the shepherds was renewed. Their barking was like the clatter of applause. This time when they rushed him, Bob trotted away. Now they

changed their tactics and began to chase. In a
moment they were running around the courtyard.
Bob was astonished at himself. He could run like
the wind. In fact he ran so fast he was soon behind
the slowest dog, the one with the hurt leg. Then he
leaped on that dog and felt his muzzle probing for
its throat. He thought about it, thought about
aiming his teeth, finding the right place in the
fur—and in an instant was at the bottom of a heap
of snarling, snapping killers.

Again he got to his feet, but this time he could
feel his own blood leaking from a hole in his neck.
He needed a doctor; what if the wound was close
to his jugular? Still just the one dog was wounded.
He noticed, though, that their chests were heaving. He was barely tired.

A voice said from the dark wall: "He can run,
man, but he slow in the clinch."

"He strong."

The dogs were wary now, keeping their distance, very intelligently using their superior ma-
neuverability to worry him. Every few moments
there would be another excruciating pinch and
another wound. If this kept up, they would slowly
tear him to pieces. When they came close, he
would try to bite them, but he inevitably missed.

It was not long before their circle had tightened.
They were crouching low, their heads against the
ground, their hindquarters in the air, tails flying.
He had a dozen wounds. Between them they
shared perhaps four, only one of them serious
enough to reduce the victim's efficiency.

He shook his head to get the blur of blood out of
his right eye. His muzzle reeked with his own
blood when he inhaled, and he seemed almost to
be floating. The battle went far away.

Instantly they leaped at him, biting wildly. They were going to eat him alive, to tear him apart. He screamed in agony as teeth dug into him.

Wolf: the gleam of the careful tooth, the mind calm in the mayhem, calculating a death blow and then the snick of the jaw, a shocking flash as the tooth passes through flesh and a dog howls its last, its bowels splashing from the hole Bob had made.

Wolf: leaping on the back of a squirming dog, gobbling at his bones, gnashing down on the gristle, feeling tooth slide against backbone, tasting the soft sweetness of the spinal bundle. Another one dead.

Then the wolf stopped, scented the air, tossed his head to clean his ears of the wild screaming, the thundering drum, to clear his eyes of the flicker of the torches. Two dogs remained, one dragging a leg and constantly shaking its head, the other shrinking against the far wall.

He had a vision, and he knew that he could make the vision true. Quickly he trotted to the near side of the courtyard. Between here and the back wall there was a twenty-yard run. He tossed his head and catapulted forward, a bullet of glowing fur. His legs carried him, took him upward, soaring, flying in the screams of the crowd and one scream in particular: "Bob, Bob, Bob!"

Cindy was in the courtyard. The vet was behind her, his face flushed. Beyond her was Monica, angular in the light cast from the building. He glimpsed Kevin, too, his beloved son!

Bob's claws reached the top edge of the wall. He pushed, the timing perfect, and cast himself up onto the scree of glass shards embedded in the concrete. Below him there was an alley, and in that alley a panic-stricken crowd was falling wildly over itself in its urgency to get away. A shot exploded, a blue, blinding flash, a rush of hot air, a stink of powder and hot oil.

Bob learned forever the smell of a gun.

Then they were gone, all of them, the doctor, the mama-san, the worshipers at the altar of the game.

"Bob, Bob, come down. You can come home now, honey. We'll take good care of you."

It was hopeless. There would be no peace at home, not with the press blitz that was probably breaking on the eleven o'clock news just about now. Atavisms would be brought up in the marginal people; there would be men with high-powered rifles, poisoners, trappers, and of course O'Neill and his lawyers.

But there would be Cindy and Kevin, and the chance to be a little bit human in the privacy of their home.

"Bob, please."

He hesitated, drawn by the night and the freedom, and by the soft, familiar scent of his wife. The moon paced the clouds, the wolf paced the high wall. "I'll get the dart gun," the vet said softly. Hearing that, the wolf won.

Bob leaped off into the wild, free night.

CHAPTER ELEVEN

WHEN HE DISAPPEARED OVER THE WALL, CINDY BRACED for another shot. Instead there came the high-pitched screams of the voodoo worshipers still in the alley, who cared not at all to have their wolf-god join them.

Rage broke in Cindy like a bloody foam of waves. She ran her fingers in her hair and shrieked.

"Shut up," Monica bellowed. "Pull yourself together."

"He's going to get killed!"

"Ma'am, we'll get him back."

"You were using him, you were treating my husband worse than I'd treat an animal. You're vicious, inhuman *monsters*! I swear, if he dies I will come back and I will kill you one by one!"

The vet's mouth had dropped open. The word "husband" formed and died silently on his lips. Then a glance askance at Monica.

Cindy roared on. "I know what you're thinking, you bastard. You're thinking I'm crazy. You're hoping I am. But I am not crazy and I have a superb lawyer, and you and the city and the ASPCA are going to suffer for this! Your career is over, buddy, dead and in the dirt. And as for this bunch of cigar-chomping weirdos—look at them, you ought to be ashamed, for Chrissake—you talk about cruelty to animals, my God, you oughta be closed down!"

Cindy's words flashed into a silence. Even the dogs quieted down. The voodoo practitioners who had been in the windows were creeping away. As for the vet, he had gone to attention. "Yes, ma'am," he said in a voice he had probably learned during military days, "there have been irregularities. They'll be corrected at once, ma'am!"

Cindy laughed, harsh and derisive. "I don't care about your irregularities." Now her voice rose to a cutting quaver. "I want my Bob back, and I want him back alive!"

"Bob? Is that the wolf's name, ma'am?"

"Yes, of course it's his name. Bob Duke."

"He responds to the name Bob Duke?" The vet's face was now impassive, very carefully so. He definitely scented craziness, perhaps even amusing craziness, but this lady was so mad he couldn't risk the smallest sign of mirth. She was going to be complaining loud and clear, and the voodoo ritual was going to be very difficult to explain to the board of directors.

For the first time Cindy saw the reporters, who had flowed out into the courtyard and were now trying to scale the wall. Realizing it was hopeless, one astute camera team came thundering back

through the pound itself, camcorders swinging.
"Fan out," shrieked a tiny man in a Hawaiian
shirt, his face purple, the veins in his temples
pulsing like fire hoses.

"Who are these people?" Cindy asked.

The vet brightened. He was looking forward to
being on TV. WCBS and Channel 5 had already
interviewed him. "The media—"

"You're kidding!"

"No, this is big news. I'm sure I can get them
interested in talking to you, too. They don't just
want expert opinion. Human interest has a place,
too."

Monica grabbed Cindy's arm. "Let's get out."

As they left the building police cars started
roaring up, their sirens wailing, their lights jumping red against the dun girders supporting the
elevated part of FDR Drive. Radios spattered
codes, uniformed men jumped from the cars and
sprinted off down the street. A van disgorged a
SWAT team decked in full body armor and carrying 12-gauge riot guns. "They'll kill him," Cindy
moaned.

"Come on, Cyn, let's find a cab. We've got to get
out of here. We need the media like a hole in the
head."

Outside of the vicinity of the pound, the streets
were gray and lonely. "What will he eat?"

"He'll find what he can. Bob's a resourceful
man."

"Oh, he is not! He's about as resourceful as—
as—" She stopped, considered. "A three-year-old
would be more resourceful!" Her poor husband,
he couldn't camp out, couldn't even hike without
getting hopelessly lost. Even around the house he
was a disaster. "Last week he glued himself to the

dishwasher with Krazy Glue trying to fix a knob. When I found him, he'd been there for two hours. The phone was within easy reach the whole time. He knew where I was, but it never occurred to him to call me. Do you think the man who did that can survive alone on the streets with no money, with no clothes, with no hands, with no way even to talk to people?"

"He'll hunt, he has the capacities of a wolf."

"Bob Duke will hunt. I've been hunting with him, so have you. He'll starve and he'll get wet and cold and confused and make mistakes. Meanwhile every man, woman, and child with so much as an air rifle is going to be hunting *him*!" She stared up and down the street. "Bob," she called, "Bob!" A camera crew began running toward them.

"Uh-oh, we're recognized," Monica said. "Let's get a move on."

Just then the vet burst out of the pound, his white coat flying. "*Live at Five, Live at Five*, they want us all on *Live at Five*!"

A cab rolled around the corner. Monica waved at it even though it was occupied. "I am doctor," she hollered, "matter of life or death." The driver gunned the motor, a New Yorker's seasoned instinct to get away, but he lost the light and a line of cars coming off the FDR Drive prevented him from running it. As Monica and Cindy crowded in with the surprised passenger the driver hit his steering wheel with the heel of his hand.

"Sorry," Monica said to the passenger, "gotta take a little detour. This woman is having a heart attack."

The driver turned around. "Listen, bitch, I gotta fare."

"This woman is dying. Now step on it."

"I don't give a damn who's dying." He produced a baseball bat. "You get out of here."

"The hell we will. You don't do exactly as I say, I'll haul you up on charges."

"Taxi commission, taxi commission, I've heard that shit a thousand times. Lady, you get out of this cab or I'll beat your goddamn brains from here to Scarsdale, now move!"

It was obvious to Cindy that Monica couldn't handle this. She took over. "We're not talking commission, gorp-face, we're talking five years in jail for uncooperative manslaughter. Five years, and you *will* serve that time! We will not stop, Mr. Czlywczi, until you are in jail and the key is thrown the hell away. You see those cops over there? If you don't help us, I am going to scream, and when I scream, those cops are coming over here, and they will see your baseball bat—"

He threw it out the window. It clanged on the street and rolled into the gutter. "Step on it," Cindy said.

"I get out," blurted the passenger, a stunned Japanese businessman. He leaped from the cab just as the light changed.

"Kill the meter," Cindy commanded. "We'll make it worth your while. Monica, give the man ten bucks. Take us to Mercer and West Fourth."

The driver became happy now that he had the ten. "God knows what'll happen to that Jap." He laughed. "From here he'll have to swim down to the UN Plaza if he doesn't want to walk."

For a time they rode in silence. The driver was studying Cindy through the rearview mirror, his eyes twinkling. "Look, no offense, but I want to know something. Do you ladies always pull this routine? I mean, every time you want a cab? Or what?"

"Every time we want a cab," Cindy growled.

"Jesus, I been hackin' twenty years and I never seen shit like that. I mean, you gotta admire shit like that!"

"Step on it."

As the cab pulled up to her building Cindy saw a crowd lurking around the entrance, their silhouettes dark against the glow from within.

As they exited the cab a klieg burst on, and Cindy found herself confronting a bright impenetrable wall. A familiar TV face came into view. A microphone was thrust at her. "Dr. Wilcox at the ASPCA says Bob is one of the largest wolves on record, and the largest ever held in captivity. Can you tell us where you got this wolf?"

Cindy heard him, but she was totally unprepared to answer. Her mouth was so dry it tasted like a cedar closet. She learned, in that moment, the true meaning of the term "tongue-tied." What could she say? The camera eye gleamed, moths fluttered in the hissing lights. Sweat beaded up through the reporter's makeup.

"Cut a minute, Jake. Look, Mrs. Duke, we're going to find out one way or another. We're going to find out everything."

"My God, help me," a male voice screamed off in the dark. Instinctively, Cindy whirled. Flashbulbs popped, somebody scuttled off.

"Don't worry about that," the reporter said, "it's just the *Post* going for a reaction shot. You and Bob are their front page tomorrow."

Cindy rocked back on her heels. Front page! All it meant to her was Bob's body, full of bullet holes, being held up by a proud SWAT team.

"How long have you had the wolf?"

"A day," she finally managed to answer. "We found him on the street. He was hungry and alone and he needed help. He's such a gentle creature—"

"You found him on the street? Where?"

What had she said before? Was it Fifth Avenue? She couldn't remember. She'd be vague. "Uptown. On a corner. He's so gentle and sweet, so tame. I'm just terrified that—" Her chest ached, her throat all but closed. She looked at the camera, and for an instant she was looking into a million faces. They were not hard faces, they were faces of ordinary people, watching her blankly. Right now they were impassive, but at a word from the reporter they were all going to turn into cavemen. "Please don't hurt him. Don't hurt my Bob." She could not go on. Before that savage crowd she felt so weak, so helpless, all of her bravado collapsed and she buried her face in her hands and gave way to tears.

"This is Cynthia Duke, ladies and gentlemen, the distraught owner of the giant savage wolf that is now roaming the streets of New York. Again, police have urged that people stay indoors, that any and all suspicious-looking stray dogs be reported at once. Remember, this animal is fast moving, intelligent, and savage. It has already seriously injured one of the Dukes' neighbors. You could be next. John Lye, Newswatch Five."

Monica dragged Cindy through the hectoring crowd. Cameras were flashing, microphones were being jammed into their faces, questions were being shouted. The sheer energy of it all dulled Cindy, so when Lupe silently handed her an envelope in the elevator, she took it without even much curiosity.

She was still holding it when she put her key in the front door. No sooner had she done that than the door flew open and Kevin leaped into her arms. "It was on the newsbreak, Mama. They're saying we had a dangerous wolf and it's on the loose."

She groaned, hugging him to her. There might have been things she could say to her son that would comfort him, but she could not think of them. It helped her to hold him, and she trusted that it helped him to be held.

They went arm in arm into the living room, Monica following behind. The television glared at Cindy, a sheer gray eye. "Turn it on," she said.

"Don't you think perhaps you'd better not?"

"Turn it on, Monica, it's nearly eleven. We don't want to miss the news."

"Cyn, I'll tape it and you can look at it in the morning."

Cindy went over and turned it on. She sat down and crossed her legs, staring blindly at the last few minutes of *Thirtysomething*. The envelope lay on her lap. She looked down. The return address was Weisel and Dobson. The landlords. She opened it. Legal papers. She read with quickening interest. "We regret to inform you that under paragraphs 14 and 23 of your lease we are compelled to initiate summary eviction proceedings against you. We were willing to negotiate with you about the matter of nonpayment of rent, but this harboring of a dangerous animal in total disregard of the safety of your neighbors has led us to respond to the dozens of complaints we have received, and ask you to leave."

"God, they're prompt. Monica, I'm being thrown out."

"Give me that." She snatched it away from Kevin, who had grabbed it from his mother. He was white, his eyes following the paper as if it was a cobra ready to spit. Kevin had never known a home other than this. The room where he had grown up was filled with his things, his books, his art, his stamp collection, his coin collection, his computer, his very secret collection of girlie magazines. "I wish Dad would come home."

"This is outrageous. They can't do this. Why haven't you paid your rent?"

"We're dead broke, Monica."

"You're kidding. I thought Bob was doing so well."

"He hasn't made a dime in months. I thought you knew that. I assumed you did."

"He never mentioned financial problems."

"Well, he sure as hell had them."

Monica regarded Cindy and Kevin with tenderness. "I don't have any big answers, Cyn, but at least I can help you with money."

"I don't like to ask."

"No, that isn't your way. Bob married you because he was attracted to your strength."

"I'm too damn strong! I drive people away. I scare men to death." She did not add what she thought, that she only scared the strong ones. The weak came to stay.

"Don't worry about that now. I'm going to write you a check, Cindy. How much money do you actually have?"

"What's in my wallet. Eight dollars, plus three Bob gave me yesterday. That's somewhere in the bedroom."

"I have twelve dollars in my box," Kevin said.

"But what assets? What can you draw on?"

"Nothing, unless you consider the furniture."

"You're kidding."

Don't get defensive, Cindy cautioned herself. She's your good friend. "We don't have a thing."

"I can lend you five thousand dollars, Cyn. I wish it could be more."

"I haven't seen that much money in months."

Just then the news started. Cindy turned up the sound, and they all watched the story of the wolf unfold. It was the lead item, preceding the president's operation and the crash of a commuter plane on Long Island. There were terrible, lurid pictures of Bob glaring into the camera, his face lighted to look menacing. To see him made Cindy groan aloud. What was it like to *be* that? What was the poor man thinking, what hell was he going through?

They talked about the "enormous, very dangerous animal." An "expert" named Dr. Bert Choate from the Fish and Game Commission appeared and warned the public that while wolves were normally not particularly dangerous to man, in an unusual situation like this, "anything can happen." He leaned into the camera. "This animal is frightened and alone. It feels cornered. The first chance it gets, it will lash out. And believe me, I've seen what a wild animal can do. Its teeth are a razor-sharp weapon. And it's so skilled at using them, it can catch a floating hair out of the air and split it."

Then came Cindy. The camera made her coarse and heavy of face, her skin glue white, her eyes dark, sunken holes. She looked like an inmate in a fluorescent nightmare. "How did they do that?

John Lye looks great."

"It's the lighting. They're trying to portray you as evil and callous."

She was seen in her initial anger. When she said Bob was gentle, Lye smiled ironically. Rather than show her weeping, they cut to a shot of Bob standing on the examining table, glaring at the camera with what Cindy knew was almost total confusion.

"The wolf lady says she found the animal on a street corner right here in Manhattan. Who knows where she actually got it? Given its tremendous size, experts at the Zoological Society theorize that it may be a wild wolf from the Soviet Union."

Then they went on to other stories. Cindy was amazed. She had come across looking like an ogre, vicious, hateful, uncaring. She wanted to throw something through the TV. If she'd been able to get her hands on Rivera, she would have turned him inside out.

Monica handed her the check. "Thanks," she said. She knew it would be gone tomorrow noon. Four thousand rent, five hundred to her loudest creditors, five hundred for food to keep her and Kevin for the next few weeks. Rent or no rent, she'd probably get evicted anyway.

After the news Monica went home, pleading exhaustion. Soon Kevin nodded off on the couch. She tried to smooth his fists, to somehow make the terror leave his exhausted body. She kissed him. Now came the time she had really been dreading. The apartment was empty and there was no one to help her.

Her mind went to thoughts of Bob, out there alone, disfigured, confused, chased. "God make him come home." Her voice filled the room with brief, helpless sound. Seeing herself in the mirror, a slumped shadow, she felt very small. She had been yelling at people, making demands, cursing, for hours and hours—in fact, ever since Bob had his problem. What good had it done?

She went into her bedroom and threw herself down on their bed. Her mind kept running images of him hurrying along streets, him hit by a car, him shot. She saw that big, furry head, those eyes, and she thought she was going to be sick to her stomach. "Where is he? Bob, where are you!"

She turned over on her back, stared at the ceiling. Obviously she had been too hard on him, making demands that he couldn't possibly meet. Bob was a poet. His business ability was nil; he couldn't even remember to put bus fare in his pocket when he went out. Anybody could sell him anything. When he was a broker he was always getting stuck with the customers the other brokers didn't want to bother with, the idiots, the deadbeats, the complainers. He would be ceaselessly patient with them, and was always ready to overlook their faults. Naturally he didn't make a penny brokering. But he spent anyway. Bob didn't understand the concept of credit. He looked upon loans as presents from banks grateful for his custom. Checks were simply a means to an end, usually a means to getting rid of creditors for a few more days—until the checks bounced and it was time to write new ones.

She turned on the light. There was a copy of *Travel and Leisure* at her bedside, and a library book she had been enjoying enormously, Doris Grumbach's *The Ladies*.

She stretched. "Oh, Bob." She did not miss him physically, although they were often intimate.

Love was more central to their relationship than sex. She seduced Bob whenever the mood struck her. It was always easy. She wanted to do it now.

What a good talker he was. His wit was dry, sardonic, and he had brought a wonderful deadpan humor from Texas. His lies could be completely convincing, and if you believed them, you were in peril of the surreal. Once he had made a brilliant case for eggs separating back out of brownies if they were cooked too fast, and had gone so far as to slip an egg into a pan of brownies she was baking. She had found it, perfectly poached, in the middle of the pan and had told the story in all seriousness for years. People were polite. They generally didn't comment, thinking that she was perhaps a little odd.

She laughed aloud, remembering how many times she'd told that story. Monica had finally stopped her and made her think. "It's scientifically impossible, Cyn. The physics just aren't there. It can't happen."

"But it did happen. I saw the egg—oh, my God, Bob, you creep!"

Her heart raced when she heard gentle tapping at the bedroom window. "Bob!" But no, it was not him, miraculously having climbed the six stories of sheer wall. A thin rain had started, and she watched it blowing in clouds around the streetlight. It was very late, and no cars passed. A man hurried along, the collar of his raincoat pulled up, a hat down over his eyes. The night sky glowed pink, flaring from the city lights. When she opened the window she felt a cold clamminess in the air. Autum was definitely here, with its long, gray rains.

If he had any sense at all, he would come home.

Suddenly she thought again of being evicted. Even if she paid, they might get her on the animal angle. Then where would Bob go? He would have no way of finding her and Kevin. They might never see each other again. "Bob," she whispered, her word making a faint haze on the window glass.

Then she saw him. He was trotting right up the sidewalk, his tail between his legs. He stopped, stared at the building, then hurried on. The fool! Didn't he recognize the place? She threw open the window. "Bob! Bob!" There was no time to waste. With what seemed the slowness of nightmare she dragged on a pair of jeans, tore her nightshirt from her body, and pulled on a sweater. Still in her slippers, she ran across the apartment and out the door. There was no time to wait for the elevator. Lupe was off duty and she couldn't run it well. She'd spend five minutes just getting it to stop close enough to the lobby floor to enable the doors to open.

She rushed into the green, echoing fire stairs with their perpetual faint tang of incinerator smoke and took the steps three at a time. The lobby was unattended at this hour, the front door inaccessible from outside without a key. As she raced through it she hit her pocket, confirming the presence of the keychain. Good girl, you did that right.

The street was as quiet and empty as a closet in an abandoned house. She looked up, down, past the row of trees, beyond the swirling mist. The dank cold sank through her sweater. "Bob," she shouted. Her voice echoed against the blank face of the high rise across the street, which responded with a faltering echo of her cry.

Then she saw movement among the parked cars

at the far end of the block. She took off, running for all she was worth, her arms flailing, her feet slapping the wet pavement. There was a thickening of shadow under a BMW parked at the curb. She leaned down. When she did she jostled the car, and its antitheft siren promptly began to warble. "Damn!"

The shadow under the car darted out into the street. It slid across the pavement and halted. The creature stood on the far sidewalk looking over its shoulder. Cindy held out her hands. "Honey, it's me." She could see him twitch his nose, and had the awful thought that even his mind might have been dissolved into the animal form. Maybe he was just and only a wolf now, here in obedience to an urge he no longer understood.

She went between the two cars, ignoring the outraged shouts coming from windows on both sides of the street. If people didn't like car sirens, they could damn well get earplugs. Manhattan is the world car-siren capital. Moving slowly, her hands open before her, she progressed toward the wary animal, which backed off as she came closer. "Bob, Bob . . ."

It was a matted creature, wet and bedraggled, just like Bob would be. "Bob?"

She was almost close enough to touch him now. He put his ears back. His eyes were teared pools, swimming with fear.

For an instant her hand came into contact with his head. He crouched, drawing back, baring his teeth. Then, with a flash of his tail, he turned and dashed off.

She started to run after him, but the rain was getting harder and she was freezing cold, and she knew she could not catch him.

For a time she stood watching the dark. Then the siren wound down and the street returned to its quiet.

Had it been Bob, or just another stray? Unable even to hazard a guess, she turned and went home. She slept the worried sleep of the lost.

CHAPTER TWELVE

BOB HAD LEAPED ACROSS THE SCATTERING CROWD INTO the alley. There came an animal shriek when his fall broke against the back of one of the spectators, the one with the gun. The man never got the second shot he'd been trying for. Instead he threw his gun aside, bellowing in agony. Dark red trenches appeared in his back where Bob had accidentally dragged his claws. The man crumpled.

Bob ran the other way, soon coming to a fence at the end of the alley, cinder blocks topped by three feet of Cyclone. He raised himself up. Beyond were gardens, a pretty decorative landscape surrounding the lobby of an expensive apartment building. He climbed to the top of the fence, carefully putting one paw above the other, forcing himself to remember to control his body. Along the ground it could go like a glider, but it was not structured for acrobatics.

Behind him there was a loud cry of alarm. He saw two uniformed men sprinting toward him, heard their quick breathing, heard the clink and rustle as they withdrew their guns from their holsters.

Then they stopped. They were bracing to fire.

One paw up, then another, then the first again. He reached the top of the fence.

A click resounded in the silence. Bob knew that it was the hammer of a pistol being cocked. Then another click, and another. Bob scrabbled at the far side of the fence, seeking purchase. A shot thundered, then more shots. Hot wind passed him. One of them brought searing heat to his thigh. With all of his strength he launched himself into the darkness. He fell hard into a flower bed. The cops behind him reached the wall and started scaling it. "We got 'im now," one of them said. "That garden's not open to the street."

Hearing that, Bob almost despaired. His impulse was to lie down, to curl his tail in against his body and close his eyes. Then he saw a glass door that led into the lobby. Bob ran to it—the damned thing pushed out, not in. A thud followed by the whoosh of breath and a curse indicated that one of the cops was already over the wall. Bob worked at the door with the claws of his right paw—claws, he noticed, that had a lot of blood on them. He had hurt that poor man in the alley terribly.

"Holy shit, that thing is *smart*!"

Bob got the door open enough to slip through. He dashed across the slick marble floor, his claws ringing, then silent when he reached a huge Kerman rug. "Good heavens," a doorman in dark blue livery cried. "Oh Lord." He grabbed a telephone as Bob rushed out into the street. He trotted down the curved driveway, then broke into a run again, dashing toward First Avenue. He knew that Carl Shurz Park wasn't far away, but it was too small to hide him. His objective was Central Park. He could crawl down into the brushy part of the Ramble and hide, and nurse this throbbing thigh. He hoped that it wasn't just adrenaline driving him, and that there was only a graze wound.

Ahead of him another police car sped into view. It screeched to a halt at the corner of First. The doors flew open and five cops leaped out for all the world like clowns coming from a circus car. Deadly clowns, though. He could see the somber gleam of the streetlights on their pistols.

He was not a man of action. It took him time to figure out how to deal with situations like this. He kept trying to talk. Explanations clogged his mind. "Excuse me, I've had a slight accident. . . . Pardon me, but I'm not nearly as dangerous as I look. . . . Ah, the police at last! Could you return me to my home?" To a listener, though, his most civilized, reasonable words sounded like chilling snarls. A repertoire of barks, growls, whines, and howls was totally inadequate to the delicate clarifications his predicament demanded. And that last human vestige, the scream, didn't help a bit. It drove the ignorant to blind panic, and made even decent people vicious.

The wolf, the traditional monster, was on the loose. To live through this, Bob was going to have to concentrate completely on the situation at hand. He could not wonder at the evil miracle that had afflicted him. Right now he had to put a line of cars between himself and those police pistols. The cops would blow his heart out if they could, and mount his head on the wall of their precinct house.

Behind him an entire SWAT team appeared in the street, all running like maniacs, waving shotguns, tear-gas grenades and pistols. Regular cops were closing off the intersection ahead. He'd have to rush somebody, and he chose the street cops. On them he smelled at least a little fear. The members of the SWAT team had an unpromisingly solid odor: sour beer, gunpowder, steel. They weren't even nervous.

For all his soul was worth, he ran. The air roared around him, his ears swept back, his dewlaps parted, and wind rushed coldly past his tongue. It was exhilarating, it was like flying— right into the barrels of five pistols.

Just then, though, there was an intervention: a stocky man burst out of a building ahead. He was carrying an aged 30-30 rifle and wearing a blue bathrobe. His slippers plopped as he ran, his glasses danced on his face. "He's mine," he screamed, "he's goddamn mine!"

Bob passed right between the churning legs and the man went up into the air, his gun describing the arc of a windmill. The man hit with a soft, painful crunch. Then the rifle struck the ground and went off, its report cracking the air, the bullet ricocheting off a wall. "Goddammit, move your fat ass," one of the cops yelled.

It was like flying, or being a ghost, and Bob knew where all the flying dreams come from, those escapes of the night when we leap the houses and the fields: they come from the past, when we could truly run.

"Move! Move! Move!"

The cops were in trouble, their guns glaring straight into Bob's face, unable to shoot because of the civilian still floundering around behind him. He rushed the cops and this time his bark worked. It worked fine: it was a thunderous, primitive bark. As a wolf he was neither clumsy nor timid.

Their faces folded and twisted, they turned away as if from something loathsome, they began to scramble back into their car. Whining, one of them worked a back window, slammed the door, pounded the lock with the heel of his hand.

Bob jumped upon the sloping shoulders of another of them and launched himself straight up like a rocket. Below him the man slammed into the ground. Bob soared up and up, glimpsing into second-story windows before he came crashing down onto the top of the car, denting it deeply.

Another jump took him to the street behind the police car. He ran full speed down the middle of First Avenue. Traffic was heavy and slow, and he found he could keep up easily. This body could run, could lope, could leap. He could not dislike it anymore, not after the past few minutes. He'd never been much of a physical specimen, not before now. This was quite wonderful! He had gotten past those cops beautifully. He was excited, elated—and then coughing, shocked by how strong the fumes of the cars smelled.

At Ninetieth Street he made a turn and trotted up the dark sidewalk. He was breathing harder, but despite his wound there was still plenty of run in him. He lolled his tongue and breathed across it fast, moving the air and spreading delightful little tendrils of coolness through his entire body. This is panting, he thought. This is how it feels to pant.

Had he been able to laugh, he would have laughed
with the wonder of this new body and the exhila-
ration of his escape. All he did was toss his head
and pull back his rather immobile lips. He did not
make a sound.

A car slowed. Pale faces peered from behind
rising windows. Excitement sparkled in their eyes,
but when he met them they glazed with fear. The
car sped off, its occupants silent, haunted. No
doubt they would stop at the nearest phone to call
in their sighting.

His excitement was fading. The thought of the
whole mechanism of the city hunting him down
was depressing in the extreme. He moved on, now
slinking through fine mist. Stray dogs always
seemed to huddle close to the buildings, and as he
walked he felt the same vulnerability that they
must. A moving shadow startled him and he dove
down under the stoop of a grand old brownstone.
Beyond the kitchen window he saw a woman in a
silk dress and a Kenneth hairstyle talking to a
maid who carried a tray of canapés. From farther
up in the house there came a spill of laughing talk.
How Bob would have liked to be in there among
them, drinking and snacking, ready to sit down to
a beautiful dinner. Smells assaulted him. They
were as powerful as actual blows, these explosions
of roasting duck and braising celery, of smooth,
thick goose liver and saline, marine caviar. Also,
he smelled wine, and the comfortable odors of
bourbon and gin and whiskey, of vodka.

He leaned against the iron basement door,
moaning to himself, dreaming of a nice little glass
of Stoly, frosty cold from the freezer, freezing the
throat and warming the heart. Then he would take
a caviar canapé like Communion, and when it was

time for the duck, he would get a breast piquant
with sauce, covered with dark, crackling skin, and
he would wash it down with glass after glass of
Chateau Latour '69.

There was a garbage can off in a dark corner of
the understairs. It had a sticky, old-food odor. He
went over, sniffed more carefully. There was bread
in there among the rancidities, the old butter, the
greasy gravy, the wet cigarette butts. He nosed the
top of the can. Stuck tight. He pushed again.
Angry frustration made him whine. This was just
hell, this whole thing, and being without hands
was a special hell! He stared at the can. Just like a
hungry dog, he was drooling.

He made a loud sound and was astonished at
himself. The whine had built into a yap. If he
expected to survive much longer, he was going to
have to get into control of his own noises.

His stomach tormented him with muscular
heaves. Was it eating itself? He trembled. Was this
how dogs felt when they were hungry? If so, food
was an awful lot more important to them than it
was to humans. Dogs weren't slaves to men at all;
they were slaves to regular meals. There was really
only one choice: he was going to have to knock the
garbage can over and hope the lid flew off.

He shouldered it, which had an effect far greater
than he had intended. The can seemed to leap
from the floor. It smashed against the door with a
ringing crash and a fountain of garbage flowed
out. Another thing Bob needed to do was get used
to his own strength. He had to find the measure of
himself, but not now, not when he was standing
amid coffee grounds, butts, rotten fruit, bread
soaked in vinegar, soy sauce, and sour milk, and a
bag of Almost Home peanut-butter-chip cookies

that had somehow gotten covered with what smelled like liquid Wisk. Was this to be dinner?

Then he noticed the cold cuts. There were slices of Hungarian salami with little spots of white mold on them: these he gobbled up, chewing slowly, letting the rich saltiness fill his muzzle, closing his eyes with delight. The presence of the food in his mouth banished all reserve. Now he gobbled wet bread, tore into the cookies and damn the Wisk, ate some mushy grapes and a piece of fiercely hard Parmesan slopped in peach yogurt.

It was while he was breaking up the Parmesan with his powerful jaws that he noticed that the lights had come on and the door was open. The elegant woman stood there. "Oh, Mary, a goddamn dog has broken into the garbage." She stamped her foot. "Tell Jake to get down here and get it cleaned up. Honestly, I'm going to have to get a lock for that can."

Bob was backing away when he heard quick footsteps in the street behind him. He had lingered too long on this block. He should have run like a maniac the moment that carload of people recognized him. But the food . . . he was so hungry he wasn't thinking straight.

The woman waved her hands at him, shouted "shoo, shoo!" A man in blue workclothes came hurrying out of the house. "Jake, I want this cleaned up, and I want poison put out from now on."

"Yes, ma'am."

"This neighborhood is overrun. I don't know— what in the world?"

Two cops were running up the street. The homeowner shrank back into her kitchen. The cops stopped when they saw Bob, who was still attempting a retreat to the sidewalk. He was trapped between the police and the woman. He did not like the feeling of being trapped, did not like it at all. A surge of raw terror coursed through him.

He turned away from the cops—into the sight of the iron understair door being pulled closed. Without even thinking about it, he dashed through that door into the hallway. The elegant woman cursed, Jake blurted an automatic "Sorry, ma'am!" and the two cops came rushing in.

"It's the wolf," one of them yelled. "Take cover!"

You would have thought he was a neutron bomb with four legs and a tail. A glance back revealed the woman, her eyes popping out of her head, Jake cowering behind her, and the two cops, their own faces carnival masks of horror.

If only he could talk! "This is all so silly," he would say. "I'm about the least offensive person you could meet. Ten-year-old muggers practice on me."

At the top of the stairs was a butler's pantry. He went through, hoping that he would find a hallway, but instead he walked into the middle of the party. "I didn't know you had a dog," a woman shrilled.

"I don't," the hostess bleated.

The guns began to follow Bob as he leaped around the room, upended the coffee table, turned over a couch, caused an explosion of ashes out of the fireplace.

Then he saw the street beyond the front window, silent and free. There was no time even to consider. He ran for that window, his feet scrabbling maddeningly on the highly polished floor. Then he leaped, his tail whirling, his paws grabbing air, and sailed out through a cascade of leaded glass. Behind him alarms started clanging. Shapes darted back and forth behind the broken window.

Bob left it all behind, running as fast as he possibly could. For once the police made a slight error: the backup teams came roaring around the corner from Madison. Had they been smart, they would have gone down Fifth, knowing that they would head him off on his way to the park.

He might be able to run like the wind, but his thigh hurt when he did it. Without the anesthesia of desperation, the wound was getting painful.

When he at last reached the park, it took almost all of his remaining strength to leap over the rock wall. He fell down the other side, landing with a soft thud in a mat of moist leaves, and another world.

Suddenly there was silence, there were smells that seemed to penetrate instantly to the core of his soul, smells that he remembered from some childhood, perhaps his own, perhaps that of the wolf, or all childhood. His body urged him to burrow down into the redolent leaves, but his mind demanded more of him, that he get deeper into the park. He was about at Ninety-second Street: travel due west would soon bring him into the thickest part of the Ramble. He pulled himself to his feet, yelping a little at the spikes of pain that came from his thigh.

Movement in the park was much different from movement on the streets. It was a lot better, a whole lot better. There seemed to be a sort of electricity between his paws and the ground, and the air was tightly packed with odors that he could almost understand.

There came to him the weighted thought that we must have known the world from this perspective before Eden, before we climbed down from the trees. He tossed his head. When he saw them, his heart leaped toward the towers that shone on all four sides of the park. He looked toward the rich far windows of Central Park West and yearned as he had at Kissinger's party for the hiss of luxury.

He was passing the baseball diamonds now and turning in to the Ramble. As he moved he noticed one odor that stood out above all the others and gave him greater alarm than had the police or even the pound employees. It was a musk, deep and tart. What did it mean? Here it rose from a bush, there it covered a patch of browning leaves. He found the bones of a bird and gnawed them, but they were too dry to be of any use. Deep in the Ramble, down in the dark where roots tangled like ropes of distressed muscle, he moved swiftly and silently along. He passed a derelict sleeping under a bench. Then he smelled that odd smell again, so strongly that it stopped his easy slithering through the undergrowth.

He crouched, very still. A cold understanding crept into his mind: this smell was a warning. Other canines were not wanted here. Something had claimed the Ramble as its own.

He knew then that he was being observed, and from very close by. He had blundered into the middle of a pack of some kind, and it did not want him here.

As if in response to his thought, they flooded him with their smell, a straw-blood odor shot with urine and feces. It revolted him, and their dark little eyes revolted him more. Two of them came prancing stiff-legged out of a blackberry thicket.

They bared razor teeth. The eyes with which they regarded him were astonishingly intelligent. One animal stared him down while the other glanced constantly about, keeping watch. Their ears moved with method back and forth. These wary beings never ceased to test their environment, not for one instant.

They were the size of scrawny sheepdogs and a lot thinner. Their heads were wide and their ears big and pointed, like giant cat ears.

This was no motley pack of stray dogs. As more of them slipped into view Bob found himself stopped by awe and understanding. These were wild animals who made their living off New York City. They were the legendary coydogs of New England, a strong cross between the coyote and the dog, among the smartest animals nature has ever produced.

They were notorious dog murderers. And they obviously did not like big, wheezy wolves too much either. They were wiry little monsters, their faces sharp with hate and hunger. It was clear to Bob that they would kill him if they could. He could locate six of them in the shadows around him. He noticed the bones of a dog scattered about. It had not been a small dog.

He could sense movement all through the dark shrubbery, ahead, to the sides, behind. The only thing that prevented them from attacking him was the locked stare he was giving the leader. If he broke the look first, he was going to be torn to pieces.

Every whisper of fur against leaf, of paw in loam registered in Bob's ears. The breathing of the coydogs sounded like tiny pumps hissing. When he cocked his ears toward the leader, he could hear his heart beating faster and faster. And his scent was changing, rising to greater sharpness. He was a creature cocked, ready to dart like an arrow for the throat of the big, slow animal before him.

There was a frisk of movement just at the corner of Bob's eye, and a high-pitched squeal as one of the coydogs snatched a bat from the air and gobbled it down, the wings fluttering against its chin.

For the edge of an instant, the leader glanced at his companion. It was enough: feeling as clumsy and lethal as a tank, Bob ran at him. The little creature did not expect this. Bob shouldered him aside and took off running as fast as he could toward the lights of the Transverse Parkway.

As he ran one of them dropped down from a tree, its claws spread, growling rage. Bob took it on his back and felt the hot touch of its claws before he managed to scrape it off against an overhanging limb.

Then he was at the reservoir and the coydogs were still with him, slipping dangerously along nearby. If only he understood this situation, but he did not even begin to: if he had any wolfish instincts at all, they were a vague mental stubble. Bob was no more a part of this secret wild than he was a part of humankind.

Thirst made his tongue feel like a wooden paddle. His nose was tight and he longed to dip his muzzle in clear, fresh water. His hunger made his insides seem like a hollow shell. The feelings were astonishingly intense, much more than they had been before he changed. Even the various diets Cindy had tried out on him had not created burning, passionate hunger like this.

The coydogs attacked as swiftly and silently as

Indians attacking a prairie schooner. One moment he was loping along, aware of their odor around him but more or less minding his own business, the next moment he was in the middle of a dusty, snarling, snapping crowd of the vicious little killers.

One of them nipped his belly, and it hurt like a blast from a blowtorch. He screamed his miserable, human scream and rolled, covered with coydogs. A small one wailed as his weight compressed it, but the creature was like rubber, and it was digging its teeth into his neck before he even got to his feet. Dragging five or six of them, he struggled on. If only he could get to the Transverse Parkway, surely the cars would scare them off. A terrific flash of fire exploded in his breast. One of them was lodged just below his chin, his dewlap in its mouth. It shook its head, furiously tearing the meat of his neck.

He went to his foreknees, biting air, flailing and kicking. Now the one on his belly bit down. The heat of it made him scream again. He gnawed the ground, he knew that death had come to him: they were tearing him apart. He was big but he had no idea how to fight them. Involuntarily, he tried to use fists that weren't there anymore.

A few minutes ago he had been congratulating himself on his newfound wolf prowess. Now where was he—being eaten alive by a pack of really skilled killers. They gnawed, they tore, he snapped and thrashed. Soon one of them was going to open an artery or disembowel him. Then this odd traverse would end, here in the night and dirt.

They melted away, disappearing like dreams in morning light.

He stopped growling, stopped his futile snapping, stopped his kicking. Then he heard the rhythmic thudding of human feet. Shakily, he stood up. He was near the reservoir. Through the bushes was the jogging track. A man and a woman came pounding past, Walkmen on their heads, their bodies pouring off odors of sweat and various perfumes. Bob had never been so glad to see anybody in his life. Gleefully, he followed along behind them. The coydog odor dwindled and soon was gone.

South of the reservoir Bob adopted a long lope. Obviously he couldn't hide in the park. As soon as the joggers disappeared around the far curve of the track, the coydogs would be back.

Bob had decided to go home. If the media wasn't too crazy, maybe he would have some chance. There was no place for him in this world, not as a wolf without instincts, or as a man without the form of a man. Home, though, was different. Cindy and Kevin would care for him and love him, and give him what comforts they could. Of course, if the press was whipping up real hysteria, the apartment could turn out to be a death trap.

He reached the Park Drive and hurried south, his various wounds all demanding attention even as his tough new body kept at its job. The creature he had become was a real survivor, it appeared able to stand a great deal of punishment. But it had an end, he knew that. The beast would fail.

He was down an awfully lonely crack in the world. If he had to die, let it happen at home, in Cindy's arms.

Before he reached the zoo, he moved out onto Fifth Avenue. Zoos were dangerous.

He huddled along the streets, keeping to the shadows cast by parked cars. Seen from his new angle the city was a very different place, menacing, darkly looming, fast and full of surprises. Dogs on these roaring corners must be grateful for their leashes.

Because it is a street devoted to business and not well tenanted at night, he chose to go south along Madison Avenue. As swiftly as he could manage he went through midtown, scrabbling under cars twice as patrols passed. The second police car had four men in it, and a rack of hunting rifles. He had never seen rifles in a police car. The only logical conclusion was that they were a special detail assigned to him.

It was a strange thing indeed not to feel that the law was backing your right to live. He had no rights.

He kept on, reaching the end of Madison and proceeding south on Park. He finally got into his own neighborhood.

Just as he was turning onto Fourth Street, he was spotted. A pretty girl of about eighteen with a shaggy green punk hairdo put her fists to her cheeks and screamed like a thing gone mad when she saw him slide across the sidewalk. "The wolf, the wolf," she cried, and the cry spread.

He rushed along, his tail down, his head low. Maybe he ought to just let them catch them.

The prospect of home kept him going. His mind fixed on that one, single, true place. His place, the place of Robert Duke. He wasn't much of a provider, not much of a success, but there was love there for him.

He rounded a familiar corner. Even the graffiti was familiar, that and the black plastic bags neatly stacked for tomorrow's garbage pickup, the line of five ginkgo trees, the ironwork in front of his own building with the newspaper machines chained to it.

He looked up. His windows were lighted. Lupe would be off by now. Maybe he could break down the glass door and get into the lobby, somehow punch the buzzer, somehow call the elevator. Or, Cindy might come out. Once, twice he paced the block. He'd hide under a car until—

He saw her. His soul, his blood, yearned toward that silhouette in the sixth-floor window. She stiffened, leaned forward. He cocked his ears. Just barely, he could hear her saying something. But the window was closed and he could not make out the words.

Then the silhouette disappeared. Bob moved away from the building and crouched under a car.

It was from that vantage point that he saw the headlines on the *Post*. It was a red-banner extra, and it said:

KILLER WOLF STALKS CITY
POLICE WARN: IT'S A FREAK

What he could read of the story described him as a giant, marauding wolf so dangerous that he was to be shot on sight.

It sickened his heart. This was just the sort of thing he had feared. He wasn't going to be safe anywhere in this city, not even at home. Perhaps especially not there.

Then Cindy appeared, hobbling along in a single slipper, her hair a mess, her robe flapping in the wind. "Bob," she called. Her voice was music.

Sadly, he remained hidden. When he could, he

slipped away from her, moving quickly under parked cars.

She called and called, her voice echoing in the street. Her tone agonized him. She was suffering so terribly. He wished he could take her in his arms and kiss her, and bring her some measure of comfort.

He hadn't really thought of where he would go. His only destination was away from here. Cindy's cries grew long with despair. They followed him down the streets, catching him, driving him deep into sorrow. He'd been a fool to try this, to subject them both to this anguish. He made his way west through the intricate and hidden streets of the Village.

It was a long time before he lost her in the silent streets. Then he was as far west as you can go, standing on a ruined pier. Before him was the black, muttering Hudson, wide and swift and cold.

CHAPTER THIRTEEN

SHE'D BEEN LOOKING OUT THE FRONT WINDOW, WATCH-
ing the grim, blowing mist when she saw his
shadow dart out from under a car. For an instant
their eyes met and her heart thrilled. "Bob," she
said, "Bob!"

She ran down to the sidewalk in her robe and
slippers, but when she arrived he wasn't there. She
also saw the *Post* in its machine, was drawn to its
cruel, lurid headline.

Her hands shaking so badly she could barely
manage to put the coins in the slot, Cindy bought
a copy.

She stood there, stunned, staring at the picture
of Bob. Blown up to cover half of the front page,
even his wolf face communicated the gentleness of
his soul. This was despite the fact that an airbrush
had been used to make his teeth look larger and
sharper and to heighten the gleam in his eyes.

She knew him well enough to see how lost and sad he was. Slowly, reading the story, she sat down on the curb. When she turned to page two, she stifled a scream. Her skin prickled. There was a photograph of her stepping out of a cab, her face pinched, her eyes glaring. WOLF LADY TERRIFIES CITY said the headline above the picture. Below it was a garbled version of her lie about finding Bob on a street corner. She was portrayed as unwilling to meet the police and the press halfway. She was pilloried.

The silent buildings seemed to frown down on her. People do not like to be frightened. They distrust the wild, and she had unleashed it in their midst. "God help us," she whispered.

Then she thought she saw a flash of Bob in the distance. Her paper under her arm, she set off after the shadow. But by the time she reached the corner he was gone again. "Bob! Bob!" There was no answer, no movement in the silent street.

A nobility of love possessed her. "I'm going to find you!"

She looked up at the blowing, cold sky, at the low, pregnant clouds. "*What did you do to him*! Answer me! God, you answer me! I know you're there, you can't hide anymore, not after what you've done. Answer me, damn you! Don't you dare keep silent, you haven't got the right!" She broke down completely, right out in the middle of the empty sidewalk, weeping bitterly, her paper fluttering down, a crowd of white bat pages around her feet. "God, don't turn out to be a creep. I will sacrifice my life if you will change him back."

She hurried off after him, calling his name again and again, seeking him through the streets. Once or twice she glimpsed a shadow. That was all.

She did not notice that a car had stopped near the sidewalk, nor that a big, expressionless man had gotten out. He put his hand on her shoulder. She looked up, startled, into a face that was very disturbing. There was a red scar running up his tan, hollow cheek. His lips were cruel, his eyes tiny and black and thick with sin. Slowly, sensuously, his hand came up her cheek, tickling her, and something sparked in the black eyes. "May I help you?" he asked.

She turned away from him, wishing she was closer to home. She could imagine his mayhem, the ripping, the snarls: this was a violent man.

"You're the wolf lady," he continued, his voice soft. "I know you from the TV. I've been looking for you. I can give you some help."

His words seemed to penetrate as if from a great distance, words of fate and solace coming from this huge, horrible creature. She had expected rape in the small hours. Instead a weighty, careful finger slipped along the line of her tears, and she saw that the eyes were not cruel at all, or at least not all the time. For a moment they became merry, and he was a great benevolent elf. Then what she now recognized as an expression of fundamental anger returned. "I am Joe Running Fox," he said. "I know a little bit about the old ways." He glanced again at her, as if willing her to accept him. When he continued, his voice had acquired a tone of pornography. "There was once something called shape-shifting, that medicine people could do. A long time ago. They lost their power when we were thrown out of our land."

"Are you going to hurt me?" How little she sounded, a whining girl.

Tired air rattled through old lungs. He closed his eyes. "I'm an ugly cuss but I never hurt nobody. I have some medicine in me, the old-time kind. You get where I'm coming from?" She did not. He had conjured images of Lydia Pinkham's and Castoria. "Indian medicine," he added.

She looked him up and down. "You're an Indian?"

"A medicine Indian. Power. It's what you need, power to lead your heart to understanding."

In an instant her fears, her suspicions evaporated. A shock brought her snapping to her feet. "You know."

He nodded. "I have a pretty good idea, hawk woman. Is he your husband?"

She wrung her hands in frantic eagerness. "You know, you know all about it!"

"So I'm right. Your husband is the one who shifted out." He stood up. "We need to talk."

She glanced around. "My place—"

"No, a place where I am comfortable. A bar. Do you mind an Indian bar? Drunken savages?"

"My son is asleep in our apartment. I've got to get back."

"Is he wolf clan?"

"What?"

"Is he like his father, especially attracted to wolves?"

"No, I don't think so. He likes Kafka."

"Oh, Kafka. Everything in Kafka happened to the Indians before Kafka was born." He looked up at the sky. "I ought to meet your son. I will find out what kind of child he is."

He took her home, his bar proposal apparently amended by the presence of Kevin. Cindy let him into the building, thinking to herself, You fool. His back was extraordinarily wide, covered by a threadbare and not particularly clean charcoal knit sports jacket, the sort of thing one might get at the Salvation Army. He was wearing ancient, cracked army boots and baggy khaki pants.

She recognized that she was absolutely crazy to be letting this man in her house.

And yet there was something stolid and earthbound about him. He seemed too old, too wide, and too decrepit to be of any danger to anybody. Then you looked at his eyes and there was a sense of spreading wings, of sunlight in the midnight hour. Those eyes were wonderful with love, reflecting back the light that entered them, at once menacing and gentle. She could still feel the delicate touch of his huge sausage finger on her cheek.

His presence was overbearing in the elevator, his odor a mix of beer and beans and thoroughly ripened sweat. There was also, though, something sweet—quite fresh and pleasant—that brought to mind new flowers. Standing beside her, silent, staring at the elevator door, he gave no sign of what might be happening in his mind.

They got off together and Cindy opened the door of the apartment. How did it feel to be forced? Would he make it hurt? Would it last a long time? Fear had strengthened her senses. She felt with great acuity the coolness of the key in her hand, listened fascinated at the rasp of the lock, inhaled the familiar home scents that blew out through the opening door.

He stood shyly in the foyer, his hands folded over his broad waist, his eyes down.

"Come on in. Sit down."

"No. I have to get something from the place. Let

me walk around." He stared at her. Seeing that she did not dissent, he began a slow, rocking progress, his brow wrinkled, his lips pursed. He crossed and recrossed the living room, circled the dining table, moved through the kitchen. Then he proceeded down the hall to the bedrooms. Occasionally he made a guttural sound. He passed thrice around her bed, then lay down on it, dropping so hard it all but went through into the Steins' apartment below. After a moment he sat up. "Lots of love here," he said. When he smiled, she saw that his teeth were rotted to stumps.

Then, with a grunted sigh, he got up and went to Kevin's room. Cindy followed him avidly. She was now convinced that she had been insane to do this. He might hurt her little boy. He was someone off the New York City streets; she didn't even know his name. "Owl boy," he said absently.

He returned to the living room. "Hawk woman, owl boy, wolf man. And wolf man has been stolen." He ground out a laugh, dropping down to the couch. "You think I don't know what I'm doing—it happened over there." He pointed straight to the spot where Bob had changed. "That's where he entered the wolf clan."

She was astonished, excited. He was either very clever or schooled in disciplines hidden to her own eyes. "What do you mean, 'entered'?"

"The wolf clan is dying. They are calling all the ones whose spirits will help them. The people who have a special affinity for them. The Wolf People. Do you understand?"

"No."

"Everybody implies a certain kind of animal. Each human soul contains a little dust from some other species."

"We're descended from apes."

"It's much more complicated than that. Remember the philosopher Whitehead? He stressed that there is no 'nature.' Only details. Millions upon millions of details. Concentrate on any one, or any group, and your whole reality changes to support your new focus of attention."

"I thought you were an Indian. What in the world does Whitehead have to do with it? What about Black Elk or somebody like that? Chief Dan George?"

"We get what we can where we can. Injun Joe's been a beggar for a while now. I'm from a culture that went under."

This was leading nowhere. "What do you want?"

"I want to help you understand what happened to your husband. From my own understanding, from the cultural tradition I represent, I might have a few answers."

He was beginning to annoy her. "So, I'm waiting."

"You're very impatient."

"I don't think you know what you're doing. You made a lucky guess but now you're ad-libbing. You probably aren't even an Indian."

"I'm a full-blooded Mohican."

That answer chilled her. She had been taunting him for more information; she had not believed that he was an imposter.

"The last of the Mohicans?"

He gave her a long look. "The last one around here. I was a Mohawk, but what the hell, there's a family tradition that we were Mohicans until the Mohawks stole my great-grandfather eight times removed. So why not? Let old James Fenimore

Cooper turn over in his grave if he wants to, I don't give too much of a damn."

Once again he had surprised her. You thought you had captured the measure of this man, only to discover a moment later that your conclusions were still wrong, but in a new way.

"I could use a beer, if you've got any."

Her mind went to Bob, Bud in hand, reading a novel in Sunday-afternoon sunlight. "Help me get him back."

"Why don't you join him?"

"Don't be ridiculous!" The way the Indian looked at her made her furious. "I have a child to raise!"

The Indian laughed. "Him too."

"I want help, not this superstitious nonsense! People don't just turn into animals. That's ridiculous, it doesn't . . . happen."

His eyes were twinkling. "Have it your way, white eyes. But I'd like to keep talking about reality for a second, if you don't mind."

She closed her eyes. He went on: "I was trying to tell you about the fact that the animal kingdom is dying, and because it is dying, it is beginning to take heroic measures to save itself. That's why the spirit of the wolves beguiled your husband. The animal kingdom is after the mind of man."

"I want my husband back!"

He leaned forward, clasped his hands between his knees. "So, follow him. You're his squaw."

"Crap!"

"Well, I don't mean it in a demeaning way. It would take great courage to follow him. He is a hero. You would be a heroine if you did it."

It was time for a family conference. She went in and woke Kevin up. He was flushed with sleep, his hair tangled, his smooth skin warm and sweet. "I don't know what he is," she told him, "but he's saying things that make a kind of bass-ackwards sense. He thinks we should try to find Dad."

Kevin regarded him down the shadows of the hall. "He looks like an old drunk, Mom."

"Well, he's most definitely that. But he also knew the truth about Dad, from the very first. He has the idea that the wolves are in such desperate trouble that they sort of seduced Dad into becoming one of them in order to gain the power of the human mind."

Her son's hand came into her own. "I wonder what the truth is about Prometheus," Kevin said. "What did he steal, to make the gods so mad? Was it only fire?"

"Wasn't that enough?"

"My guess is that he stole their inner fire. Their godliness. That's the point of the myth. And the wolves want to steal our inner fire, our humanity."

"Is that bad?"

"Mother, the animals are beautiful." Squaring his shoulders, he went into the living room.

The Indian got to his feet. "You are a young brave. I salute you!"

"Hey, Mom—"

"Let it go. Just listen to what he has to say." Catching a glimpse of herself in the dark window, she saw the sharpness of her face, that angular, questing shadow that seemed to fight her beauty, but was in fact its center. Her psyche had claws: she remembered last night, waiting in the middle of the bed for Bob, waiting like a wolf in the secret dark, to devour him with her demands. Wolf woman.

"You know the old idea of types? In the West, it

used to be thought that there were seven types of personality. There are more than seven types! A type for every beast in the animal kingdom. We are reflections of the whole of reality. Among us there are shrew types, porcupine types, owl types, frog types, lion and zebra types, eagle types. On and on. Often people change types when they get dogs. That's why old people and their old dogs look alike. A bulldog owner becomes a bulldog type. You have to understand the universe as it really is. A hall of mirrors, and we are the mirrors. I hate to sound like a broken record, but I would be able to do this better if I had a beer in my hand."

He was and wasn't a fraud. She got him a Bud. They'd been out. When had she bought more? She didn't remember doing it. But there were also three new Lean Cuisines in the freezer, some apples and grapefruit in the fridge, and another half gallon of Tropicana Premium OJ. She'd done the shopping automatically, sometime in the black struggling hours.

"Can you dance, boy?"

"I can waltz."

"That isn't dancing. What's dancing is what attracts spirits. Ghost dancing." He began to shake, leaning from foot to foot. "You have to jiggle your insides so your soul jiggles. The spirits hear that and they get curious. They're like fish that way, coming up when you jiggle the bait. Only be careful, because your soul is the bait."

Kevin started the same movement. The man began to chant, "eaah, eaah, eaah ea*ah*." He repeated the simple rhythm, his eyes closed. Then he had a little packet in his hands, made up of fur and bones and bits of skin. "Wolf medicine," he said. "Very powerful. Medicine of the Thunder Wolf."

For fifteen minutes they danced. Occasionally the man went around in a little circle, hopping and chanting. Once he whooped. He took a small rattle from his pocket and shook it. He handed the wolf medicine to Kevin, took it back, handed it over again.

Finally he stopped and took a long pull on his beer. "They aren't coming," he said. "My magic's not powerful enough. I could hear them laughing, though."

"Who?"

"The wolf clan. They're very happy. I don't want to upset you, but it looks to me like they've got him for good."

A rocket blasted into the center of her gut and exploded with phosphorus fire. "Nobody got him for good! He's mine, do you hear that! He is mine and I am going to have him back. My God, Bob was one of the gentlest, most humane people I've ever known. He was this boy's father. He's ours. I'll curse the whole species of wolf unless they give him back to me."

"Stealing's never a good idea, I guess."

"Get out of here, you old idiot! You're like some quack with a fake cancer cure. And if you tell the papers that the wolf is really Bob, I will come after you and personally kill you, and believe me, I will do it slowly."

He smiled, the whole bottom half of his face cracking open in a paroxysm of black pits, gnarled stumps, and yellow teeth. "What will you use, the claw or the tooth?"

Shaking like a disturbed longleg spider, she guided him to the door. "Get out."

"Thanks for the swallow of beer."

She slammed the door behind him. Kevin came and put his arm around her waist. That felt awfully good. Now if only Bob was standing on her other side . . .

"I'm going to find your father and bring him home and turn him back into a man."

"Yes, Mom."

"You'll help me?"

"Mom, of course I will."

She told him how close she had been to him earlier. "He's been hurt, he's all scruffy. The last I saw of him, he was heading for the far West Village."

They made bacon and eggs and coffee together, and opened the fresh orange juice. Sitting at the kitchen table, in the thin light of dawn, they laid plans, gardens and castles and clouds of plans, to go down the labyrinth that had claimed husband and father, and lead him back to his humanity.

CHAPTER FOURTEEN

THE STREETS OF NEW YORK ARE ALLEGEDLY NEVER quiet, but they were certainly quiet tonight. An occasional siren wailed, mist billowed, shadows moved behind windows. After seeing the *Post* extra Bob understood why: this city of seven million lethal human creatures was stifled with fear. The beast of apocalypse prowled its streets. Ancient terrors were invoked. All was quiet.

To Bob, slinking along hurt and cold and famished, it seemed absurd. In his present mood he would gladly have let a child kill him. Smelling Cindy so close had been too keen a sorrow. He could bear no more of this. As he paced the banks of the Hudson, he contemplated jumping from one of the ruined piers and bringing this whole bizarre experience to an end.

The city around him could not have seemed

more oppressive or unfriendly. He had no way of explaining himself, not even in his own mind. His only thought was that ours is an age at the far limit of time, and it is at limits and extremes that the impossible can happen. Or maybe the mysterious fifth force that physicists speculate about had something to do with it. Maybe it was a disease, psychological or otherwise.

He stood looking down at the waters. They were black and smelled of creosote. Lapping and sighing beneath the pier, the river surged in its course. Far out, a magnificent yacht moved in stately passage, its portholes all alight, the sound of its engines coming faintly on the wind.

Bob inhaled, almost believing that he could still smell Cindy's special odor. People's smells were as distinctive as their faces or fingerprints. Were there two smells exactly alike? He suspected not. They hung in layers in the streets of the city, millions of them. He had just noticed this, and was beginning to be able to tell them apart.

He looked down at the water again. How would it feel to die in that murk? Would he struggle, or just go to sleep? It might be a painful death, indeed, like the death of smothering. Once when he was ten, another boy had smothered him in a plastic shower cap, a large, vicious boy. To this day he remembered the gnawing agony.

And the water was cold. He did not know how this miserable body might react to that. Normally he shunned even slightly cool swimming pools. Cold showers, cold days, snow sports were all abhorrent to him.

He could see things floating in the water, big, amorphous things, like great masses of sewage. Doubtless that's what they were. So he would not only drown in the river, he would drown in sewage.

His ears back, his tail down, in his anguish he snapped at the air.

He smelled Cindy again, this time much stronger, as if she was somewhere nearby. It was the perfume of her spirit, this, or the trembling scent of memory. Until he had been blocked by this new body from his relationship with her, he had not understood just how much a part of him she had become.

Then he heard a noise, a tapping on the pier. Figures approached, moving silently side by side, by their smells a man and a heavily scented person, probably a woman. She was so powdered and perfumed that her real smell was almost obscured. There was a faint underlying odor of pus and scabs. He was fresher, the scent of healthy sweat, the remains of deodorant put on many hours ago, a touch of Afta still clinging to his face. The blue odor of oiled metal was chief among those he noticed coming from the woman's purse. He knew she had a pistol hidden there.

There was a quick round of bargaining between them, obviously further to an earlier conversation.

"This ain't exactly a hotel."

"You're gettin' off easy, ten bucks."

"It's cold. I wanna do five."

Her voice, exhausted. "Seven."

They came closer, the prostitute and the john. Bob stayed absolutely still, embarrassed and ashamed to be witness to their humble and private business. Closing his eyes did nothing to shut them out: he smelled them, he heard them. The woman was kneeling before the man, the man leaning against a piling, his fingers working in her hair.

In a merciful few minutes it was over. There was a stink of hot bodies. The woman made a rustling movement. "Take off your clothes," she said in a low voice. The gun was in her hand.

She tossed everything into the Hudson—the underpants, the socks, the shoes, the cheap suit. "Please, lady."

She opened the wallet. "Eighty fuckin' bucks," she said in a new, harder voice. No wonder all the powder: she was a man. "I oughta blow you away."

The transvestite turned and marched off the pier, leaving his john cowering naked. "What am I gonna do?" he moaned. After a short time, he also hurried back toward the darkness of West Street, a pale flash in the night.

To Bob that poor man seemed the luckiest of creatures, normally formed, his body the key to the whole list of human freedoms and powers.

The wild was not freedom at all; the wild was a terrible bondage. Man was free.

He remembered the wolf in the zoo. That had been the message in his eyes.

Was that wolf like me, a lost man? Was he warning me with his eyes, or cajoling me?

His eyes had been so beautiful. Too bad being a wolf was such hell.

He could escape, of course. All he had to do was let himself fall, then take a single, deep breath after the water enclosed him.

Before he jumped, there was one thing he had to do, if only to satisfy himself that his situation was indeed hopeless. Many years before he had been

interested in meditation. TM had been popular
when he was in college, and he had tried it. He had
met a girl who was involved in the Ecstatic
movement within the Catholic Church, and he
had gotten high on repetitive prayer.

They had joined together, Bob and Lorelei, on
the Way of Flesh and Prayer—their own name for
their Catholicized sexual freedom—and had
learned secrets of meditation known, if at all, to a
few adepts of the *Kama Sutra*.

Bob wondered if he could still sense his body in
the old way. Could he perhaps re-create his human
body by creating a vivid enough image of it in his
mind?

With all the will he could bring to it, he concentrated on turning his left rear paw back into a foot.
He visualized a foot—his own foot—just as he
remembered it, complete with the scar from his
bunion operation and the ingrown second toenail
he had been meaning to show to Al West, his
podiatrist.

Nothing happened, nothing at all. He kept on
trying, raising the paw off the ground in the
intensity of his effort. Nothing seemed to happen,
but when he put the paw down, he was amazed
and shocked to feel ordinary human toes and heel.
He looked back, and there in the shadows was a
pale, naked man's foot attached to his wolf leg.

Pure excitement made his blood rush so hard he
started to faint. The foot felt a little like rubber, a
lot like gelatin, and it seemed as if a lessening of
attention might make it dissolve once again into a
paw. The moment he shifted his attention to his
upper leg, the foot indeed began to disintegrate.
There was no sensation, but his contact with the

ground began to change. Then he returned his concentration to the foot. At once it was human again.

But it wouldn't stay like that, not without a Zen master's ability to concentrate on it and keep it human. A very real force was urging his cells into the wolf shape. When he fought it, he could feel it resisting, striving to recapture the shifted part.

Then he learned another thing: By keeping some attention on his foot and extending it up his leg, he could transform the leg as well, and include it in the new fortress of his human being. He labored, striving to fix the quicksilver of concentration, until he was a human torso with a wolf's chest, shoulder, and head. There was war inside him. His organs battled the confusion of juices. He vomited and the wolf body regained the torso for a moment. Then he recaptured his attention from his pain and dragged it up his midriff. It slipped, concentrating suddenly on what he wanted most, which was hands. They popped out of his paws, new and slightly wet, knuckles closed against the ground. Then the wolf tail slipped out again. He fought it down, felt the fur of it tickling against his buttocks as it was absorbed.

Now, holding in awareness all of his human parts, he made a great effort to draw his attention up both forelegs and then across his chest and neck. With a rush as of swirling snow his whole sense of smell disappeared. He was shocked to realize how dependent on it he had become. For a moment, shaking his head, he thought he was blind.

Then he saw a flush of color, the crystal world that human eyes see. He was lying, wet and new on the dirty slabs of the pier. He raised himself up.

Shaking, he stood slowly to full height, and felt the sharp airs of night on naked skin. He clapped his hands, he swooped and swirled.

He had to be careful, though. The wolf itched just beneath the surface of him, waiting to pop out the moment he stopped concentrating on his shape.

He remembered a paraphrase of the physicist Richard Feynman, that reality is plastic, that it is essentially dependent upon the observer.

Speaking of whom, he found himself lit by headlights, which proceeded slowly down the rattling pier toward him. He began to back up, momentarily terrified. But why? He was human again. He was safe. Smiling with relief, he ran forward toward the car. "Hey, I need help."

A light bar flashed: it was a police car. "You couple of fuckers," a voice said, drawling easily. "Come aaannn." Two young policemen emerged from the car. Sitting in the back was the dim figure of the man the prostitute had mugged. "What is this, a new thrill?" one of them asked.

"I don't think I—" He stopped. The moment his attention had gone into the effort of speaking, the wolf had leaped up inside, ready to surge out.

"You guys stay at home. We don't want any funny business out on these piers."

"I—I—"

"Get in the goddamn car. We're runnin' youse in. Two creatures start a naked trip out here, pretty soon all the creatures are doing it, am I right?" The officer made a move toward Bob. A strong hand connected with his arm. Bob jumped away: where the cop had touched grew a tuft of fur. "Oh, come on," the cop said in a bored tone. "We'll beat you up if you make this a pain in the ass." He grabbed again.

Bob still felt loose and unreal, like a jelly. He skittered away, dragging a paw on his left arm, then with a dry hiss a whole left foreleg. When he tried to bring back his arm, it would not come.

"Halt, you're under arrest," one of the cops shouted. The other came at Bob, his arms outstretched. Bob backed up, warding off those awful hands with his one human fist.

He saw the misty sky and heard a rush of air around him. Then he hit the water with a whooshing splash. Cold, stinking river water poured down his throat, making him choke. Choking, he sank deeper and deeper, until there was no sound but the pulsing of distant marine engines. Something big and clingy wrapped around his midriff. He struggled to release himself from it, arching his back, clawing, trying to paddle.

His attention was shattered, and he knew that the wolf would win if he didn't regain it. The wolf leaped, struggled, twisted. There was nausea and the seething of skin. He fought: foot not paw, flesh not fur, and then he felt the eerie swinging of the tail. The pressure of the water was slaughtering his ears. He concentrated his whole attention into a single dot of consciousness. And he knew he had won: down in the depths of the river, he was human again.

There came the pounding of blood, shock after shock, the hammer of suffocation. He had to breathe. The agony was amazing, total, all-involving, far worse than what he had imagined.

He felt his flesh popping like sausage skin, felt the emergence of the reborn thing as it climbed out of him and became him. Each quake of his heart brought a flash to his eyes. In a moment he was going to take in a heave of water, cough, and commence the unmanaged panic of his dying.

Cold water rushed past his face. He drew back his lips, felt his mouth opening, felt his every muscle straining, his legs churning, his lungs expanding to whistling, airless balloons, then a gust of water blasted down his throat. He gagged, his body contorting to a knot, then he coughed it out, expelling it through his nose, helplessly breathing again—but this time it was cold, dank air.

His head had broken water. Again he breathed, choked, coughed, gagged, breathed, fought the waves, raised his nose high, and swam along, sweeping the water aside with his four powerful legs.

He was an amazing distance away from the pier, and his nose took in the myriad scents of the watery world, the fish, the creosote from all the rotting timbers, the sewage and trash, the skim of oil on the water's surface.

He cocked his ears toward the pier. The two cops were standing there calling, playing their flashlight on the near waters. They were looking for a blubbering human swimmer, though, not the sleek creature who watched them.

He was a wolf again, thoroughly and completely. His concentration had been shattered at just the wrong moment. He screamed out his rage, but this time even that vestige of his humanity was gone. It seemed that his return to the wolf form had worked more perfectly than the first transformation. He was now smoothly wolf: an animal howl echoed across the Hudson waters.

Dog-paddling steadily, he turned himself around and around, seeking the closest shore. But there was no close shore. He was being taken by the tidal current, and taken fast. Manhattan was already farther away than Jersey. He could see the lights of cars emerging from the Holland Tunnel. Far upriver the George Washington Bridge glimmered. A tug sounded its mournful drone. The mist sometimes obscured the riverbanks, making it even harder for him to orient himself.

He had lost sight of the police on the shore. Manhattan was now an anonymous grandeur of lights, coldly self-centered, indifferent to the mere animal that was going to drown before its glow. Dog-paddling was an exhausting way to swim, but if he stopped he sank. He kept his muzzle just above the water, held his ears back to keep the cold out, and dug at the water with his tiring legs. The cold made him ache, the pain distracted him, the spinning lights on the shores made him fear that he was swimming in circles.

It would have been easy to just stop paddling, but there could be no question of that now. His experience of drowning had cured him of any desire to do so; the closeness of death had ignited in him a hunger for more life. He worked furiously in body and mind, trying to find some way to survive.

He had entered that state beyond exhaustion, where the flesh is supported only by will. It is a condition of rapture that seems while it lasts that it might go on forever. It doesn't. The end is always complete and total collapse. Bob swam on. There were lights ahead, but he could not tell if they were a ship at anchor or the Jersey shore.

Then he heard a bell ring loudly and he understood that one of the lights must be a buoy, and perhaps quite near. He cocked his ears—water ran down inside, roaring and causing these fine wolf ears excruciating pain.

There was a flash of white noise in his head. His chest constricted, he gagged. Dimly he realized that he was now completely submerged, still paddling but no longer powerfully enough to keep himself afloat. He remembered a morning long ago, fishing for perch at the John O. Fishing Camp with his father, looking down into the green water, wondering that there were creatures who needed it as we need air. He remembered the flopping struggle of the caught fish, the astonishment in their golden flat eyes.

Then he surfaced, heard the bell, and knew he was soon going to stop swimming. No matter how hard he tried, his legs were slowing down. For relief he let his back legs stop and churned with his forelegs, just keeping his nose in the air.

The bell rang again, a clear, sharp peal. Before and above him he saw a flashing green light, and he heard the river sloshing against the buoy. He flailed with his paws, touched the bouncing thing. Its sides were smooth, but there was a superstructure that housed the bell. Conceivably he could lodge his front paws up in there and hang on.

He tried to grasp the side of the buoy but his claws scratched helplessly. For hands this would be simple. He tried to concentrate, to picture a hand where his paw now scrabbled, a hand with its flexible fingers, its reach, its power.

No change occurred. It was as if his earlier efforts had drained a battery. Change now seemed completely impossible. He was as much a wolf as he had been a man. He snorted, yapped, tried to hug the buoy with both paws. The buoy was rusty above the waterline, and he dragged slowly down until he reached the algae that clung to the base, whereupon he slipped and splashed off into the water.

Excited, snapping, frantic, he came to the surface and tried again. This time his forepaws held. He scrambled with his rear paws, trying for at least a little purchase in the goop that adhered to the buoy's underwater surfaces. Again he kicked, and again failed, and came slowly down the side. Then one claw caught what was probably the rough edge of a weld. For an instant he was poised, unmoving. He could feel his forepaws beginning to slip. Another inch and he would topple backward into the water. Slowly, carefully, he began to straighten the rear leg that was holding. First a bare quarter of an inch, then another quarter, he slid up the buoy. It was working, definitely. Higher and higher he slid, stretching at last to his full length. He felt the edge of the cage that enclosed the bell. Then he was falling, twisting, splashing, turning beneath the waves. He came up fast, slamming his head against the bottom of the buoy so hard he saw a pink flare behind his eyes and was for a moment stunned.

Then he made his way out from under and surfaced again. His swimming was slow. He might as well have been wearing saddlebags filled with lead. If only he could shed this soggy fur, if only he could rest just for five minutes. He could actually hear cars on the shore, horns honking at the tunnel entrance, the sigh of the roads, even a radio playing on the bank, entertainment for some lonely fisherman.

He wanted life, his blood hungered for it, his breath sped through his lungs for it, he yearned toward the shore. He did not think he could make it. There were now just two choices, either he could try the buoy a last time, or he could attempt another fifteen minutes in the water. If he failed at either, he was dead.

The buoy rang again, its sound deafening and yet also peaceful, reminding him of a church at dawn, of the flat seascapes of the world. He smelled coffee and hot dogs. The fisherman had opened a snack.

Desperate now, Bob struck for the shore. The buoy was useless to him. Every few moments he would find himself underwater. It would take a burst of energy to get him to the surface, and every time he did that he was a bit less able. Soon he was spending more time below the surface than above it. His ears were roaring, his muscles were frantic, he wasn't getting enough air.

Then the water was suddenly very cold and the lights were whirling again. He was in a powerful current. He relaxed, realizing that this was the end. The lights, which had been no more than a few hundred feet away, began to get smaller. He sloshed with listless paws, waiting for his body to give up its struggle. The water caressed him. He closed his eyes.

As soon as he sank he found himself rolling against rocks. Rocks! They couldn't be more than five feet below the surface. He paddled again, reached the surface, flopped and splashed, looking for a place shallow enough to stand. But he was rushing along so fast he couldn't even begin to get purchase. The rocks tantalized him, sweeping by just below the tips of his paws.

Then he came to something quite solid. The current literally shoved him against it. He found himself clambering over cutting stones, clambering and swaying. He stood, astonished, his head hanging, too weak even to look up. Then he toppled to his side, his legs still weakly paddling, but they paddled air, for he had come up on a rocky promontory of the shore.

"Oh Lord, who—" Bob heard the voice of the fisherman, smelled his food, his coffee. His impulse was to run, but he was beyond anything so draining. All he could do was lie on his side just where he was, and stare with one open eye up into the dank gray-red sky of fog and mist.

"You is a dog. Lord, you done swum out of the Hudson, ain't you? Lord, Lord."

He took off his own coat, the fisherman, and rough-dried Bob's freezing, soaking fur. Then he stroked his head.

"All I got is the end of a wiener," he said. "Ain't much food for a big dog like you, but it ain't air either."

Then there was meat at his lips, meat and bread and tangy hot mustard. Even a little kraut. Bob gulped down the food. His eyes closed. The fisherman threw an old, dank tarp over him.

Soon there was a slight warming of his body, which was an infinite comfort. At once he slept, and he dreamed that he had come to the reefs of heaven, and found there an old black man with a hot-dog end and a rotting square of canvas, who was an angel of God.

PART THREE
COUNTRY LIFE

The country has been amputated, its soul
is bigger than its place.

The country has perfect mist, morning light
that reconstructs what is true.
The country is where you go to find what you lost,
and find what lost you.

—Robert Duke,
"Country Life" (1989)

CHAPTER FIFTEEN

THE MORNING SUN HEATED THE CANVAS TARP. WHEN Bob awoke, it was from a nightmare of the gas chamber at the pound. His fur was steaming, his body sanded with pain. It was as if every muscle had been wound with barbed wire. His stomach was tight and sour. He was ravenous. In his mouth there lingered a maddening temptation of hot dog.

He got up, shaking the canvas off his back. All around him were dank, twisted rocks. Beyond rose a cliff of the lower palisades, tall and complicated. He moved forward, sniffing the crisp air. Everywhere there was the sour sweetness he was coming to recognize as the ground odor of human bodies. Above it was the stink of the river, the nostalgic rot of autumn leaves, warm asphalt, faint car exhausts, and a musty odor of animals, no doubt the rats that lived along the riverbanks. His stomach knocked and a film of drool covered his tongue.

He was damned if he was going to eat a raw rat.

And yet he found himself imagining a lovely steak tartare, the way they would serve it at the Palm, one of his favorite restaurants. It had been a long time since he could afford lunch at the Palm.

Would he get rabies from eating a rat? Well, that was nothing to worry about. He would never eat anything alive. He was going to be the first noncarnivorous wolf.

His real desires were for a cup of coffee ground at home from Jamaica Blue Mountain beans, some flaky croissants from Patisserie Lanciani, and a nice stupefying Sunday morning with the *Times* and WBAI's *Music of a Sunday Morning* in the background. Add to that some fresh-squeezed orange juice from the Korean market on Bleecker, and perhaps—just to be bad—a couple of slices of bacon.

Even so, the rats smelled kind of good.

He couldn't see them, of course, but he knew they were there, and he sensed that every rat eye was on the monster that had intruded on their domain.

Maybe there were delis with salad bars here in Jersey. He could burst in and start gobbling down the *kappa maki,* the endive, and the *olivata.* He'd be shooed away, of course, but what the hell. Hit three or four delis and he'd be full.

There was movement before him, back near where the old road passed under the cliff's face. He cocked his ears and was rewarded with a richly detailed scuttle of noises: the chugging of rat breath, the silver rustle of rat paws on stone, the swallowed whines of rat fear.

They knew what he could not yet admit, that in the end he would hunt them, that among them there was one who soon would die. He drew deep, exploratory breaths, hoping that the fisherman had left some bits behind. Even one of the greasy, tumor-ridden Hudson fish would be preferable to a rat. For God's sake, rats were nothing more than reprocessed garbage.

His body's motives were not those of his mind. His body simply wanted to eat. It was also efficient. And it was working on the problem. While he worried, it had targeted a hole that was full of rats. His ears said that they were seething there, uneasy, noses pointing toward him. When he moved forward, there was a tensing. He stopped. Soon the tension died down. He found that his tail had lifted, and he felt some sparkle in himself, a glee as sharp as glass. He pranced forth on the hunt—and saw not just one hole but a dozen explode with fast gray shapes. They skittered about, their tails swirling behind them, their little voices shrilling. It was a dance of dread, and he suddenly knew the source of all dance.

His body twisted, skidded, turned, and leaped. Then there appeared in his sight a long rat crusted with offal, its teeth yellow, one eye filmed gray. His nose smelled the saline freshness of its blood, sensed the heat of its body, and he tasted in his muzzle the minute hurricane of its breath, which reeked of wet cigarette ends, pigeon droppings, and bugs.

His muzzle was a quick weapon. Once he had the rat in his vision he was able to follow it with the dexterity of a radar guidance system. A flush of wet filled his mouth. His belly churned, becoming blazing hot. This was a stomach far more powerful than its human counterpart. As he matched the rat's staccato march he noted fierce acid fumes rising from his own throat. Probably his stomach could digest damn near anything.

There came a moment when the rat's neck would be just where he needed it. He reached down, snapped, and drew the scrabbling, screaming creature into the air. It had heft, it was no small rat. When it tried to turn around and bite him, he cracked the whip with its body. As if turned off by the will of God, it went limp. He had killed it as easily as that. It fell from his jaws with a wet thud. Now all the other rats, who had become indifferent as soon as they realized they had not been singled out, took a new interest. There would soon be carrion to scavenge.

Bob sniffed at the thing. Up close he could smell so many different varieties of unpleasantness that he was unable to count them all. The worst, perhaps, was a distinct odor of benzine. The rat also had a scaly growth on the side of its head, that looked almost like the plates of a lizard's brow. A bizarre cancer.

His humanity told him not to touch this diseased thing. His wolfhood wanted to gobble it up and have done with it. He pushed it with his nose. The surviving rats gathered eagerly around, waiting for him to finish.

He wanted to get out of here. But the dead rat kept him lingering. Without hands, how would he skin it? How could he bear the crunch of the bones? His stomach was molten iron. Without any conscious decision at all, he gave the rat's soft underfur a smart nip.

His jaw seemed to go off like a cocked pistol. Entirely without his conscious participation, he had ripped the rat down the middle. Its blood flowed out, steamy and quick, causing eager scurrying to break out among the others. They followed their brother's blood down the cracks and commenced drinking at once, their little lapping filling the still, expectant air.

He recoiled at the sight of the slick, purple guts spilling over the stones. How could he be doing this? A thrill of fascination went through him—this curiously automatic and quite skilled behavior must come from instinct. Becoming a good wolf was like learning a musical instrument.

In this case, though, success would mean actually eating the ghastly mess on the rocks in front of him, something he did not at all want to do. The smell of it, so intense and bloody and alive, made him step back. Then, quite suddenly, one of the rats dashed in and grabbed some offal. That made him growl and lunge forward, and before he could stop himself, the warm meat was going down his throat. He felt it on his tongue, fur and skin and muscle, little rat bones, he tasted it and the taste was absolute meat. Then it was gone, the whole damn rat, even the tail.

He stood there, his head lolling, his mouth open. The revulsion that crawled through his body made him turn up his lips and snarl. When he exhaled, he smelled essence of rat, the freshness of the meat as well as the hollow rot of the filthy fur and whatever horrors had been in the stomach.

He gagged. But he did not bring up what he had eaten. On the contrary, it was perfectly acceptable to his stomach, which was comfortably digesting it.

Good God. He had done something truly unspeakable and yet lived. He was so sensitive, such a careful eater. As a child he had been amenable only to hamburgers and carrots. Over the years his repertoire of foods had expanded, but slowly. Not until he moved to New York had he acquired a taste for real exotica. Now he relished everything from snails to raw abalone.

A great, low booming distracted him from his thoughts. He looked out at the river, and there was the *QE2* flanked by tugs, her white superstructure shining in the morning sun. His heart almost stopped to see her and behind her the jeweled towers, Manhattan in a splendor of glass and spires. He could see people on the decks of the *Queen,* a man in a blue blazer with white trousers, a woman beside him wearing a hat, her mink shining darkly. She raised one hand and held her hat against the wind.

For him it was a bitter sight. The corner of life he had entered was a place of adventure in the deepest sense of the word, where every step was a step into the unknown, where all of his human intelligence and his animal instinct would be required to see him along the way.

His muzzle raised itself to the blue sky and he made a long, high tone he found quite fine. He did it again, this time adding a tremble at the end by relaxing his throat. Again he did it, throwing all of his feelings into the note, his loneliness, his despair, his disgust. These were the feelings that he put into it, but something very different came out. He heard in his howl the voice of a deeper freedom than he had ever imagined, and the sky seemed more blue, and the smells of autumn more poignant, and the booming of the liner more grand. He stopped, excited, his tail waving. The wild was in him, the very wild, the unchained, the innocent, the terrible wild. He knew it from the farthest reach of his human heart, it was the old, old truth come forth in him, resurrection, Eucharist, a new world being born.

He realized with the force of cold water on morning skin that he was feeling a primitive emotion that was essentially and totally human. The ancient human wildness had reemerged in him, cohabitant with the wildness of the wolf.

To have been human at the beginning of the species must have been like this. His first impulse was to run and tell people, to tell anybody he could find, that the wild is waiting for us.

Obeying both sense and instinct, he trotted off up the road, seeking a way to the top of the palisade. Somewhere out there across the human land lay the forest, constricted perhaps, but still the forest. He wanted to race this body against the closure of the suburbs, to seek the quick eye and the savage tooth. As it mingled with his own blood the blood of the rat taught him the morality of the carnivore. Every act is a poem, sniffing the scent-touched leaf, disemboweling the faun.

He was filled with so much energy that it seemed almost like magic. The rat had been just the good food his body had wanted. His instincts had been right. His tail high, his head thrust smartly forward, he moved up and up, making his way among the stones. It was easy to keep to the path: all he had to do was follow the scent of men and fish. This was where they came down, this collection of crevices and rough-hewn stones. Here was a Welch's grape drink bottle, there a Trident gum wrapper. And over it all was the smell of fish and the smell of men, many men, some young and sharp and fresh, others old and covered in sodden wool.

When he reached the top of the palisade, he found himself in a park he hadn't even known existed, a dramatic park overlooking the Statue of Liberty and the harbor. People stood at the edge of the balustrade just above him, some of them leaning into ten-cent binoculars and looking at the *Queen,* which had reached the center of the harbor and was just dispensing with its tugs. Farther east a Staten Island Ferry left its slip. It was rush hour, and a traffic helicopter sped up the Hudson, a green and white bug spewing noise. He looked over this great vista and picked out his old neighborhood. He couldn't see their building, but he could just see the top of the structure that hid it.

He blinked his eyes. His vision was not as good as he would have liked. The colors were muted, the details obscure. But when he cocked his ears, he heard a wonder of sounds. The world's noise was no longer an aural fog. Rather he now heard all the detail of it, the pulsing deep in the *Queen's* engines, the excited voices of the people on her decks, someone hammering in the scaffolding on the Statue of Liberty, somebody else scraping, the engines of the ferry and the splashing of her thick bow, the suspiration of wind around the towers of the World Trade Center, the click of a sea gull's wings, and the hiss of fish rushing in the harbor.

He was a generous man, and at that moment his heart burst with one wish, that all human beings everywhere could just for one instant experience the old world in this new way. He had not known it was like this, had never dreamed what a difference really powerful senses could make. Human eyes were strong, but not so strong as wolf ears, nor nearly so discriminating as a wolf's nose.

A smell startled him, the familiar odor of human fear. When he realized where it was coming from, his heart almost stopped. One of the ten-cent binoculars was pointing directly at him. Two froglike eyes swam in the dark lenses. For an instant he captured them with his own eyes.

He saw deep into them, into the empty soul behind them. He could push, he could twist, he could *alter!*

He could make her into a wolf with his eyes!

But the pupils dilated and then drew back. He saw a pale mask of a face peer past the shiny aluminum housing of the binoculars. The face was rapt, closed, the lips tight, the eyebrows knitted. Bob was in too awkward a position to cringe, to cower to this young mask of a woman in her vaguely red sweater and wind-rushing skirt. If only he could make people see him as the inoffensive being he was.

Behind him was the tumbling palisade. He dared not go down, because he knew there was no escape down there. Unless he was willing to try another swim, that was nothing but a trap. Too bad he couldn't fly.

The young woman had darted away from her binoculars without uttering a word. He struggled up the final thirty yards and scrambled over the balustrade. Here was a cobbled esplanade backed by a road, and beyond it a stand of trees. There were perhaps a dozen people on the esplanade, some of them sitting on benches, others strolling, others at the binoculars. Simultaneous with his appearance, there came a cry across the quiet scene. The young woman shouted in a clear, stern tone, her smooth hands cupped around her soft lips: "It's the wolf! The *wolf!*"

The whole scene froze. People stopped walking.
Those on the benches turned their heads. A man
rose up from behind a pair of binoculars and
began to hurry across the esplanade, his shoes
clicking in the silence.

There was nothing to do but race across the
pavement. He ran as fast as he could. This particular movement aggravated last night's thigh injury,
sending hooks of pain deep into his leg. But he was
still fast. He shot along close to the pavement, his
nose down, the cobblestones speeding past. It was
only a moment before he was in the trees and
racing between their thick-grown branches toward
the far end of the park.

Then he was through the park and finding
shelter in some reeds. A police car screamed past.

Ahead was the invincible barrier of the New
Jersey Turnpike, eight lanes of certain death. He
trotted along, trying to see a way across. But there
was no way across. The turnpike stretched for
miles. From his vantage point low to the ground
he could not see a single break in its featureless
expanse.

He had to cross, and at once. He'd never seen so
much traffic, never realized just how fast cars
could go, never understood the barrier of the road.
Not far away lay the stinking body of an opossum,
skinless, torn, its jaw gone. The school bus, his dog
screaming, the shotgun in the gentle afternoon.

There was hardly even a median here. He would
have to find a lull on this side and cross, then jump
the divider and huddle on the other side until
another lull. Only then could he manage the four
southbound lanes. He'd come dozens of times
along this route, dozens and dozens of times,
never thinking how totally devoted it was to

human needs, how indifferent to the needs of other creatures. Had they bothered to build a few low tunnels under it, the opossum need not be dead, nor the wolf trapped.

He stepped onto the shoulder of the road. Cars roared past. Then he encountered a terrible and unexpected phenomenon. One of them swerved onto the shoulder, aiming directly at him. He could see the driver hunched over his wheel, a young man with a green smile. Beside him another man had just raised his head and was beginning to laugh.

Bob leaped back, catching a blast of hot exhaust fumes and the angry wail of a horn.

They hated his freedom, or perhaps it was their own helplessness that made them do it. Crushed, oppressed, miserable men—killing something granted them power. That they could take life pushed back the fear that they themselves had lost their value.

A hole appeared in the traffic. He darted out into the road, one lane, two. Then he felt the pavement trembling like a hot pan. Bearing down on him was a huge thirty-two-wheeler, its grille a wall of steel. Its driver sat impassive over his wheel. Bob was transfixed by the face, the slow, steady chewing, the plug of tobacco bulging in the jaw, the aerodynamic sunglasses. Beside him a woman smoothed her hair with her hands, looking down, a smile on her face of almost ineffable purity, her lips slightly parted, the sunlight shining on her fresh skin. Then the truck was upon him. There was no escape. He crouched, pressing his body against the pavement as it screamed over him, blasting off down the road, its slipstream almost lifting him into the air. Behind it a Buick was coming up fast. Seeing him, the driver swerved away.

Bob wasn't hit, but he had lost the lane he had gained. Another space between cars, perhaps three seconds to a VW Sirocco. He dashed forward, his tail slapping against the car as it passed him. The impact sent a shock wave through his body that made him yelp. Then he was at the median, crouching flat along it as the traffic billowed by in both directions. He raised himself, leaning against the steel fence that separated the lanes, found purchase, and drew himself to the foot-wide space between the beams.

He was tempted to trust luck and just dash out into the traffic on the far side of the median. He felt trapped here, and the rushing of the cars confused his eyes. It was easy for him to observe details up close, or to follow a single, moving object against a still background, but this was just a blur.

Under these circumstances his nose and ears were useless. To function in the world of man requires a sharpness of eye most other land animals do not possess. This place was as dangerous as poison to a creature such as himself. Even his instincts fought him. Being trapped here was like being cornered. He wanted to lash out at the cars, to run wildly.

He fought himself, begging the wolf to listen to the man this time. Standing where he was, he could see another opening in the traffic, this one also in front of a big truck. They tended to be slower than cars. Ahead of them the road was often clear. Behind them, though, there would be a glut of traffic.

The wolf did not listen to him. He was just

tensing himself to jump when he popped off the median like a spring. It was too early. He landed in front of a van, which tried to miss him. Desperate, he rolled. The van passed as hot wind. Now he felt nothing. He was on his back against the concrete base of the median. There was no more than an inch between him and the tires of the cars. He couldn't even turn over without risking his paws being smashed.

He was a creature at war with himself. The instinctual part was not in touch with the intellectual. It seemed unaware even of the existence of reason. Out here in the middle of the turnpike, though, either reason was going to win or instinct was going to get him killed.

Thanks to instinct he was lying on his back, his tail curled over his stomach, his paws clenched against his body. He could no longer see the cars. Now he had to go by the vibrations of the road and the sound of the traffic. The trouble was that there was so much noise that his ears didn't work right. What would in a human ear have been an ebb and flow of sound as each vehicle passed was to his wolf ear a continuous roar.

Because there was no other way to deal with the situation, he finally did the only thing he could and rolled over. Cars were whipping by so close he could feel heat pulsing up from the road. He managed to get to his feet. Leaning against the barrier, he waited. The cars continued. Twice people swerved toward him, but they missed because they were afraid of scraping the barrier.

Then an ancient van came rattling along, much slower than the rest of the traffic. Its lights were on, it hung askew on its frame, and it was being driven by an old woman who looked as if she was dressed in handkerchiefs. She slammed on her brakes. He would have gone to her but he simply could not trust human beings. Probably she stopped out of kindness, but it might be out of fear, because she realized that he was the terrible wolf. Maybe there was a bounty on his head and she was fumbling for a tire iron. Unlikely, but he could not know. He ran in front of the stopped van and, using it as a barrier, managed to cross to another lane. Now he could see clearly, and his progress to the far side of the turnpike was smooth.

Before him was a sea of reeds interrupted far to the north by the tall bulk of the People's Gas and Electric power station, and to the south by the rusty hump of the Pulaski Skyway. He stepped into the marsh. At once he sank to his knees, but fortunately no further. He took a step, then another. Like an envelope closing, the world of the marsh embraced him. It might be in the middle of a brutal traffic pattern, it might be viciously polluted, but it was alive, and as long as it lived it spread its magic over all who entered it.

The roar of the highway was replaced by the click of insects and the busy fluttering of birds. Driving along, he'd always thought of this as an empty world, reeds, muck, that was it. He now found rich life pouring into his ears and nose.

The smell of the man's world dwindled fast. For the first time since he had entered this new life he did not smell a single human presence.

He sloshed along, thinking that he might soon scare up a rabbit or another rat. Given how the last rat had gone down, he no longer found this a particularly unpleasant notion, although he did hope to find a cleaner victim.

Soon he was moving through shallower water. Then he came to a bald place. The sun was high, the day warm for autumn, and it occurred to him that he was free to lie down. He curled up in the reeds, drawing his tail almost to his nose.

It was peaceful here, but he knew that these marshes did not extend very far. Beyond them were suburbs full of peril, then the Poconos and beyond them the Catskills. He would have to go far to the north before he found the forest that his wolf soul and wolf blood sought.

Lying still, he could hear the traffic's faint wail, a hungry ghost half a mile away. When he slept he dreamed that a helicopter was nosing about in the reeds, looking for him. Then his dream changed, and in it he was matching the turns of a rabbit, delighting in the prospect of a meal.

He awoke sometime past sunset. The western sky was deep orange, and the evening star hung on the edge of the horizon.

For a long moment he considered the young woman on the palisades. Had he *really* been able to turn her into a wolf? No, surely not.

But it had happened to him.

When as a young man he would lie on the ground in the deep country and look at the stars, he would think that their light must have been purified by its journey. So also souls are purified by journeys, and it was time for him to move on.

He set out to cross the marsh, moving toward the jeopardy of the lights, and the dark promise of the hills beyond.

CHAPTER SIXTEEN

IT MIGHT BE TWO O'CLOCK IN THE MORNING BUT HE WAS
a fool to be standing on a street corner in Morristown, New Jersey, peering at a newspaper through
the wire of a rack. He was aware of a car cruising
slowly up the street, but he was so fascinated and
horrified by his picture in the paper that he didn't
retreat. It was remarkable to see himself like this.
He really was a wolf, a perfect wolf. His mind had
conjured a more muscular, vaguely human shape
for him—a sort of man on all fours with the head
of a wolf. He wasn't like that. There was nothing
at all human about him.

Below the picture he could see the first few
words of the accompanying news story. "After
critically injuring one man, the animal escaped
across the Hudson . . ."

The words froze his blood. He stared, stupefied,
as his shadow defined itself beside him. Even the

gentle rumbling of the car's engine did not break his attention. He had injured somebody, hurt them bad. But who? Maybe the man he fell on in the alley. It had all happened so fast, he wasn't sure.

The poor man.

When Bob looked up, it was into a flaring explosion of brilliance. These eyes were wonderful in the dark, but he discovered that they did not work at all well under an assault like this. He was staring into a glaring, impenetrable curtain, behind which he could hear an engine idling, doors opening, and the shuttle of weapons from holsters to hands.

He shrank back, one ear cocked toward the clicking of the pistol.

A shot seemed to explode in his face. He reeled, twisted, scrabbled wildly to the middle of the street. Then there was another shot and the slap of wind against his head.

He ran for all he was worth. Up the street he raced, past an Italian restaurant with a full garbage bin waiting for dawn, past a hobby shop, a drugstore.

Then he stopped, panting. Behind him there were pattering footsteps. He crouched behind some trash cans. What was in them? They smelled like heaven. Then another police car swept past, its lights flashing. There was no siren, not in this suburb of high executives and broad, quiet lawns. Nixon had once lived around here.

Bob went on, trotting close to the storefronts, slinking across streets, taking advantage of every bit of foliage he could find. He left Morristown on a long, straight road. Every so often he would see a police cruiser and crouch down. The car would glide past, and he could hear the men inside.

"Man, I haven't had this much fun since deer season."

"Who gets the head, the guy that does the shooting or the mayor? That's my question."

Horrible!

As he neared Morris Plains Bob turned west and began to make his way through a more densely populated neighborhood.

Something happened that he hadn't taken into consideration, something very bad.

The houses around here were closer to the street, and the dogs inside were going mad. One, which had been asleep on a porch, came running up and went into a paroxysm of barking, leaping, and snapping. Its lips wrinkled back over its teeth as it crouched down, ready to attack. He watched its hackles, its muscles, waiting to absorb its charge. The creature went off like a shotgun, blasting into him with the full force of its body.

He let himself relax into the blow, dropped his chin to protect his throat from the fury of the jaws, then followed the dog down as it fell in a scrabbling heap at his feet. Once he would have merely wounded it, and sent it screaming away into the night, but he knew he could not afford the attention the screaming would attract. Sadly, he tore the dog's throat open. Its barking at once ceased, replaced by the sound of air whistling and bubbling in the wound. The creature bit wildly, running in the air as it did so. Bob jumped away from it, his heart beating hard, and then he heard a boy's voice call "Frito." The dog shook and gibbered. The voice repeated, "Frito?" Bob slipped into the shadows, miserable but safe.

Scared now, the voice repeated, "Frito!" Bob

could see a profile in a front door, a boy of about eleven dressed in pajamas and floppy sandals. "C'mon, Frito, come home." Sadness now, the voice cracking.

An engine muttered beyond the trees at the end of the block, and a squad car wheeled around the corner, its lights searching through the thin fog of the night. Concealed in a bush, Bob stood very still.

The boy waved and the car stopped. "There was a dogfight," the child said. "My dog is hurt!"

The two policemen got out of the car, their guns drawn. The pistols smelled cold. This was not the same pair that had shot at him in Morristown. A flashlight worked the ground, coming to rest on the body of the dog.

"Frito!" The padding of small feet across grass, the sobs. There is no love like this, Bob thought bitterly, no love so noble or so true as that between a dog and a child. He hated himself. His only excuse was that life was sweet also to the wolf.

The flashlights began to poke about in the bushes. One of them swept the bush he was in, paused, came back. "Go inside, son."

"My dog—"

"It's the wolf. Go inside." The boy needed no more prompting. Bob heard the slippers pattering frantically on the dew-wet grass.

Inside the house the child's voice was raised: "Mom, Dad, it's the wolf! It's here, it killed Frito!" Lights came on, joining other lights from houses where dogs were still barking. Bob had already understood that his end might come anywhere, down any innocent street, anytime. It could come down this street, now. He wanted to be reconciled to this but he could not accept it.

There was in him an almost overwhelmingly urgent need, one he had never felt in such a raw, terrible form. Bob the man might be tired and sad and ready to give up. But the wolf didn't feel that way at all. The wolf wanted to live, and he wanted it desperately. Bob was still his gentle old self. But the wolf had tasted blood; the wolf would kill to live.

The two cops had already radioed for help and lights were now coming on in virtually every house in the neighborhood. These wealthy families would probably be well armed. The police, with their notoriously inaccurate .38 Specials, might miss a quick target in the dark, but the hunting rifles and target pistols that were about to be brought into play would not miss.

"Work around to the other side of the hedge," one of the cops said softly. "It's just standing in there. Maybe it doesn't realize we mean it harm."

As soon as the second cop came around the bush Bob was going to be trapped. Without another thought he jumped up and took off down the street, causing a massive upsurge in barking. Doors slammed, people shouted. A shotgun roared, its pellets whining over Bob's head.

"I hit it," a man shouted, "I got the wolf!"

The tip of Bob's tail stung, but the old wound in his thigh was far more painful. His tail might have been grazed by a pellet, but as injuries went it was minor.

He dodged down a driveway and jumped a Cyclone fence into a yard inhabited by two cats, which began shooting around like fur-covered hockey pucks, their tails fat with terror, their eyes blazing. Then he was through the yard and into the alley, trotting fast, but not running. This could be a long chase and he had to preserve his strength.

As he moved along he realized that he was not nearly as scared as he had been before. The wolf and the man had come together again. He had begun to be very interested in the process of combining his reason with his instinct, which was the key to preserving this unique life.

He smelled not only woods around here but flowing water. There was a stream where he could drink, maybe even enough woods to harbor a meal.

He trotted to the end of the street, throwing himself under a car as the police and a crowd of enraged citizens came puffing around the corner. Powerful lights plunged about, seeking the tawny spot of fur among the fallen leaves and the naked bushes. A little earlier in the season and it would have been a lot easier for him to hide. They passed him and he started off again, heading for the smell of the water.

Soon he came to the stream. There was nothing behind him to suggest danger—no smell of dogs, no off-the-road vehicles. He lowered his muzzle and began to lap the sweet, iron-tasting water.

A shot split a limb a few feet to his right. Far off in the street he saw a man with a rifle and some bulky equipment: a starlight scope.

Bob hastened up the middle of the brook, trying to run in the water as much as possible. He was worried about dogs being put to his scent. As a boy he had seen the Lone Ranger ride down streams to throw them off, a trick taught to him by Tonto.

He left the stream bed for a jumble of rocks. Another shot echoed in the woods, but farther away. Starlight scopes or not, people couldn't follow Bob into this tangle. Beyond the rocks the land sloped steeply upward. He was soon on a ridge, looking down over the wood he had just crossed. His ears and nose told him that he was alone. Without trained dogs, they were helpless.

Bob loped now, following an abandoned deer path. There wasn't a fresh scent along its whole length, not even droppings. The deer had died out on this ridge. As he moved he glimpsed a dark hulk off to the right. Then, through the trees, he saw that it was a house. This one was huge, a great, Gothic monster with a dozen chimneys and hundreds of blank leaded-glass windows.

He altered his course toward thicker woods. He wasn't precisely sure where he was anymore, just that he was moving in a northwesterly direction, and his nose told him that the human population around him was growing less dense.

He trotted steadily, easily, putting as much distance as he could between himself and the human world.

As the western sky began to grow light he lengthened his stride, trying for a final burst of speed before he stopped and hid until dark. He was also hungry.

Sniffing as he moved, he sought the rotted-grass odor of a rabbit or the garbage smell of rats. The woods seemed empty, though. He would have considered bugs, but it was past their season.

Was this to be his new life, scuttling through the woods searching for food or seeking escape? He wanted to lie back on a grassy hillside and think. He wanted to have a discussion with his son, or go out with his wife and talk and sip espresso.

He was the running wolf, the wolf of desolation, lonely wolf. To man he was now the gray cloud in the morning, the shadow worrying the bones. Overhead he heard a helicopter popping. He ignored it. They weren't going to spot him from that thing, but its presence meant they were really hungry to catch him.

The helicopter circled back, louder this time. As a precaution he stopped in a dense copse of hemlock. As far as he knew there was no way for them to detect him. Unless—what about infared, or a starlight scope?

A bullet whizzed down through the trees, splitting a fat branch not three inches from his face.

There was no time to hesitate: he started running.

He tried to remember the terrain he had crossed. Were there any gullies that went down to the stream? No, he thought not. As a matter of fact, he didn't remember any place he might hide from starlight scopes or infared, unless it was behind the waterfall he had seen on the creek. The waterfall was miles back, though. Slow as they were, even his human pursuers would have reached there by now.

He did the only thing that he could do, the thing any ordinary animal would do: he ran blindly, hoping for the best. Maybe he would reach deeper woodland, maybe he would be shot. All he could do was hope that his nasal and aural technology would somehow outwit man's sight technology.

The helicopter kept with him, fluttering like a massive insect in the glowing sky. From time to time a bullet smacked through the trees.

When he mounted a rise, he knew exactly why he was alone here. The wind was blowing from behind him or he would have known much sooner. Before him there was a pit full of rusty steel drums, some of them leaking stinking orange goop, others intact, still others surrounded by scums of green jelly. This close he could smell them despite the direction of the wind, and the odors were awful: powerful acidic scents as if of Clorox mixed with gasoline, airplane glue, and roach spray. A rivulet trickled sadly along, scummed with silver oil, making its way through tired, brown grass. There was a smell of death: two buzzard corpses lay twisted beside the fulminating ruins of a 'coon that had apparently dropped dead while drinking the water. Then the buzzards had died while eating the 'coon. Nature is designed to work in cycles. It dies in cycles, too.

The dump seemed to have no borders. Bob had no time to get around it. He would have to cross it, out in the open, the helicopter on his back. There was no reason to wait; caution would gain him nothing. He moved into the clear space. The land was just being touched by the gray light that precedes the dawn. The eastern sky was now a faint green, Venus low on the horizon. Grackles and jays were beginning to scream in the woods; the feathers of a dove lay in a puddle that Bob carefully avoided.

Inside the dump the smell was shocking. The ground was spongy and his paw prints quickly filled with scum. The odor reached deep into his muzzle and clung there. He was sure that it was in itself poisonous, it was so strong.

Then the helicopter came in low, raising a mist from the standing pools. Bob ran hard. He was more afraid of getting exposed to that mist than he was of the bullets that now came steadily from the copter. In his mind's eye there was an image, maybe from a *National Geographic* special or a

Sierra Club program, of a wolf seen from above clambering through a snowbank, being chased down by a helicopter. And then the wolf's head explodes and it tumbles back down the bank, its tail gyrating like a broken propeller.

Behind him there was a terrific thud. For a mad hopeful instant he thought the helicopter had crashed, then he felt heat on his back. One of the bullets had caused a drum of chemicals to explode. So much for their infared scope now. That blaze would white it out. Unfortunately, dawn was on their side. Shimmering lines of light were spreading from behind low eastern clouds. Bob could hear birds rising from the trees on the distant horizon, and could smell even above the stink of this dismal place a sterling, rich burst of autumn breeze, the beautiful dry odor of the hanging leaves, the sweetness being exhaled from the ground.

Another drum of chemical exploded. Intense heat made Bob skitter forward, then gallop. The whole place started thudding and popping. The fire was furious and spreading wildly. The helicopter rose into a billowing mushroom of orange-black smoke and disappeared off toward Morristown. Bob wondered if the citizens of that worthy community even knew that this mess was here, leaching slowly into their water supply. Well, they were certainly going to find out.

He managed to stay ahead of the flames by running himself hard, finally reaching a high Cyclone fence. He ran along beside it, thinking for an awful moment that it was going to trap him. But it hadn't been maintained; he managed to go through a hole as big as a Lincoln.

He rushed back into the scrubby woods. The

area had been logged within the past ten years, and the hemlocks and white pine were still saplings, and stunted by the near presence of the toxic dump. He kept moving, always choosing the uplift of the land, seeking less populated regions.

He was tired and hungry and wanted badly to hunt. As if on command, his nose and ears promptly became hypersensitive. All he could smell, though, was birds. They seemed to be more able than ground dwellers to survive near the chemicals, probably because they spent relatively little time exposed to the poison. He'd seen one of the coydogs in Central Park catch a bat, but he didn't think his own paws were adapted to such extraordinary skills. Nature had created coydogs in the past fifty years or so, breeding the new species from the best of the dogs and the coyotes. The coydogs belonged to the future. They were smart enough and supple enough and adaptable enough to live right in the middle of the human world. People had them in their backyards and never knew it. In the small hours the Central Park packs probably hunted midtown from the Hudson to the East River, and nobody saw them, not ever.

Bob stopped long enough to lift one of his paws and examine it. It wasn't going to grasp anything. The toes were long, but not as long as those of the coydog. And he could not move them independently. He would eat no birds.

There was a flutter and a sudden pang along his spine. Snapping, he twisted around just in time to see a jay flying off with a tuft of his fur in its beak. As a child he'd disliked them because they got to his feeders and scared away the songbirds.

To rid himself of the jay Bob moved into a

thicker copse. Screaming, the bird flew off.

Then Bob became aware of a pungent and absolutely magnificent aroma. As it filled his muzzle he trembled with delight. He was hungry, very hungry, and he smelled bacon.

The odor was warm, too, meaning that the bacon was being fried nearby. He followed the scent up a low rise and through a thick copse of saplings. It wasn't long before he saw a ruined cabin with smoke coming from the chimney. The roof was half-off, the walls were peeling tarpaper, there was no glass in the windows. Bob approached warily. He could hear the bacon sizzling, smell the two people clearly. Bob was a reticent man, but he could not ignore the fact that he smelled the odors of human sex. There was also an odd smell of fresh earth. He stole forward on his belly, trying to ignore what he was smelling, all except the bacon.

Then he heard a female voice, softly pleading. "Please, please . . ." He pricked his ears. Something told him that this was not right. Close by the cabin wall, he could hear deep male breathing, very soft female breathing. It was almost the gasping of a child. Bob raised himself up on the window ledge and looked in. There was a man of perhaps forty frying bacon and eggs in a skillet on the hearth. Behind him there were some dirty, crumpled sheets on the dirt floor of the cabin, sheets that stank of sweat and the uses of night. Bob was horrified to see, hunched into a corner, a terrified and naked girl of perhaps thirteen. Her arms clutched her beginning breasts, her legs were twisted around one another.

Around the front of the cabin Bob saw a hole, a

shovel lying beside it. On the man's hip was a .45 automatic. But for his pistol belt, he was as naked as the child.

Bob had never seen such a depraved situation. The poor girl was in awful trouble. This vicious monster had obviously raped her repeatedly. Bob was no longer one to waste time about these things. He leaped at once through the window and knocked the man on his side.

"Aw! Holy shit!"

He grabbed at his gun but Bob bit his wrist hard. The man yelped, twisting and turning until Bob felt his own teeth scraping bone. Then there was a crunch and the man shrieked. The girl sat absolutely still, staring. With a snarl the man came at Bob, swinging his closed left fist. The blow connected with Bob's nose, causing him a fierce blast of pain. He screamed, thrusting his head up, snapping, trying to reach the man's throat. Instead he connected with his chest, took a gouge out of his skin and fell back. The man also fell, but in the opposite direction, landing with a high scream on his dangling right arm. He kicked at Bob, who was trying to straddle him.

The girl, who had seemed almost catatonic, now rose from her corner and moved to the hearth. The man grabbed Bob's muzzle with his good hand while he forced his bad one to fumble for his pistol. It was no good; Bob was heavy and took full advantage of his weight. Again and again he hurled himself against the struggling man.

At the hearth, the girl took the skillet in her hands. Bob felt a blow from the man to the side of his head. Another one, much harder, landed on his skull. The man was built like a tank. Despite the pain of a broken wrist, he was becoming a wheezing, furious juggernaut. He crashed into Bob's side, throwing him to the ground. A spike of pure fury made Bob roar. He dug his teeth into the man's floppy belly, feeling the little pops as his incisors broke through the flesh to the fat within.

There came a clang. The man sank down. He and Bob were both covered with sizzling bacon and eggs. The girl stood over the inert form of her captor, the skillet held in both hands. Then she dropped it and, grabbing a dirty sheet, took off into the woods, looking like a ghost as she swept off among the trees.

Bob ate the bacon, which was only a little burned, and lapped up the eggs.

CHAPTER SEVENTEEN

WITH A DETERMINED JAB CINDY STUCK ANOTHER RED pin in the map, at the location of the smoldering dump site northwest of Morristown. "I'm convinced," she said to the others. "It was him."

Monica still disagreed. "The police say it started during a high-speed chase. They don't mention Bob."

"Of course not, he got away. But look at the media. 'Killer Wolf Invades Silk Stocking Suburb.' We know Bob's in the area. Who else would they have been chasing out in the woods? The poor guy is heading directly away from civilization. He's trying to escape, he must be so scared!"

Joe Running Fox stared at the map. "My guess is he'll go back into the Poconos, up through the Shawangunks to the Catskills, then on into the Appalachians and Canada."

Monica stared at Cindy, a slight smile flickering

across her face. "I'll bet he's going to the hunt club!"

"To meet me," Cindy said. She even thought it might be true. Even Bob had the occasional flash of practical insight.

Joe Running Fox put his hand on Kevin's shoulder. "What about you, Kevin?" Her son was comfortable with this man. Joe Running Fox had told Kevin about the Way of Silence and won his heart. The two of them had spent hours together sitting face-to-face, totally silent, their eyes locked. Last night Kevin had told Cindy that it was the most intimate experience he had ever had. "We can all see each other's souls any time we want. We just have to look at each other. Not for a minute or two, but the way the Fox does it, for a couple of hours. Then you see the soul."

She had managed to share her eyes with Kevin for about three minutes. Her love for her vulnerable, inquisitive little boy had burned high, but there had come a point when what she saw, and what of her she felt was being seen, was simply too much to bear. You see the whole of a person's time in their eyes, from the first shattering infant moment to the darkening swells of age.

Over the past few days Kevin had undergone almost a complete change. Although children shine very bright, it doesn't take much to dull their fragile spark. More even than the loss of his father, Cindy thought, her son was suffering from a loss of his own faith in reality. His Kafka shelf was now abandoned. Instead he read the Bible. She found him absorbed in Ecclesiastes and Job, and the Book of Revelation. He had also bought a book about multiple personalities, and another about the Spanish Inquisition. He sat sometimes for hours staring at this last book, looking at a facsimile of a poster announcing an auto-da-fé in which thirty people were to be burned at the stake.

His identification with the persecuted had always been deep, arising, she liked to feel, from the powerful ideals that animated her own and Bob's thinking. Yesterday she had discovered him staring into the eyes of a picture of a wolf. "Can you share anything with a photograph?" she had asked.

"No, but I think I know how the wolves captured Dad. They did it at the zoo. Remember that old wolf staring at him? That was when they captured him."

"It's that dangerous to look into another's eyes?"

"'A child goes forth each morning, and whatever that child first sees, that thing he becomes.'"

How many times Bob had read Whitman's poem to Kevin. "Whitman was referring to a change of spirit, not a physical change."

"How do we know that? Maybe he was talking about a real change. I think Kafka was talking about a real change in the *Metamorphosis.*"

"Whitman was writing about a child. Dad isn't a child."

"You never accepted that a child is exactly what he was. In some ways I'm more mature than Dad."

Fox came over. He folded his arms, looked down at Kevin, who had tossed aside the wolf photo and was examining a woodcut of a man having his feet burned off in an Inquisitional dungeon. "Few people are more mature than your father," Fox said. "Maybe now, nobody."

"You never knew him," Kevin replied in an

intensely charged voice. "He could get excited about the same flower every time he saw it, day after day, until it died. Then he forgot it so completely it might as well never have existed. Dad had no mature emotions."

Cindy could not agree. "He loved us."

"We frightened him, I think. Life was too much for him. And we drove him. We created the conditions that enabled this to happen."

It was grief that was behind these hard words. His brilliance was working against him now. Cindy sensed that what he really wanted was to cuddle up in her lap and cry.

Fox might have known it, too. He touched the boy's cheek. One thing the man knew was when not to talk.

In the silence Monica drew a line on the map, connecting the red pins. Beyond the last pin she continued the line to the hunt club deep in the Catskills. "Maybe we ought to just go up there and wait for him."

"Unwise," Fox said. "We're better off tracking him. If he doesn't go to the club, we won't miss him that way."

"You can do this?"

Fox nodded. "I can track a wolf, if I can find the trail."

"And you're sure you can? I'd hate to be traipsing around Ulster County while Bob sits at the hunt club. He might not wait long. It's bird season and we got a huge stocking assessment, so the place is full of grouse and therefore hunters."

Cindy interrupted. "We'll split up. You go to the club, Monica. The three of us will do the tracking."

"I want to do it alone. With the boy."

Cindy wouldn't have that, not for a moment. She wasn't going to agonize the days away at the club. The miseries of camping and hiking would keep her preoccupied. Anything was better than the ordeal of waiting. "I'm going."

"Women have other power. Not this."

"Oh, nonsense. I won't hear that. He's my husband."

"I won't track with a woman."

She almost couldn't believe what she heard. The man was worse than a chauvinist, he was an unreformed Neanderthal. "You have no conscience," she said. She'd always found personal discrimination surprising and confusing. His eyes were brown and flint hard. She pleaded on her own behalf. "He'll respond to me. If he knows I'm there, he'll be much more likely to stop running."

"His son will be there. A man will do anything for his son."

That was it. He'd have to learn here and now who was in control of things. "If you imagine for one moment that my boy is going without me, you're very much mistaken, Mr. Fox. You're not lord and master of this house, no man is, not even my poor husband, God help him. I intend to go out there into that wilderness and find him."

"A northeastern second-growth forest is hardly wilderness, ma'am. I want my medicine to work, and with a woman around it might not. It's no reflection on you. It's just the damned Indian culture. Woman has her role and man has his, and the two are different. Equal but different. I know it's another stupid Indian idea, but I can't help respecting it, dummy that I am."

"The hell it's an Indian idea. I don't hold with all this idealization of the old Indian culture. You say you've got Mohawk blood? The Mohawks considered their women slaves."

"They loved them. It was all stupidity, though—"

"Shut up, and can that false self-deprecation. It makes you seem like a bigger ass than you probably are. Now, let's quit bickering and lay our plans. The more we talk, the farther away Bob gets."

Fox didn't say much more after that. It took only a few minutes to plan their journey. Largely it was a matter of making sure that the available hiking boots passed Fox's meticulous inspection. "I thought Indians used moccasins," Kevin said. "I don't mean to be condescending, but it is what I thought."

"Boots. Indians used moccasins because they couldn't afford anything better, not to mention the fact that the dopes never invented the shoe on their own. Indian high-tech consisted of beaded wampum. Life was diseased, dirty, violent, and short."

Cindy wondered if the man was trying to be insufferable, or if he was so involved in his posturing that he really couldn't see himself at all. She needed him to track Bob, and she wasn't going to let anything stand in the way of that.

"We have no camping equipment," she said, "beyond the boots and Kevin's sleeping bag."

"I need a blanket. What do you need?"

It was a dare, she supposed. At best she found it boring. "I need everything I can get. A tent, preferably air-conditioned and equipped with a full kitchen and all necessary supplies. Why?"

"Just asking. So I'll bring two blankets."

"Waterproof."

He nodded. "Let's go."

"You're kidding. Right now, at eight o'clock at night?"

"We can stay in a motel tonight. In the morning we start. Early, four A.M."

She found herself eating a fatty breakfast in an all-nighter on Route 202 at 3:30 in the morning. Her head was pounding. Poor Kevin looked like a corpse, he was pale and very slow. Cindy made sure he drank a couple of cups of tea. Fox advised a big breakfast, and she obliged with scrambled eggs, toast, sausage, 40% Bran Flakes, coffee, and a slice of melon that tasted like dishwasher detergent. "You can eat," Fox said. "That's good. Once we're tracking, there won't be much time for food, and game's scarce these days."

"We'll hunt?"

"I make traps. You'll see. They work good."

The detailed area map showed a road ringing the dump site. It was a lozenge-shaped two hundred acres of smoldering, noxious ruins when they arrived, their headlights dispelling the faint glow that persisted from the fire. The car moved slowly along, Fox peering out into the dark as he drove.

"Somewhere on this side, I figure." He drove for a time in silence. "I hope your husband had a good sense of direction. He's not a fool, is he? He wouldn't go south?"

Bob was not a fool in the sense that Fox meant. She did not think he would go south. He knew the direction of the wilderness in New York. His love of it had taken him deep into the Catskills and the Adirondacks. If only he could get away from civilization, he might well have a chance to survive. "He knows the country."

"Can Dad kill things with his mouth, like

rabbits? And I wonder if he can eat a raw rabbit?"

They were upsetting questions. "I have no idea how your father is coping. I can't even begin to imagine it."

"They acquire the secrets of the beast," Fox said. "That's why men try shifting in the first place. They want to learn the secrets of the animals. Such secrets used to be very valuable."

"The cave paintings at Lascaux," Kevin said. "They don't show any people because the people are the animals."

"It's an ancient way. In all my life, in all the legends I've known, I've heard of only one other case where it really happened. Where somebody really, *really* changed into an animal. And that was many generations ago." He stopped the car. His hands went toward Cindy, took hers. "I want to thank you. You've given me a chance to meet this man in person, the man who was seduced by the wolves."

The three of them got out of the car. Cindy could see absolutely no trace of him in the dark blotchs of undergrowth that hugged the ground this side of the woods.

"There." Fox gestured toward a place that seemed no different from the others. "He went in right there. He was moving fast, you can see that by the number of leaves that are broken." Bending low, he hurried over to the spot. "He's favoring his right rear leg, toes digging in left to right. That says he's got a thigh wound. The way the left foot is hitting, I'd say the bone's not broken. It's a flesh wound, probably infected. Hurting him, but not too dangerous. He's moving very strongly for an animal that's lost weight."

"Now, how can you possibly tell that?"

"The paper said he was weighed in at one-sixty. These tracks in this dirt—he weighs more like one-fifty." He stood staring at the ground, thinking.

"Where is he?" Kevin asked.

"Your father is well away from here. He passed this spot at least twenty-four hours ago."

"The dump fire started at five-fifteen yesterday morning. That's when he was here."

"Well, nearly twenty-four hours then. With his thigh and general weakness, he's covering about twenty miles a day. That's if he hunts on the run. If he can."

"What do you mean, if he can?"

"If he has the skill. You're hunting like he's got to hunt, running the animal down, it doesn't go in a straight line. It goes in circles, backtracks, anything to get away from you. Once he's killed and eaten something, then he has to reorient himself and cover lost ground. So we can assume he's getting maybe fifteen miles a day out of it. Moving sunup to sundown, maybe a couple of hours at night. My guess is he's about thirty-five miles from here."

She didn't want to ask the next question; she felt Bob slipping through her fingers. But she did ask, she had to ask. "What are our chances of catching up with him?"

"We can cover maybe fifteen miles a day. Twenty, if we work like mad. We don't have the four legs, that's our trouble. And we're tall. The undergrowth will slow us down."

Maybe they should all go to the hunting camp and just hope for the best. Bob would know the camp was crowded, though. There was a good chance that he would bypass it. He was hurt, she knew he was scared. If it was her, she'd be desperately unhappy and in a state of extreme panic. She would not make rational or courageous decisions. Her tendency would be to get to the most isolated place she could find, and hide there until she died.

It had occurred to her that he might commit suicide. She could only hope that the thought wouldn't cross his mind. Sometimes, though, he had fallen into deep, deep troughs. His despair was pitiful, at once bitter and full of sardonic humor. When he got an especially good poem back from one of the magazines, or endured some epic business humiliation, he could drop into one of those states.

She kicked a stone.

"There might always be another sighting," Fox said. "You never know."

Wave after wave of sorrow broke in Cindy's soul. She hunched her shoulders, fighting back the tears until her throat felt like it was being wrapped in leather thongs. Then she burst out with huge, gasping sobs. Kevin clapped his hands over his ears. Fox stood impassive. When she stopped, he merely headed into the woods. They moved along easily at first, passing between tall trees and through stands of mountain laurel.

Soon Cindy became uneasy. They seemed to be going in an almost perfectly straight line. This was fine, but it didn't strike her as the sort of thing Bob would do. He'd get confused, double back, fall down gullies, end up at the edge of cliffs. But she had to trust Fox; he was the expert.

Even so—Bob in the woods? He'd practically gotten himself killed trying to track wolves in Minnesota back in the early seventies. And then

there was that camping trip where he'd forgotten
the matches and failed to pack the tent in the tent
pack and brought the wrong hiker's map and
missed the bus, and then laid their campsite at the
edge of a pretty waterfall which had become a
raging torrent during the ten-hour downpour that
had taken place that night.

And the poor guy was out here with no hands,
trying to keep himself alive with half the population of the northeast cheerfully hunting him
down.

Lost in her thoughts, she wasn't aware that she
had fallen behind until Fox was standing in front
of her. "Look, Mrs. Duke, we can't keep breaking
stride for you. Either you keep up or you don't
keep up. The car's half an hour behind us. You can
go back if you want to."

"No. I'll keep up."

He started again, twisting and turning through
the trees like some sort of ghost, followed by
Kevin, who was almost as swift. "I've been thinking," Kevin said as he moved, "we need to hit a
town and buy a Walkman. One of us has to be
listening to the news at all times in case there's
another sighting reported."

Fox grunted. Twigs were scraping Cindy's head,
she had leaf dust in her right eye, she'd practically
shattered her knee slipping on a toadstool the size
of a pancake, and now she was tumbling head over
heels down a ravine she hadn't even noticed.

She did a complete somersault. When she saw
the top of the forest rush past, leaves against a pale
pink streak of dawn, she forced herself to relax
totally. Then she hit with a thud. There was a
jagged rock right under the center of her back, but
she had managed to loosen up enough so that she

flopped over it rather than breaking in two. "I'm good, no problem," she shouted. Then she was on her feet and up the ravine and running to catch them.

As he talked Kevin hopped from stone to mossy stone in a little brook.

"Listen," Fox said. "I think the water has a message for us. He passed this way. The brook remembers him."

Cindy could not keep her mind on the water. She was more interested in her own ragged breathing and the excruciating pain at the back of her left heel, where her boot seemed to be grinding down to bone. She flopped back in a bed of leaves and mushrooms, and stared up through amazingly tall trees. It was now full dawn, and the orange and red leaves were clearly etched against a blue sky.

When she listened, the brook did indeed speak to her. She sort of understood what Fox meant, that the water had a message. It wasn't a direction, a piece of information, it was another kind of message, vibrant with obscurely useful meaning.

"I tell you one thing," Fox said, "the way this water smells, there's a town upstream."

"I don't smell anything. The water's fresh."

"You don't know the meaning of fresh water, then," Fox replied. "I've drunk perfectly fresh water. Bathed in it. The more filth you can smell, the farther along you are on the road home. That's the message of this water."

"What he's saying, Mama, is that we need to get to the town."

Nonlogical thinking was what they called it. Or was it nonsequential thinking? Cindy sighed and got up. "I hope there really is a town."

"Hell, just through those trees is a gigantic

condo development. We're in New Jersey, ma'am, one of the most densely populated states in the nation. The only reason we don't see it is that Bob avoided it. This forest is a thin strip of green between armies of housing developments, believe me."

Half an hour later they were walking along a road. A mini-mart stood next to an Exxon. Rite-Aid Drugs and Wendy's had occupied the center of town, hard on to the lawn and garden center and the drive-in bank. Kevin picked out an inexpensive Walkman at Rite-Aid and Cindy was elected to listen with one earphone.

When they started back to the woods to reconnect with Bob's trail, she found herself walking to the drone of WINS, all news all the time. The Brooklyn–Queens Expressway was jammed from Grand Central Parkway to the Gowanus Canal, due to a disabled tractor-trailer. It was now 9:14. In sports, the Oakland A's had beaten the Orioles.

Torture, torture, torture. Slog through the woods while listening to this drivel. She was bored. She wanted a cup of tea and a good book. She wanted to lie down. She wanted to cuddle Bob up tight and make love to him.

"In other news, the escaped wolf has been sighted along the New York–New Jersey border. Waldemar town Supervisor Richland Frye and his daughter were camping at Braemar Park Site 12 when the wolf leaped in the window of their shelter, menaced Mr. Frye, and knocked him unconscious. Young Miss Frye wrapped herself in a sheet and ran the four miles to Waldemar to give the warning. Mr. Frye was treated and released at North Orange Hospital in Waldemar."

Cindy was sitting on the ground by the time the story was over, her hands pressed against her ears in order to drown out her son's frantic questions.

"It's him, there's been another sighting!" She repeated the story.

"Waldemar. My God, your husband's doing damn good. He must be covering more like twenty-five, thirty miles in a day."

To make a long story miserably short, it now became necessary to hike all the way back to the car in order to drive to Waldemar.

Lying in the backseat, inert with exhaustion, Cindy vowed that she was going to take control of this expedition. Fox wanted to do what he was best at, which was track. But good strategy and good detective work were more important. If only she could anticipate Bob's own thinking, she felt sure she could put herself in his way instead of trying to chase him, which was obviously hopeless.

Waldemar. He was now traveling due north. The question was, what did he know about the region he was entering? He would be bound to use that knowledge to his own advantage.

Her mind returned to the early seventies, to those ridiculous camping trips.

She knew. Just like that, she knew where to intercept him. Sitting up, she told Fox. When Bob got there—and he would get there—she would be waiting.

CHAPTER EIGHTEEN

A HUGE WILLOW TREE GAVE BOB HIS NIGHT. NEVER, not even as a child, had he felt as small and vulnerable as he did now, sheltering in the tree's silent, protective fronds.

He dreamed of deep woods, the trees stalwart and concealing friends, and in his vague, shadowy dreams he ran after slow, fat rabbits. Then he dreamed of an enormous old cruise ship, and he was his old self. He and Cindy were taking a cruise through cold, islandless seas in the dead of winter aboard this ramshackle vessel. Like the other passengers she was dressed to the elegant beckoning of the past; she wore white flowing silk, the whispering evening clothes of the turn of the century. She smelled like wysteria, and indeed her jewels were their color, cunning glass earrings and necklace believed by the awed, hissing passengers to be priceless.

Bob was restless on the ship, frightened of its rough progress and the deep clanking of its engines. In his exploration of the dun ballroom, the weathered dining room with its frayed chairs and chipped Spode, the algal swimming pool, the cold, musty cabins with their sagging beds and their hair-choked bathtub drains, he became less and less sure of the vessel.

Then the others went parading in to a dinner of grapefruit halves with withered maraschino cherries and some sort of very dubious curry, chicken or rabbit, cat or rat. Bob found the fourth level, the deck where the crew lived. It was a brown, awful, rotted mess crawling with rats, spread with feces and bits of unidentifiable rot, and from its portholes he could see that the bows of the ship were plunging so deep that water was pouring down the smokestacks.

The crew were worse than zombies, listless, their vigor escaped with the last heat of their bodies. Some of them lying in their bunks had become almost flat, and when you touched them, their skin turned to dust.

They had to leave the ship. To get to the dining room Bob had to crawl through a squishy, musky tunnel. It disgusted him, all the intimate wriggling that was necessary, and the sins of the woman, her exhaustion, her poor diet, her fear, were contained in the stink of the canal.

Emerging, his tuxedo flowing with a slick substance, he confronted Cindy, telling her the truth about the ship, and saying that they had to get off at the next island.

"But there aren't any islands, and this ship won't sink." She surrounded him with her smooth arms and buried his face in softness and wysteria.

Then he heard water gulping in the bowels of the ship and ragged, exhausted cries.

He awoke to a rushing morning. In the night a northern storm had come, bringing with it long gray arms of clouds and icy flecks in the air. The fronds of the willow whipped his broad head with armies of yellow leaves. As he staggered to his feet, unaware yet of hunger and thirst and pain, this was one of those moments when he thought he understood some elusive secret, when perhaps a poem could come from him that would be nearly good, the very lines of the ship rendered into words. But then he became aware of the stunning, overwhelming beauty of autumn's smells, how very subtle and rich were the aromas of the ground, the leaves, the fust of mushrooms, the dirt, the sour little smells of insects, and through it all a wild freshness, the north wind coming down the Catskills.

He knew exactly where he was. This morning he would take the path up past Veerkeeder Kill Falls on the south face of the Shawangunks and proceed into the fastness of the chain of preserves and parks that protect the mountains and all that live upon them. As long as fifteen years ago he had come up this very trail with Cindy, taking her camping, trying to teach her his own techniques for living off the land. She never learned, though; to her, camping consisted of hauling the whole twentieth century into some corner of the woods and re-creating it there, with a wood fire for effect only. One cooked on a portable alcohol stove. One ate dried food reconstituted in boiling water. One drank not from the fresh-flowing streams but of flat city water brought in canteens and bags.

Bob sniffed the air. There wasn't a human smell

in it. It seemed almost as if his body was becoming wider and bigger, encompassing more space. As he left mankind, the world opened out to him. Wolves are creatures of small society. They are not like ants and men, living in vast hives, entirely surrounded by their own kind and odors. On the wind Bob smelled ice, leaves, the bloom of the witch-hazel plant, cold stone, water. There was hardly a single detectable tang of smoke, no undertone of chemicals, little odor of human bodies, no smell of cold steel and oil, the sign of the gun.

He felt exultant—and he wanted to tell Cindy. He wanted so badly to say to her that he'd—but he couldn't say anything. He couldn't talk to her, couldn't share his life with her, never again.

Cindy. It was the most beautiful of all the words he could no longer say. Dear, sweet Cindy.

He moved off in the predawn, traveling slowly at first, then, as his thigh loosened up, going faster, slipping under the low-reaching boughs of saplings, through stands of hemlock, upward and upward. After an hour of steady trotting he came to Veerkeeder Kill, which was merry and fast, speeding down from its mountainside. The water was full of iron and seemed almost to catch in his teeth, leaving them vibrating. It was fiercely cold, so cold that it seemed to clarify his breathing even more than had the air. His sense of smell grew ever more powerful.

Raising his head, sniffing deep to find a rabbit or some other small creature, he smelled something that made his heart twist on itself and his tail droop.

It was her. Unmistakable. She was somewhere up on the mountain. He threw back his head, his thoughts dark with recognition and longing. She had been thinking and planning very carefully, to anticipate his route.

He wanted to get to her, to feel her arms around him, to take her and give himself to her.

His mind whispered, God help us, and the wolf threw back its head and howled through the rushing autumn morning.

Her scent lay close to the ground, wrapped in other smells, Kevin's humid freshness, and the old, smoky odor of another body. Had she hired a guide? It was certainly possible. After her experiences camping with him, her distrust of the woods had become profound.

As he climbed the path beside the spraying falls he became more and more uneasy. What would happen when they met? Could there be a real relationship? He imagined himself sitting in the living room, Kevin reading to him in that fluttery boy's voice of his. Or his dinner, pretty on one of the yellow checked place mats and a china plate, on which might be beef stew with a side of endive salad and a bowl of red wine, all neatly laid in a corner of the kitchen floor. There would be signals, nod to turn a page when he was reading by himself, a couple of taps to open a door, and it was all a pipe dream because in fact there would be no money and all the problems with the police and the ASPCA and heaven only knew who else.

But Cindy was a terrific person, she could solve problems. The only thing she'd never been able to do was hold down a job. She was too stubborn and proud to get along with bosses.

He climbed so easily, a free wolf in the air of morning, that he reached the top of the falls far more quickly than he had as a man, and with no gasping, no scrabbling, no skinned hands or dubious pains in his knees. This body was wonderful to feel and be.

Now their odor became strong. His nose directed him to their sleeping forms. Going softly closer, he inhaled the most amazingly intimate odors from them. He could smell everything, their sweat, the grease of the hamburgers they had eaten for supper, the light acidic content of his son's stomach, the fouler odor of the man's belly with its must of digested beer, and Cindy's contents, sour dairy: she'd had ice cream for dessert. He loved her harder; when she was sad she ate ice cream.

He did not want her to be sad.

With the total clarity that these things sometimes bring, he knew exactly what he had to do. There just couldn't be any question about it. This woman, this poor little boy, were his family. That meant more to him than life itself, than anything that had transpired. His skin crawled when he remembered his desire to commit suicide. How great a sin that would have been against these beloved sleepers. Look at them: Cindy with that amazingly pure skin of hers. How madly he had loved that skin. He could smell it now in heady detail. The lives of scented beasts were so intimate.

Odors that might once have seemed foul to him no longer seemed at all bad, not even the sour, unwashed stink of the man who was with them. Odors were not characterizable as good and bad. They were too complex and interesting. Just the smell of that man—he couldn't even count the number of separate odors involved. There were thousands.

A whole art must exist in potential around the selection and orchestration of scents.

Still, though, as much as he enjoyed his wolf, it was time to make a final and heroic effort on behalf of real life. As soon as he had smelled Cindy there came to him the definite sense that the wolf was on some level less real than the human had been. It was a wonderful body, true, but it was also primitive, totally unsuited to a man of poetry and thought. He, who sometimes spoke well, had been reduced to a rude state indeed, given this minor voice, capable of no formed words, and the crude paws for hands, paws that could never write a line.

And yet he was in here, full of thoughts that ought to be written, love and hope to speak, defenses and challenges, all made of words. He wanted to love his wife, to love his son, to somehow apologize to them.

When the man with them moved, Bob knew he was awake. How long had he been lying there watching him snuffle his family? A great moon face came oozing out of the blankets, rimmed by black hair. The eyes were tiny and as dark as obsidian. What was this man, Hispanic? No, Bob knew an Indian when he saw one.

An Indian. How interesting that Cindy had gotten an Indian. Where in the world had she found him, this man who moved so slowly that it was hard for wolf eyes to follow him?

Then he was on his feet. A swift, watery motion. Scary. Up close, human beings were tall and alien, their heads so far away, their faces terrifying with knowledge.

The Indian stood absolutely still. His face, though, was dark with staring. He was absolutely

concentrated on Bob. His stillness made him hard
to keep in the eye; this man knew something of
wolves.

One reason that men were so scary was obviously that they were dangerous. There was another
reason, though, one it was hard to put into words.
It had to do with the very animation of their faces.
They looked too aware. And he knew they were:
the human mind has gotten lost; it has strayed too
far from its wild origins. Animals were distin-
guished by their concentration on what was in
front of them. The human mind went back and
forth, in and out, complicating. It could not find
anymore the shadow upon the grass.

The wind soughed across the mountain, the falls
sounded like glass. In Bob's nostrils were the
smells of water and stone, and of his beloved
family. The light had taken on a rosy grayness, and
a sparrow twittered nearby. Why in this sweet
morning was the man moving like that?

He wanted to kiss Cindy, to hold her, to feel her
snuggling against his breast.

The Indian came closer, oozing like heat-
softened plastic, his arms and legs seeming almost
jointless. "Shape-shifter," he whispered. "Shape-
shifter, please tell me your secret."

To calm the man, Bob sat firmly down on his
haunches. He let his jaw drop and his tongue hang
out. His face was not very mobile but he thought
he must be smiling. He yapped once, trying to
awaken his family.

"Shh! Tell me before they open their eyes.
Think what it would mean to my people, shape-
shifter. Think what it would mean!" He squatted
before Bob, his hands open and pleading. His face
tightened, his lips drew back. Bob could see his

skull, and his death, and the long quiet years in the ground. He had a clear notion: The body belongs to the ground, and the ground knows it. "Please, shape-shifter, give me a sign." He screwed his eyes closed, his hands were begging claws. "Think what it would mean to us. We Indians could change into wolves and foxes and deer, and we could go back to the forest!"

Bob was startled enough to growl sharply. The man's eyes bulged wide open. "You—you understood?" The wind swept down, ruffling Bob's fur, making the man squint. "Snow's coming!"

Kevin leaped out of his sleeping bag and threw his arms around his father's neck, kissing him wildly, his tears filled with the smell of the ocean and his skin with the fragile scent of youth. Then Cindy was there, too, and she kissed the side of his muzzle, his lips with careful, determined sensuality. "You never run from me again," she said, her voice going low. "Never!"

He looked at her. Before the knowledge that he now faced, he felt ashamed.

He could not live in the human world, not as a wolf, not as a dog. As much as he missed Cindy and Kevin, he didn't even want to become human again.

You, wolf, will be back to making cold calls from that stuffy office, the man at the bottom of the Empire State Building.

He snarled at the Indian, who had produced a little straw packet, which he was opening.

"We've tried shifting a million times. I used to do it when I was a kid. I wanted to be anything except an Indian. If I'd been able, I think I'd willingly have turned myself into a lawn mower. As it was, I tried for hawk, for eagle, for wolf, for deer, for panther. All I got was burned hands when my ritual fire blew up."

He spoke as if Bob could not understand him. Bob had gone up on all fours, and made sure he was between the people and the mountain. His instinct wouldn't let him be comfortable with the falls behind and three human beings blocking escape.

He was ashamed of himself when the notion of simply trotting off flashed through his mind. The Indian could probably track him, but he could never catch him, not without an off-the-road vehicle or an airplane.

He heard Cindy muttering to herself, her words inarticulate. It would hurt so much less if she wouldn't pray. Her religion, like his, was indifference. They were lapsed Catholics, both of them, full of quiet pride that they had solved the algorithm of guilt so well that they could enjoy the croissant Sundays that kept them home from church.

Until now Bob had not understood quite what it was that distanced him from the church. A few days in the bright shock of a new form had made it all clear, though: on a planet that so obviously needed the love and protection of its most clever species, a heaven-directed church seemed anachronistic, its indifference to the welfare of the earth fundamentally invalidating.

When the Indian began shaking a carved stick over a fire, a fine pin of unease entered Bob's mind. Religion may or may not be invalid, but rituals aren't hollow. In the hands of the believer, the ritual is a powerful force indeed.

On its deepest level Bob's change had been a matter of the wall against this kind of belief breaking down in him. His first transformation, in the hotel in Atlanta, may indeed have been imaginary. Because it was so realistic, though, he had believed in it. After that, everything else had become inevitable.

He stared transfixed at the Indian's preparations. Western culture had destroyed the Indians because it had destroyed their ability to believe in their own magic.

All the Indian had to do was to transform Bob back into a man and all of his magic would work for him again, because his success would strengthen his belief. The tribes, broken in spirit, would spring back to life.

At the end of the stick that danced in the Indian's hand was a tiny dancing man. He stared at the naked thing. Was it wax or real? It had no face, or perhaps the face was simply too small for wolf eyes to see.

He thought of the ritual deaths of kings. To give the Indian back his birthright, the wolf would have to die. The man at the end of the stick danced, a slow and regular dance, as graceful as the drifting of a finger in the sea. He was a weed of a little man, down at the murky bottom.

His arms rose and fell, his legs flashed in the spreading light. Kevin cried aloud, clutching down into the folds of his mother. A crow landed nearby. Bob smelled rabbits on the wind, and wondered how far away they might be.

He didn't wonder long though. The Indian kept chanting, shaking his stick, and Bob knew that there was another smell in the air, a human smell, small and intense. There was a suffering, real man at the end of the stick. He wept as he danced, the same awful, universal mourning that made Lewis

Carroll's Mock Turtle such a figure of childhood dread. The weeping without reason and therefore without consolation, reflected in the tears of the Indian.

Bob felt the movement within and knew that the man was striving to escape as the wolf had escaped. He sensed the crow alight from its food gathering, sensed the rabbits across the mountain grow still, sensed the failure of the wind and the stopping of the leaves. He had known a body that saw by eyes and one that saw by nose. It was difficult to imagine how the planet saw and felt and knew: the whole of life was its mind, its nerves, its vision. The earth was a great cyclopean eye rolling through space, looking out into the void. What awful consciousness had urged the spawning of man, or more, had ordered him to become what he had become?

He felt anger rushing through the stillness. No wonder the tiny man cried, no wonder the Indian cried, no wonder his son hid in his mother and the crow became silent. Within him the man rose and clambered, stuffed himself into the shape of the wolf, and he felt his muscles longing to stretch, his skin longing to shed its stuffy fur and spread to the caressing air. His stomach did a grotesque turn. Green-flecked vomit burst out of his mouth and he stood tottering, a tall, naked man who could not help but dance to the command of an Indian with a stick.

The Indian threw the stick down and screamed. Cindy cried out, Kevin shrieked, and Bob saw a chance of madness in the poor child's eyes.

His scream, his father's anguish, spread through the silence as quickly as an atomic expansion. Then, as quickly as a trap taking a rat, the wolf

snapped back around Bob and he fell down, his
jaw working, growls scumbling in the thick mucus
that was the waste matter of these furious changes.

"Bob, Bob!" Letting her boy fall aside, Cindy
rose up. Her face was distorted to a Hydra gri-
mace, her hands were working in his fur like
snakes, her body bursting with thick panicky
stench.

"Bob, please come back to us." Her voice was
not steady. She was thinking fast. "I never expected you wouldn't want to. You don't though,
you *don't!* Oh, Bob, you got a rejection from the
Poetry Review, but it was a personal letter. Bob,
they asked if you were aware of the Imagists. I sent
a reply, I said yes, but you didn't care for Amy
Clampitt. Was I right, Bob? Oh, come back to your
life. Come back to us." Then her voice broke and
she sank down, miserable on the stones.

The world seemed not to have noticed. The falls
still spattered, the crow still worried a berry bush.
But Bob knew the lie in that, he had sensed the
tension in its watching.

"Dad—"

It was agony to hear their pleading. Even to
glance into his son's eyes was torment.

"Dad, please. Please. I need you, Dad, I miss
you. I can't even read anymore, not without you at
home. I can't draw. All I draw is black."

The Indian was lying on his back, staring at the
sky. His breathing was so even, Bob thought he
might be in a coma.

He must not prolong this torment. With a bitter
heart, hating himself for what he did, he turned
away from them. There was no sound behind him.
Over his shoulder he saw Cindy slumped on the
ground. Kevin was watching him with a sorrow in

his face that no child should know. Bob could not say why, but his deepest instincts, wolf and human, were all telling him to do this, to leave them, to run into the wild.

He did run, farther and farther, until the last edge of their scent was gone.

All day he ran, stopping only to steal a chicken from a yard in High Falls, New York. Toward afternoon it began to snow. He ran as much toward the wilderness as away from his family and his former life. Somewhere in him a brute voice shouted that it was free, shouted down the driving snow.

He heard the flakes hiss on the hemlock boughs, felt them snap cold on his nose. As he ran the world changed from the last of autumn to the first of winter, and all memories, all desires, were covered with a kindness of snow.

CHAPTER NINETEEN

DAYS STRETCHED ON DAYS AS BOB MOVED STEADILY north. He became a cunning hunter, quick and mean, and clever at avoiding men. Winter came, wet at first and then rich with snow. Sometimes he heard Cindy's name in the wind, or saw the sorrow in Kevin's eye, but he ran on, obedient to the wolf that he was, and the wild.

He was in the deep north now, and the snow hissed in the hemlocks and pines, it roared past the naked limbs of oak and maple, it swirled in the glades and blew hard against his flanks.

His coat had grown thick and full. Only his nose was cold, and it was tormented. When he could bear the twirling knife of the wind no longer, he would curl up with his back to the blizzard and bury his muzzle in his paws. He could remain like that for hours, until he was entirely covered by a blue, icy translucence. Then it was quiet, and he experienced a deep feeling of safety.

Every morning, when thin light would penetrate the sky, the urge to move would possess him once more. He would break out of the snow and shake himself, feeling the cold air penetrate all the way to his skin. Thus refreshed, he would sniff the air, seeking the musk of an opossum or the rabbit odor.

The colder it got, the less often he smelled anything beyond the smooth aroma of the snow.

There was something in his soul that was urging him north. He did not know what it was, but it drew him, dragged him, forced him when he was tired. His nose ceaselessly tested the air for something he could not name. Cindy and Kevin had become glowing statues in his memory. The brutal labor of his journey, the snow, the clarity of his struggle had sliced away all sentiment. His blood was no longer attached to his family; it belonged to whatever goal lay at the end of this journey.

But then he would hear the wind, and her name. . . .

He loved something out here, something he could not name. Maybe it was the wild itself, the whole complex, restless personality of life, or maybe it was his new wolf nature—so urgent, so fundamentally decent—or maybe it was wolves in general, even the beautiful act of hunting.

Finding and killing game was the highest experience he had ever known, higher even than riding Cindy in the soft summer nights. There was something at once so terrible and so beautiful about biting the life out of a little creature that he quaked inside just to think of it. In his life before he had never seen sorrow like the sorrow that entered the eyes of an animal he was killing, nor had he ever felt the fire that eating a kill gave him.

It is the life of the killed thing that is eaten, as much as the blood and meat and bone.

By the time he reached the high Adirondacks the weather was so cold that the fur framing his face froze at its tips. The pads of his paws had fissures in them that revealed deep red wounds, and he left pink flecks of blood in his tracks. Game was scarce indeed, and he was becoming famished.

Despite his doubts and the conditions, his progress had taken on a kind of hypnotic quality. From the gray hours before dawn to the gray hours after sunset he would lope steadily along, stopping to hunt when he scented the opportunity. He would eat anything—rat, opossum, rabbit, raccoon. He avoided skunks and porcupines. Deer were too fast for him, and the idea of trying to attack something with sharp little hooves was unsettling.

In the past few weeks he reckoned that he had come at least five hundred miles. As he moved along he altered his course to the northwest. Sooner or later he knew that he must cross the St. Lawrence Seaway. He would not attempt to swim. He was hoping that he would reach it after the seasonal ice had closed it. If not, then he would have to wait on the American side until it did.

He had been without food for six days when he detected a powerful, greasy odor coming out of a tumble of rocks. He'd never smelled anything like it before. Strong smells delighted him, and this one was so strong that it made him shudder all over. His impulse was to rub himself with it, to wear it like a sort of talisman. It was extremely rich with meat and blood.

He looked toward the rocks. How odd that the

odor came from there. Such a powerful smell, rolling over him in waves, had to emanate from a large animal. But what could it be? He would see a deer or a moose. Stiff-legged, he stole closer. Still there was nothing, and yet the odor was literally pouring out of the rocks. It was strange enough to be frightening. Had he not been so hungry, Bob would have left this place.

The rocks were contorted razors. They cut painfully into Bob's paws, and he slipped on the ice, skinning his spindly lower legs. But that scent: he visualized a whole mass of animals, rich game, incredibly rich. His drool froze on his chin.

It was not long before he located a den in the roots of an enormous hickory. The den opening was large enough for him to walk through.

A large black bear came swarming out at him, its eyes beads of fury and hate, its voice booming against the snow-muffled land. There was no warning, no waiting. Before Bob could do more than utter a bark of surprise, the bear had taken a hissing swipe with the claws of his right paw. Bob narrowly escaped the speeding, black nails. He skittered back, fell, tumbled backward. The bear literally leaped through the air in its mad urgency to attack. For a moment the whole huge beast hung above him, its front paws spread wide, its lips revealing yellow, vicious teeth.

The smell that cascaded down from the bear was lovely, an art of meat and wonderful, rich grease and blood. As Bob tried to tumble away the bear landed on him with a thunderous crash. Now Bob was under the creature, his breath knocked out, half-stunned by the power of the blow, feeling his bones bending to break beneath the horrendous weight of the animal.

Beneath his compressed body he could feel a tangle of frozen brush. It was a crack in the rocks. As the bear struggled to get its huge forelegs around him, he tried to dig down, grappling at the twigs with clumsy paws. Frantically, he scrambled out from under the bear. A swipe of one of its paws connected with his injured thigh, reopening the wound with a flash of pain so great that he almost lost consciousness. He spun round and round, tumbling down the rocks, stopping only when he landed upside down against a spindly rowan.

The bear stood in front of him, swaying from side to side. He could hear its claws clicking, and the moaning of the wind across the top of the ridge behind it. Looking into the bear's blank, glittering eyes, he felt very alone and very lost. In all the wild he was, after all, the only truly aberrant creature. This bear was savage, its eyes said. And its eyes also said that it had no mind. If he died here, it was going to be a lonely, hard death. But were not all deaths in the forest such? And he would die having had one of the highest of experiences: to be a raw animal, in the body of the animal, with all his human consciousness intact.

Cindy . . . the wind said. He shook his head and snorted. At a moment like this, the human world must not be allowed to intrude. If he was to survive, he had to fight as a wolf.

The bear sucked him up in its deadly hug, and began dancing ponderously through the snow-choked clearing that bordered the stony hill. He smelled its breath and heard the dark thudding of its feet in the soft snow. Then sun came out, and shone golden on its coat. In the rich new light Bob struggled and snapped, trying to connect with some vital part of the monster, while it crushed out his life.

His chest was closed off and his nose began to pulse with trapped blood. He could no longer breathe, and it felt as if his head was going to explode. A torment of air hunger made him writhe. He felt his bowels give way.

His teeth kept meeting air, but the bear's claws did not meet air. Instead they twisted and dug under the skin of his shoulder, piercing toward essential gristle. In great agony, he screamed. The bear replied with a mournful, inexpressibly savage moan. It tightened his grip on him, and he saw Cindy coming up the clearing with a gun in her hand.

His heart battered against the walls of his chest, he felt his legs scrabbling through the bear's fur. Cindy raised her rifle—and then disappeared into the crystal air. At that moment he came close to complete despair. The bear was killing him, and she had been a death dream, nothing more. Had he been able to shout, he would have called her name, but in the event, all that escaped from him were high, sucking cries.

His body turned and his legs kicked frantically. The bear danced round and round, moaning as it brought its muzzle closer to his neck. He could feel its bear breath on his face, could smell an intimacy of berries and old fish. His body was wiped in the animal's grease. The odor of bear that had drawn this ignorant wolf too close now became a loathsome smell.

He probed dismally into the wall of coarse fur, snapped with half his strength. To his surprise the bear tossed its head back, then bit at him angrily. For a moment the two of them were cheek to cheek. He could see his own reflection in the bear's savage eye.

Twisting his head, he drove a canine deep into that eye. There was a loose pop as of a finger jabbing through many layers of tight, wet paper and this time the bear screamed horribly, throwing its head back, the remains of its eye dangling along its cheek. A claw drew across Bob's back, the nails going deep. It would have been less painful to have his skin trenched by hot irons.

The pain was so great that he forgot himself. His head shook from side to side, his jaws snapped and snapped. All control was gone.

Then he was lying on the ground and the bear was glaring down at him, shrieking and gasping. Half of its face was torn away. Bob could see teeth and muscles, and the tongue working in the mouth. In his own mouth he tasted filthy hair and rich, rich meat.

Almost without being aware of it he leaped right at the creature, driving his furious muzzle deep into the flesh of the belly, into reefs of sticky fat, then deeper into the wall of tight muscle beneath it and the steaming organs at the final depth. With a roar the bear grabbed him in both paws and heaved him away. Bob slammed against a boulder, was covered in a cascade of snow, and came forth wild with a fury he could neither control nor understand.

Shaking, his ears back, the skin of his neck stiff and full of shivers, his tail close down, he ran at the tottering bear and grabbed a purple loop of intestine protruding from the hole in its belly. The gasping creature savaged him again, kicking him away. This time, though, he drew the bear's vitals with him, his jaws clamped hard around them.

By pushing him away, the animal had gutted itself. It stood to its full four feet of height and waved its forelegs in the air, looking very much like a man wearing a bearskin. Then it began to claw at its own belly. A torrent of dark blood poured out of its mouth. Surprised, it snapped its jaws shut. Its eyes were sad now. Slowly, it sat on its haunches, swaying from side to side, staring at the wolf that had killed it.

With a final moan of rage, it threw itself toward him. By the time its great, bloody body had covered him, it was dead. Bob lay beneath it, in the heat of its blood and offal. He struggled a time to free himself, but a tiredness so profound that it seemed itself a kind of death overcame him and he closed his eyes.

He dreamed of the kindness of a balmy goddess, who touched him mercifully where he hurt. She touched him with long, golden fingers, probing so gently into his wounds that he felt naught, filling them with the sparkling medicine of heaven.

When he awoke, it was from coldness bothering his nose. It was snowing again, and the bear was no longer covering his body.

He opened his eyes to piercing gray light. The blizzard had blown itself out, leaving a residue of flurries drifting down from high clouds. When Bob raised his head, he was astonished to see the remains of the bear scattered all around him. He snorted, stood up.

At once he yelped; every part of him ached, especially his chest and back. His old thigh wound was better, perhaps because the bear's clawing had lanced it and drained away some of the infection.

He took personal inventory: he had at least two cracked ribs, possibly a broken one. His shoulder was hard with swelling and scab. When he shuddered his skin, his back felt as solid as a board. Looking as far as he could over his shoulder, he saw a mass of scab there. He was literally encased in dried blood.

The bear was in pieces around him. The huge creature had been pulled apart by experts, and eaten. The organs were all gone, most of the meat and fat had been consumed, even the bones of the legs had been cracked and the marrow eaten.

Bob saw in the snow tracks very much like his own, dozens of them. His heart started racing: wolves! Then he smelled the finest, the sweetest, the most exciting odor he had ever known. He barked five or six times, he did a crutchy dance of excitement. Wolves, he was in wolf country! Sheer happiness burst up in his heart, making his injuries seem light, his trouble seem small. Wolves, you could feel them, all around. His heart was weighted with love and longing.

This was the nameless thing that had come to dominate his life, had separated him from his family and drawn him all of these brutal miles. They smelled wonderful. It was much more than an odor or a perfume, it was a scent connected directly to his soul. There was no way to describe it, except to say that it was to normal odor as the sight of heaven must be to hell-weary eyes. Again and again he inhaled. Wonderful. Love. His heart burst with joy.

Then he found himself throwing back his head and howling. The sound that came out was not restricted as it had been before, controlled by the uneasy human consciousness that was so quickly becoming a supercargo. Now the sound rose fine and tight as a needle piercing the sky. It shaped itself to a long sonic spire, then spread out like a flower in the light air, flowing softly across the frozen land.

It evaporated into silence. Bob was disappointed. Where were the wolves? Why wouldn't they answer?

Then they did.

Echoing across the far hills, sweeping past the naked limbs of the trees, as cool, as sharp, as delicate . . . the answer came, and his tail twirled wildly.

He had been spoken to across the miles by a real, living wolf! He had spoken wolf-to-wolf! As a wolf he was here in this place, and he was one with the whole kingdom of the wolves.

The howl died away, ending on a low note that carried in its tone a text of warning. Bob howled back at once, all of his excitement and joy flowing into the soft, curving sound.

The reply came as quick, from the north and from many wolf throats, a high scream of a note, speaking volumes of subtle language, building pictures in his mind of limpid eyes and fast teeth. Was this alien speech rejection or welcome? He listened and their voices touched him to the bottom of his life. He wanted to be among them, to be one with them, to love them and live among them. Cindy, they're wonderful, they're like gods! Cindy, I—

I still miss you.

But he started out at once, tracking them with a competent nose.

Even though he was still in New York State, he'd encountered a wolf pack! A big one too, judging from the number of different voices in their howl. He found himself looking around for a pay phone

to call Cindy and tell her to get in touch with the
Department of Environmental Conservation.
Wolves in New York: what good, what happy
news.

Then he thought: maybe DEC already knows.
What if they *did* tell the public? Would not people
come forth with their guns, eager for trophies,
eager to kill the evil thing of the forest? No, the
presence of these wolves must remain a secret. In
their world they were powerful, they were kings,
but in man's world he had to remember that they
were vulnerable little creatures without a future.

He smelled them again, this time when the wind
blew from behind him. This scent was stronger
and he detected in it something new, something so
exciting that he almost collapsed. A female odor,
definite, musky, deep as wood, so intense that for
a moment he could actually see her, the face of
perfect beauty, its sleek snout, its fine, black ball
of a nose, and the heartbreaking line of the eyes,
so expressive and subtle. He was embarrassed,
confused. This was not a woman's face, but it was
the most feminine face he had ever seen.

All of his knowledge of wolves arrayed itself
before him. The books sped past in memory: *Of
Wolves and Men*, Erik Zimens's *The Wolf: A
Species in Danger*, the work of Dan Mech. He
remembered his time in northern Minnesota, the
wolf he had seen, and his dreams of wolves, his
lifelong wandering in the shadows of his own
desires. Now he ran, a wolf at last, seeking what
his soul had wanted, maybe from the very beginning of its existence, which was to fulfill this odd
destiny.

The wolf pack is a tightly knit organization,
made up of animals who have known one another

from birth. It is not generally open to strangers. Wolves are fierce territorialists, protecting their hunting grounds from outsiders. They are expert fighters. They have a strict and elaborate hierarchy.

He followed the trench of tracks in the snow, never losing it for more than a few seconds, his nose drawing him after them with great accuracy. As he moved along, he thought he could smell other wolves much more clearly than he could anything else, almost as if his nose was more perfectly adapted to this odor than to any other.

He did not move fast. If he ran, his back, shoulder and thigh hurt, and when he breathed deeply, his ribs wrapped him in a band of pain. Trotting along, he again scented the female. Something turned in his loins, and he moved faster despite the pain. He was astonished at himself. He was having a strong sexual stirring. This was the mating season for wolves, or the beginning of it. He did not feel the steamy sense of desire that Cindy evoked in him. This was more pure than the inventive love of humans: this was lust in a form so simple that it was perfectly clean; it was sex devoid of all but purpose.

His desire made him imagine the gentle aroma of cubs, feel their soft fur. He had to father cubs, *had to*! He gasped as he ran, he panted even in the cold. His desire came cracking through the layers of self: cubs, cubs, cubs. She was in heat, she was a goddess, and he had to have her. He stopped, raised his muzzle, and howled. In that howl he knew that there was more than quest and loneliness, there was also a challenge he was helpless to suppress.

The replying howl washed over him, a tumult of

passion, and it was not kindly passion. It was
fierce and immediate and full of snarl. Behind it
was fear, and he knew that he was approaching
them too directly. A pack of wolves is an ancient
and very subtle social structure, governed by
rituals and laws that must go back in an unbroken
tradition to the very origin of the species.

There were things in that howl that made Bob
stop and listen most carefully. Terrible things,
anger, bitterness, suspicion. There was also a
pride so great that it awed him. The howl was rich
and full and decisive, beginning and ending with a
single, great tone. It was the voice of the leader.

Bob ignored the warning in the howl, the impli-
cation of murder. He had to; he could not bear to
think that the wolves would do him any injury.
After all, had not that wonderful female in her
kindness licked him? Hadn't she? What healing
she had in her—were it not for her, he would have
awakened in great anguish. As it was, her tongue
had accomplished significant healing. He could
move and he was certainly not going to die.

For hours and hours he followed the trail of the
pack. They were going north, farther and farther,
never stopping, never even reducing their pace.
He had prided himself on his speed and range, but
these wolves were much faster than he. He believed that they had gone as far as forty miles last
night. Evidently the odor of the bear had been
strong enough and unusual enough to bring them
out of their normal territory, to which they were
nervously returning.

It was just getting to be evening when he found
himself at the edge of the forest. Before him was
the St. Lawrence.

He looked out across the tumult of ice.

The seaway must be at least a mile wide here. It was a white, tumbled emptiness, cracking and thundering as the current underneath shifted the ice floating on top.

On the far edge of the ice, where it softened into a smooth, snowy strand, he saw something that stood his hair on end. There were at least a dozen black dots there.

On a nearby bush there were a group of strong scent marks, pungent, redolent with the particular urine odor of this pack. It was not a bad scent. It was sour and warm and penetrating. Interesting. He sniffed carefully.

Then his body did something that he did not expect: it raised its leg and urinated, obliterating the territorial marker.

The wolves on the far bank had become very still, and were now hard to see, a fuzzy clutch of black blurs in the winter emptiness.

He smelled them, raised his head, and howled again. They howled back, angry, afraid, full of warning.

His answer was the only one he could give: he trotted out onto the frozen water. Whatever happened, he had to try and join these wolves.

They were the center and purpose of his life, he now understood that clearly.

They howled again. The sound was frank with menace. Bob lowered his head against the vicious wind. The time had come to face them.

CHAPTER TWENTY

THE STACK OF FILTHY DISHES TEETERED ON THE EDGE OF the counter. Cindy turned, snatching at them. Her uniform snagged against a loose corner and she went down amid a cascade of plates, cups, silverware, hamburger crusts, and wet cigarette butts.

She sat there in the rubble contemplating a half-eaten pancake that had adhered to her apron. From the other end of the counter Louie Parma, the owner of Parma Lunch, clapped, a series of dismal pops. Misery swept Cindy. She got up, murmuring a "sorry, Louie," and started picking up the shards. A piece of glass jabbed her finger. A convulsive jerk caused her morning's tips—a dozen or so quarters and dimes—to fall out of her pocket and roll away among the chipped and broken dishes. "Sorry, Louie, sorry."

She shook the tears from her eyes. As she started organizing the rubble into a pile she saw

Louie's neatly polished shoes appear. "How much?" he asked, pointing a toe toward some of her coins.

"Six dollars."

"I'll take that and dock you another twelve, we'll be even."

"Okay, Louie." Her salary was five dollars an hour and she'd been here since 6:00 A.M. It was now eleven, which meant that less these deductions, she'd cleared only seven dollars on the morning. That was important, vitally so: Kevin would have to eat the last of the spaghetti tonight; she would skip the meal.

No matter what, she was not going to call Monica. The woman was slowly coming undone, tortured by her inability to understand what had happened to Bob, and unable to enlist the aid of any of her fellow scientists and doctors in her research. Monica was now a haunted woman, her practice in ruins, her wealth disappearing into the well of what the rest of her profession saw as an insane quest.

Monica was no longer a source of money, support, or anything else. Cindy felt so sorry for her, but there was nothing she could do. Her concern was finding Bob again and really communicating with him. Only then, with him and understanding him, could she and Kevin hope to have any peace.

Joe Running Fox, also, was obsessed with him. He had guided them to Olana and then disappeared—when was it, in February? Yes, and here it was the end of March.

Joe knew that Bob was somewhere near here. If Joe found him, Cindy knew that he would be back. As it was, he lived out in the snow, a

frostbitten ruin of a man, almost an animal himself. He prayed to the old Indian gods. He
searched.

As she dumped the remains of the plates into a
gray busman's tray, she remembered that she
would still be able to keep her lunch tips, which
might be as much as eight dollars if those darned
highway engineers didn't take up table one the
whole time and not leave anything again.

She took her mess out back herself, not caring to
confront Willie Clair, the dishwasher and busman, with the results of her mistake. He'd scream
at her, then subside, walking back and forth
slapping his hands against his thighs and cursing.

When she opened the back door, a blast of wind
made her stagger. She glanced up, into the clear,
frozen air. Immediately beyond Ontario Street the
forest began. She looked into the blue, shadowed
fastness of it. Week after week she had walked this
forest, through what seemed an endless winter.
She had come to see it as intractable, hostile, and
joyless. It was devoid of poetry, of hope: in all the
weeks of her searching she had heard wolves
howling exactly once.

She and Kevin were fugitives from ordinary life.
He was no longer in school. He had become fierce
and domineering. Night after night he awoke
screaming, so often that they could not keep a
room for long. They'd about used up Olana, as a
matter of fact, moving from the Gracey Hotel to
Mrs. Winslow's to the Indian Inn, where the puffy,
woebegone Sim Jones was beginning to shake his
head whenever he saw the boy.

"Cindy, you got customers," shouted Louie.

"On my way, Lou!" Table one was occupied by
two people, a thin, sallow woman with a cigarette

between her fingers and a big man who looked like a wax effigy of himself. That table was the big one. "Hi, folks," Cindy said, "sure you don't want a booth?" Seeing two people at his big table would put Louie into a funk for the rest of the afternoon.

"This's fine," the woman said. "Gimme coffee and one of them nut rolls."

"Coffee and you got cherry pie?"

"Yes, sir, we sure do."

"I want apple. Cherry's too damn sweet."

The woman laughed. "What do you do that for, Bud? You always do that. 'Got coffee?' 'Yeah.' 'Gimme tea.' I couldn't believe that when you first did it." She looked up at Cindy, smoke rising from her wide, tight smile. "Can you believe this man?"

Cindy smiled. She did not laugh. It would take an extra tip to get that out of her. She turned and posted the order on Louie's turnstile. His face, already dark over the loss of the big table, darkened further when the highway engineers came blundering in, knotted in the doorway, and stared at the table. There were mutters. One of them nodded his head and the group left, tramping back into the snow, headed no doubt for Clasby's down at the other end of Ontario, or for the McDonald's that stood near the high school.

Louie shook his head. "You got no sense," he said bitterly. "There goes twenty-five bucks if it's a dollar. What the hell am I gonna do with all the extra hamburger I got in for those guys?"

"Eat it."

"Gimme a kiss, cutie."

She thought how nice it would be to take a whip to Louie's great lardbag of a rump. She could imagine his flesh rippling and his voice cracking while she did to him in the body what he was doing to her in the soul. He's paying me and I hate him, she thought. Isn't that typical, ungrateful bitch that I am?

"C'mon." He made yet another halfhearted snatch at her. Then his eyes met hers, his big animal eyes. The Indian had called her hawk, Bob wolf, Kevin owl. This was hyena, this sweat-sheened short-order cook with a fleck of tobacco from his long-chewed morning cigar still adhering to one of his front teeth.

She shook her head, backing away from Louie. There was no use yearning for Bob. Even if she managed to find him again, he would no doubt run away once more.

At first she had been furious with him, but time had made it more clear that he'd seen no alternative. How could she house him, feed him? And what about their love?

There was a man in that wolf body, and she loved the man. But the animal—it was mysterious and, frankly, horrible.

There was no time to think about these things now: she had another table to work: Big Charlie Tolner had just come in with his brother Little Charlie from their garage over on LaSalle.

That made Louie happy again: the Charlies tended to favor Clasby with their business. "You guys walk? I ain't seen a car."

"My truck's busted," Big Charlie said. "So's his. We's out last weekend after us a moose, ha-ha. Almost got us a wolf. They're comin' down farther every year. Not enough deer and moose up in Ontario, I expect."

Cindy might as well have been dealt a blow to the side of the head. She took a large, unlikely step, slopping coffee out of both mugs, ruining the piece of cherry pie she had just cut.

"Wolves," she managed to croak. "Charlie, did you say you saw a wolf?"

"Big black fella, thin as hell, standin' up beside the St. Lawrence. Just stood there, lookin' at us. We got two good shots at him."

Her skin felt like a sheath of snow. "Did you hit him?"

"Nah. He's a smart sonembitch. Most wolves, they start runnin' like hell, you shoot at 'em. This old guy, he see's he's got the St. Lawrence behind him. He runs out on that ice and we can just take our time. We got a wolf pelt. This fella takes cover, like. See, he goes up behind a big chunk of crack ice." The Charlies both stared at her, their left eyebrows raised in identical expressions of astonishment at the memory. "We run after him, but he got away," Big Charlie said.

"Slunk through the ice mounds near the bank," his brother added.

It was Bob. It had to be him. She could picture him: thin, scraggly, smart.

Out on the St. Lawrence. "Where?"

"Oh, well . . ."

"Please tell me, you guys."

"The DEC—"

Her mind was twisting and turning on itself. She had to know, had to get it out of them. "I don't care if you were poaching or whatever it's called." Both Charlies looked away. She went for the dumb one. "C'mon, Big Charlie," she said, "tell me where you saw a wolf. I think it's so exciting." She hated the fake sex in her voice. Big Charlie didn't hate it, though. His ears turned red.

"Oh, well, we were out about twenty miles up from the bridge. We were on that piece of land owned by those city people."

"The Jews," Little Charlie said, as if this would excuse their trespass.

Cindy didn't know a thing about who did and didn't own land around here, and she didn't give a damn. All she could think of was Bob. She squared her shoulders and raised her chin, thinking of the nobility of her love. It was always the men who embarked on quests in the old stories, Piers Plowman, Sir Gawain. Women stayed at home and raised the children. Well, she wasn't that kind of a woman. Her quest was clear, as fine and perfect as Sir Gawain's: she had a grail, too, the sacred body of her love.

"Cindy," Big Charlie suddenly blurted, "you care to take a drive over the border Saturday? Maybe go up to Voix and have a little supper at Antoine's?"

Louie stared, openmouthed. Little Charlie began giggling silently.

Without a word she turned away from the table of the two gargoyles. "Sweet," Big Charlie said as his brother collapsed into open laughter.

"Willie won't bring in the damn potatoes," Louie snarled as she came back to the counter. "You go get 'em."

He was referring to the two-hundred-pound sacks of frozen french fries that were due to be delivered today. "Lou, I can't possibly! I can't drag those bags."

"You do it, or you've got your walking papers. And I want them in the back of the freezer, not all jammed up around the door like he does it."

Feeling hopeless, Cindy put her beautiful blue cardigan from Bloomie's and better days on over her thin nylon uniform and went struggling out into the glaring, icy light of noon.

She tugged miserably and quite hopelessly at one of the big gray sacks. Louie was a cruel man. They were all cruel. The women around here were huddled misanthropes, slaves and sloven whores. What a misbegotten place.

It came to seem even more misbegotten a moment later, when both of the Charlies appeared, one at each end of the restaurant. She stepped back, only to see Louie's shadow in the doorway. He had locked the door.

So that was what this was about. When had they had time to plan? There hadn't been a word spoken between them. Without another thought she started running, wobbling across the snowy parking lot in her cheap flats, the wind eating at her body, making the cardigan seem almost imaginary.

They came along behind her, moving heavily but with surprising speed, the two Charlies. "Come on, Cindy," Big Charlie cried, "won'tcha? Why won'tcha? A little blowjob ain't nothin' to a woman."

"Oh, God."

They appeared beside her. She did not like the sweat sheening Big Charlie's face or the clicking wheeze that Little Charlie developed when he ran.

Big Charlie's hand brushed her shoulder. "Them shoes are no good in this hardpack," he said absently, as his arm closed around her neck. "You had no chance."

She could see Louie's shadow in the back door of the diner. He waved at her, a hesitant gesture, as if he was seeing her off on some undesirable voyage. Her impulse was to kick and bite and claw, but she controlled it. She was not a weak woman, but these two men were certainly her physical superiors. Quietly, carefully, she reviewed her options. She was being walked along, Big Charlie tugging her by the neck, Little Charlie with his horny fist around her wrist.

Taking a deep breath, she screamed. The sound was high and thin, more like the squeak of chalk on a blackboard than a human noise. Little Charlie looked up at her out of the corner of his eye. "That wasn't too good," he said happily.

When she was a kid, she had been able to scream marvelously well. She closed her eyes, tried to calm herself enough to organize some more effective noise. They were passing her rooming house. If only their room wasn't at the back, Kevin might hear. He'd be there—because she did not want to put him in one of the local backwater schools where he'd be taught nothing more challenging than Gum-Chewing 101 and probably beaten to a pulp as well, they had decided he would go into hiding for the duration of the search.

He spent his time reading. He was on *Remembrance of Things Past* now, and he wanted to get the walls lined with cork like Proust had.

Big Charlie's hand pushed against her left breast. The sensation was disgusting, a nauseating thrill that churned to pain when he squeezed. This time she screamed with fierce energy. In response the two men began moving faster down the freezing, silent street. "Somebody help me!" Was the whole town dead? No, more likely everybody around here except Kevin was off at work or at school, Kevin and that inert old man who inhabited the little house at the end of the block. He wouldn't come out. If the world ended, he would meet it staring out that window of his. "God help me! God help me!"

Big Charlie moaned. "Come on, Cindy, we won't hurt you. Please, I just want you to treat me like a man. Honey, I could give you a good life."

"Let me go, you filthy creep. You smell like a wet cigar butt."

"I'll stop with the cigars if that's what it takes. You don't like 'em—done! Howya like that? Cindy, I got nobody, I'm getting older. You're young. I'll leave you everything in my will. I got money, Cindy! Marry me."

"Help! Help!"

The door of the old man's house flew open. Astonishingly, Kevin came rushing out. Behind him was the old man himself, carrying a tall, rusty halberd. In his hands Kevin brandished a volume of the *Encyclopedia Britannica*.

"Oh, Lordy, now look what you done, Cindy! Hold on, fellas, she don't need help. Lord, what is that, an ax?"

"Unhand her," Kevin shrieked. "Mr. Forbes has been trained on his weapon!"

The old man, who was tall and emaciated, wearing a tattered herringbone sports jacket and plaid pants, took a spread-legged stance and lowered the halberd. "Let her go, Charlie," he said. "I can cut off balls with this thing just as clean as heads."

"That's gotta be an illegal weapon or something." The two Charlies complied, though, and Cindy felt a great relief. Kevin stepped forward and slammed the encyclopedia down on Little Charlie's head, whereupon he sank into the snow without so much as a sigh. "Aw," Big Charlie cried, "why'd you do that?"

"That's my *mother,* scumbag!"

"Oh Lord. All I wanted was to talk to her. I want her to consider me a suitor, that's all. I need a wife. Eileen died, damn her, and I need a wife, oh, God I do. I've got love in me. Yes, I've got love in me."

The old man jabbed with the halberd, and Big Charlie became silent. "I'm tired of men like you, you brutal fool," the old man said. "I ought to hurt you." The halberd whistled and Big Charlie had to jump.

Little Charlie raised himself up, squinting and rubbing his head. "Somebody oughta whip that kid, he's a damn sonembitch."

Louie came running down the street, shouting and waving a large knife. "You let them alone, Gilford Forbes! It's just their way."

"The hell, Louie, nobody drags women off like that, not in my sight. This is the civilized world, and if you don't like that, you can damn well move to South Africa or someplace."

"Come on, Mother, it's time to go."

The tension between Louie and Gilford Forbes seemed ready to erupt into a battle. Cindy was not sure what would happen if the spindly old man actually began to use the halberd, which was obviously as sharp as a razor. She wasted no time following Kevin, who was already on his way back to Forbes's house.

Forbes backed up, marching like a spider, rather than turn away from the other men.

The house was an old one, really no more than a cottage, with a wooden porch populated by an ancient swing and choked in the tendrils of what in spring and summer must be a laurel. Beyond the front door was a living room full of bulky furniture, overstuffed chairs, a large and complicated Wurlitzer organ, and on the walls prints of familiar Impressionists: Van Gogh's *Starry Night*, Renoir's *Bathers*, and four or five others. They added an altogether incongruous note of intense cheer to an otherwise drably comfortable scene.

"Please make yourself at home, Kevin's mother," Forbes said. He bowed. "The altogether estimable mother of a most remarkable young boy." He smiled, his cadaverous face cracking into a grin so wide that it seemed about to cause his lower jaw to disengage itself and flop down along his neck. "I am Gilford Forbes, former don at Christ Church College, Oxford, former tutor at Harvard—alas, all very former. Presently Kevin and I are engaged in setting ponderous poetry to light music and light poetry to ponderous music. An interesting exercise, Pound's *Cantos* chanted to the tune of 'A Rock and Roll Waltz' and the works of Rod McKuen intoned to Beethoven's *Missa Solemnis*. Your screams did not fit, and I must apologize to you—"

Kevin rushed forward and hugged her.

Gilford Forbes smiled a little nervously. Kevin glanced just sharply enough at Cindy to communicate the message that he had kept his father a secret from this man. The boy must already have told the old man some story—some lie—that explained their presence here in Olana.

"A broken life," Kevin murmured sadly. His face was grave. Cindy saw again the stoniness that more and more often appeared in his eyes.

She nodded. "That ends at Parma Lunch."

"You'll get back on your feet. You're young!" There was an extended silence after the old man's remark. "It's cold," he added. "Would anyone care for tea?"

Wordlessly, Kevin went with him into his tiny kitchen. "Where did you get this Darjeeling?" she heard her son ask.

"In Toronto. I've also some scones. Your mother might like one."

"She hardly eats anything."

The man did not answer. Cindy sat in an old Morris chair. This was an extraordinarily comfortable room. The wood stove crinkled softly, beads of snow tapped against the window. Beyond it, in the darkening afternoon, the sinister little town seemed about to settle into the woods that surrounded it. Nothing moved in the street, no car, no pedestrian, not even a wandering dog. Idly, Cindy picked up a magazine, a literary journal called *Prometheus*. Bob had bought it from time to time, and the look of it brought back memories. She glanced through it, impressed mainly by the beautiful printing and layout. Then she saw a poem by Gilford Forbes.

> *The snow trumpets silently down,*
> *Hurrying the shadows in*
> *The terrible land,*
>
> *Enforcing the migration of bones,*
> *This snow, laboring with the force*
> *Of dangerous old laws.*

The fire shuffled again, and the snow pinged on the window. Cindy realized that in this moment she had come face-to-face with the mystery. It stood revealed before her, as if a door had at last opened—but only into endless night. Tears collected in her eyes. She could not look again at the magazine. Instead she pushed it to the floor with her knuckles and wiped her hands on her dress. A tiredness akin almost to death stole over her, dropping around her shoulders like a cloak of cold chain. She bowed her head, aware only as her glance passed over it of a tiny cross hanging on the wall, a priest's black cross.

"So you see," Gilford Forbes said, "I'm broken, too." He put her cup of tea into her hands. On the saucer there was a scone cut in two and buttered, and it looked awfully tempting. "Before you, woman of the broken life, stands a ruined priest. I will tell you my story if you will tell me yours."

How could she? His story would move, it would touch, it would enlighten in a fine and decent manner. Her story would sound lurid and absurd.

Even so, Bob was out there in the snow, or he was dead, a pecked hulk on a roadside, or a pelt in some trapper's winter storehouse. "I was caught in flagrantibus delictis. I pluralize because I was with two of my students, a young woman and a young man. We were in the dressing room, in the bottom of a cupboard. The shaking of the cupboard attracted the attention of the choir, which was just coming down after singing High Mass. One of them opened the thing and there we were, wallowing naked in a pile of vestments."

Another silence developed. Kevin looked steadily at his mother, his eyes intractable. She was not to tell.

"You were thrown out?" she asked.

"Difficult to do to a priest." He held up his

hands. "They will still bear the Paraclete. I was hustled out of Cambridge and posted to an obscure boonie parish. No more Newman Club for me, no more students. The trouble was, that incident—which was my only transgression of celibacy—assumed such enormous proportions in my mind that I could no longer bear to abide by my vows. Night after night I thought of the wonders of that time in the cupboard, how good they had tasted, smelled, how warm and lovely it all was. Dear God, I still do. It was the central experience of my life. I've never tried sex again, for fear of disappointment."

"They must have been marvelous people," Kevin said.

"Marvelous looking. They were a team. I got their number out of a singles paper. They were undergrads doing a little whoring to make their lives more comfortable. God, they were wonderful." He sipped his tea. "Your story, please."

"No," Kevin said. "You have to be careful of him, Mother. He never had that experience. He wasn't even a priest. He's trying to trick you."

Gilford Forbes smiled, this time a little thinly. "Your point, Kevin. I suppose that you must remain a mystery to me, too."

Cindy would have told him everything. Why not, what did it matter? Look at the Indian—he understood more about what had happened to Bob than she had imagined possible, but he had not the strength for the journey. And Monica: "Call me if you need me. I love you." In other words, good-bye.

Only she and Kevin remained, in this difficult time. She bit into the scone, which was still cold in the middle. As she chewed she heard shouts outside, more than one shout in the muffling snow.

Forbes frowned, looking toward the dark gray window. Kevin put his teacup down and stepped over to the door. He opened it, stepped onto the porch.

Another shout, this time accompanied by the shape of a man running down the street.

Kevin returned. His face was horribly twisted, his eyes were darting with fear. "Wolves," he whispered, "they've seen wolves at the north end of town."

"Really! I had no idea there were wolves in New York State. In a way that's lovely, if they don't just shoot them."

Without another word, forgetting how lightly dressed she was, forgetting her fearful experience with the Charlies, Cindy jumped up and dashed out into the snow.

Up the dark streets she raced. She could hear Kevin beside her. Whether Forbes had come or not, she did not know.

As she ran she heard it. She stopped and looked up. Kevin looked up. Ahead of them a man carrying a high-power rifled stopped also, and he looked up. A cat, which had been sitting in a window, darted away.

The howl rose and rose, a plasma of dark pealing echoes, powerful and loud.

Kevin's hand came into her own. That was Bob, she knew it in her freezing bones. Bob was here, and the town was turning out to meet him. Bob must stand against a town full of sharpshooting roughnecks.

She ran, Kevin ran. Far behind them Forbes— who had been running—dropped to a walk with a gesture of annoyance.

Bob was here. At last, at last she had found him. With a frantic little scream in her throat, she made her way through the snow, determined this time to find a way to share life with him as best she could, on whatever terms he would grant.

PART FOUR
HOMECOMING

We left when we were too young
to know.

Now we are far away and going farther.
Home, we say, home. . . .

We watch the empty dark.

—Robert Duke,
"Home" (1985)

CHAPTER TWENTY-ONE

BOB HAD GONE DASHING ACROSS THE FROZEN ST. LAW-
rence Seaway, his claws crackling on the ice. He
had leaped over floes and cracks, slipped, got up,
and slid forward, barking joyfully.

The eyes of the other wolves had followed him.
None barked back, no tail wagged. For his part,
Bob had been so excited that he couldn't stop
barking. Smelling the wolves this close made
thrills sweep up and down his body. Their odor
was sensuous, incredibly attractive. It was far
richer to his nose than any human odor had ever
been, more so even than Cindy's beloved scent. As
he ran, his mind cast about for meaning in this
odor, but there were no words that described the
experience of smelling it.

These wolves lived in this heaven of smell; they
were used to it. Beyond their individual smells—
the sharp, shocking aromas coming from the pack

leaders, and the sweet smells of the lesser wolves, there was another odor, which was the combination of them all, the majestic smell of the pack as a whole, a fine old spirit of an aroma.

When Bob was about ten yards from the pack, the wolf at the lead had barked once, a sound as sharp as a shot. It went deep into Bob, exploding in his heart. It was a warning and a command: it said stop.

Bob had stood, his tail wagging, his tongue slopping out of his mouth. He gathered himself together: he was a man inside, after all, and he had his dignity.

The dignity of a man, though, is nothing before the dignity of a king of the wolves. Human governments rise and fall across a few generations. This king was the inheritor of ten thousand generations. His pack was an ancient kingdom, and he ruled it by traditions that extended back into the mists. He had come forward, his legs stiff, his ears cocked, on his face a look at once curious and fierce. Bob could see his nose working.

Bob's whole attention had gone to this wolf. By degrees he was realizing that he would not be welcome here. It hurt him. He had come an awfully long way to get a reception like this. He might be a man, and feel he was a man, but he was also a *wolf,* every inch of him. If he had any rights at all, it was among these creatures.

In his rising anger he had made a mistake: he barked loudly. It was a challenge, it couldn't be interpreted any other way. The king of the wolves snarled horribly, lifting his lips to reveal startlingly effective-looking fangs. His pack seethed behind him. A strong musk came from them, as if they were spitting odor at the interloper, trying to cover his unwanted scent. Bob could feel his own glands working, could smell his own anger and excitement. His neck tickled: his hackles were rising.

The king strutted, ears back, eyes fairly cracking with rage. Bob had to think, but he was getting too scared to think. He was acutely aware of the fact that he was out here alone in this wilderness, and the only creatures he could trust, the only companions that were even close to his own kind, were rejecting him out of hand.

What to do? He couldn't explain himself, he didn't know the language of the wolves. And they had a language, he could see, hear, and smell that. It was a thousand, a million times more rich than anything he had ever read about. Tails flickered, expressions rushed through faces, complicated waves of odor and sound flashed through the pack like little storms. They were so incredibly integrated, they were like one person.

How could anybody have ever thought that these were simple beasts? Bob was faced with the shocking realization that the wolves had evolved an intelligence and a sense so great that it was literally incomparable, and yet so different from man's intelligence that it was all but invisible to the human mind.

There was no rational shape to it, no sense structure. It had words, though, sentences that were songs, and through it all there was creeping what he could only describe to himself as angry, rejecting prejudice.

His heart ached. He knew that he was going to have to fight again. It was so damn sad. He lowered his eyes and tail.

When he did, the whole pack erupted at him,

barking with savage fury. Then their leader, their arrogant, strutting king, was at his throat, bellowing, his jaws flashing in the white, snowy light. There was more fury, more wildness in this assault than Bob had ever known before. It was literally fantastic in its energy, like a hurricane, like the explosion of a mountain, like some holocaust come down from heaven. The wolf snarled and snapped and slammed directly into Bob's chest. Bob was bowled completely over, his own growl sticking in his throat.

In all of his previous battles, with the shepherds at the pound, the coydogs in Central Park, with the bear, this had been the moment when his wolf instincts took over and carried him to victory. But this wolf was so powerful that it shattered all instinct. As he rolled and tumbled beneath its attack he was swept by aromas that stunned the very center of his being. He was awed, humbled, titillated by the smell of this wolf. He could not fight back, he just could not.

The wolf bit him hard in the throat and he found himself turning over on his back. He felt an awful, delicious stirring of what could only be described as ecstatic humility. He spread his legs and turned his head, baring throat and genitals to the powerful creature that dominated him. The wolf was not large, nor was he old, but he was so lordly, so proud, so certain of himself that Bob simply could not stand up to him.

For a moment he held Bob's throat, then he released it. Still full of strut and anger, the wolf suddenly did a most intimate and embarrassing thing. He bent down and nuzzled Bob's penis with his cold, damp nose. The contact injected a fiery vibration of purest pleasure into Bob's body, a pleasure so great that for a moment he was incapable of thought, of motion. As the wolf continued its exploration wave after wave of sheer, delicious enjoyment rocked Bob's being.

Then the pack leader tossed his head, snorted as if contemptuous of the gift he had given, and walked away from Bob. For a moment Bob lay there swooning, helpless. Then there came to him another aroma, this a scent he could identify from his old life: it was the smell of a woman.

She moved forth over him, circling him. He had never seen such beauty as the king's mate. She was young and strong, her fur shining white and light gray in the sun. Bob's own chemical essence poured desire through him. He almost wept to see such female magnificence. Hers was a new esthetic, of rich odors, deeply satisfying, the kind of smell Bob could imagine living within forever, intimate and sweet, conjuring images of furious passion. He recognized her odor: this was the wolf who had licked him after the fight with the bear.

When she stood over him, Bob again felt the same helpless wave of submission the king had given him. Then she also touched her nose to him, most intimately and without a trace of what he had once called shame. At once his body reacted, bursting with pleasure so great he thought it might actually kill him. For a long moment she continued, extending the examination, learning him.

When at length she was done with him, he was more in love than he had ever been or dreamed possible. The complex, equivocal coupling of his human life seemed a mutant shadow compared to this. She was so beautiful, so grand, so calm and magnificent—he could hardly believe her an earthly creature.

He knew the secret behind the feeling of the dog for its master. Canine love is not like human love, not at all: it is all rapture.

She stepped off him and, growling in her throat, strutted about with her tail high, as if enjoying her conquest. Her mate looked on warily. The tension coming from the other wolves was high. They whined and strutted, some of the lesser ones snapping at each other. One or two barked. Bob realized that the pack was in heat. Coming upon them, he had gone into heat, too. What a small word for the largest emotion and the greatest pleasure he had ever known. He found himself lying there on his back in the snow and thanking whatever God there was that he had been freed of the bondage of being human. Something in the air had changed. The wolves were no longer holding him captive, no longer humiliating him. He was free to rise, and he got up, to stand hangdog before the king and his queen, too much in love ever to leave them, too alien ever to be accepted.

The queen regarded him. Her face—all soft fur and glittering, passionate eyes—seemed not unwilling. He circled her, his nose drawn to the center of her magic, the spot beneath her tail from which there flowed her nectar.

Up close the smell was so good and so fascinating that he simply could not quit inhaling it.

With a little growl she moved away. She had sniffed him, too, but in a perfunctory manner, an act perhaps of protocol or at best mild curiosity. He was being rejected. How was that possible? How dare she drive him to such a pitch and then turn away from him?

With a quite involuntary snarl he leaped on her back. He felt his penis strike at her like an arrow.

Instantly she was out from under him. So quickly that he could not tell how she had done it, she upended him in the snow, and he found himself once again with his legs in the air. His throat hurt; she had grabbed him by the neck and turned him over.

Again she dominated him, this time licking his exposed penis and causing an explosion by doing it that actually did make him faint. For a few moments he was on another ground. The she-wolf seemed serenely regal. Far off Cindy stood, and in a thin voice called his name.

This time when she had finished with him, he found that he could not arise, not until every one of the other wolves had had his or her way with him. They strutted about in a kind of ecstasy of domination, one after another threatening him, standing over him, then examining him.

At the end of it there was not one of them to whom he would not roll. He would do anything to be with them, he adored them. To him they had acquired in full amount the magic he had always suspected was possessed by the nonhuman beings of the earth. They were living close to the central truth of things, their passions unencumbered by the cluttered mental hodgepodge that afflicted humankind.

When he got to his feet and went strutting toward them, the smallest and least of them, a scruffy little female wolf with a kink in her tail—the last one to have sniffed Bob—ran at him and snapped fiercely. Even though Bob was twice the animal's size, he turned away. The wolf wanted him to roll, and she barked furiously, then went for Bob's throat. Bob rolled, but another wolf had snapped at his attacker, who disappeared back into the milling, nervous pack.

Bob realized what had happened to him with these animals. Stunned by the unexpected intensity of the pleasure they were giving him, he had let himself be dominated by all of them. Instead of fighting for a place, he had wound up outside the pack's order altogether. He cursed himself for submitting to them. But how could he have avoided it? He would do the same thing again.

The little wolf, who was a female not in heat, bland smelling, returned to worry him. He wondered what would happen if he fought her. Or should he fight the lowest male, or go back to the king? He really had no idea. All he did know was that they had at once seduced and rejected him.

It was a more profound event than he at first realized. Night came on and he wound up sleeping some distance from the other wolves, outside of the inner border of their scent, the line beyond which they had to use scent marks to define their territory.

He would have thought they would huddle together in the snow, but each wolf slept alone, tightly curled in on himself, nose beneath tail.

Bob was not like them; he had neither their peace nor their confidence. Again and again in the night he remembered the extraordinary ecstasy they had granted him. If they could all evoke such powerful sensations in one another, how did they survive, how did they bear one another's presence? He was mad with lust and love, a trembling little creature beneath the cold stars, ignored by those whose touch he craved.

He raised his head in the middle of the night, alert with an idea that made him weak all over again. Perhaps, if he challenged the alpha female, she would once more carry out the ritual with him.

He had no trouble finding her: her heated scent made her a constant beacon to any wolf. None of the other females were like her. Bob got up and walked across the creaking snow. He bent over her motionless form and sniffed, smelling the sweet beneath the unwashed dogginess. Her muzzle was soft, her fur glowing in the starlight.

Then, with a snort, she leaped to her feet. Not an instant was wasted: she attacked Bob with snarling, barking fury. The whole pack awoke and jumped up, but he was already lying on his back. He was rewarded once again by the whole strutting, delightful ritual, and was again passed down the pack and out to the rear, being finally dominated by the scruffy little female.

He crawled away, besotted, crazed with a hunger for more. Some of them had been a little perfunctory this time, though. He suspected that he would bore them if he challenged too often. A wolf pack was a psychosexual Gethsemane for the rejects, a bed of love and torment. For its members, though, it was Eden.

God curse the serpent and the tree of knowledge of good and evil. Compared with the animals, man is numb, and it is knowledge that has made him that way. Bob looked up at the sky, and learned in that instant more about the whole wheeling of the universe than all science knew. Without words, he understood the subtle indeterminacies of the laws and saw the endless frame upon which time is woven. He knew the true purpose of thought: It is not to process information, but to seek the law. Modern science is the burned stubble of ancient magic. Once we flew: now we struggle sadly along.

Curled up tight, he slept fitfully in the snow. When he woke up, it was with a lingering impression that some sort of kindness had soothed him in the night. Then he saw the wolves moving. They were cast in golden light. They were deities. Highest among them was the heated goddess, who undulated, wagged her tail, and gobbled snow.

The wolves were excited, yapping and running about, dashing off into the snow with their noses to the ground, then coming back, tails high, eyes agleam.

When Bob smelled a clear, clean odor of deer, he knew the reason for the excitement: a hunt was on. The pack was like a perfect machine. Led by the alphas, it moved off into the woods. Fifteen wolves disappeared as if they had been shadows. But Bob was not lost. His nose and ears worked, too. He could follow them, which he did at once. They ran along beneath the snow-heavy hemlocks, ducking under low-hanging boughs of pine. He wished that he was part of the pack, but that was not to be. By light of morning he cringed to remember the liberties he had allowed them. Every one of them knew him intimately, while he knew none of them. Such knowledge was an important part of their ritual life. Unless he could make them roll before him, they would never consider him one of them. Even then, he wondered if he would ever acquire that almost indefinable odor of belonging that they had, the special undersmell they all shared.

As they moved along, Bob began to smell the deer more and more clearly. He could identify the odor of the breath: the deer had been gnawing a sassafras plant.

The wolves proceeded quickly and efficiently. As far as they were concerned, Bob simply didn't exist. He was there, though, running along behind as fast as he could, his mind swarming with thoughts and speculations, his heart brimming over with love.

They came upon the deer suddenly. The wolves were quick and efficient. They burst out of the woods into the tight clearing where the deer were tearing bark. There was a whistle of alarm, then the flash of a tail. Deer screams, as soft as the blowing of clouds, filled the air. There were three animals: a buck and two does.

The buck bounded off into the forest, followed a moment later by one of the does, who had a red streak on her left leg. Wolves were barking, leaping, snapping. The one remaining deer broke wildly for the woods. Her body twisting in the air, the alpha female leaped for the throat. She missed, falling back into the snow with a thud and a spray of white.

Bob found himself face-to-face with the doe. He didn't hesitate a moment—he leaped right at the throat of the beautiful little animal. He was a big wolf. The doe struggled, dashing him with her front hooves, but it was no use. He had the flap of skin on the underside of her neck. When he worried it she shrieked, a gentle and lovely sound. This was like killing Bambi. But something drove him on. He would not stop for Bambi, not even when her heart rending whistles changed to bubbling sighs, and then stopped altogether.

She stood, her head hanging down. The nearest of the pack wolves, which was the one farthest to the rear, had reached her. It was the shabby little female with the broken tail. She clambered up the doe's side, trying to get on her back and bring her down.

This seemed to break the doe's trance. She proved to have more fight in her than Bob had imagined possible. Despite her torn throat and the little wolf clinging to her she began to run. Soon the wolf fell off. The doe plunged through the woods in plumes of snow. She was swift. Bob could also run, though. He was big and his thigh was healed; he could run like the wind.

The deer plunged on through the drifts, Bob just behind. He was hungry now, and the smell of the blood sent mad thrills of excitement through him. The deer reached a long meadow and picked up speed. Bob ran as hard as he could, stretching his whole body, nipping at the flying hooves.

Then someone was beside him—the alpha female. He was fast but she was much faster, a wolf of lightning, her muzzle stretched tight, spittle flying from her mouth, the whites of her eyes showing as she sped forward.

She shouldered Bob aside, ducked her head under the side of the leaping deer, and with a toss of her muzzle opened a huge hole in the creature's abdomen. Guts spewed out as the deer tumbled over and over. By the time it stopped falling it was dead. The alpha female strutted, her lovely face drenched in blood, and then she plunged her mouth into the still-heaving entrails and began gobbling huge gulps of the steaming organs.

Bob took a bite. A raw flash blinded him. Both she and her mate were on him, biting savagely. He screamed, scrambled away, felt her jaws tear his flanks as he ran.

He was forced to watch, drooling, in an anguish of hunger, while all of the other wolves ate their fill. They did it in strict rank order. To the little female was left the brain and some skin. To Bob was left gnawed bone.

While the others trotted off into the woods, full and happy, Bob bit at the bones, trying without success to crack them for the marrow. It was useless—all he succeeded in doing was cutting his tongue on a bone splinter.

Finally he went hunting alone. He was surprised to find such a lack of game. Then he understood why these wolves had come so far south. They, also, were suffering from the shortage of game. This was an exceptionally snowy winter. They had moved south with the deer.

As he sniffed about for sign of raccoon or opossum, he reflected on his passion and their seeming injustice. He shuddered, remembering the pleasure they had accorded him. Nobody but Cindy knew him that way, Cindy and now these wolves, who were so beautiful that he could not help but let them do their bidding with him. He knew the truth—that they had humiliated and rejected him. But they had done it so sweetly. Did they make their pack important by creating in others a desire to join it? Or would what they had done to him have felt different to a real wolf? He suspected that a real wolf would have found their nosing about an intolerable humiliation and put a stop to it as soon as a beast weaker than himself tried.

He mounted a ridge. From here there was a view for miles. The St. Lawrence glimmered on the northern distance, a jagged tumble of ice. Far to the south rose the Adirondacks. For a moment Bob thought he heard music—a harpsichord, perhaps Scarlatti or Bach. The sound made him cock his ears, but then he lost it, gone in the immensity of the view.

He was hungry. In fact he was damned hungry. Sooner or later, he had to find a kill of his own. He sniffed the air in the careful, searching way he had learned from experiment. It was possible to sort out the different smells not only by odor but by an elusive texture. The ubiquitous smell of snow was crisp except where there was melt, which had a much smoother feel.

Besides the snow, he detected ice, frozen plants, a wisp of smoke, cold stone. No smell of game, not a trace. He was disconcerted. In all of his travels he had never encountered a day when he smelled no animals at all. The image of the winter wolf, its ribs like bars, came to him, and the image of the starved wolf, curled in death agony.

He paced the ridge, taking deep breaths, analyzing the air for any trace of food, any carrion even, any garbage. He wasn't revolted by these things anymore, at least not so much that he wouldn't eat them if necessary. He let his body decide what to eat and what to pass up.

Then he stopped, cocking his ears. This time it wasn't music he heard, but the grinding of gears. The sound came from behind the line of ridges to the south. His estimate was ten miles. He turned, cocking his ears, and listened carefully. When he did so, a welter of tiny sounds came into focus: cars moving on snow, voices, various snatches of music, doors slamming, children shouting. So there was a town over there.

A town meant garbage and it meant the chance of stealing some animal, a chicken or a goat, perhaps, from a farm. The other wolves would shun the town, but they did not possess the human lore that Bob did. He felt that he could sneak in and out quickly, and get himself fed. A guerrilla attack.

Without further ado he set off down the ridge, going straight toward the source of the human clatter. As he dropped lower the sounds faded, but he knew they would be there when he mounted the next rise.

He was halfway up it when he heard a sharp bark behind him. He turned and saw the alpha female standing in a clearing. Her tail was high, her face was stern. She was commanding him to turn back. She trotted up, whining. He was surprised, he thought the pack had rejected him. Apparently not, because she was treating him just like one of her other wolves. Whining, she rubbed her cheek against his. She began wagging her tail. At that, his interest in the town evaporated. She was far more important to him than food. Hunger could wait, journeys could wait. To have her come near him, to notice him, even touch him, drove him to a joyous pitch of excitement. He practically danced around her.

She played. She barked and tussled with him, growling in mock challenge. To say that he was delighted was to understate the feelings that washed over him, the rich, mysterious, enormous feelings. It was as if the basic creative energy of the earth was flowing right through him. When they tussled, he smelled and tasted her. Beneath the odor of her fur there was a sweetness so pure that it was shocking, and then the powerful female musk.

When it grew suddenly much stronger, he felt his loins contract. There was a sensation as if of a tickling, delightful fire between his legs. He found himself mounting her, felt himself thrusting at her, saw her eye shimmering with amusement when she glanced over her shoulder, felt her expertly pull herself away. He tried again, whining for her to stay still, pushing, trying in his clumsy way to make this new practice of sexual union work. Never before in his life had he mounted like an animal.

He was hurled off her into the snow by a snarling, biting streak of enraged alpha male.

Where the devil had *he* come from? And with him the rest of the pack, all barking, all threatening, their anger wild.

The next moment, though, he thought the alpha male was going to forget him, so intense were the odors coming from his mate. But he didn't. The alpha male attacked, leaping onto Bob with savage fury.

Even as they fought, both of them made involuntary sexual thrusts. One of the younger wolves mounted the female. The alpha male stopped beating Bob up long enough to turn and bark him away. This alpha was not enormous, but he was a devil of a fighter. His pack mate knew it, and the barking was quite enough to make him rush away.

Bob realized something in that instant of respite. He had to beat this wolf if he was going to have a place in the pack. Now was the time. The alpha female's heat had precipitated the confrontation.

If he won the battle, he was going to be able to make love to her. The male grabbed for his throat and sank his teeth into the much-scarred skin. Bob yanked away, managing to bite the other wolf's ear hard enough to draw blood and a high scream of pain.

His eyes gleaming, the alpha took Bob by the scruff of the neck and shook him. Bob skittered away, feet digging the hard, old snow. So far he had always lost fights with the wolves, but he did not want to lose this fight. He had to find a way to succeed. The wolf was so fast, such an expert at this, so relentless and wild and passionate. Bob had never encountered such powerful will before: it mattered to this wolf, it mattered terribly.

They separated and Bob ran at him, forcing himself to be more aggressive than he felt. To his surpise the weight of his body completely unbalanced the smaller animal, who went flying into a snowbank with a scream and a great windmilling of paws. Bob was on him instantly, biting, growling, clawing. For a time there was nothing but a jumble of flashing fur and fangs, then Bob found himself on top, and his opponent was screaming.

He backed away. His heart hurt—he did not want to do injury to this magnificent creature.

The alpha wolf clambered to his feet. When he would not meet Bob's eyes, a rush of triumph filled him. He could not help himself strutting. His tail went high, he yapped in excitement. The female leaned against him, and her odor was strong.

He mounted her, causing a tremendous explosion of excitement among the other wolves. They yapped, whined, ran about, paced. Some of the males snapped at each other. Then Bob found her secret, and thrust, and was rewarded with the most exquisite sensation. It was a perfection of feeling: soft love mixed with electrifying pleasure. Lying on the back of that wolf, he found the edge of heaven.

It was not a quick thing. He burst open like a

flower within her. His body collapsed from the sheer intensity of the sensations that were roaring through it like storms come down the mountains of love. Her back was strong. She stood like a stone, receiving him in her milky center. The other wolves kept coming up and licking at him, sniffing under his tail, adding to the pleasure he was already experiencing.

His heart beat so hard he thought it would explode. But it didn't explode. Instead his loins exploded, and he saw flashes of stars, and smelled coming from her an odor so sweet that he could not but be humble before it. Then he was finished. He dismounted. For a long time, with quiet waves flowing back and forth between them, they stood linked.

He thought when it was finally over that he knew this wolf better than he had ever known any creature. In her dark and gleaming eyes, he saw that she, too, shared the knowledge. The total intimacy still shocked him a little. Privacy, secrecy were not known here. All the wolves had participated. Now some of the younger males were mounting each other. There was much intimate licking and much barking.

The alpha male went a little distance away, curled up, and slept. Bob also slept, and the alpha female midway between them.

Bob thought, on awakening, that he would become pack leader. She soon disabused him of this notion. By the operation of laws he did not begin to understand, all that had happened was that she had somehow changed places with the alpha male. She was now leader. The scraggly little female at the end of the line reasserted her dominance over Bob, making him roll to her. He did it because he sensed that ignoring her demand would lead again to total rejection.

That he could not bear. To be near them, to be included in their love, was the only thing Bob really cared about. That and food.

He cared about food. And there was so little food. No more deer, no possums, no coons.

There was that town, though, and on mornings when the wind was right, Bob was sure he heard the calling of a rooster and the bleating of goats. This was lumber country, so there weren't any significant farms, but that didn't mean that people in the town wouldn't be keeping chickens and goats, maybe even a few cows.

Of course they were keeping chickens. On the first morning of the south wind, Bob heard them clearly. He smelled melt, too. For three weeks he had eaten exactly two rats. Some of the wolves had eaten nothing at all.

He cocked his ears, he got up, shook himself. Despite the obvious danger, even the foolhardiness, of going into a human place, Bob trotted off south. He had to eat, they all did. It was especially important for the alpha female. Shortly after her encounter with Bob she had gone out of heat. The sexual intensity of the pack had immediately disappeared and they had become a band of companions, flawless in its balance and organization. Day by day Bob watched the nipples grow on her thin body, and when the days were longer and the sun returning from the south, he saw a roundness to her belly.

He was going to hunt down the town's chickens and goats, and damn the consequences. The pack could always escape across the St. Lawrence if they had to. Canada was far more empty. These wolves had come from there, after all. Only the presence of the town kept them from moving even farther south in search of game.

Well, with him in the pack they could confront the town. He understood towns. Maybe that was why all this had happened, why he was here. Suddenly there was a wolf pack that could survive in close proximity to human beings—indeed, could control its whole relationship to mankind. He glimpsed the edges of a magnificent design here, perhaps even another step in the process of evolution.

Wary but eager—no, desperate, for the pack was starving—he set out toward the town and all its dangers, and its chickens.

The first trip in was a great success. Bob ate two perfectly delicious Rhode Island Reds and took one back to the alpha female. She gobbled it down, leaving only feathers for the other wolves to lick.

When Bob returned to the town a week later, two of the other wolves came with him.

Again they were successful, although only Bob would return with food in his mouth. That was not a wolf tradition, and they could not be made to do it.

Through the last months of winter, the pack gradually moved to within striking distance of the town. They took goats, dogs, more chickens. Sometimes they got rats, once an opossum.

Through the lengthening days the alpha female grew heavy with her burden of cubs. Bob's cubs. He remembered Cindy when she was big with child. They were happy then.

Oh, Cindy, I am so lost.

One night, when the snow was grown soft and

the breeze was again in the south, the alpha female gave birth to four magnificent cubs, and one small one. The birthing was abrupt and simple. She expelled the little bundles of fur one by one. Then the afterbirth folded out. She ate it, along with the cub that was too small.

There was happiness among the wolves. Everybody was awake, yapping and sniffing the babies. Bob and the two alphas licked them clean. Bob thought they were the most beautiful things he had ever seen, so soft and tiny, mewing and shaking their heads. They nursed their mother, who lay on her side in a kind of rapture.

It was a good time, with spring coming and plenty of chicken. The cubs grew quickly. Soon it would be time for the thaw. That night all the wolves howled together, and the strongest of the new cubs yapped.

Bob wondered about his cubs. What would they be like as they matured? They had wide heads and quick eyes, and they gazed at him sometimes with the love eyes of children. He began to want to be across the St. Lawrence and away with them.

They loved their mother, nuzzling her, playing in the warm enclosure made by her reclining body. He had thought at first that the cement of a wolf pack was sex, but that had been true only during the time of heat. Now things were more settled and more simple. These creatures were together because they were friends and blood relations, and because they loved one another. The pack was a band of lovers, adoring, gentle, accepting, full of fun and play.

Bob was totally involved now, a bottom wolf still, but he accepted that. He had gained the highest of rights, to impregnate the heated female, and his cubs were his cubs. They crawled all over him when he was still. One little female liked to chew ears, and the sensation was so tickling that Bob could barely stand it.

He would lie very still, until she had crawled up on his muzzle. Then he would snort and jerk his head and she would go tumbling off with a great deal of mewing and snapping. They would lie face-to-face. When they were sleepy, he would lick his cubs, tasting their sweet taste.

One day he found a roach for them to play with, and it was a fine morning. What joy they took in the chase, what merry pleasure!

The presence of the roach should have warned him.

The danger it represented never crossed his mind, though. On a moonless evening, he made his way again to the town. There was a good coop of chickens as yet undisturbed, and he planned on raiding the garbage behind the diner.

No other wolves were with him. Raiding the town was not like hunting. They tended to do it alone or in small groups. Since Bob brought food back, the alpha female never went at all, but relied on him to feed her and the cubs.

Bob was standing just at the edge of town when he realized that everything had changed. He'd always assumed that people would notice the missing livestock, but he felt sure that they would attribute the losses to feral dogs, an annoying problem in any isolated community, but the sort of thing they would put off doing anything about until spring made it easy.

The evening air was soft and almost warm when Bob reached the outskirts of town.

What he smelled stopped him right in the

middle of the street. He stood there, paralyzed by deep emotions. The aroma brought crowds of memories: voices, dreams, sunny days. A woman's smell, rich and strong and familiar. That and the scent of a little boy. He knew them, and when the scents reached his heart, he was filled with longing.

Cindy and Kevin were here.

Bob's second mistake was to stand there, staring down the dark street, trying to see into the past. He lingered a moment too long.

CHAPTER TWENTY-TWO

THE TOTALLY UNEXPECTED PRESENCE OF HIS HUMAN family froze him.

—Sunday mornings with the *Times*.

—Watching *Mystery* with Kevin and Cindy.

—Reading Kafka, the *Metamorphosis*.

—A good cup of coffee. A good play. Laughing, singing, listening to music. Music, talk: pastries in the afternoon, discussing poetry with Cindy.

—Cindy in the night, Kevin's face when he slept. The life of the family, intimate, infinitely private, gentle.

—Rooms, heat, beds, food on demand.

—Privacy. Being alone. Being naked. Bathing. Being touched by Cindy, touching her. Sharing secret knowledge. The richness of human life.

It all came back, assailing him, sweeping him away on a tide of longing. He had become, truly, a lover: he loved the wolves, the cubs, but he also loved Cindy and Kevin.

The old wolf seduced you with his eyes.

Bob was torn, his heart ached, and when a wolf's heart aches, he is as inspired as when he is joyful or lonely, and he howls, forming with his throat and tongue and lips the music of the wild.

The howl swept down across the town, chilling the March twilight. Men, shining with eagerness, loaded rifles and fueled up snowmobiles. This was an event: wolves in Olana for the first time in living memory. What horror, what fun!

All winter there had been livestock thefts. At first they had attributed it to dogs left behind by summer people. But then they had realized it was wolves. Right there at the end of Ontario Street where the Tucker property began, stood a big, black timber wolf. No doubt about it, they'd come down from Canada because the winter'd been so hard.

Bob stood in confusion as Cindy started to run toward him. His skin quivered—he was repelled by the odd human odors, but also attracted to her, loving her again, that creature from the bright improbable past.

"Run, Bob, run!"

What was she saying? It had been a long time since he had heard words. She was speaking too quickly.

"Bob, run, run for your life!"

Her fear communicated what the words could not. They were simply too fast. In fact the whole town was fast, engines roaring, a siren blaring, people darting about.

He skittered away a little. Had he been seen? He'd come here so many times, he'd gotten used to not being seen.

He had gotten careless.

He knew it for certain when a phalanx of snowmobiles came screaming around the corner, jammed with men and guns.

Oh, God.

He turned and ran, leaving his wife and son and a large part of his heart behind. They had reawakened the man in him, a man who had gone peacefully off to sleep. He loped, choosing a wide, easy stride, the kind that was best for long runs. He could do forty miles like this if he had to. Initially, he wasn't afraid.

His plan was to head straight up the ridge behind the town, then cut through the dense forest just beyond. The snowmobiles wouldn't be able to follow him there. He would get back to the pack and draw them north toward the St. Lawrence. The ice might be getting loose. It was time and past time for them to return to Canada. They could not afford to be caught on this side of the seaway. There just wasn't room in New York for wolves, not even in these relatively empty regions.

The climb up the ridge was hard. He was moving a lot faster than usual, and he felt his wind coming quicker and quicker as he struggled through the sticky snow. If only it hadn't suddenly turned warm!

Behind him the snowmobiles never slowed down. They growled and screamed on the ridge, but they did not slow down.

It was horrible, being chased by such relentless machines. Once a shot rang out, but he wasn't worried about that—nobody was going to hit a moving wolf from a moving snowmobile.

The next shot, though, smacked into the snow not a tail's length from his head. He redoubled his efforts, bounding along, increasingly desperate.

Voices now mixed with the scream of the engines. Men were calling back and forth, their voices gone high with eagerness. "Two hundred pounds," somebody shouted.

"Two-ten," came the cheerful reply.

At the top of the ridge Bob began to be able to go faster, but the snowmobiles also broke out. They raced along behind him. The woods were not a hundred yards away, but he knew they were going to close the gap before he was safe.

He was frantic, running with all the force he could muster, the wind sweeping past, his fur flying, his paws grabbing the ground with practiced efficiency.

The snowmobiles were on him in a matter of a few minutes.

A rifle butt slammed down across his back. He yelped and snapped at it, but he did not stop moving. There were snowmobiles on both sides of him now, and rifles were weaving in the air.

A shot rang out.

Bob, by a miracle, had been missed. Then he saw why: the shot had not come from the snowmobiles, it had come from a man standing off to the left.

"Leave that wolf alone," the man thundered, "in the name of the Mohawk Nation!"

An Indian, by God, and where had he come from? Another gun butt hit Bob, making him roll once in the snow.

Then the Indian fired again, and one of the snowmobiles peeled off, rattling horribly, its occupants diving off into the drifts. It turned over and burst into flames just as Bob reached the edge of the woods.

"You goddamn fool," a voice screamed behind him, "what the hell's the matter with you, that's a damn *wolf*!"

"I am not a fool. My name is Joe Running Fox and I'm the last of the goddamn Mohicans. That wolf is sacred to my people."

As Bob twisted and turned among the hemlocks and the pines the voices dwindled behind him. He could have listened but he wasn't interested. The Indian might stop those men for a few hours or even a few days, but they would be back. The pack was in immediate danger of being killed.

The cubs would die.

He raced on, his breath coming in hurting gasps, his blood thundering in his temples.

An hour later he reached the pack in a state of happy relaxation. The cubs were playing with the big alpha male and the little female with the bent tail, still Bob's immediate superior. Better, the middle wolves had taken a raccoon, which lay where it had been hunted down, a deliciously bloody ruin.

Bob's fear caused a little restlessness. The alpha female wagged her tail inquiringly. Others watched him, looking for some signal that would explain his distress.

Their language did not allow for explanations, though. They would have to hear the snowmobiles and smell the men before they would run. Bob dashed north a distance, barking frantically. Some of the younger wolves yapped, infected by his state. The alpha male, who had obviously eaten his fill of raccoon, stretched out on a bare patch of ground and went to sleep.

Night fell. The wolves were happy, and they howled together. Bob felt sure that the hunters were close enough to hear them, and he yapped helpless protest. The howl was so good though, so charming with its racing highs and soaring, laughing combinations of voices that he joined it, too, and when it was over, he almost wanted to leap for the rising moon, he was so full of the gladness that is being a wolf among wolves.

His beloved daughter cub curled up with him this night. He lay with her softness under his chin, listening and sniffing. Although he smelled smoke and may once have heard a faint murmur of voices, the men did not appear.

Next morning Bob arose before dawn, to the protests of the little cub. He nuzzled her and she licked his face, making complicated little noises of love in her throat.

Especially when he was with his cubs, Bob thought he could sense the loving force that was behind the change in him. He sensed it now, and he sensed that it was both uneasy and excited.

His mind went to Cindy and Kevin and he thought, *if only*.

But surely it was impossible. No, he was alone in this. People don't change into animals.

He stood, then ran a distance into the deeper woods. He did not like the fact that the thickest forest was to the south. Northward there was a daylong run to the seaway, through mostly scrub woods, over ridge after ridge. The climbing would quickly exhaust the wolves.

From the middle of the woods Bob heard them. The Indian had not been able to turn them back. Now they roared, now they snarled, at least a dozen of them, each carrying one or two armed men.

The wolves had no chance.

He barked furiously, and there was such fear in his voice that every adult wolf in the pack leaped to his feet also barking. In the quiet that followed, Bob heard the snowmobiles again, this time muttering in the far side of the woods. They were tracking him, moving slowly because of the trees.

He took his daughter cub in his mouth and started trotting north. Behind him a few wolves yapped, but the alphas soon heard the snowmobiles also and took flight, each carrying a cub. The scraggly female carried the fourth, a scrappy little male who had once made a neat line of twigs, nosing them through the snow.

The wolves trotted steadily along, the alphas in the lead, then the middle wolves, then the female, and at the end Bob with his daughter, who had obediently fallen asleep.

The snowmobiles came screaming out of the woods not a mile behind them, and fanned out across the wider field they had just left, sending up silver plumes of snow in the dawn light. Bob could not make out the words, but he could hear the delight in the voices. The men must be almost beside themselves, seeing the whole pack. Probably these were the first wolves any of them had seen in the wild.

Shots sounded, snowmobiles shrieked and bounded across the land, eating up the distance. The wolves moved steadily along, going from a trot to a lope, the alphas conserving their strength.

It was a hopeless flight. Before another hour had passed the snowmobiles were flanking the wolves. A shot rang out and the little female ahead of Bob, whom he had faithfully obeyed since they met, whom he loved, to whom he often rolled, exploded in a splash of blood and bone. The cub flew out of her mouth. She lunged, grabbed it, and started trying to pull herself along with her front paws. Then her head was blown apart. The cub was hurled screaming into the air. No sooner had it landed than one of the middle wolves grabbed it.

There was no longer any question of conserving strength. The alphas were running hard now, desperate for anything that could be called shelter.

It was slaughter. They were still miles from the seaway and there was nobody to help them. Again the shots rang out, and this time a middle wolf collapsed, dead of a bullet through his heart. Bob closed the line, slinking low, his daughter cub in his mouth, running as hard as he could. He was thinking little, just following the alphas, hoping he wouldn't get shot.

Another middle wolf was hit. She screamed, blood spurting from her side. The cub she was carrying was picked up by another. She lay down in the snow, panting. Like the others Bob went around her. Her eyes were on the wolves, and he knew why. In her dying there was nothing else she cared to see but the long gray line with its waving tails.

"Don't shoot the fuckin' heads!"

She screamed. Then again, louder. She was dying in agony.

"Don't shoot again! You'll mess up the pelt. It'll die in a minute."

Her agony, though, lasted longer than a minute. In her tortured end she gave the others a little time. But they were terribly tired, so it was time not for more flight but time for rest. They trotted until they heard the snowmobiles grinding gears and starting off again. Then they began to run.

Bob was right behind the alpha female now. The middle wolves remaining were behind him. Pack order was in confusion. Even if the killing stopped now, it would take days for them to sort themselves out again.

Bob could smell her beautiful musk. God, he loved her. He loved her more than he ever had Cindy—or at least differently. His love for her was without equivocation. It was adoring, plentiful, unashamed. But it was not exclusive: it included the whole pack, male and female alike. Only in time of heat did sexual differences really become important.

The snowmobiles were back. The wolves had fanned out, though, in a hunting spread, and so they could not so easily be flanked. A few shots were fired, all misses.

Then there was some luck: one of the snowmobiles hit a tree and its driver fell off and started screaming. He was holding his head when Bob looked, dark blood coming out between his fingers. The wolves kept running.

As he ran Bob cursed himself. Despite his place at the rear of the pack, he had been subtly leading it just as certainly as if he had been at the front. The wolves did not have his intelligence. Pinned into a wolf suit, he was as deadly to them as if he had been a normal human being. It was he who had roamed too far south, who had discovered the town, who had started the chicken raids. Now the wolves were paying the full penalty for his lack of caution.

The cub in Bob's mouth was beginning to squirm and mew. It must be painful, bouncing along as she was. Then Bob heard the mad buzzing of the snowmobiles again. The other wolves put on a burst of speed but it wasn't long before the hunters were back, firing at the remaining wolves.

Another male went down, crying as he fell, his body pierced in the anus. With a whoop one of the hunters leaped from his snowmobile and began to follow the struggling, dying wolf on foot. Bob knew it had been a good shot; no doubt the only damage to the pelt would be a wound under the tail. The wolf dragged himself along. Bob remembered him playing with the cubs through long, happy hours, letting them climb up his back and then shaking them off amid squeals of cub delight. The dying wolf had not had a cub with him now, which was fortunate because there would be no saving it.

He gurgled and gasped. Looking back, Bob saw his lips twisted back, his legs digging at the snow. Then he went down. Once he barked, and then he was too far behind to watch without slowing down.

A bullet whistled past Bob's skull. He dodged and ran on, slinking to get between some close trees. Another shot cracked and there was a heartbreaking shriek. It was her, she was hurt! Carefully, his mind washed with great clarity, Bob put down his cub and ran for all he was worth to help her. She had a grave wound in her belly. A terrible realization came over Bob when he saw her blue guts dragging in the snow. She fell to her side, gabbling pain. The cub she had been carrying dropped from her mouth.

A laughing, happy man leaped off his snowmobile and scooped the cub up. Bob thought fast. He might be a wolf, but he knew a few things that were going to surprise this man.

"I got me a—"

Bob jumped up on the snowmobile.

"What in hell?"

He surveyed the controls. Handlebar throttle, wouldn't you know. If it had been a pedal he might have managed to drive the thing. He broke off the key and jumped out amid a fusillade of shots. A bullet grazed his back like a hot poker, tumbling him over in the snow. But he jumped to his feet and rushed the man, who was not ten yards away and reloading.

While his beautiful friend died in agony, biting her own guts to speed her end, all of her grace and dignity spattered as blood on the snow, Bob savaged another human being mercilessly. He bit the man's face, he raked his cheeks until he could see bones and teeth, he bit the scarf-protected neck so hard the screams became popping whispers.

Then he grabbed the cub the man had dropped and took it to where he had left the other. The rest of the wolves were already far away, followed still by four snowmobiles.

Bob left her dying, her murderer sitting in shock in the snow, his face a pulp. He would live, scarred. She would die.

She whined and Bob stopped. He could not bear to leave her, nor could he bear to leave one of his cubs. He yapped miserably, hopelessly.

He went to her and gently licked her gaping wound. At first she resisted, then her great head flopped down and she made no further sound.

Her eyes told him that she was dead.

He howled over her, raising his soul's dirge. The man he had injured moaned, his hands fluttering in the ruins of his face. Bob could have killed him, but he would not. Already he had done too much.

Carefully, he picked up one cub and set it beside the other, then he took the two of them in his mouth as best he could. They did not like this at all, they squirmed and yowled. But when he moved, their instincts saved them—or perhaps their understanding—and they became quiet, bearing their discomfort.

About a mile to the north there were more shots, followed by whoops of pleasure. Something snapped in Bob, to hear the easy delight. For the hunters this was nothing more than fun.

But it was so much more. It was so terribly immoral, so fundamentally wrong that Bob almost could not bear that it was happening on the earth. Evil is not entropic, it is not a winding down: evil disguises itself as decay. In truth it is an active force in human life, active and clever and tireless. Evil laughed with the laughing men, and the wolves died.

When Bob reached the top of a low hill, he saw them, a scraggly line of six animals with snowmobiles racing round and round them. There was no hope, but still they ran on. Bob could see cubs dangling in the mouths of the alpha male and one of the middle wolves. They were trying so hard to save themselves and their infants. For the wolves this was an occasion of the greatest possible suffering and the highest seriousness. How could it be debased to fun by the whooping hunters, now riding their snowmobiles like cowboys on dancing mares.

Stunned by the horror of the scene before him, Bob had stopped almost without realizing it. The alpha was a clever wolf, and he suddenly turned away from his northerly direction and into a dense thicket that fell quickly away to a rushing kill, the torrent foaming with spring runoff. The snowmobiles could not follow. Within the thicket, Bob saw them put down the two cubs. No doubt they hoped to fly as fast as possible, then come back later for the cubs. Or maybe they were simply too tired to carry them farther, and were hiding them as best they were able, with no plan for the future.

The snowmobiles stopped in a line at the edge of the thicket. A couple of shots were fired but it isn't easy to hit a target running as fast as the wolves were running now that nobody had a cub in his mouth.

Bob saw a chance—not much of a chance, but a very definite chance. He could distract the hunters, draw them away from the other wolves and the two cubs left in the thicket. Without a moment's hesitation he put down his own two cubs and began barking furiously.

Faces turned with alacrity. There were excited shouts. Sure enough, the easier game was more interesting to the hunters. After all, they had already gotten themselves eight wolf pelts and seven fine heads. A ninth—and such a big one— would surely be enough for one day.

Taking up the miserable cubs, Bob started moving north and west, still in the direction of the seaway, but away from the other wolves, who were going east and, Bob felt sure, would soon turn north again.

He ran as fast as his spent, trembling body would allow. The snow was in full melt beneath the noontime sun, and it made movement hell. The snowmobiles had been designed to handle it. They roared easily forth.

If only the men would find their companion

with the ravaged face, they might call off the whole hunt. His was far more than the minor head injury the other one had encountered. But he was too far back. They wouldn't discover him until they turned for home.

The engines got louder and louder, the whoops and laughter higher and more excited. Soon early shots were ringing out and Bob saw the snow fountains of bullets all around him. Ahead of Bob was a long, drifted ridge—just the sort of situation that would punish him the most. His cubs were crying. At least the other two were with the main pack. They would live if the pack got across the seaway.

Bob realized that he was going to die. Maybe, somehow, his two cubs would make it.

Not two days ago one of his offspring had made a line of sticks. Made a line! They *had* to live!

He turned to face the snowmobiles, his head down, barking furiously.

There came out of the south an amazingly unlikely caravan. First was an ancient car, slipping and sliding through the snow, driven by the Indian who had called himself Joe Running Fox. Beside him in the car sat a woman. Bob smelled Cindy. The car had chains on its tires and was a total mess, covered with snow, both lights put out by collisions along the way, the windshield cracked. Behind it was an even more outrageous sight, a spindly old man on a brand-new Kawasaki snowmobile. Sitting behind him was Kevin, who carried a shotgun.

The procession drove right between him and the oncoming hunters, and there it stopped.

Bob could hardly believe what he saw. "You're all under arrest," Cindy shouted. "What you're doing is a felony. You're wantonly killing an endangered species without so much as a permit."

"These damn things have been taking chickens and goats all winter. They're being exterminated." With that one of the hunters took aim on Bob. Kevin's voice came over the noon thrall: "If you shoot, I do, too!"

"Oh, come on." The rifle clicked ominously.

Kevin fired the shotgun high. Thank God Bob had taught him something about shotguns. Otherwise he might have misgauged the spread and given one of the men a face full of buckshot.

"The next one will be for you, Mike Lispenard," the old man said in a thin, slightly English voice.

"You old queer!"

"Maybe so, but you're a murderer."

"Hell, this is a hunt. The worst we're gonna get is a fine, if that. And one of these pelts is worth a lot more than what we'll have to pay."

Kevin fired again. This time one of the snowmobiles leaped back and its occupant climbed down, ripping off his jacket. "A pellet! I got a pellet in my goddamn chest!"

"That's a lot more serious crime than killing a few chicken-thieving wolves, lady."

"The worst he'll get is a fine," Cindy snarled, "and it's worth it to see you creeps suffer."

Bob did not wait for the end of this confrontation. He took his two cubs and set off toward the seaway.

All afternoon he loped, his heart still far to the south where the other cubs lay hidden in the snow. He wished mightily that he could go back for them, but he knew that the alpha had been right. Grown wolves could be risked for cubs only up to a point. Bob knew that there would be other seasons and other mates, and many litters.

At least he still had the two. In many ways that was a triumph.

Early in the evening he reached the seaway. For an hour he heard it booming and cracking. He had been sick with fear, but confused, because the ice seemed to be breaking up awfully early.

Then he saw why: there were icebreakers on the water, long, gray ships plunging and rearing along, leaving dark blue tracks of open water behind them. Bob remembered the roach—the fact that it was out should have warned him that spring was proceeding. The sailors knew it: like the insects, they gave not a moment more to winter than necessary.

Bob ran as hard as he could, but it was not hard enough. By the time he reached the seaway the water was blue down a trench in the middle at least fifty yards wide. And the ice for a hundred yards on either side of it was shattered and thin, floating precariously on the current.

Bob sat down on the bank. A wave of blackest despair washed him. Putting down the two cubs, who immediately began to tussle and play at his feet, he raised his muzzle in a disconsolate, lonely howl.

From the far bank he was answered. He counted six wolves. Since he was the seventh, it meant that they had ultimately killed nine. A terrible toll, more than half of them. But the survivors were over there, not here, and for that Bob could be glad.

He decided to hide these cubs in a snow den and go back for the others at once, so that they wouldn't have to spend the night in the cold. As long as he lived, they had a chance, all four of them.

As he dug his den, he heard the howling from the far bank of the St. Lawrence, and thought that it was the saddest sound he had ever known, far more sad than the deepest human sorrow, because it had to do with the final tragedy of their species, and they sensed this.

Miserably, Bob dug the snow den. These were such early cubs, maybe they were never fated to live, any of them. Bob had been so randy that he had interrupted the dance of heat with an impregnation weeks before it would normally have occurred. Again, his human nature had unbalanced the delicate life of the pack.

He nosed the little cubs into the den and turned south, counting on the rising dark to conceal him. He had not gone a quarter mile before, quite abruptly, he collapsed in a heap. For a moment he was confused. Why wouldn't he go? He tried, but he got nowhere. It was fully fifteen minutes before he could get himself to move again. And then he could barely manage to walk back to the snow den.

He lay down beside it, curling his nose under his tail. Soon he had two very happy and relieved cubs cuddling into the warmth of his fur, tugging and snuffling for the best position. He knew they must be hungry. He'd deal with hunting in the morning. God willing, the thaw would bring out some squirrels.

He dropped to sleep thinking of the other cubs out there in the night alone, the poor children of his body. And her, he thought of her, how beautiful she had been, the most beautiful female creature he had ever known.

But when he slept, he dreamed of Cindy's arms around him.

The light that woke him was not the sun. It came stealthily through the woods, and brought him to his feet.

"It's us, Bob."

They came forth out of the scrub forest. Bob smelled a hot car nearby, and he also smelled something else, an odor that made his hackles rise even as his heart was charged with hope.

"We have the cubs. We saw you carrying the other two. We know how important they are to you."

Cindy and Kevin loomed up out of the dark, each carrying a cub cuddled in their arms. Both infant wolves were curled up, motionless with fear.

When they smelled Bob, their heads began to wobble. Then they started mewing, and his every instinct was aroused. They were so precious: they bore the spark of intellect. Such cubs as these were destined to save the wild!

The cubs were put at his feet, and soon all four of them were scrambling about together, their fears forgotten in the protective shadow of their father.

"Bob, do you still understand?" Cindy was a perceptive woman. He'd heard enough language this day for it all to have come back to him. One tap was yes, two was no. He tapped.

"Oh, Dad, you're still in there, you're really still in there!"

Kevin's voice, so full of loyalty and love, practically broke Bob's heart. Before he realized what he was doing, he raised his nose and howled out his combination of joy and sorrow. From the far bank there almost immediately came a response. He felt the longing in their voices: they had lost lovers and cubs. Also, though, they had heard his joy and there was an undercurrent of hope in their sound.

He looked at his son. For an instant, their eyes met. Then Kevin looked away.

Bob thought, I can do it.

"The seaway trapped you, didn't it," the elderly man said.

Bob tapped once.

The old man looked at Cindy and Kevin. "Amazing. Can it *really* be true? Every word you've told me?"

Bob scratched again, hard, and wagged his tail.

The old man made a sound like a sob. "I see this as a very hopeful sign," he said.

"If you'll get in the car," Joe Running Fox said, "we'll take you across the seaway at the Lightforth Bridge. We'll leave you within striking distance of the other wolves. Do you want that?"

Bob scratched yes and yapped excitedly. How desperately he wanted that!

"Bob," Cindy asked, "you must answer me a question. Please, Bob, do you want to stay with us? We'll give the cubs to the other wolves. But Bob, come home. There is love for you there. And maybe someday——"

He spoke with his heart: *Look at me, Cindy! Look into my eyes!* She did not hear. Within himself he was still her husband, still Kevin's father. But he was also the father of these cubs.

He was anguished.

He loved his old family and the life of man, but he belonged to these cubs, and to the future they represented. He knew why he was here, to save the ancient race of wolves by giving them a spark of man's devastating intelligence.

But Cindy, dear heart, how can I ever leave you! For God sake, look at me! Kevin, look into Dad's eyes!

The cubs, grown hungry, mewed in perfect unison at his feet. Normal wolf cubs do not mew together like that, not ever.

In the car the cubs became quiet after eating some beef jerky offered them by Joe Running Fox. Bob slept with his head in Cindy's lap, waking occasionally to take a long, lovely sniff of her.

It was a long drive down to the bridge and back up the other side. Through it Cindy stroked Bob's head. He smelled tears, but she made no sound. He waited to lock glances with her or Kevin, but it never happened.

Then the car stopped. "It's time," Joe said. Bob got to his feet. Kevin and the old man were sleeping on one another's shoulders. Gently, Bob nosed his son awake.

"Good-bye," Cindy said. Kevin bent down and kissed him.

No, it must not be! For God's sake, look at me!

He imagined them changing, fought to see them as wolves, Cindy's face soft and full of courage, her scent unimaginably perfect.

She moaned, and then, quite suddenly, she was looking back into his eyes.

There came a shaft of golden light from the sun. The old man screamed, the Indian sighed, Kevin's voice swept high with terror. "Mom, Mom!"

Oh, there—perfect, just perfect! He leaped into her, rushing and roaring, filling her with the essence of the wolf, the magic of the wild.

She rolled, growling and muttering, still trying to talk.

She was one god-awful beautiful wolf!

"Mom, no!"

Kevin, come on, look at me, look at Dad!

"Mama, I'm scared! Please, Mama, *please*!"

She leaped up, resting her paws on the boy's shoulders.

"They do it to you," the Indian shouted. "Kev, they do it with their eyes!"

He was young and full of life, and that life recoiled in fear.

When his mother looked into his eyes, he whimpered, then cried. His whole body shook, shimmered as if behind a wall of heat, then his arms, his legs began to twist, his hands to curl in on themselves.

It wasn't easy for him like it had been for his mother and father. Perhaps this was because he was young and full of human hope for his human future. Or perhaps it was simply because youth loves life, and this felt too much like death.

But once the process started in him it would not be stopped. The change continued relentlessly on. His head burst with a great crackling sound into the head of a fine young wolf.

Out of the writhing blur of his body there came the naked stalk of a tail, the skeletal sticks that would be his legs, then beneath the ripping, tearing clothes, a blur of fine, gray hair.

He was a lovely young wolf, his soft eyes crackling with intelligence.

He stood beside his mother, his tail circling, his very stance speaking promise. When Bob went to him to sniff under his tail, he leaped forward, yapping.

Had it been possible, Bob would have laughed. But he taught them both the wonders of their new sense. In a few minutes of sniffing each other the little family knew each other better than human beings have since we left the forest.

When he lifted his head from his wife and his son and his cubs, Bob could smell the other wolves not a hundred yards away, hiding in a stand of pine.

"I'll never forget you," the Indian said. He would not look at Bob, though, when Bob sought his eyes. "It's too late for me," he added, "I'd be a waste." Then he dropped his eyes. His fists were clenched, such was the pain in his heart. "You go on, find others, many others! Find the young and the strong. God bless you and bless the race of wolves!" He and the Englishman withdrew so that the other wolves could come out of hiding.

When they appeared, the pack reunited with much sniffing and joyful yapping. Because of the losses, the two new wolves were more easily accepted.

The pack remained there through the night, sometimes fighting, sometimes not, and in the morning there was a new order established.

The alpha wolf was still alpha. Behind him came Cindy of the high tail, who had turned out to be a fierce fighter. She had taken second place against all of the other female wolves. Then came a thoroughly beaten Bob. He had tried hard to be alpha. He was Cindy's husband, for God's sake, married in the Catholic Church no less! But the leader was clever in the ways of wolves, and he was strong. Behind him were the young wolves, included among them his own beloved son.

Not long after dawn the Indian and the old man returned to the pine grove. He watched them in silence. There were tears on the Indian's face, but he would not meet Bob's eager eyes. "Under God's heaven," he said, "make something new in the world."

Bob knew what was finally happening, knew the grandeur and the wonder of it. The spirit of man had finished its ages-long journey through history, and was finally returning to the wild from which it had come. But it was returning triumphant, bringing the gift of intellect with it.

The two old men stood watching as the pack left. When they mounted a rise, Bob looked back. He saw their car creeping away like a beetle, moving toward the Lightforth Bridge and mankind's old, dark world.

At last Bob turned north. He bounded forward, taking his hard-earned place as third wolf. He followed his alphas, deep into the freedom and safety of the wild.